Praise for Richard Roper

'Funny, moving and thought-provoking – I loved this'
Clare Mackintosh

'A charming, humorous and life-affirming tale about human kindness' *BBC News Online*

'This perfect, quirky summer page-turner [is] a life-affirming debut' *Sunday Times*

'A magnificent read. Tender, funny, compelling' Lucy Foley

'I loved this novel with my whole heart' *New York Times*

'I adored this! It warmed my heart, broke it a little, then put it back together' Beth O'Leary

'Endearing and delightful' *Prima*

'Heartbreaking. Hilarious. Life-affirming' Holly Bourne

'This is a story that gets under your skin – a must-read' *Sun*

'Funny, moving and uplifting . . . I loved it' Libby Page

'A wonderful debut that's heartbreaking, uplifting and laugh-out-loud funny' *Woman's Weekly*

Richard Roper grew up in Stratford-upon-Avon, before studying English at the University of Sheffield. He now lives in London, where he works as an editor. His first novel, *Something to Live For*, has been translated into nineteen languages.

He is @richardroper on Twitter and Instagram. He can also be found at www.richardroperauthor.com

Also by Richard Roper

Something to Live For

WHEN WE WERE YOUNG

Richard Roper

ORION

First published in Great Britain in 2021 by Orion Fiction,
This edition published in 2022 by Orion Fiction,
an imprint of The Orion Publishing Group Ltd,
Carmelite House, 50 Victoria Embankment,
London EC4Y ODZ

An Hachette UK company

1 3 5 7 9 10 8 6 4 2

A CIP catalogue record for this book is
available from the British Library.

ISBN (Mass Market Paperback) 978 1 4091 8566 6
ISBN (eBook) 978 1 4091 8567 3

Typeset by Input Data Services Ltd, Somerset

Printed in Great Britain by Clays Ltd, Elcograf, S.p.A.

MIX
Paper from
responsible sources
FSC® C104740

www.orionbooks.co.uk

For my nephew, William.

PART ONE

PART ONE

Chapter One

Theo

I was being evicted, which wasn't ideal. The fact that my land-lords were my parents definitely rubbed salt in the wound. That my residence happened to be the shed at the bottom of their garden was perhaps the biggest sign that things weren't exactly going brilliantly for me.

The eviction news had been broken to me with a letter posted under the shed door, my name scrawled on the envelope in my dad's scratchy handwriting.

Theo,
I'm afraid this has gone on <u>long enough.</u> You cannot simply continue living here without showing any signs of wanting to move on. It was only supposed to be a temporary solution. Therefore, we are giving you until the day after your birthday this Saturday to find somewhere to go.
*   It's for the best.*
*   Love,*
*   Dad and Mum*

We'd had the 'moving out' conversation a hundred times in the last two years since I'd slunk home from London, but a formal eviction notice – even one written on the back of a church newsletter touting a 'guess the weight of the cake competition' – did feel like something of an escalation. I decided, after a brief two-hour nap, to tackle the situation head-on.

As I made my way up the garden, I saw that Dad was teetering dangerously at the top of a ladder as he produced some lethal-looking garden shears with which he began to hack at the ivy clinging to the side of the house. He was wearing his self-styled 'garden shoes' – old slip-on office brogues that gave zero protection against things like, to pluck an example out of thin air, garden shears. I wasn't sure what had got into him since he'd retired. He had taken to filling his days with what Mum had started calling 'your father's little projects' – a majority of which seemed to place him squarely in danger. This meant I'd had to keep up a state of constant vigilance: throwing windows open to release soldering iron fumes; pretending I'd just happened to find some safety goggles from my old chemistry set and leaving them on his workbench, before discreetly discarding the Amazon packaging. I wished he could have taken a leaf out of Mum's book: Agatha Christie's backlist and a robust exchange of letters with an orthodontist in the local paper about the new one-way system seemed much more on brand.

I had no choice but to brave the chunks of ivy raining down so that I could stand on the bottom rung of the ladder, holding it steady to make sure it didn't slip.

'Morning,' I called up to him.

'Afternoon,' he replied.

A glance at my watch told me it was 12.01 p.m. First blood had been drawn.

'I presume you received our letter?' Dad said.

I rolled my eyes. 'Yes, it reached the trenches at dawn. And thank you for the chocolate and cigarettes. Morale is strong as we prepare to go over the top.'

'Ah, that'll be one of your famous jokes. Not your funniest, I'm afraid.'

'I'd say it's about as funny as my parents evicting me.'

I just managed to keep both hands on the ladder while avoiding a particularly vicious chunk of ivy that came whizzing down just past my ear.

'Yes, well, I'm afraid you've given us no choice. We have been having this conversation for two years now.'

'Twenty-three months, actually.'

'Hairs. Splitting. Rearrange. Et cetera.'

'Well, what about the fact you're doing this *a week* before my birthday?' I said.

'Oh come on, don't sulk.'

'God, I'm *not*,' I said, sighing, rolling my eyes and folding my arms – quickly unfolding them again to grab the ladder, which had wobbled dangerously to one side as Dad stretched to dislodge something from the gutter. (Moss, it would seem, most of which was now in my hair.)

To my relief, Dad decided to have a break. When he got to the bottom of the ladder, he put a hand on my shoulder. I noticed what looked like liver spots near his wrist. How long had they been there? Had they arrived at the same time as the last patch of brown bristles had departed his beard, leaving it a dirty-snow grey?

Gently ushering me off the foot of the ladder, he said, 'Look, as we have discussed many, *many* times . . . I know you went through something of a tough time in London. We all wish that the TV stuff had worked out, and as for Babs – the break-up and whatnot – that was a shame, and we were very fond of her. But moping around here isn't going to fix things, is it?'

'But I'm happy here, Dad. Doesn't that count for anything?'

He carried on as if he hadn't heard me. 'The longer you stay here, the harder you will find it to rejoin society.'

'Rejoin society? You make me sound like I've just served a ten-year stretch for armed robbery. Or I'm some sort of . . . hermit.'

'Well, you're doing your best impression of one. I mean, look . . .' He pointed down to the shed. 'Turning my garden shed into your little grotto like that.'

'Hey, don't have a go at the shed. I've just put fairy lights up.'

Dad rubbed his eyes.

I sensed weakness and moved to capitalise.

'Would you not say I'm a model lodger? I mow the lawn. I unload the dishwasher. I . . . I pay rent.'

'Not for the last eight months you haven't,' Dad shot back.

'Well, no, not technically. But I put change into Mr Pigglesby nearly every day.'

We both looked through the kitchen window at the piggy bank on the sideboard. The treacherous little bastard seemed to be avoiding my eye.

'Besides,' I continued, 'as soon as one of my scripts comes off, I promise you I'll buy you another shed.'

'And how *are* the scripts going?'

'Spectacularly,' I said, though, in truth, I'd not written a word for months.

'I'm sorry,' Dad said, sounding worryingly resolute, 'but we've decided. You've been here long enough. No more excuses. As we explained in our letter, we're giving you until your birthday. After all . . .'

Oh god. He was going in for the kill. I braced for the headshot.

'. . . you *will* be turning thirty.'

Chapter Two

Joel

The letter had changed everything. Although I'd learnt the news it contained in person the day before I'd received it, it was only when I saw everything in stark black ink that it actually sunk in. From that moment on, the letter hadn't been out of my sight, hidden away in my left jacket pocket. In the month since it had arrived, I'd been guarding it just as closely as what was in my right jacket pocket – the ring which I was clutching now, checking for the hundredth time that morning that it wasn't lost.

I glanced at my watch. It was just after ten. By the time those hands had looped around and were back to the same position, the ring should have a new owner . . .

Never had I felt more certain of how much I loved Amber Crossley than one rainy summer morning just over two months ago. The city was stirring, and everything was peaceful. I had turned to face Amber, who was still asleep. My eyes were drawn to the faint, pencil-thin scar on her chin, the legacy of when she'd fallen off her bike when she was seven. I remember thinking how much I hated the idea of her being in pain, even more so when I thought of how much of that had been my fault. Well, from now on, I thought, things were going to change. I'd never hurt her again, and if anyone else thought about it, they'd have to get past me first. The little rowing boat we had been on that had weathered furious storms was now drifting through still, clear waters. I knew then in my bones that, at last, everything was as it should be. At that precise moment, Amber had opened her eyes, as if she'd been listening to my thoughts all along. As her eyes had met mine, a smile spread out across her face; slowly, like a ripple on a perfectly still lake. And that's when I knew I was going to marry her.

I put the ring back in my pocket and pictured the little cottage in Tuscany I'd booked for the occasion. Its stone walls were being warmed by the rising sun, swallows were darting overhead. I'd carefully planned a spontaneous picnic where we'd head out to watch the sunset later that evening. That's when I was going to ask her. Amber was on her way there from Rome, where she'd been visiting Charlotte, an old friend. My flight from Heathrow taking me to her was leaving in a couple of hours. It was going to be the most perfect day . . .

. . . Except it wasn't going to happen.

Instead, I was sitting in an airless, creaking train, surrounded by screaming babies and self-important businessmen, heading deep into the heart of the English countryside on my way to see someone I'd not spoken to in a decade, who, as far as I knew, hated me with every breath in his body.

The train plunged into a tunnel. I rested my head back against the seat and closed my eyes, but the motion of the train made me feel nauseous. Then, just as we entered daylight again, came the phone call I'd been dreading. I made for the vestibule. For a moment, I considered not answering, but I cracked after the next ring.

'Hey.'

'Buongiorno, m'darlin'! I can't wait to see you. Please tell me it's raining in London? It's so gorgeous here today.'

I glanced out of the window at the cloudless skies.

'Yeah,' I said, 'bucketing down.'

'Perfect. Are you at the airport yet?'

I felt my mouth going dry.

'Hey, you still there?' Amber said.

'Yes, I'm here. But, I'm . . . This is so shit, but I'm not going to be able to come out.'

There was a moment where Amber digested this.

'What do you mean?'

I tried to push past the disappointment in her voice.

'Something's come up.'

'With work?'

'No, it's not that. It's . . .' I was floundering already at the merest hint of interrogation.

'Wait, Joel, please tell me you're not . . . Listen, if you've had a slip-up, then it's fine.'

'No,' I said quickly, 'I promise. Not had a drop.'

'Because you can tell me and I won't be angry.'

'It's not that,' I said.

'Well then, what?' Amber sounded a little exasperated now.

At that moment, the train began to slow and the guard's monotone voice came over the speaker:

'*We are now approaching Kemble.*'

'Did I just hear Kemble?' Amber asked. 'Jesus, it's not your mum? Has something happened?'

'No, nothing's happened,' I said. 'But . . . she called me in a bit of a flap. She's having one of her down days – but worse than usual.'

At least this was true, not that it gave me any satisfaction to

10

recall the conversation with Mum where I'd told her about the letter. She'd had some tough days since I'd left, and I knew that she got upset sometimes – especially when she went for long stretches without seeing me – but I'd never heard her cry like that before.

'Oh the poor thing,' Amber said. 'OK, well, I guess I'll fly straight back from Rome then.'

'No, you should go on still – take Charlotte with you. You've probably got loads to catch up on. I'll come out when I can.' If things went well today then I knew that was almost impossible, but I couldn't stop myself.

'I suppose . . .'

Amber was trying not to sound disappointed for my benefit, which made me feel ten times worse.

'I'm sorry,' I said. 'I wish things were different.' And Christ how I did.

Just then my signal wavered, before cutting out completely. I felt guilty at how relieved this made me feel. I'm not sure how much longer I could have kept up the pretence.

We'd reached the station. I saw the Kemble sign go by, its letters rusty brown on the dull white background. As the doors opened, I hesitated. I could just stay on the train, go one stop on to Stroud and Mum's house. I didn't have to get off here at all. But at the last moment I stepped down and the train moved off, leaving behind the smell of diesel.

I walked to the end of the platform and climbed up onto the footbridge, pausing at the top, the tracks below me now. I turned slowly on the spot, taking in my surroundings. A bi-plane was making its uncertain descent towards the Cotswold airport. To the south, I could just see the top of the church spire above the trees. To the north, the Thames Head pub, the site of my first legal pint. It was just a short walk from there to the field in which two teenage layabouts without a care in the world had made a promise to each other.

If I'd not had the letter, I might have forgotten about that moment – it would be a regret, but just a footnote. But the words contained on that one page of A4 paper had brought into focus things I hadn't thought about in years. There were wrongs from the past that had never been righted. People who had once been an ever-present part of my life, only to fade away. And one of them was the curly-haired boy I'd watched teetering on the edge of the Thames Head monument, talking about a future that seemed a million miles away. An idle teenage promise, once forgotten and faded as quickly as the footprints in the grass we'd walked home through, now felt like something I was compelled to honour – even if it meant I was about to become the most unpopular surprise birthday guest of all time.

Chapter Three
Theo

'Happy birthday, you big silly prick.'

I leant down to receive my sister's deliberately crushing hug. Her arms – built up from years of wheelchair propulsion – were now perfectly suited to squeezing the life out of me. Alice's house was next door to Mum and Dad's. They'd bought it when the couple who lived there had moved out, and used all their remaining savings to adapt it for her: ramps, wider corridors, a specially designed bathroom – the works.

I flopped down onto the sofa and let out a long, deep sigh.

A week had passed since the conversation with Dad about me moving out. It was clear that he and Mum weren't backing down this time, so unless I wanted today to feature my birthday celebrations followed by my eviction, I was going to have to do something drastic.

'Mum and Dad are actually serious about kicking me out,' I said. 'So they've left me with no other choice.' I couldn't resist a dramatic pause. 'I'm going to have to sue them.'

Alice's response was just to look at me, unblinking, a tactic she employs when she wants me to realise just how absurd what I've said is.

I folded my arms defensively, but as usual my little sister was right.

'OK, fine, I'm obviously not actually going to sue them,' I said. I pictured their little faces in court. It'd be like telling Paddington Bear he'd developed an allergy to marmalade.

'Good,' Alice said. 'So now that we've quashed that idea, do you not think that this could finally be a bit of a wake-up call?'

'How so?' I asked, as innocently as possible.

'Well, you've just turned thirty . . . and you live in a shed. I'm not a life coach or anything, but I'd suggest that means you're not exactly flourishing. In fact, I'd go as far as to say that – no offence – but you seem to be completely wasting your life, consumed in a cocoon of self-absorption and point-less vendettas.'

'Right,' I said. 'Normally I think you're supposed to say "none taken" when someone prefaces a criticism with "no offence", but, to be honest, there was quite a lot of offence taken there.'

I'd managed to sidestep the truth of what Alice had said, deliberately bogging things down in semantics, which had become something of my forte of late.

'But aren't you bored out of your mind here?' Alice asked, not to be dissuaded. 'I mean, don't you want to see the world? Not to put too fine a point on it, but not all of us have the luxury of stress-free, go-wherever-the-fuck-you-want explor-ing that you do.'

Guilt washed over me at this, and I looked away. There had been a time after Alice's accident where I'd made myself promise I'd never leave her behind. She'd practically had to beg me to go off to uni when I'd tried telling her I wasn't going to go. That might have been a noble gesture at the time, but these days the idea that I was sticking around because of Alice was something that – to my shame – I was hiding behind. Because, the truth was, the idea of leaving home again terrified me. I could pretend all I wanted that I was being forced to curtail my dreams of travelling, or my grand plans to make a difference in the world, or even climbing to the top somewhere and making a load of money. But, in actual fact, my ambitions stretched as far as seeing how many sausages I could eat in a single sitting, and the idea of having to face reality again by leaving home was about as appealing as nailing my face to a windmill.

It was only in the last couple of months, as I approached the thirty milestone, that a nagging voice at the back of my head forced me to take stock of my life. And the more I thought about it, the more I realised that when I summed everything up it didn't make for pretty reading, especially in the form of an early 2000s MSN questionnaire:

Name: Theo Hern. BA Hons.

Age: Urgh. Thirty.

Relationship status: Single. A mutual decision. Definitely mutual. Incontrovertibly. OK, 60–40 her decision. 70–30 tops.

Appearance: the lovechild of Screech from *Saved by the Bell* and a disinterested court bailiff in a true crime documentary.

Interests: The writings of Soren Kierkegaard, impressionism, chess, the music of Chopin and Stravinsky, opera, calligraphy, tae kwon do, geocaching, glassblowing, powerlifting, millinery, volunteering.

***Actual* interests:** Accidentally-on-purpose positioning myself on trains so I can read people's texts.

Main strengths: Being really good at guessing the time. Remembering jingles from early-1990s TV adverts. Good hair (2009–2012).
Main weaknesses: Soft hands. Catastrophising.
Things I would ban if I were to become emperor of the world: Fracking. Street performers.
Occupation: Social Media Manager for a budget burger chain.

It was the last thing on the list that was proving the most demoralising.

After university – and following a disastrous failure to make it as a comedian after something of 'an incident' at the Edinburgh festival – I'd moved to London with the girl I loved, determined to move on. I threw myself in to a series of marketing jobs, eventually landing a copywriting gig, in which I progressed steadily, managing to find enough ways to be creative day to day to make up for the more soul-crushingly corporate parts of the work. So far, so sensible. But then I began to develop a bit of an itch. Had I been too quick to throw everything away? I had been utterly obsessed with making it in the world of TV comedy since I was a little boy – and now here I was: a total sell-out. But then something happened which I managed to convince myself was clearly A BIG SIGN. One of my clients in the communications team at Sky had apparently found some of my copywriting so (and I quote) 'hilarious' that he'd decided to pass it on to his friend in the comedy department there. The friend, Bryan, offered to meet me for a coffee. He hadn't been the whip-smart laconic creator I'd expected (and I was put off to some extent by his T-shirt bearing the slogan i-Pooed), but after our meeting he told me I was welcome to come to the writers' room for a new pilot he was working on. 'That would be cool,' I said, shortly before clenching a sachet of ketchup so hard it burst all over my T-shirt, as if I'd been shot by a sniper. I floated home that evening, celebrating with a pint in every pub I passed on the way. And when I got in, I fired up my laptop, opened my emails and informed my boss that Theo Hern was no longer a slave to the corporate pigs in copywriting – he was going to be a proper writer.

I might have been all right if I'd not handed in my notice with such convincing vitriol. But when it turned out that Bryan had made something of a mistake, and that I wouldn't actually be allowed to sit in with him on the pilot, and in fact he was probably quitting to retrain as an actuary because he was skint and living in a narrowboat with no windows, my former boss decided they'd rather not take me back on.

And so began the chain of events that led to me returning home from London two years ago: jobless, friendless, with a broken heart and an ugly, misshapen scar by my right elbow, the origins of which make me cringe to the point it's more painful than the injury itself.

When it came to finding employment again, given that the chances of a glowing reference seemed slim, there weren't that many options left for me. In the end, I'd somehow lucked my way into the job of running the official Twitter account for a budget burger chain called 'Captain Beefy', that inexplicably has over a hundred thousand followers. My job, my brain-numbing nine-to-five, is to tweet out stupid jokes and puns and interact with followers. And if it's a national holiday or something newsworthy is trending, then I'm supposed to relate it to that. I do try my best to match the enthusiasm of

17

my kind, zany boss, Jake, but the other day he asked why I hadn't tweeted something about the joys of 'being English on St George's day', and I couldn't bring myself to tell him the truth, which was that all I could think of when it came to 'being English on St George's day' was a single shoe on a top of a bus shelter. In the rain.

'Oi, are you listening to me?' Alice launched a pistachio shell at my head.

'What?' I said.

'I was in the middle of telling you how much you're wasting your life.'

'I do apologise. By the way, you know about the guests who've invited themselves over for my birthday drinks at Mum and Dad's later?' (I'd realised I had another distraction up my sleeve.)

Alice narrowed her eyes. 'Guests? What guests?'

'Why, our delightful neighbours of course. Beverley and Roger.'

'Oh God,' Alice groaned. 'The most boring people in the world. What time is it? Actually, I don't care. I need to start drinking now if I'm going to get through a conversation with those two later. You sit and think about your dreadful life while I go and find some booze.'

I watched Alice manoeuvre herself to the kitchen – struggling as I always did with whether to offer to help and risk seeming patronising, or not and seem unhelpful. I felt a huge rush of affection for my sister. Despite her rather brutal bedside manner, I knew she only had my best interests at heart. That went for Mum and Dad, too. Really, I was stupidly lucky that they were my family. They were the best kind of safety net a person could ask for, and I loved them all dearly. Truthfully, sitting with them in the garden on a nice day having a cup of tea was when I was at my happiest. I don't care how boring or sad that makes me sound, because it's those times where my worries melt away, even if Dad chooses that moment to scale the roof in his slippers to adjust the TV aerial while thunder rumbles in the distance. The problem was that they had all decided that I should get back out into the world, no matter how much I tried to explain that I'd been there and done that and it really wasn't for me.

'You talk about life like a child who's tried an olive for the first time,' Mum once said, in a rare moment where her frustration with me got the better of her. But as hard as it was to feel like I was disappointing her, and Dad and Alice too, I still felt too fragile to try out the real world again. I'd just have to find a less mental course of action than taking them to court to make them forget about the eviction for another year.

As Alice handed me a glass of wine, she accidentally nudged the remote on the sofa with her elbow and the TV sprang into life. The final scene of a repeat of that week's episode of *The Tooth Hurts*, BBC One's smash-hit sitcom, was in full flow. Alice and I had watched the entire thing in stony silence the night before, and here we were again, looking on without the hint of a smile as the show's loveable protagonist, played by Amber Crossley, fell backwards into a wedding cake, and the studio audience erupted with laughter.

'The worst yet,' I said.

'Pitiful,' Alice agreed, and I felt a guilty stab of pleasure, as I always did when I stoked Alice's anger enough for her to direct her ire at the screen.

'Shall we?' I said.

Alice nodded.

'Wait for it . . . wait for it . . .'

The credits began to scroll, and we waited until we saw the name flashing across the screen before we rolled out our catchphrase in unison:

'Joel fucking Thompson.'

Chapter Four

Joel

Kemble's one claim to fame is marked by a small, vaguely embarrassed monument and a jumble of stones a couple of fields away from the station. The spot denotes the source of the River Thames, and the start of the Thames Path, a 184-mile trail that ends at the Thames Barrier in east London. I'm always struck by how there's no mention of this anywhere at Kemble station, particularly given how happy we usually are to shout about the most minor of local attractions: *'Alight here for the Uttoxeter Bread Museum and changes for London St Pancras and onward journeys to Paris.'* Maybe Kemble hiding its light under a bushel is part of its charm. And, even though I'm an irregular visitor these days, from what I remember of growing up here it can be very charming. The fields are lush in the summer but do winter well, too, when they're capped with frost. As a teenager, I celebrated the bucolic beauty of the place largely by throwing stones at it.

As I came out of the station, I felt the violent assault of the past. The hedgerows were alive with birdsong, combine harvesters hummed away in the distance. The perfect August Saturday in England. Awareness of my surroundings isn't my strong suit. I tend to walk with my head down. But recently

21

I'd found myself trying to take as many mental snapshots as I could. And today, everything was pure gold.

I paused, wanting to take it all in. Though, if I was being truly honest with myself, my lingering might have had more to do with why I was here and who I had come to see. I had resolved to let all the guilt and regret I had for what happened slowly drain away, but now I couldn't rely on time to heal old wounds. If I was going to try to make up for things, try to make things right, then I was going to have to do it now.

As I approached the bottom of Theo Hern's driveway, I took steadying breaths. I remembered the many nights I'd stop at the end of this drive and look back – thinking about the warmth and love enclosed behind that front door, and dreading what was waiting for me at home. It was jarring to feel that same sense of trepidation here.

I walked towards the door, rehearsing my opening gambit. 'I was passing through and I remembered it was your birthday,' I'd say. 'I just thought I'd come to say hello.' As I reached towards the doorbell, heart pounding in my chest, I allowed myself a smile at the irony of that. Because even though I wasn't going to tell Theo this, if anything, I'd actually come to say goodbye.

After the second time ringing the doorbell with no response, I felt relief mingling with my disappointment. Maybe I'd got the date wrong. But then, out of the corner of my eye, I saw the curtain in the living-room window move. Someone was definitely there. I tried the doorbell again. Still nothing.

I went around to the garden. At first the glare from the sun meant I couldn't work out what was happening on the other side of the French doors, but as I got closer, I realised that there were people in the living room crouching down, facing away from me. As I spotted Theo's parents, and then Alice, I felt the breath catching in my chest. Theo was at the far end of the room, peeking out under the curtains – the twitch I'd seen earlier. Just the sight of his mad bird's nest of hair gave me a rush of nostalgia that hit like a punch to the stomach. As I got a little closer, my heartbeat quickening, I realised that Theo and his family had been hiding from me. That didn't exactly bode well.

Eventually, I had no choice but to tap politely on the glass door.

Even as I saw Theo turn slowly around, his face contorting with shock and anger, I couldn't help but smile. He might have just turned thirty, but he hadn't changed much. For one thing, he was wearing a T-shirt I swore I recognised from our schooldays. How I longed for him to throw open the door, a grin on his face, laughing as he asked me what the fuck I was doing here.

As he marched towards me and wrenched the door open, he said the words I'd wanted him to, except they were delivered with pure venom.

'What the fuck are *you* doing here?'

The hatred in his eyes actually made me take a step back.

'H-hi,' I stammered. I cleared my throat, suddenly unsure of what to do with my hands. Clasping them behind my back seemed too solemn. Putting them in my pockets too casual. 'Sorry, I didn't mean to shock you like that. I was just passing by, you know?' I could hear how absurd this attempt to sound casual was, but it was too late to go off-script. 'Thought I'd come and say hello, and happy birthday of course.'

'You, what . . .?' Theo was staring at me, baffled now, like I

23

was a stranger who'd just asked him for directions in a foreign language. 'You were just . . . passing by,' he repeated.

'Yeah,' I said.

'On the way to . . .?'

'Oh, you know.'

'Ummm no,' Theo said. 'Not really.'

'Maybe we could have a quick word in private?' I said, aware of the others' eyes on me.

Theo let out a strange sort of yelp, a derisive bark of laughter perhaps, which under other circumstances might have made me laugh, but that feeling was quickly dampened when I saw the now truly murderous look in his eye.

'Sorry, not really up for a chinwag. But thanks ever so much for dropping by – you know, unannounced, uninvited, un-*welcome* – but if there isn't anything else, then perhaps you'd kindly like to fuck off.'

I paused for a minute, gathering myself.

'Well, actually there is something else,' I said. 'Something important. I know we've not spoken for a very long time . . .'

'With good reason.'

'. . . and that this must be a bit of a shock, but please . . . just hear me out? You'll want to listen to what I've got to say, I promise.'

Theo pretended to think about it.

'Umm. Nah, I'm all right thanks.'

He went to shut the door, but I stuck my foot in the way. We both looked with surprise at my squashed foot.

'Please,' I said, 'it won't take long. Twenty minutes, that's all I'm asking for.'

As I looked into Theo's eyes, I could tell he was conflicted.

He obviously wasn't glad to see me, but he was curious to find out what this was about, I was sure of it.

At last, he pulled the door open, releasing my foot. He stomped back into the house and returned a few moments later with his coat under his arm.

'OK. Fine,' he said. 'But ten minutes, not twenty. And definitely not here.'

Chapter Five

Theo

As Joel carried our pints back to the table, I realised that this could well have been us in another life. Here, in our teenage local, on Christmas Eve perhaps – judging all the old lot from school sitting around us, remembering the stupid nicknames and the apocryphal stories that got more absurd every time we told them.

I made an exaggerated show of drinking half of my beer in one go. I'd left my coat draped over my shoulders, too, rather than taking it off properly, to show him I wasn't getting settled. I still hadn't even begun to process that Joel – Joel fucking Thompson – was actually here in the flesh. I'd not known quite what to do when I saw him outside. Which might explain why I'd panicked and just told everyone to hide. I'm not sure whether they thought there were Jehovah's Witnesses outside, or aliens about to attack, or perhaps this was a new parlour game I'd invented for my birthday, but there was clearly enough authority in my voice for them to do as I asked without questioning it.

Joel looked unusually nervous, fidgeting away with a beer mat. None of the easy charm I was used to. It was oddly unnerving. Joel had always been someone who could adapt to any situation and take things in his stride, one of a number of his traits I'd been envious of. It had taken me years to get to the heart of the difference between us, but in the end, I had settled on the realisation that Joel was a man who could pull off any hat you were to give to him, no matter how novelty, whereas I was a man who never fully trusted that an automatic door would open as I approached it.

Aside from looking nervous, he also looked, well, like shit. I thought he'd have had the full Hollywood treatment by now, but his skin was waxy and dull, and he looked rather gaunt. There had been rumours, once he'd started getting semi-famous, of coke binges (such a cliche!), and lost boozy weekends in Soho. I'd even seen him on a tabloid website coming out of some awful-looking club appearing 'worse for wear', amongst other euphemisms.

I could already feel the beer I'd necked going to my head, and I wanted to get whatever this was over with before I started making a prat of myself.

'Come on then. Out with it. Why are you here?' I asked.

Joel scratched his chin, then puffed out his cheeks.

'Do you remember the first time we got high by the Thames Head stone?' he said.

Well, that wasn't what I'd been expecting.

'No,' I replied flatly, but an image of the two of us that day flickered in my mind all the same. Why that, of all things? Was mentioning that day at the Thames Head just his clever little way of leading me down memory lane to happier days? What an infuriating tactic, I thought.

Nearly as infuriating as the fact that, with every passing second, I was starting to realise just how much I'd missed him.

Chapter Six

Joel

I was finding it hard to focus. I couldn't work out whether Theo had seen me asking the barman to pour two bottles of non-alcoholic beer into my pint glass. Also, him sitting there with his jacket around his shoulders like a grumpy Napoleon was so peak Theo it made me want to hug him.

I sensed he was lying about not remembering that day at the Thames Head stone, but I decided to take him at his word, and launched into the story as best I remembered it. We'd acquired what we'd been told was cannabis resin but what could just as likely have been a stock cube. We were rebels without a cause, we weren't going to be told what to do. And what said 'fuck you' better to 'The Man' than smoking what could well have been gravy at the beginning of a National Trust trail?

'We should walk this path, you know,' Theo had said, blowing a smoke ring into the chill winter air.

'What, now?' I'd yawned. 'I think it's about 200 miles, isn't it? And I *am* very hungry.'

'Not now, but like, in a million years, when we're thirty or whatever. We'll wend our way through the country, stopping off at all the taverns, copping off with . . . you know . . . wenches.'

'I'm not sure you'll "cop off" with anyone you call that.'

I'd ducked as he threw a twig at me.

'Imagine it though. Just you and me tramping along. We'd bring some of this weed.'

'Obviously.'

'I could learn the accordion and bring that too.'

'OK, I'm out.'

Theo had ignored me and scrambled to his feet, climbing on top of the stone, where he balanced precariously, arms wind-milling. 'We'd end up in London, weary from our travels.'

'Riddled with chlamydia.'

'Riddled with *experiences*.'

I'd pretended to snore.

'Come on, are you in?' Theo had said, jumping down from the stone.

'If I say yes, can we go and get pizza?'

'Yeah, OK.'

'Fine then. I'm in.'

We'd walked off, arms around each other's shoulders. Any embarrassment that this outright show of affection might normally have caused was masked by the pretence we were too stoned to walk straight – though I hadn't realised cannabis tasted quite so much like a Sunday roast.

Now, in the pub, Theo was looking at me sceptically as I recounted the story.

'And then what happened?' he asked.

I frowned. 'I think you pushed me into a hedge.'

'Oh yeah.' Theo smiled, then saw me notice and took a big gulp of his drink to hide it.

'You remember then?' I said.

He shrugged. 'Maybe.'

'So . . .?'

'So what?'

'So let's do it! Think about it: you and me, tramping the Thames Path. Oxford, Runnymede, Windsor, Henley. Look!' I took out a book from my back pocket that I'd bought the previous day. 'I've got a guidebook and everything.'

Theo just stared.

'Are you serious?' he said. 'Leaving aside I've got a job, so I can't just go toddling off on long walks, you think you can just waltz back into my life and pick up on some stupid promise we made each other when we were fifteen? After everything that's happened!'

'OK, OK, fair point,' I said, holding my hands up. 'I should have warned you I was coming. And, it goes without saying, you know how sorry I am about Edinburgh still, and obviously, what happened with . . . with . . .'

At this, Theo stood up. 'You can't even say her name. Can you? It's Alice. My sister is called Alice.' He drained the last of his pint. 'Well, thanks for the offer and everything, but I'm afraid I'd rather jump off a very tall building, onto a very big spike, than spend another second with you.'

I watched him trying to leave, straining furiously to get his arms through the right holes in his coat. Even when he'd managed that he made a typically undignified exit as he attempted to barge his way through a door with 'pull' written on it at eye-level.

Well, that had gone about as badly as it could have done. I didn't really know why I was expecting anything different. To think I'd be able to trick him into the walk on the strength of one happy memory already seemed ridiculous.

The pub seemed to have grown oppressively hot. I went to the gents' to splash some cold water on my face. As I lifted my head from the sink, I saw Amber staring back at me from a faded poster. It was from the short live run we'd done of *The Tooth Hurts* after the end of the first series. After all these years, even on a smashed poster in the grim men's toilets of this knackered old pub, the sight of her smile made me ache. I fought the urge to call her and unload everything.

Out of the window, I saw Theo stalking off, hands clenched at his sides. But just as I went to turn away, I saw him stop and glance back, before he carried on. And it was that hesitation that gave me renewed hope. He was tempted. But he clearly felt he couldn't indulge me any further on principle. What I needed was some other incentive to offer him. Something he couldn't resist.

I looked again at the poster, and an idea began to form. If I was going to convince my old friend to overlook the past, and let me back into his life, I was going to have to offer him his dream on a plate.

Chapter Seven

Theo

I was back onto the road when Joel caught up with me, breathing quite heavily despite the short jog. He wasn't spending his TV money on a personal trainer then.

'Theo, slow up.'

'Not interested,' I said.

'Look, OK, I haven't told you everything,' he panted. 'There's another reason why I'm here.'

'Still not interested.'

'*Theo*.' This time, he grabbed my elbow. The shock of him taking hold of me like that startled me. I felt a flash of anger and wrenched my arm away.

'Look, unless this other reason is that you've invented a fucking time machine, then I don't want to know, all right?'

A dog walker came around the corner, her whippet trotting along in front.

'Afternoon!' she said, brightly.

'Afternoon!' we responded in unison, because even when you're having a dramatic showdown, you're still aware that this is England and there are *rules*.

'The thing is,' Joel said. 'I had a meeting with the BBC the other day.'

'Good for you.'

Joel ignored me.

'A show they'd commissioned for next year's been cancelled. They need a replacement – another show. Six-part comedy. BBC Two, 9.30 p.m. slot.'

'And?' I said. 'So what?'

'Well, they put me on the spot there and then. Asked me to pitch something. But I hadn't got anything. Not even the kernel of an idea. But I couldn't say that, could I? So I was wracking my brains and then suddenly I remembered: *The Regulars*.'

My heart skipped a beat. *The Regulars*. The best idea Joel and I had ever had. It was something we'd come up with one underage drunken night. Set in a pub (because write what you know and all that), the show would follow an eccentric gang of regulars and their attempts to keep their local run-down boozer from closing. But then we'd gone our separate ways, and nothing had ever come of it.

'You remember it?' Joel said.

'Of course I do. So . . . what did they say when you pitched it?' I was trying not to sound interested, but from the way Joel was smiling I'd obviously failed.

'Theo, they loved the whole thing so much they told me there and then they want to make it.'

I gaped at him, all pretence gone now. 'Are you serious?'

'Yep,' Joel said. 'I know. Mad, right? But, well, the only thing is, because they want it to replace this show that got binned, they need scripts by the end of next month, otherwise they'll just scrap having a new show in that slot next year.'

'Next month? Isn't that . . . surely that's cutting it too fine?'

'It is. Or at least it would be if I was doing it on my own.

That's why I told them I'd need a co-writer. And that I knew just the man . . .'

As it dawned on me what Joel was saying, I had the strangest urge to burst out laughing. It was ridiculous. Things like this just don't happen.

'Think of it,' Joel continued. 'We walk the Thames Path, writing the scripts as we go, and then we get to London, casually drop off the script at the Beeb in person, and then mosey on to the end of the path. It couldn't be more perfect.'

As I struggled to comprehend what was happening, Joel rambled on animatedly about casting and wrap parties and that this was only just the start for me and my career. And you know what the worst part was? I was instantly softening towards him, feeling my anger subside, realising that actually I could probably get to a point where I could forgive him for everything after all. How horribly fickle I was.

Joel spun around in front of me and grabbed me by the shoulders. 'Are you listening to me? You do realise what I'm saying, right? This is what we've always dreamed of. And the walk! I know things have . . . well, changed, since we came up with the idea, but wouldn't it be good to actually go through with that plan?'

I chewed my lip. Given the way I knew Joel worked, the Thames Path was actually perfect. He'd have to be disciplined about it. He couldn't just wander off or get distracted like he always used to. The time frame was tight, but I knew we could do it. I mean, he could have said we only had half an hour and I'd have probably given it a shot. Because what he'd said was true. This *was* all I'd ever dreamed about. But as I looked at Joel's face, wide-eyed with expectation, a part of me – the part that had told him I never wanted to see him ever again – felt the need to stay firm.

We'd walked as far as the station. A train was just pulling in.

'Look,' Joel said. 'I tell you what. I'm not going to ask you to make a decision right now. I'll be at the start of the path tomorrow morning at ten o'clock, OK? If you're not there, then I'll know you've decided against it, and I won't try to contact you again. No pressure. But . . . at least tell me you'll think about it?'

Him telling me there was no pressure would have felt believable if he hadn't still got his hands clamped down on my shoulders. There was a palpable desperation in his eyes that made me feel uncomfortable. This was far from the insouciant, bordering-on-arrogant Joel I used to know.

'I'll think about it,' I said, reaching up and taking his hands away one by one.

'Great!' Joel replied. He took a step back, looking a little embarrassed that I'd had to loosen his grip like that.

We looked at each other for a moment, neither quite sure how to part. We hadn't been huggers, even before things had gone to shit. But we'd never shaken hands, either. That was something we'd always agreed was for bank managers and football referees.

I'd just shifted my weight onto my back foot, about to turn and leave, when Joel, his eyes to the ground, said, 'It's really good to see you, Theo.'

With that, he was off, head down, hands in pockets, straight through the gate, up onto the platform and then through the closing doors of the train, which promptly moved off, as if it had been specifically waiting for him. Speaking as a man who's at least half an hour early for every journey, length or significance immaterial, I could only stand back and admire him.

I looked down at the spot on the ground where Joel's gaze had fallen, shiftily, as he'd said his parting words. He may have thought he'd just pulled the wool over my eyes, but I knew Joel Thompson far too well not to realise that there was something about all of this that he wasn't telling me.

As the train rounded the bend, my thoughts turned to *The Regulars*. I tried to imagine how ten-year-old me would have reacted had he been told this was what lay in his future: his very own sitcom on the BBC. On balance, I suspect his head would have almost certainly exploded.

∞

I was a funny-looking kid. My growth spurts were haphazard, in that they seemed to happen in different parts of my body at different times, so I never looked at home in my own skin. I capped off the look with uncontrollably curly hair and a mildly lazy eye, or 'forgetful', as Mum used to say, when she tried to cheer me up about it. That was one of the things that led to my defining characteristic at that age: my shyness. One of my earliest memories is being taken to visit some cousins I'd never met before in Norfolk, where I was so consumed with white-hot embarrassment simply at being in the same room as new people that I spent the entire afternoon with my face buried in the sofa, playing dead. As long as nobody knew I existed, then everything would be OK.

I did my best to enjoy primary school, but I never made what you'd call a proper friend. I just found being around groups of people too much, especially at break and lunchtimes. It was all so overwhelming – the shrieking and the constant chasing and shirt tugging. Why couldn't everyone just be a bit quieter? A bit calmer?

Things came to a head on the last day of term before Christmas one year when I was seven. We'd all been herded down the street into the village hall and separated out into groups, where a teacher told us we were about to play 'the chocolate game'. Before I knew what was happening, a large bar of chocolate had been dropped in the middle of our group, and immediately it was chaos. A pair of dice and a hat appeared. The boy next to me – who seemed to know exactly what to do, as if he'd been training for this his whole life like an Olympic athlete – grabbed the dice and swiftly rolled two sixes. At this, everyone began to scream and yell as the boy scrabbled to pull on the hat, as well as a scarf and gloves, before tearing with utter desperation at the chocolate packaging with a plastic knife and fork, trying to get to the gooey mess within. People were shrieking with excitement. Similar scenes were happening all around the room and I just could not bear it. Then the dice were thrust into my hands. A posh little blonde boy screamed at me to roll them, but instead I threw them down and made a break for it, ignoring the shouts of 'Come back!' and 'It's only a game, Theo!' as I ran. I just about managed to pull open the heavy village hall door and throw myself out into the freezing dark.

My mum was called to collect me. I remember her kneeling down in the snow and hugging me tightly, as I tried to explain why I was upset. 'Hey, love, it's OK. Let's get you home, shall we?' The car was warm and Slade was on the radio. And soon I was back home on the sofa, sandwiched between Mum and Dad, with four-year-old Alice sitting on the floor, carefully building a Lego tower before knocking it down and starting again, giggling at her own destructiveness. The fire was crackling in the grate. Dad ruffled my hair. There, I was loved. There, I was safe.

The BBC must have decided to show a rerun of some old comedy classics as a bit of pre-Christmas TV filler. Mum and Dad were chuckling along here and there, but it was the Peter Cook and Dudley Moore art gallery sketch that completely floored them. Never before had I seen my parents helpless with laughter, and even though I didn't really know what was so funny, watching Mum and Dad fall about like that made me laugh too. There, in that moment, I was so far from the misery of the village hall I may as well have been on another planet. All it had taken was these two fools on the screen, fuzzy in black and white. How happy they had made Mum and Dad! It was like a superpower, to make someone laugh like that. And so began my obsession.

From that moment on, I would insist we listened to 'something funny' whenever we were in the car. Dad dug out some classic Radio 4 sitcoms and sketch shows of yesteryear: *Round the Horne, Hancock's Half Hour, I'm Sorry I'll Read That Again*. Most of it went completely over my head – there were references and innuendos I was far too young to understand – but it didn't matter. I may not have got half of the jokes, but over the next few years of forensic attention to detail, I grew to understand the rhythms and the timing, the ebb and flow of set-up and punchline.

We were never more carefree as a family than in Dad's old Saab, trundling along the motorway, listening to those shows on holiday. When we got to the beach, it was the same routine every time: Mum and Dad would fall instantly asleep; little Alice would draw and colour, while I read script books and wrote my own terrible copycat versions. If we were feeling brave, we'd swim in the sea, Alice laughing maniacally in the face of the icy water like a Viking chieftain celebrating a rival tribe's demise.

There was one moment on the beach that still stands out. We were in Whitesands in Wales, and an entire swarm of non-poisonous jellyfish were washed up, neglected by the retreating tide. Dad began picking them up and tossing them back into the water, and Alice, Mum and I followed suit in an uncoordinated rescue attempt while I gave a running commentary like a football commentator. What must we have looked like, the four of us – side by side, hurling squelchy sea creatures back from whence they'd come? I suppose we'd have looked like a carefree family – untroubled, protected by a force field of our own happy eccentricity.

That particular summer seemed to stretch out for ever. I'd just left primary school, and while I hadn't got any friends to play with, I found my own fun in a battered old Walkman of Dad's. I'd lie on my bed, headphones clamped over my ears with both hands, mumbling along until I had each episode of the radio adaptations of *Blackadder* or *Dad's Army* learnt off by heart. I think what I really loved about it was that there was a very simple contract between performer and audience. *You sit there and listen, and we'll try to make you laugh.* So when the occasional cloud of sadness drifted over me when I heard other kids playing on their bikes in the road by my house, I knew exactly where to turn to make myself feel better. I'd even found the perfect place to hide away: the shed at the bottom of the garden. There, I'd prop myself up on upturned paint cans or sweet-smelling firewood, listening to Basil berating Manuel, or Corporal Jones telling everyone not to panic, and for those twenty-eight minutes all was right with the world.

Chapter Eight
Joel

I was banking on Jane Green working late at the BBC as usual, even on a Saturday. As the call rang out, I looked through the train window at the meadows and fields flashing past. I caught a glimpse of the familiar stone roundhouse building between the trees. How many times had I gone past that place on the train and never thought to look up what it was?

Jane picked up, but I knew I had at least ten seconds to wait before it was my turn to speak.

'Joely-poly! How are we, sugarplum? Bear with me if I start effing and fucking blinding over here. Shitstorm brewing with *Doctor Who*. Apparently one of the Cybermen went on a massive bender last night and lost his helmet in a Cardiff Wetherspoon's. So things are a total fucking mess as per. Head of props is shitting feathers. Anyway, where are you? How are you? Who are you? Et cetera, et cetera. Tell me everything.'

'I'm all right,' I said.

Jane chuckled, her smoker's lungs rattling like a child's home-made musical shaker. 'That's obviously bollocks, but I shan't pry. You taking a break before we shoot the Xmas special?'

I paused before answering. Lying to Jane Green wasn't advisable.

'Yeah, something like that,' I said. A train flashed past on the adjacent track. I had the briefest glimpse of hundreds of blank faces. Then they were gone.

'So what can I do for you, dear boy?'

'Well, you know how you'd asked for a new idea for next autumn?'

'Indeed.'

'Well, I think I've got just the one.'

'Aha! Do tell.'

I launched into a pitch for *The Regulars*. I was slightly hazy on the details, so I had to keep it to the point. This had to be a no-brainer for Jane.

'Innnnnteresting,' she said, once I'd wrapped it up.

I breathed a small sigh of relief. If she'd hated the idea, she would have told me straight away, most likely using at least one swear word I'd never heard before.

'Well, matey, leave it with me. I'll run it up the flagpole. But I for one like the sound of it.'

'Great.'

And now for the other part . . .

'It's a co-write, I should say.'

'Really? Unlike you, my little *auteur*. Who's the other bod?'

'Guy called Theo Hern. Catalogue of stuff under his belt, but all very much under the radar. He's brilliant, but modest. A real one-off.'

In truth, I had no idea how much Theo was still writing these days. But what I did know was that he was easily the more talented out of the two of us, and that this had been something he'd always wanted much more than me. If I could help him pull this off – at least to get his foot in the door – then maybe that would go some way to making things up to him.

'Hmm. Well, I'll take your word for it, J-Pole. Right, the time has come for me to go and tear this Cyberman a new metal arsehole, but promise I'll get back A-sap to you and . . . Tim, was it?'

'Theo,' I said. 'And honestly, Jane, trust me – the guy's a total genius.'

Chapter Nine

Theo

I'd had my finger stuck in the bottle of Fanta long enough that I was really starting to panic. Thankfully, I managed to free it before I knocked on Alice's door. She wouldn't have let me forget that in a hurry.

'My god I've been dying for you to come back,' she said. 'Come on, spill the beans – what the hell did he want?'

As I came into the living room, I saw Alice's kit laid out for her next wheelchair basketball game.

'Big match tomorrow?' I asked.

'Vital,' she said, handing me a glass of wine. 'Kemble versus Chippenham. Huge stakes. Now come on – spill.'

'And is that guy you fancy playing?' I was stalling for time, and this line of attack seemed to have worked, as Alice pulled an appalled face. 'One doesn't simply *fancy* Dan Bisley. He is a work of art.'

'Oh yeah,' I said. 'What is it, again? Arms like . . .'

Alice rattled it off impatiently: 'Arms like two pylons wrapped in elephant hide, eyes as pure as azure lagoons and a smile so bright—'

'It could power vast galaxies for a million years. Yes, I remember it now.'

'So—'

'You up for my b-day tradition?' I said, crossing to Alice's DVD shelf.

'Oh, *Withnail*, you mean?'

'Yeah, that OK?'

As I looked for the film, I felt Alice's eyes boring into me. But she didn't ask about Joel again. I got the impression she was giving me the benefit of the doubt, letting me tell her about it in my own time. But we were only ten minutes into the film when she cracked.

'OK, you can't hold out on me any more – are you going to tell me what happened with Joel fucking Thompson or what? It was so weird, him standing there all mournful. Still annoyingly handsome, though. Mum and Dad were pretty thrown. Roger and Beverley pitched up about five minutes after you'd gone but Dad just sent them packing, thank God. So what did he want?'

'Well, it's . . . complicated, really.' I stopped, grappling with shame. Blinded entirely by the promise of my own stupid dream coming true, I'd managed to conveniently forget about my sister.

'Come on – spit it out,' Alice said.

I shifted on the sofa, keeping my eyes on the TV.

'Well, it was just . . . he reminded me we'd made this silly promise when we were kids, where we said we'd walk the Thames Path together when we were thirty.'

'Yeesh,' Alice said. 'I'd forgotten how cool you were.'

'Mmhmm.'

Alice widened her eyes expectantly. 'What, and that was it?'

'Yeah. Well, kind of.'

Alice threw her head back and groaned with frustration.

'OK, OK,' I said. 'But before I tell you – just to be clear – I've told him no. Well, I haven't yet. But I will.'

Alice's eyes flashed dangerously. 'Theo. Will you please just get on with it before I kill you with . . .' – she searched around for a weapon and grabbed something – 'this spatula.' She brandished it menacingly. Why a spatula was in the living room I wasn't sure, but the incongruity only seemed to add to the threat.

'Right. So. The thing is. Years ago, Joel and I came up with an idea for a sitcom called *The Regulars*. He had a meeting with the BBC the other day and happened to mention it and . . .' I picked up my glass of wine and spoke the rest of the sentence very quickly into it: '. . . they've commissioned it and want us to write it and we'd write it together on the path and then it'd be out on the BBC next year.'

For the longest time, Alice didn't say anything. When I finally glanced over, she was staring at me, open-mouthed, still aiming the spatula at me.

'Holy. Fucking. Shitballs. What channel?'

'BBC Two,' I mumbled.

'Time slot?'

'Friday, 9.30 p.m.'

'BBC Two. Friday, 9.30 p.m. My god.'

'Yep.'

'The holy fucking trinity.'

I shrugged. 'Yeah, well . . .'

'So, wait, hang on. You . . . said *no*?'

'No – I mean, I haven't done yet. But I am going to, obviously.'

'Really?'

'Yes,' I said. 'After what happened with you . . .'

Alice went to say something but stopped. I waited for her, but two minutes passed, and then five, and soon we were watching the rest of the film in silence, lost in our own thoughts. Every now and then, I glanced over and saw Alice, her brow furrowed – and I was pretty sure it wasn't anything to do with the film. By the time Withnail was delivering his Hamlet monologue in the final scene, Alice was asleep, head lolling forwards.

I got up, popcorn cascading from my lap, and shook her gently by the arm to try and wake her.

'Time for bed, pal,' I said.

Alice responded with a noise I initially interpreted as either 'Wimbledon' or 'Wigwam', before realising it was probably 'wanker'. (Alice didn't particularly care for being woken up.) I made another couple of half-hearted attempts, but it was no good. So, as gently as I could, I scooped her up out of her wheelchair and into my arms. I wobbled slightly – it had been a while since I'd done this. I was out of practice. As I carried her over to her bedroom, I could have sworn I saw her look up at me, but the next second, her eyes were closed. I took the rest of the journey slowly, partly not to wake her, but mainly because I was enjoying a rare moment where I could be a useful older brother.

I managed to kick the duvet aside and laid Alice carefully down before tucking her in. I was about to leave when I spotted a mosquito lying in wait on the wall. I carried out a commando-style mission to kill it, creeping around the bed, squashing the thing successfully and silently, only to clatter my knee against a cupboard as I made the return journey.

I heard Alice stir, but I didn't seem to have woken her. But then as I was tiptoeing out of her bedroom, she cleared her throat.

'Listen, fuckface, I think you should do it.'

I looked around. She still had her eyes closed. I wondered for a moment if she was dreaming.

'Do what?' I asked.

Alice opened her eyes. 'The TV show. The Thames Path. All of it.'

'No,' I said. 'I don't want to. I should have just slammed the door in his face.'

Alice sat up.

'Now, you listen to me very carefully, OK? What happened, happened. It was a very long time ago.'

'Maybe,' I said. 'But that doesn't mean you should forget it.'

Alice shook her head. 'Sorry, but you don't have a say in how I should feel. The truth is that I am happy with my life. I love being a teacher, I have friends who I am completely obsessed with, and once a week I get to stare at Dan Bisley under the guise of playing basketball. You, on the other hand, are not happy.'

I opened my mouth to retort, but I'd got nothing.

'Think about the last year of your life,' Alice continued. 'You've basically turned into an agoraphobic.'

I rolled my eyes.

'Sorry, I know you hate talking about it, but, Theo, the longer you stay cocooned here, the less chance there is of you getting on with your life. And, look, it's obviously not a bad thing how close we are as a family – but Mum and Dad aren't going to be around forever. That shed's not either. I know Joel fucked things up for you too, with Edinburgh, but that was a decade ago, and at least he's trying to make amends. Aren't you curious to hear him out? Not to mention that it just so happens he's casually dropped the most insanely exciting opportunity of all time at your feet.'

'Well yes, but—'

'Nope. No buts. I'm not saying that everything will suddenly magically fix itself in your life if you do this, but what I do know is that if you aren't waiting for Joel at the start of the path tomorrow morning, it could well be something you regret for the rest of your life. Do you really want to take that chance?'

Later, I wandered back to the shed, pausing to admire the spectacular blood-orange sunset. Alice's words were playing on a loop. I could tell there was no way I'd be able to concentrate now on a book or whatever was on TV, so I dug out the emergency wine.

After a few moments where I built myself up to it, I fought through the bike pumps, linseed oil and tennis rackets to find my old boxes, which I'd labelled 'my old boxes', because I am hilarious. Inside were hundreds of script books, their pages creased, corners bent back, and crammed full of my own handwritten notes: *'Good example of pull back and reveal'. 'Note: rule of three'*. And to think I didn't lose my virginity until I was eighteen.

Digging down further, I found some of my own offerings – at least two dozen notebooks (most of them exercise books pinched from school), each one full from cover to cover.

By the time I'd finished looking through everything, it was nearly midnight. Just as I thought I'd gone through the lot, I found one final exercise book, saw the words written on the front – '*Joel and Theo: Quite the Little Double Act*' – and I found myself hopelessly lost to the past.

∞

On my first day of secondary school at Atherton Comprehensive, I felt uncharacteristically hopeful that I might make some friends there. I'd managed to overcome my shyness a little, and I was determined to find a little gang of my own. I imagined it like in comic books – we'd catch frogs in jam jars and get into adventures on our bikes. I'd be the wisecracking leader, always ready with a funny line. There'd be a gifted nerdy type with thick-rimmed glasses who we'd affectionately call 'The Professor', or 'Prof' for short. Someone exotic – an Australian or American, perhaps. Maybe even a girl! We'd establish ourselves as the Kemble Revue and perform a daring takedown of teachers at the end-of-year panto, the other kids carrying us on their shoulders out of the hall, chanting our names.

It's funny how life works out.

What actually happened was that on my first day I couldn't find my form room, and by the time I had – late – my nerves were shredded to the point that I got stomach cramps so bad I had to sit hunched over. I'd made it barely ten minutes before I had to run from the classroom holding my stomach, asking anyone I saw where the nearest toilet was. There wasn't any coming back after that start. The other kids were naturally suspicious of me. I was like a character in a zombie movie trying to hide he'd been bitten.

I decided to embrace being an outsider instead. It wasn't that I couldn't make any friends, it was that I was actively choosing not to. I'd been watching Hugh Laurie playing Bertie Wooster in the old ITV series, and I persuaded Mum to take me to the charity shops in Gloucester, where I used my pocket money to buy a tweed blazer and a tie. Later came an old broken pocket watch on a little chain, and a cigarette case in which I'd keep fake sweet cigarettes, often tucking one behind my ear. Given that all this went against school uniform rules, the teachers made me change as soon as I got off the bus. But after a while they stopped caring – or maybe it was pity, given my lack of friends – so I'd carry the look into lessons too. The other kids laughed at me first, of course, but eventually everyone got used to seeing this strange little Edwardian throwback shuffling around the place, and people stopped paying attention. Everyone, that was, apart from Darren Brighouse.

Darren had seemed to work himself up to being the class bully – like it was a hobby he'd decided to learn in his spare time. There wasn't anything that sophisticated about his attacks. He was bigger and stronger than everyone else, so if he took a dislike to you, then you got thumped, and that was that. Suspiciously, he had ignored me up to then. Perhaps having to lay a finger on me was just unpalatable. But out of the blue one lunchtime, he came up to me and asked if I wanted to play football with him and some of the others.

'Um, OK,' I said.

Darren laughed and clapped an arm around my shoulder. 'Why do you look so worried, Theo? It's only a kick around.'

'Ha, all right, OK then,' I said, returning Darren's smile. Maybe I'd got him all wrong, I thought, as we headed out to the PE field. Small shoots of hope stirred within me as I pictured dinner that evening, leaning back in my chair and saying, with a casual yawn, 'I might have a friend around sometime, if that's OK, Mum?'

Mum would sit down and take off her apron. 'Oh, love, yes of course!' she'd beam, eyes full of pride, slipping out to call Dad with the good news.

I should have known better when Darren asked me to go into the cricket pavilion to get the football. When I teetered on the edge of the door, realising that something wasn't quite right about this, he shoved me inside and padlocked the door shut. The boys hammered on the dusty window, laughing and whooping. I felt the air swoosh near my head, as what I thought was a bird flew past. But when it landed on a beam and splayed its wings, I realised that it was a bat. I threw myself to the floor and crawled under a bench, shaking with fear. The boys watched on jubilantly until eventually they got bored. After they'd gone, I yelled for help until my throat burned. But nobody came. I'd been trying not to think about how badly I needed the toilet, but eventually the pressure on my bladder got too much. I felt the hot trickle between my legs and began to snivel. When the caretaker, Mr Marstens, finally unlocked the door, I didn't stop running until I was out past the school and into town.

When I got home, I was desperate to hide that anything was wrong, but as soon as Mum asked me brightly how my day had been, I couldn't hold back my tears. I only began to feel better later when Alice skipped over and presented me with a drawing she'd done of the two of us, with a caption she'd written underneath – 'Theo, my brother, the bravest idiot I know', which made me laugh and cry at the same time.

If I thought the pavilion was a one-off, then I was mistaken. I became Darren's go-to target all the way through year seven and into year eight. At first, I tried fighting back, but he seemed to relish that even more because it gave him an excuse to hit me harder. So in the end my tactic was to ball myself up like a hedgehog, waiting for it all to be over. I would hear people walking past, barely stopping their conversations. That was what hurt the most. Maybe I hadn't tried hard enough not to be so weird. Maybe I deserved it.

Then, one lunchtime, Darren sportingly told me in advance that if he saw me again during the next hour, he was going to make me cry. I decided I wasn't going to take any chances. Rather than spending lunchtime out in the sunshine with everyone else, I holed up in the boys' toilets in the music block. I was safe, but I found the whole thing so shameful – sitting there eating my packed lunch in a toilet cubicle, listening to someone murdering 'Smoke on the Water' on an out-of-tune guitar next door. My Walkman was on its last legs by then. It only played the tape if the deck itself was secured shut with two thick elastic bands, but it still did the job. I listened to *Blackadder* with one headphone, leaving my other ear free to listen for anyone approaching. It was inevitably at the moment I began to relax when Darren and his goons decided to explore the music block.

'Where's Theodore got to then?' I heard Darren say, as they bundled their way into the bathroom.

There was the sound of aggressive pissing. The roar of the hand driers made me jump, and, to my horror, I felt my Walkman slip from my sweaty hand and clatter to the floor. The sound had been drowned out by the drier, but one of the batteries had come free and was rolling towards the cubicle door. I scrabbled to grab it, but it was too late.

'Look!'

'Where'd that come from?'

I shrank back, trying to work out which was the most likely point of attack.

'Who's in there? Is that you, Theodore?'

I heard the adjacent cubicle door bang open, and a moment later a face appeared above the door.

'Oh my god, it is!'

I looked wildly around for something to defend myself with. But all I had was my Walkman, and I really didn't want to damage that.

It had gone momentarily quiet outside the cubicle. But then, chaos. I was being pelted from above and under the door by water-soaked paper towels and handfuls of liquid soap. I threw my arms over my head and assumed the brace position. My attackers' voices got louder as they egged each other on, like hyenas consumed by bloodlust. During a brief respite, I managed to pull my blazer up over my head, though I couldn't stop the cold soap trickling down my back. But then, as soon as the attack began, it had stopped. There was another voice. One I didn't recognise, quiet and calm.

'I said, what are you doing?'

'And I said, piss off.'

The response was meant to sound aggressive, but it was too hesitant. Darren was clearly wary.

'I don't think you should be doing that to whoever's in there.'

'Whatever.'

I heard feet shuffling. Some quiet sniggering. To my relief, it sounded like they'd all left, but then someone knocked on the cubicle door.

I got to my feet. My hands were shaking. My eyes stung from the soap. But whatever was waiting for me outside, I felt resigned to it. I just wanted to get it over with. I pulled open the door, determined to stare Darren down before he attacked. But he was gone, taking his gang with him. Instead, standing at the sink was a tall, wiry boy I hadn't seen before. He didn't react when he saw the state I was in, as if he'd barely registered that I was covered head to toe in a gloopy soap paste.

'You all right?' he asked, passing me a wedge of dry towels.

'Yeah. Fine,' I said, pressing the coarse paper to my face, holding it there for a moment to hide my tears. Whether they were from relief at the ordeal being over, or just because the boy had been kind to me, I wasn't sure. But by the time he'd introduced himself as Joel, and asked if I was sure I was OK, in a way that made me feel like I was a normal person, I felt that strange, ungraspable feeling that steals over you when you realise the ground has shifted under your feet, and that everything is about to change.

Chapter Ten

Joel

I could count the times I'd been back to my childhood home on the fingers of one hand. Admittedly, one of those times had ended up with me staying for months, but I had been in too much of a state to remember much of it. The memories that lingered were only unpleasant ones.

I paid the cabbie who'd driven me from the station, and crossed the road, hanging back in the porch. I could see Mum through the living-room window, hunched over her laptop. There were dull rings under her eyes, like she hadn't had a proper sleep in days. She frowned and started looking around for something, lifting a magazine, shifting a stack of papers.

I smiled. It was her glasses she was after. 'They're on your head,' I muttered. 'Like they always are.'

I shrank back as I felt a dangerous stirring of sadness. I should have come back here more often, no matter how difficult it was. I shouldn't have taken Mum for granted all these years. I clenched my fists and tried to shake myself out of it. On no account was I going to let Mum see me upset.

I rang the doorbell. As Mum opened the door I painted a smile onto my face.

'Darling!'

'Hello, Mum.'

She pulled me into a hug. It felt like I had to stoop a little more than usual. It startled me how thin she felt. Was that all the worrying?

'Something smells nice,' I said. I realised I couldn't remember the last thing I'd had to eat. I was starving.

'I'm making a curry,' Mum said, ushering me into the hall. 'Chock-full of turmeric. Brilliant all-rounder apparently. You have been taking the capsules I've been sending, haven't you?'

'Oh *that's* what those are,' I said, hanging my coat up. 'I thought they were worming tablets for the cat.'

Mum pretended I hadn't said anything. She took my jacket from the hook I'd hung it on and moved it six inches over to another identical hook.

'What about the other things I emailed you about? Did you have any thoughts on milk thistle yet?'

'Only that he was my least favourite dwarf in *Lord of the Rings*.'

'Joel, I really think—'

'Hey, come on, Mum.' I took her gently by the arms. 'Let's not talk about that stuff, eh? Let's just have a nice relaxing evening.'

'I suppose,' Mum sighed.

'Excellent,' I said. 'Now. Quick question. Are my old walking boots here?'

'They're in the cupboard under the stairs,' Mum said. She went off into the kitchen at the sound of a pan boiling over. 'What on earth do you need those for?'

'I'm walking the Thames Path,' I said, bracing for Mum's reaction. Sure enough, I heard her drop something that clattered onto the floor. When I came into the kitchen, she was staring at me as if I'd gone completely mad.

'You can't be serious,' she said. 'It's two hundred miles.'

'Not quite that, and it's basically flat the entire way.'

'Yes, for *two hundred* miles. And what does Amber think of all this?'

'She, um . . .'

I pretended to be distracted by something the other side of the room. Walking over to the fridge, I bent down to inspect the photo of me and Mum in the garden when I was a little boy. My hair was a white blond back then. I couldn't remember how old I was before the colour changed.

'*Joel*,' Mum pressed.

'Oh, you know . . .' I waved my hand airily. 'How old was I in this picture by the way?'

'Don't change the subject,' Mum said. Then I heard her let out a little gasp. 'Joel, please tell me you've told Amber about . . . everything.'

I straightened up. 'Well, not exactly. Not yet.'

'So when you said you were going to tell her as soon as you got off the phone to me, you were just lying, were you?'

I scratched at the back of my head, feeling like a teenager, as if I'd been caught red-handed stealing a beer from the fridge. 'I'll tell her when the time's right.'

Mum looked like she was going to say something else, but she turned back to her cooking and began chopping away, taking her worries out on some coriander. I crossed the kitchen and put a hand on her shoulder, giving it a gentle squeeze. After a moment, she stopped chopping and put her arms around me.

Remember this moment, I thought. *Remember how much love there is in this hug; remember how the windows are fogged with steam; remember the daffodils in the wonky clay vase you made on that school trip.*

*

I was exhausted, but I couldn't sleep. How often as a kid had I stared at this ceiling, feeling anger and sadness boiling inside me as I listened to Mum and Dad – and then, after the divorce, Mum and Mike – arguing downstairs? At times, everything would bubble over and I wouldn't be able to take it any more. As time went on, I had learned to deal with the pain by hurting myself in a different way. It had started with me scraping my fists along the rough wall, progressing to punching it as hard as I needed to until the pain drowned everything out. It had been my shameful secret for a long time.

Now, as I ran my fingers over the familiar bumps and grooves, I thought back to the moment at the end of my first year at Hescott High School when Mum and Dad sat me down and told me they were divorcing. Even as a twelve-year-old, I could sense the forced show of civility as they held hands at the kitchen table and Dad told me he was going to be moving out for a while. A fortnight later, that had been upgraded slightly, to 'moving to Australia'.

'For how long?' I'd asked him.

'Well, mate,' he said, clearing his throat, 'sort of, permanently. But you'll have to come out and visit, you know, when you're a bit older.'

'But, but . . .' I tried uselessly to stop my whimpering, which I knew he hated. 'It's not fair,' I moaned.

'Now listen,' Dad said sharply. 'Life's not fair. Stop crying, OK. You're not a girl. You're the man of the house now. Your mum's going to rely on you.'

I didn't understand what he was asking of me. He was the one who was leaving.

For the last two weeks of school, it had felt like a great

weight was pressing down on my chest. All I wanted to do was kick and punch at something, or someone. On the last day of term, we were allowed to bring in games and watch films instead of doing lessons. I sat at the back of the classroom ignoring everyone, watching the clock tick closer towards 3.30 p.m. when I could finally get out of the stifling room. But once I thought of how I'd be spending the summer without Dad, the rage overwhelmed me, and the next thing I knew I'd grabbed a stapler from my desk and hurled it as hard as I could across the room, where it skimmed off the wall directly into Oscar Tate's face. If my grades had been better, I might have got away with it. But given the threat of legal action by Oscar's parents, Mum was informed that it would be best if I were to find a new school to join the following term.

I think about that moment a lot, and how it changed the course of my life. If I'd made it to 3.30 p.m. without exploding, then I wouldn't have been kicked out of school. I'd never have met Theo. I'd never have met Amber . . .

Lying on my old bed, now, I felt the familiar, overwhelming need to punch the wall just like I used to, to let out the pain at the unfairness of it all, to release the anger. A sudden pang of nausea made me sit up in bed. I had to take slow, deep breaths until it passed. These episodes had been happening more and more. And the thing was, it was only going to get worse.

I turned the light on and reached for my jeans, pulling out the crumpled letter. The page had ripped slightly at the top, just below the NHS logo. I couldn't remember doing that. I don't know why, but it made me cross to have caused the tear. I began to read the letter yet again:

Dear Mr Thompson,

Re: Test results

Following your diagnosis, we are referring you to the hepatology department

I stopped. What was the point? The same words were there every time I read it, in black and white, sending me spiralling back to the moment I'd first known something was wrong.

I'd not felt anything other than unusually tired the day I'd suddenly had to run out of a *Tooth* rehearsal to vomit. I'd assumed it was just a bug, but when I lifted my head from the bowl, I saw blood. What I remember most about the doctor who'd examined me and then sent me for tests was how entirely humourless he was. I wasn't exactly expecting him to start cracking jokes, but he wore the expression of a man who thought smiling and laughter were things you should grow out of. Given that I'd taken against him somewhat, when he sat me down and told me what was wrong, I'd felt quite pleased to be able to set him straight.

'Ah, but that can't be right,' I'd said. 'I've not had a drink for five years.'

'That, unfortunately, is the problem with liver disease,' the doctor replied. 'Often, as in your case, there are no symptoms at all until it is at a very advanced stage. Your, er, lifestyle, has been the contributing factor, but you also mentioned an incident when you were younger, when you injured yourself falling down the stairs?'

'What about it?' I said, doing my best to hold the memory at bay.

'Your records show that you incurred a laceration, and bile duct inflammation. That is consistent with where the problem lies today. Your bile ducts never fully recovered, and, along with alcohol abuse, that has led to primary biliary cirrhosis.'

'Oh. Right. Well, what do we do then? Is it medication, or . . .?'

The doctor had breathed out heavily through his nose. Then he'd wheeled his chair around his desk so that he was closer to me. I could smell coffee on his breath. I noticed that he had two pens in his top pocket but one was missing its lid. I wondered if I should tell him.

'I'm sorry,' he said, 'but things are too advanced for that. You are in urgent need of a liver transplant. We shall put you down as a priority on the waiting list, that is very much Plan A, but I'm afraid, given the severity of the cirrhosis, time is not on your side.'

The doctor had explained more about 'Plan A', and went on to talk about a 'Plan B', but I'd already zoned out. I was picturing Amber's face, seeing her eyes go glassy with tears. The thought of her reacting to the news had made me feel faint, and suddenly I couldn't catch my breath, and before I knew it, I was gasping for air and the doctor was rushing to find me water.

A small consolation was that Amber was away with work. When the letter arrived the next day, I took it to Hampstead Heath, where I sat on a bench, trying to make sense of it all. I stayed there for hours, watching people coming and going. It seemed unfathomable that people were still carrying on like normal. Surely the world was about to grind to a halt: the birds would stop singing. Car engines would cut out. The people dotted around the Heath were about to stop what they were doing and turn as one to face me – waiting for me to stand up on the bench and confirm that the news was true: I was ill, and I wasn't getting better. I whispered the words out loud, like a guilty secret, and tried my hardest not to cry.

Later, back home, I sat at my kitchen table and laid my head on my arms, staring into middle distance. Eventually, my eyes had focused on the red light of the oven clock. I watched the static display, waiting for it to change. It was at the point where I thought it must be broken when it finally flicked over from 5:31 to 5:32. Was that how long a minute lasted? It felt like an age. Time seemed to have taken on an unreal quality now I knew my own was limited. I had an acute awareness of every second slipping past – each one wasted as I failed to do something that proved I was still alive. I jumped to my feet, inertia giving way to urgency, and began searching the house for pen and paper. I found a biro under a coffee table in the living room, but the only thing I had to write on was the back of the letter. It felt appropriate, somehow, to be planning how to best use the time I had left on the other side of the words condemning me to my fate. *I'm not done yet*, I thought, and at the top of the page I wrote the words:

My Kicking The Bucket List

I looked at the space below. I'm used to having to confront a blank page in my day job. It's the worst of enemies. Sometimes it wins and I'm forced to admit defeat, shutting my laptop and going out on what Amber calls one of my 'big serious walks'. Well, I didn't have that luxury now. The oven clock ticked over. Another minute gone. I knew at least what I *wasn't* going to write. I had no interest in an internet-assembled list of adrenaline highs, so there'd be no skydiving or bungee jumping. All that really mattered to me was the people who'd stuck by me, even though I'd done my best at times to drive everyone away. It seemed like doing anything other than trying to bring these people as much happiness as I could was time wasted. And there was only one place to start.

Amber

The act of writing down her name set off an avalanche of memories, but one in particular stood out, from nearly a decade ago. Amber was fresh out of drama school, and she'd asked me to run some lines with her before an audition. It was the first time I'd seen the script, so I didn't know what was coming. I was playing the part of her husband. I was woodenly intoning the lines, while Amber, in character, was breezy and distracted, pretending to fold clothes. And then I got to a line where my character revealed some bad news. I'd looked up from the script to see Amber's face contorted with grief and shock – and I remember just *staring* at her, like my heart might have stopped, as if I had only seconds before I'd topple to the ground . . . and then her face had suddenly snapped back to looking confused.

'What, did I miss a line or something?' She wiped the tears away with her sleeves and took the script out of my hands.

I pretended I'd forgotten I had a work call. I went to the bedroom and shut the door, sitting on the edge of the bed where I waited for god knows how long until I'd shaken the moment off.

As I looked down at her name on the paper, I knew there was no way I could tell her. The day would come when she had to learn the truth, but I would keep that pain and sadness and shock away from her as long as I physically could. That day could wait. For now I'd keep everything as normal and unchanged as possible. I was going to do my best to stop time.

Mum

Mum was the only person I'd told about my diagnosis. I felt immediately guilty at doing so, because it had sent her into a spiral where she was spending all her time browsing these mad websites that claimed you could cure cancer with things from your spice rack. What I needed to do was get her far away from all that. And that was when I'd remembered the holiday I had been promising to take her on for years. It was Lisbon she'd always wanted to go to. Her dad – my grandad – had spent time out there as a young man, and had been particularly taken with the locals and their fado music. When Mum was feeling blue for some reason, Grandad would put some fado on, especially in the winter, to help let in the sunshine. Well, now was the time for her to see the real thing up close. A no-expense spared holiday of a lifetime. A chance for us to spend time with each other in a way we'd never been able to before. A moment where we could step out of the shadows of our past, and feel the sun on our faces, finally banishing what the two of us had been through together.

Theo

I stared at the name I'd just written down. It was as if I'd done it subconsciously. But the more I thought about it, the more it made sense. Hardly a day went by where I didn't think about him. The idea of him resenting me for the rest of his life, even if I wasn't going to be around for much more of it, just felt unbearable. I longed to recapture the spirit of one of those glorious lost summers, where it felt like we were the luckiest pair of idiots in the whole world. That was the moment I remembered the Thames Path, and the promise we'd made. How wonderful it would be to find a new ending for our friendship – one that recalled when we were happiest instead. This was my final chance to make up for everything, to have my best friend alongside me again, to recover what was lost. Under the circumstances, the Thames Path was daunting. But I was determined to make it before my condition deteriorated. If I had Theo at my side from where the river started as a hesitant trickle in that muddy field in Kemble, to where it became the impatient, slate-grey mass weaving through London, I was sure that I could fix things.

As I listened to an owl hooting softly outside, I pushed away the doubts creeping in which told me I was already too weak for the journey. I might have to dig deeper than I'd ever done before, but I wasn't going to go to sleep on an argument. I wanted one last glorious adventure with my oldest friend instead.

The question was, did Theo?

Chapter Eleven

Theo

I'd finished the emergency wine and was on to the emergency gin. It was safe to say that, by the letter of the law, I was, to some extent, drunk. As I'd tried to make sense of Joel's appearance, it was like a trapdoor to the past had been opened, and I was sliding hopelessly towards it. And, as so often happened when I'd hit a certain level of drunkenness, and nostalgia appeared on the scene, I found myself thinking about the night Babs and I had met for the very first time.

∞

Everywhere I looked, people were starting to form groups, striking up conversations and taking photos with disposable cameras. How could all these people possibly be so comfortable in their own skin on the first night of uni? At one end of the student union bar, the more gregarious freshers were taking things even further. A boat-race drinking game was in progress. Two people were kissing up against the wall. It was barely six o'clock! What *was* this, the last days of Rome?!

I saw Rex, a boy from my corridor. He was talking to a girl, and even with her back to me, I could tell she was bored.

With nobody else to talk to, I didn't have much choice but to go over.

'Hey,' I said.

Rex looked annoyed that I'd interrupted him. The girl, who was a little shorter than me, wearing dungarees and scuffed white trainers, seemed relieved to have someone else to talk to.

'Hi,' she said. 'I'm Babs.'

As she smiled politely and I realised how pretty she was, I predictably lost the ability to form sentences.

'Were you named after Babs in *Acorn Antiques*?' I managed at last, immediately regretting the question, along with a lot of other choices I'd made in my life – my personality being the main one.

'What's Acorn Antiques?' Rex asked.

'It's a spoof soap opera that Victoria Wood wrote,' Babs said.

Ah, I thought. This . . . is a dream. This *has* to be a dream. She knew about *Acorn Antiques*, for god's sake! Nobody ever knew about *Acorn Antiques*.

I was struck by the vibrant hue of her eyes, which were a rich, dark brown, with a faint hint of gold. The combination of colours reminded me of something, but I couldn't put my finger on it.

Just then, a girl in a sparkly top walked past. Like a horrible little magpie distracted by something shiny, Rex darted after her.

'Well, I'm devastated,' Babs said. 'I thought he only had eyes for me.'

She lit a cigarette and offered me one, which I took, willing myself not to cough. I was acutely aware of how much cooler than me she seemed. Even the way she exhaled smoke, head tilted back slightly, was impossibly glamorous – like a rock star who'd just cut the finest take of a record they knew was going to go platinum.

I searched for something to say.

'So . . . what are you studying?'

'Philosophy,' Babs said, sounding a bit bored by such a classic go-to student question. 'You?'

'English.'

'Well, aren't we going to be useful to society in a couple of years?'

'Yeah,' I said, 'You're always hearing someone coming over a loudspeaker and saying, "Is there someone who can quote Larkin in the house?" aren't you?'

A smile spread out slowly on Babs's face. It was a smile that said, 'Maybe this person isn't *quite* as dull as I'd initially thought.'

We watched Rex talking to the girl he'd pursued. She was already eying an escape route.

'I wonder if he's trying the same line on her as he did on me,' Babs said.

'Which was?'

'"I'll cook you dinner if you cook me breakfast."'

'Wow.'

'I know.'

'What did you say?'

'Oh, I took him completely at face value and agreed. I could see him panicking about how he was going to make dinner without a kitchen.'

I laughed.

'Do lines like that ever work?' Babs asked.

'Not in my experience,' I said.

Babs raised her eyebrows.

'That came out wrong,' I blustered. 'I meant that I've never actually tried one, not that I've tried it loads and it's never worked. I'm not sure where I'd start. What is it again? You look all . . . tired . . . because you've been running around in my mind all night?'

'My word,' Babs said, grabbing my arm. 'Take me now!'

I smiled stupidly, looking down at where she'd just touched me.

People were starting to head off for new adventures, which meant Babs and I managed to secure a table. Even though I realised my early impression of her as 'pretty' was a ludicrous understatement, I just about managed to hold myself together as we talked. That was until the barman went to take my glass away and I jammed my hand on it to stop him depriving me of the tiny mouthful left. Babs found this hilarious, and her subsequent laughter turned – gloriously – into a snort.

She sighed. 'My one weakness. *The snort*. I'm quite impressed, actually. Usually only people I've known for a very long time can make me do that.'

I made a mental note to mention this at our golden wedding anniversary. Then I added a footnote telling myself to CALM THE FUCK DOWN.

At a natural break in our conversation, we kept eye contact. It was only for a fleeting moment, but I could feel my heart begin to hammer in my chest. Babs smiled, and I noticed the laugh lines either side of her mouth, like two perfect crescent moons. I thought how they suited her. And that I'd give rather a lot to spend more evenings like this, trying to make those lines even more prominent.

We left the bar, both a little wobbly, and made our way back to our halls. We paused at the staircase where we were to go to our separate corridors. This, I realised, was very clearly the moment when I was supposed to ask Babs for her number, or whether she wanted to meet up again – or at least say *something* rather than standing silently with a stupid grin on my face. Thankfully, Babs came to my rescue.

Nodding at something behind me, she said, 'I'm auditioning for that. Basically the only reason I'm here.'

I turned to see a poster for the Sheffield comedy revue.

My thoughts turned again to the very real possibility that I was either dreaming, or perhaps in a padded cell somewhere talking to a finger puppet I'd made out of a toilet roll.

'Um, are you OK?' Babs said, frowning. 'I only ever made it to one session of first-aid training, but it does look a little bit like you're having a heart attack.'

'Yeah, sure, no, I'm fine,' I said. I pointed my thumb back at the poster. 'I'm auditioning too.'

I couldn't tell if Babs believed me, but now wasn't the moment for the entire potted history of my life's obsession.

'Well, I'm very glad to hear that,' Babs said. This time, we held eye contact for a full second. Then Babs took a step towards me. 'This is a bit awkward, but I realised I never actually asked your name . . .'

I was still finding it very hard to process what had just happened. Babs knew about *Acorn Antiques*. The ONLY REASON she was here was because of the revue.

She wants to know your name, a more urgent voice in my head reminded me. *So you should say it. Quickly, say it. OK, she's starting to look very confused now. Say it, you idiot. Say it!*

'It's Theo!' I said, in a volume more appropriate for warning someone they were in the path of a runaway train.

'Right,' Babs said, understandably taken aback. Though not quite as much as I was when she'd regained her composure enough to lean in and kiss me softly on the mouth. 'Night then, Theo,' she said. 'I'm really glad we met tonight.'

As we parted ways and I turned, punch-drunk, to go to my room, I became aware of three things. One, that I'd realised what it was that Babs's eyes – the brown and the tinge of gold – reminded me of, and that it was Jaffa Cakes. Two, that I had come horribly close to telling her this. And three, that there was a very real chance that she already had a piece of my heart, and that I was never getting it back.

Lying in the dark of the shed, I pondered how on earth I'd managed to let things go so badly wrong. It had been two years now since we'd broken up, but I still wasn't over her. Part of that was because my brain had filtered out any of the bad memories. Not for the first time, I couldn't shake the feeling that we could be happy together again. And as soon as I had that thought, I realised that I was about to do something that was incontrovertibly, one hundred percent definitely, a *good idea* and had *nothing* to do with me being drunk.

It took a good degree of scrolling and jabbing at my phone until I found the right contact.

'Hello?'

'Babs! It's me. It's Theo.'

'Yeah, I saw your name come up. Phones are very modern these days.'

There was a lot of noise in the background. It sounded like she was in a bar.

'Where are you?' I asked.

'Edinburgh.'

As if to confirm this, I heard a man with a Scottish accent say, 'Babs, another pint yeah?'

My brain immediately got to work. He was a new boyfriend. Edinburgh – *of course*. She'd always had a thing for Scots. He'd be a redhead, but one of those men who properly pulls it off, with a beard that takes him about five minutes to grow. What else? He was an accomplished painter who'd turned down the chance to sell his work for millions of dollars at a New York auction house because that wasn't really why he painted. By night, he taught himself law and defended the rights of the destitute, pro-bono, restless until justice was carried out. Babs had met him at yoga, where he had achieved the impossible by being the only solo male yoga class member in history without making it creepy. He cooked things in slow cookers – seasoned with herbs from his herb garden, paired with wines you had to serve at exactly the right temperature or you lost the notes of seagull tears and griddled trilbies and spoiled its inquisitive finish. He could put up shelves and didn't own a smartphone. He was spontaneous. The kind of person to make you breathe a sigh of relief when you saw their name on an invite list. He made people feel at ease. When they talked, he listened, rather than just waiting for his turn to speak. He was happy. He was an optimist. He took genuine joy in making others happy. In short, the guy was the absolute fucking worst.

'Theo?'

Panic and despair tussled over who got to consume me first. This was quite clearly the stupidest idea I'd ever had. Alice was going to kill me with that spatula when she found out.

'Yeah, I'm here, I was just calling to say hello.' I hiccupped, like a cartoon drunk.

'Right. Are you maybe ever so slightly hammered?' She sounded wary, but I ploughed on.

'No. Well, maybe. A bit. But it's only because I've actually got some news. It's . . .' I faltered. What news did I have, exactly? I'd hoped a reason for the call would present itself, but I'd got nothing. I really should just hang up. That was so clearly what I should do.

'Um, Theo, can you maybe get to the point. Bit busy. It being Saturday night and all.'

Oh god.

'Theo?'

'OK, yes, right so, drumroll . . . I'm . . . going to have a TV show!'

There was silence for a moment from the other end of the line.

'Oh. Right. Well, thanks for letting me know,' Babs said. 'Is that it, or . . .?'

'No, no, like – this is proper. I mean BBC. Prime time.'

Everything went muffled for a moment, then the line cleared and I could hear traffic.

'I missed that last bit,' Babs said. 'What were you saying?'

Why wasn't I hanging up? There was still time to end this with a tiny shred of dignity intact. But then suddenly I was back with Babs in the student union bar, caught in the split-second where we'd held eye contact, where everything had felt alive with possibility . . . and I just *couldn't*.

'I . . . Well, it's nothing, really, but I had this good news about this show, and . . . it . . . didn't seem right you not being the first person I told.'

73

'Oh. OK.' There was just enough softness in the way she said this, as if it might have meant something to her, that it made me barrel on.

'All those days in London after the Sky thing didn't work out and I just pissed everything up the wall.'

'Theo—'

'I can't believe what an idiot I was – how much I took you for granted. But I've been thinking about the old days too and how happy we were. Remember that first night where we met? There was that awful guy Rex and—'

'Theo, please just let me talk.'

I winced. That didn't sound good.

'I think you've maybe had a few too many drinks. It's late, and I'm with my friends. If you really want to have a proper discussion about what happened, then this really is about the worst way you could have approached it.'

'I know, I know – I'm sorry. But it's just . . .'

I swigged some gin straight from the bottle.

Don't do it. Don't you dare do it . . .

'I miss you,' I said.

As I waited for Babs to acknowledge this, I thought I heard someone asking if she was OK. Then came the faint strains of a busker clinging on for dear life to the right key as he sang 'Hallelujah'.

'Theo,' Babs started. But she had to stop. I could hear the sadness in her voice. It made me well up. 'Well done on the TV show, Theo, but you really need to understand something.'

'What's that?' I said, but I knew I didn't want to hear the answer.

'I've moved on. And you really should, too.'

The line went dead.

Outside, I heard the village church clock began to strike twelve. My birthday was over.

I waited until just after eight the next morning before going around to Alice's. I'd barely slept, but I felt suspiciously OK. I assumed the hangover was biding its time, like a mugger waiting to jump out from the shadows.

'Nobody in the history of the world has ever been up this early on a Sunday,' Alice groaned, as she let me in. 'I need tea. Come on, chop-chop. You better have a good excuse for this.'

'I do,' I said. 'I've decided I'm going to do the walk with Joel.'

Alice turned herself slowly in her chair to face me. She took in my battered old waterproof jacket and rucksack. I'd hoped I looked like a noble explorer, Sir Ranulph Fiennes or someone. Judging by the way Alice was looking at me, I suspect I looked more like one of those idiots who goes up Ben Nevis in their flip-flops with half a flapjack and has to call Mountain Rescue an hour later. But then Alice grinned, and I felt a little better.

'Well, I'm shocked,' she said. 'In a good way, I mean. What made you change your mind?'

I picked at a bit of chipped paint on the kitchen doorframe. 'OK, don't shout at me, but last night, I may have got quite drunk and called Babs.'

Alice gasped. 'What?! Theo!'

'I know, I'm an idiot,' I said. 'But speaking to her was a massive fucking wake-up call.'

'Go on . . .' Alice said, frowning, but apparently willing to give me the benefit of the doubt.

'Well, it's pretty clear she's moved on,' I continued. 'And that sort of put everything in perspective. I mean, I don't know if I'm going to be able to forgive Joel, but up until I saw him yesterday I was still living as if all that shit between us had only just happened. It's like I've sort of been stuck there ever since. So if doing this with him helps me move past it all, then that shows that things can change, right? And if I can find common ground with Joel again, then I can get over Babs too.' It felt good to say this out loud. And I felt even more sure of my convictions as Alice nodded approvingly while I spoke, like a proud teacher listening to her student explain a tricky equation. 'Yeah,' she said, '*and* you're going to get a big fat TV show out of it and everything.'

I smiled. 'Well yeah, that too.' I'd emailed Jake, my boss, asking if it was OK if I took all my remaining holiday for the year over the next three weeks. That he'd signed-off on it seconds later with the message 'Sure' suggested I might not be long for the Captain Beefy world anyway.

'I'm proud of you, bro,' Alice yawned, rubbing sleep from her eyes. 'I mean, you may look like every nerdy hacker in a heist film who disarms the bank's CCTV . . .'

'. . . Right.'

'But you're actually braver than you might think, deep, deep, *deep* down.'

I leaned against the door, as if I'd taken a blow to the chest. 'I think that's the nicest thing you've ever said about me.'

An hour later, it was time to say goodbye to Mum and Dad. I took Mum aside and gave her the heads-up on Dad's newest hare-brained scheme.

'He's eying up the dining room. I think he wants to knock

through to the living room, but I googled it and I think it might be a load-bearing wall, so just keep an eye on that, OK?'

'I actually think it's you that needs to be careful,' Mum said. 'It's going to be harder than you think, this walk. It'll take its toll.'

'Mum, I'm going to be strolling through Henley with wine-in-a-can, it's not exactly Fallujah.'

Mum sighed, but kissed me on the cheek anyway. Dad reappeared and handed me some insect repellent which I was fairly sure had expired when Wham! were in the charts.

'I'll, um, tear up the eviction notice then,' he said, patting me awkwardly on the shoulder.

'Appreciate it,' I said. 'Right then . . .' The three of us went outside and joined Alice in the driveway. I saw Mum take Dad's hand and squeeze it. Alice gave me a thumbs up.

I turned around, looking at the winding lane ahead of me. This was it. As uncomfortable as I felt about leaving, not to mention the person I was on my way to meet, I was determined that the next time I came back here it would be through choice, not because I was still too scared to be anywhere else. Every time I felt crushed about Babs, I'd remember her telling me that she'd moved on. By the time I reached London, the memory of the night we met would be nothing but a reminder of the pleasant sting of first love.

I adjusted the straps of my rucksack and waved one final goodbye to my family. Then I began to walk towards the place where my past and my future were waiting for me.

Chapter Twelve

Joel

I left the house far earlier than I needed to, partly out of nerves, partly because I didn't want to get caught in another conversation with Mum where she asked me about when I was going to tell Amber about being sick, or badger me about some new miracle cure, or 'Plan B'. I left her a note on the kitchen table. *Off on my adventure! I'll be back before you know it. Love Joel x.* I wasn't feeling half as cheery as the note implied, but anything to make Mum worry less.

It was another beautiful day, the sun already strong on my neck. Sun cream was one of the many things I'd forgotten to pack. In fact, I'd barely brought enough supplies for a gentle morning stroll, let alone a 184-mile walk. I'd have to bank on Theo being overprepared. That was if he actually turned up.

I took the train one stop to Kemble and made my way to the Thames Head. As I sat down by the scratched stone monument and took out my laptop, my phone buzzed. A message from Amber.

Hey, how's your mum?

So-so, I replied, pushing past the guilt at the white lie. I'll call you later. How's Italy?

Perfect, Amber wrote. Apart from the fact you're not here. Tell your mum lots of love from me.

As two butterflies spiralled past, falling and climbing with the breeze, I imagined Amber sitting on the terrace with a coffee, feeling the same warmth from the sun that I was here – content, untroubled. Happy.

You're doing the right thing, I told myself.

It was nearly ten. I opened a new document on my laptop, and began to type.

'The Regulars'
By Joel Thompson

I looked up as I heard the iron cattle gate at the other side of the field clanging shut. I let out a long, deep breath when I saw who had opened it and, cracking my knuckles with a satisfying snap, typed three more words.

and Theo Hern

PART TWO

PART TWO

Chapter Thirteen

Theo

Thames Head to Cricklade, 12.2 miles (184 miles to Thames Barrier, London)

Joel beamed as I approached. 'All right?'

'All right,' I replied.

'Well then, here we are,' he said.

I used a hand to shield my eyes from the sun, and cleared my throat.

'Before we go any further, I want to say something.'

'OK,' Joel said, as he took sunglasses from his top pocket.

'I don't want to talk about what happened to Alice, and I don't want to talk about Edinburgh. They're both off limits. We can talk as much as you want about stupid shit from school – like, you know, that PE teacher who wore those tiny little shorts where you could basically see his balls.'

Joel grimaced. 'Mr Arkwright?'

'That's the one. But that's it. Nothing serious or heavy. OK?'

Joel smiled, but it was hard to properly read his expression with his sunglasses on.

'That sounds fine by me,' he said. 'I hereby promise that we will largely stick to our old PE teacher's balls. So to speak.'

And with that, we began to walk, settling into a comfortable pace, our boots swishing through the grass.

'This feels a bit of an anticlimactic way to start a big trip,' I said, stepping around a particularly juicy cowpat.

'How do you mean?' Joel asked.

'Well, as "road trips" go, it's all a bit sedate and British, isn't it? If this was Route 66, this would be the point we'd whack on Springsteen and rev the engine of our Mustang. Even if we were doing the Pennine Way there'd probably be some dramatic mountains in the distance, instead of . . . this.' I gestured at a sheep that had chosen that moment to wander across the path – hesitantly, like a grandparent walking into a room and forgetting why they'd gone in there.

'True,' Joel said. 'But according to the guidebook there'll be loads of interesting stuff cropping up along the way.'

I raised my eyebrows.

'What?' Joel said.

'Nothing. I'm just surprised you thought to bring a guidebook, that's all. I can't help but notice you're dressed as if you're about to open for The Strokes on the John Peel stage.'

Joel was wearing the same skinny black jeans, black T-shirt and leather jacket combo as when he'd arrived on my birthday. The only concession to the length of the walk was that he'd replaced his box-fresh trainers with some knackered-looking walking boots.

'Don't know what you're talking about,' Joel said, before taking a pork-pie hat from his jacket pocket and setting it at a jaunty angle on his head.

After about twenty minutes, we came across the muddy pool in the corner of a field, known as 'Lyd Well', the point where the river technically starts, although the riverbed that led on from it was still bone dry. As we passed it, I realised my natural walking pace was taking me on ahead of Joel. He seemed to be happy to plod along, stopping to look at anything that vaguely took his interest. I felt a bit impatient at having to hang back and wait. Part of this I realised was from nervous energy. Both because I still hadn't decided if I was doing the right thing in coming on the trip at all, and because I was itching to talk about *The Regulars*. But when we stopped for lunch in a nondescript pub in a village called Somerford Keynes, Joel still hadn't brought it up. I felt a bit cowed by how he was the expert these days. He was the one who'd made it, after all. Maybe it was a challenge – he was waiting to see if I still had what it took. I felt queasy at the thought he might have to let me down gently, sending me home with my tail between my legs because I wasn't good enough, having to hope I still had my stupid Twitter job to come back to.

I thought it might finally come up over lunch, but Joel seemed distracted, pushing his food around his plate. It wasn't until later, as we walked on through meadowland – soundtracked by crickets in the grass and buzzards keening overhead – that I decided I'd just have to go for it.

'So then – the writing. How do you want to start?'

'However you want,' Joel replied, stooping to pick up a tall bit of grass which he clamped between his teeth.

'Yeah, but, aren't there rules we have to follow? X has to happen on page Y or the focus groups will hate it and the studio will cancel it, or whatever.'

'No,' Joel said, 'because we aren't in Hollywood making an Adam Sandler film. This is England. They just sort of let us crack on.'

'Oh,' I said. And then, curiosity and excitement getting

the better of me, 'So, what's it actually like? Is it just . . . incredible?'

'What's what like?'

'You know. Having your show. Being famous. All of that.'

'Oh.'

I was waiting so expectantly for Joel to answer that I only narrowly avoided a low-hanging branch.

'Honestly?' he said at last, 'it's . . . fine.'

I didn't respond at first, assuming he was going to expand on what he'd just said. But that was apparently all he was going to say.

'That's it? "Fine"?'

Joel shrugged.

'Hang on,' I said, 'are you . . . Look, you don't have to pretend on my account. You got there fair and square.'

Joel tilted his head from side to side. 'Nope, I'm sticking with fine.'

'Oh come on,' I said. 'Really? Your own show. Are you not just walking on air the whole time, swanning into restaurants where it's all "Your usual table, Mr Thompson?" That sort of thing?'

Joel laughed. 'No! I mean, yeah there's a tiny little bit of that, although I've definitely not got a "usual table" anywhere. If anything, those sorts of places have my photo on the wall saying I'm not allowed in.'

It was my turn to laugh, but it was a slightly nervous one. I knew he'd liked a drink, but had things really got that wild?

'I dunno,' Joel continued. 'On the face of it, it seems so huge and exciting. But the best day I've had throughout all of it was when I found out *Tooth* was getting made. Almost the day after that the doubts set in. And then it's the mundane stress that comes with any job.'

'Oh, right,' I said. 'Fair enough.' I didn't know whether I bought this as much as Joel wanted me too. The idea he was holding back for my benefit annoyed me enough to press him. 'There must be properly fun parts though, right? I mean, you're not exactly working down a mine.'

'Well, the writing's still the best bit by far,' he said. 'Do you remember when we used to work on stuff together and we'd get that little shot of adrenaline, where one of us latched on to something and it was like some weird alchemy where everything fell into place?' He looked at me a little nervously as he said this, as if I might have forgotten the moments he was talking about. But I hadn't – I knew exactly what he meant. The adrenaline shot was what we always strived for, like a rare high – a holy grail. If we did get there, it usually ended with hysteria – one of us desperately trying to keep it together long enough to scribble down whatever stupid joke we'd just thought of with the urgency of someone on their deathbed imparting a final, dramatic change to their will.

I saw Joel surreptitiously pop something into his mouth.

'Hay fever tablet,' he said, when he realised I'd clocked this. 'Anyway, shall we go over what we both remember about *The Regulars* – compare notes?'

I'd been a bit worried that we might have forgotten all the best bits we'd come up with back then, but before long it all came back to us. So much of it was still there, completely fresh. It was as if we'd rediscovered buried treasure.

By the time we came up for air, it was late afternoon, the sun just beginning to dip in the sky. We clambered over a stile into a lush field where a herd of cows was mooching around where the path was.

'What are the rules here then?' I said.

'The rules?'

'Yeah. Do we just . . . walk through them?'

Joel smirked. 'Do you think they're expecting a toll or something?'

The biggest cow, which I had already decided was the ring-leader, seemed to be watching us intently, swishing its tail. I noticed there was a calf at its side.

Joel strode confidently towards them. Cursing my fearfulness under my breath, I followed. Almost immediately, the cows that hadn't spotted us got up from where they'd been lying. But they didn't retreat. They held their ground. We were now in something of a stand-off.

'Ah,' said Joel. 'I'll level with you, I was sort of assuming they'd just move out of the way at this point.' The calf was mooing plaintively.

'Isn't there something about cows getting more aggressive when they've got their young with them?' I said.

'That rings a bell actually,' Joel replied.

As the ringleader let out a long, ominous moo, and took a step towards us, I instinctively shrank back behind Joel.

This is why you don't leave home, I thought. *The only cows there come with Yorkshire puddings.*

'What do we do now?' I said.

Joel, fingers flickering at his sides like a gunslinger, suddenly wrenched his leather jacket off. I was just about to suggest that surely that particular item of clothing would only piss the cows off further, when Joel launched himself forward, swinging the jacket around and around and yelling wildly, scattering the cows.

After taking a moment to get his breath back, he turned around to me and adjusted his pork-pie hat, gesturing with his arms out wide as if to say, don't know what you were worried about.

'Um, Joel,' I said, pointing behind him.

Joel turned to see that the cows had regrouped and had started to shuffle back towards us.

'OK, new plan,' Joel said. Then he turned and ran.

'Wait!' I shouted, pelting after him.

We raced towards the other side of the field, chancing glances over our shoulders. The cows were in hot pursuit, but there was just enough distance between us and them that nervous laughter took hold of us. Giggling like idiots, we made it over the stile at the other end of the field and collapsed into the long grass just as the cows came to a halt a few metres away, huffing hotly, buffeting each other into the fence.

It took us ages to get our breath back, partly because we were still laughing. I'd forgotten what this was like. Ending up in a ridiculous drama of our own making had been our forte. I straightened up, feeling oddly thrilled by the experience.

I was ready to carry on, but Joel was still wheezing away.

'I see your cross-country days are obviously behind you then,' I said, but the joke died in my mouth as I realised how hard he was breathing, almost like he was hyperventilating. I started talking about using the cows in the show somehow, hoping Joel would recover soon, because the longer he took, the more uneasy I felt. Just at the moment I thought I'd have to ask him if everything was OK, he straightened up.

'Good idea,' he said, breathing heavily still. 'About putting the cows in. Anyway, shall we?'

He strode off and I followed, taking surreptitious glances at him as we went. A minute or two later he started talking in earnest about the show again, acting as if nothing had happened. But he wasn't fooling me.

Something wasn't right.

Chapter Fourteen

Joel

I was focusing hard on the tower of St Sampson's Church, which poked above the trees in the distance into the sky, its turrets like fingers rigid with rigor mortis. The closer it came, the closer we were to stopping for the day, and I needed that to be soon. My feet felt so swollen and heavy in my boots, it was like I was sloshing through water. The unexpected sprinting earlier might have exacerbated things, but I didn't think I'd be feeling quite this bad so early on. I hoped I'd just about managed to distract Theo when I couldn't catch my breath by rambling on with my thoughts on the show. But if I didn't get to stop and rest soon, then I was going to be in real trouble.

I could have kissed Theo when he suggested we stay at the first pub we came to in Cricklade, a tired-looking place called the Red Lion. We went in through the door that brought us straight into the bar area, and the very specific sort of silence that descends in this kind of pub when someone not born within twenty yards of the place walks in.

The Red Lion's proprietor – a flat-faced, entirely expressionless, sentient trowel of a man – led us up the creaking stairs to a twin room. I tried to keep my breathing in check as I navigated the steep staircase.

'My room's over there, just so you know,' said the owner,

nodding his head towards the door marked private, a thick peacoat hanging from the door handle.

'Right you are,' I said, though I wasn't sure why he'd felt the need to tell us this.

He looked us both up and down, looking distinctively unimpressed, like a tradesman appraising a poorly constructed wall. 'I'd appreciate it if you could keep the noise down to a minimum after eleven. And please don't push the beds together. The carpet's not up to it.'

Ah, so that explained it.

Theo and I exchanged a look, and without saying anything we moved together so that our shoulders were touching.

'Oh, don't worry,' Theo said. 'We'll be as quiet as we can.'

The man took a step backwards, as if we might be radioactive.

'Absolutely,' I added, 'well, we'll do our best, anyway . . .'

But the owner was already scurrying away down the stairs, muttering something about having to change a barrel.

The room seemed to be both damp and airless. I tried to crack a window but it was stuck fast.

'Pleased to be out of metropolitan liberal London?' Theo asked me.

'Hmm, I am feeling a bit anxious that I've not seen an Uber for a while,' I said. But just as I reached the word Uber, I felt a surge of fatigue and had to brace myself on the door frame, trying to pass it off as a casual lean.

'I'll bet,' said Theo, but he was looking at me askance. It wasn't exactly concern on his face, but he seemed to have realised that something was up.

'What's wrong?' I asked, deciding to brazen it out.

'Nothing,' Theo said. 'I just . . . Actually, never mind.'

We unpacked in something of an uncomfortable silence at

first, but then Theo started joking about what had happened with the landlord just now, and things began to feel a bit more normal again. The moments like that today, where we'd slipped into our old routines, had been such a tonic. I hoped that was a sign of things to come.

'I'm starving,' Theo said. I watched him yawn and scratch at his shaggy curls. 'Shall we grab some dinner somewhere that's not here, and then get cracking with the first script? I reckon we came up with loads of stuff today already.'

There was such eagerness in his voice. It reminded me just how much was riding on Jane Green getting back to me with good news. A more immediate issue was that I wasn't sure if I'd be able to make it down the stairs again. The doctor had warned me that the fatigue would come and go, and that my legs would swell and ache with build-ups of fluid, but I hadn't expected it to be this bad so soon.

'Shall we head out?' Theo asked.

'Absolutely,' I said, feigning enthusiasm. 'Just need a shower and to make a quick call.'

Theo grabbed his wallet. 'Righto. In that case, I reckon I'll go and get a pint downstairs and put Kylie on the jukebox just to annoy the landlord.'

As he started off clumsily down the stairs with his usual lack of co-ordination, like a newborn foal taking his first steps, I got the impression that he was enjoying himself so far, and the thought made me happy – until I had to run to the bathroom down the hall where I vomited noisily into the toilet.

I'd just made it back to the bedroom, where I planned to rest for a few minutes, when Amber called.

I nearly didn't answer it. But as much as that might have been the sensible thing to do, I was feeling scared at what had just happened, and I really needed to hear her voice.

'I was just thinking about you and then you called,' I said, forcing brightness into my voice. 'It was like I'd summoned a genie.'

'Ha. I like that,' Amber said. 'And your three wishes would be . . .?'

'Hmm. Cure world famine.'

'Borrring. Next.'

'OK. Power of flight.'

'Again not the most original, but I shall grant it nonetheless. And the third . . .'

I paused.

'That I didn't have to stay home instead of coming out to be with you. I'm sorry.'

'Don't be,' Amber said briskly. 'I'd sort of prepared myself for that being the case. Your mum still struggling?'

'She's . . . having a tough time of it, yeah.' I was starting to wish I'd come up with something that didn't mean using Mum like this.

'Don't worry, m'love, there'll be other holidays. You're where you need to be. Besides, I am actually having fun with Charlotte.'

'Great!' I said. 'Is she still—'

'Oh completely insane, yeah. Her sex life is just . . . extraordinary.' She lowered her voice. 'Joel, the other week she did it with someone in a *helicopter* – some viscount or baron or other. And, yes, *obviously* I asked her if he had a big chopper and, yes, *obviously* she didn't get it.'

I laughed hard at this. It was one of my favourite things, to hear Amber scandalised. I'd christened this side of her 'Pauline-from-next-door', because it was like talking to a gossipy neighbour over the garden fence who's been keeping tabs on the new couple a few doors down; particularly the way she mouthed – rather than spoke – words like 'threesome' or 'orgy', or, in this case, 'chopper'.

As she carried on with the story, my thoughts turned against my will to how many more times I'd get to see this side of her. But just as it all got too much, I remembered the promise I'd made to keep Amber happy at all costs. And so I listened as she told me about Charlotte's ridiculous exploits, and the script she'd been sent for some Scandi-noir drama – and then about the bakery in the next village that didn't look like much from the outside but made the most amazing bread, with rosemary and olive oil, which we *had* to have when we came back here together, and all the while I did whatever it took to keep the sadness from my voice as Amber described a future I knew we'd never see.

When I found the strength to go down to Theo later, there were three empty pint glasses at his table. Only a few years ago, the sight would have left me hungry with longing, but now I didn't feel a thing.

'Sorry, got distracted,' I said. 'Food then?'

'Sure,' Theo said, wearing the telltale sleepy eyes of someone three beers down on an empty stomach.

As he stood up, he glanced outside and then back at me, looking a little uneasy.

'Something up?' I asked.

'Oh, nothing – it's just . . . Are you not wearing your jacket? It's actually quite cold out, now the sun's gone.'

Theo's cheeks reddened just a touch. My natural inclination was to make fun of him for being so mumsy, but I was glad I managed to stop myself. I'm sure Theo was a very long way off calling me his friend again, but I'd take mild concern about me getting a bit chilly any day.

'Good point, actually,' I said. 'I'll go and grab my jacket.' But when I got up to our room, I couldn't find it anywhere, and I realised with a stab of frustration that I must have left it in the field when we'd escaped from the cows.

I'd resigned myself to bracing against the evening chill without protection when I passed the owner's room and did a double take.

It's funny how your sense of morality can change when you're on borrowed time. One day you're feeling guilty for eating biscuits when it's nearly time for lunch, the next you're calmly unhooking the coat of a pub landlord from his bedroom door handle and wrapping it around your shoulders, a wanton criminal in a wanker's jacket.

Chapter Fifteen
Theo

Cricklade was a generic if pretty market town – the sort of place where insurance companies and banks sat in disguise in amongst charming Cotswold stone houses. As we made our way down the high street, I couldn't help but notice how knackered Joel looked, and in the pub earlier, I'd heard the unmistakable sound of someone throwing up coming from upstairs.

'Something a bit odd happened earlier,' I said, as we stepped aside to let a man on a mobility scooter sweep past.

'Oh yeah?' Joel replied.

'Yeah. I heard someone upstairs having a terrible time of it – like they were trying to throw their feet up through their face. That wasn't you, was it?'

'Me?' Joel said. 'Nah. Must've been someone in another room. Now, where do you fancy eating? Our options appear to be run-down gastropub or run-down gastropub.'

'Up to you.'

I was 90 per cent sure Joel was lying. But why? It was only when we walked past an off-licence that something clicked. Those rumours I'd read in the papers about Joel's personal life must have carried more weight than I'd thought. Coupled with the waxy skin, the wheezing, the retching . . . was it all down to withdrawal symptoms?

Maybe it was none of my business. I was the one who'd insisted we keep anything serious off the table. Besides, I knew Joel well enough to know he wasn't likely to give me the whole story anyway. An image came to me of him as a teenager, looking at me with a kind of desperate longing in his eyes as he told me never to ask him if he was OK ever again.

Eventually we decided to eat in a restaurant called Jack's, the only place that seemed half busy.

'Think I'll stick to water now,' I said, keeping my eyes down on the menu. 'Still a bit dehydrated from the walk.'

'Yeah, me too,' Joel said, and I was certain there was relief in his voice. It was going to be hard not to keep doing this – pinning more evidence to a corkboard to confirm my theory.

Our waiter took our decision less well, especially when I chose tap rather than still or sparkling.

'And please might I have a knife and fork when you get a moment?' I asked – strangely stiff and polite. I was embarrassingly out of practice at even an interaction as normal as this.

'Of course,' the waiter replied, with a look on his face like I'd just asked him to sculpt a willy-perfect version of Michelangelo's *David* out of baba ganoush.

I caught Joel's eye and he smirked. There followed an awkward silence while the waiter took an age to collect up our wine glasses, and I felt myself dangerously close to sniggering. Needing a distraction, I plucked the menu from the table, managing in the process to poke myself in the eye with it. The waiter finally left and I clutched my face.

'You all right?' Joel said, looking a bit confused as I prodded my eye. And then a memory came to me which made me temporarily forget the pain.

∞

It took until the fifth time Joel sat next to me in the form room and greeted me with 'All right?', to which I responded in kind, before I finally began to trust that we were actually friends. I'd worried at first that him rescuing me in the music block would be our only interaction, but it seemed – miraculously – that he actually liked me. I quietly ditched the Bertie Wooster get-up. Now I'd had a taste of being normal, I wasn't going back . . . which is why my body choosing that moment to betray me made everything so much worse.

At a routine check-up, the doctor told me and Mum that if my lazy eye was going to have fixed itself it would have done so by now, and so treatment was needed. She called a nurse in, who presented me with a little box. I held it in my lap while everyone looked at me, and for a brief moment I actually wondered whether the nurse had just handed me a box of glass eyes. What was in there instead wasn't exactly a whole lot better. Eyepatches. Even Alice's drawing of me as a swashbuckling pirate couldn't cheer me up.

As I had expected, Darren was barely able to contain himself when he saw me with the patch on the next morning. It seemed there were so many taunts and insults available to him that they'd short-circuited his system. Dumbstruck, he pointed at me, his arm wavering like a divining rod locating water. 'P-P . . . Patch prick!' he managed at last. It wasn't his best, but the class erupted in laughter anyway. I shuffled to my desk, head down, cheeks burning, trying to ignore the jeers. Unusually, Joel had arrived before me that day, and was sitting there with headphones on, ignoring everyone – and being ignored, Darren and his goons seeming wary of someone who'd stood up to them so effortlessly. I prayed that he'd say something consoling – tell me not to worry about those idiots – but he just looked at me for a few seconds and then went back to his music.

The following morning, I knew Darren would be lying in wait, and sure enough he and his crew surrounded me as I came in, chanting 'patch prick' and shoving me as I made my way miserably to my desk. The idea of this being my life from now on made me want to run out of the school and not stop running until my lungs and legs gave out.

Joel was in before me again. He had his head down on his arms, apparently asleep despite all the noise. I sat down next to him and stared straight ahead, face hot from shame. I just hoped he'd get the 'Sorry I can't be your friend' speech out of the way sooner rather than later.

'All right?' he said, his voice muffled.

I kept looking ahead. Maybe I'd get in there first and say that I'd decided we couldn't be mates, actually, and that he needed somewhere else to sit. But then he sat up, and the class suddenly went quiet. I turned to look at him properly, and that's when I saw that he was wearing a black eyepatch nearly identical to mine.

'All right,' I said, trying not to grin too madly.

I glanced over at Darren. He was scowling at me with real menace, but for the first time, I felt brave enough to hold his gaze until he looked away first. He never bothered me again after that.

∞

Joel was still looking at me askance across the table. I hadn't thought about that moment in the classroom in years.

'Do you remember . . .' I started, before trailing off.

'Remember what?' Joel asked.

'Never mind,' I said, deciding to avoid the turn off to memory lane. 'Right then – let's get writing. Oh, you not got your laptop?'

'Sorry,' Joel said. 'I left it in the room. But never mind, we can just scribble on napkins for now if we keep it to big picture stuff. Got a pen?'

I found one in my inside coat pocket and handed it over. As Joel smoothed out his paper napkin and began to write something down, I saw his tongue poke out of the corner of his mouth, and then another memory came to me, as if ignited by the embers of the previous one.

∞

One chilly November lunchtime a few weeks after Joel's eye-patch solidarity, I felt confident enough in our friendship that I decided to let him in on my comedy obsession. It was one of my more daring moments, trying to impress a twelve-year-old boy with a 1967 episode of Radio Four's *Round the Horne*, while all the others were passing around an *FHM* someone had snuck in, or playing football. I knew the episode off by heart, so I watched Joel's face closely, eagerly anticipating his reactions to certain lines. At first, his expression was as neutral as ever, but after a while he started to smile. I'd never felt more relieved in my life.

For his part, Joel introduced me to the music he liked, and while Green Day's goofy rebelliousness didn't strike as much of a chord with me as the theme from *The Good Life*, there was something about it that resonated all the same.

One evening, I dropped into conversation with Mum that I might have my friend Joel over one Saturday, if that was OK. Mum was so surprised and flustered that I noticed the standard-issue Dorothy Perkins Mum Range sweater she was in the process of putting on was now the wrong way round and inside out. For some reason this was the funniest thing Alice and I had ever seen, and we couldn't stop laughing. Even Mum joined in after a while.

That state of giddiness continued into winter and the end of term. It snowed from early December, and for the first time in my life, Christmas looked like the adverts on TV.

Joel and I were in my room one evening when I turned round to find him holding one of my notebooks full of sketches and ideas.

'"Stegosaurus trying to enter Wimbledon",' he read.

I tried to grab the notebook, but Joel held it away.

'Yeah, that's just a stupid . . . thing, I . . . It's from ages ago actually.'

'It's not stupid,' Joel mused. 'But it's not right.'

'What do you mean, not right?' I asked, bristling slightly.

'Well. A T-Rex is funnier-looking than a stegosaurus. Think of the racket in its little arms.'

After a moment's pause, I had to concede that he was absolutely right.

That was the first time we ever wrote together – cross-legged on my bedroom floor, Joel's tongue poking out of the corner of his mouth as we scribbled ideas and jokes in the same notebook. Individually, I don't know if either of us would have been any good. But together everything just seemed to click. I remember distinctly the moment we finished that stupid dinosaur sketch, because it honestly felt like we were two scientists huddled over a microscope in a lab after just discovering a new element. *Professor, you might want to come over here and take a look at this . . .*

∞

Sitting in the restaurant tonight, our meals long since forgotten, I watched Joel – concentrating hard as he jotted something down – and I felt a deep melancholy come over me. There had been times as we'd tramped along earlier, and writing together now, when it felt just like old days. But it wasn't the same. It couldn't be.

I caught our reflection in the window. It felt like I was having an out-of-body experience, as if our doubles were looking in at us from outside, watching as we wrote away and talked nonsense as if everything was completely fine. It seemed any moment one of us out there was going to turn to the other, point inside, and ask just how the hell we'd managed to let everything go so horribly, badly wrong.

Chapter Sixteen

Joel

Cricklade to Lechlade, 10.8 miles (171.8 miles to Thames Barrier, London)

'Oh look, there's some river in the river,' Theo said, pointing to the weak stream struggling along the riverbed, which had been all but dry on yesterday's stretch.

Today we'd already been treated to a beautiful meadow just outside Kempsford, alive with bees and butterflies, though we'd been too distracted to acknowledge any of that as we were on something of a roll with ideas for *The Regulars*. I was used to the fluorescent strip lights of cramped rooms, trying to manage other people's egos when their ideas were rejected. Out here with Theo in the open air everything seemed to flow so much more naturally. But the more headway we made with that, the more concerned I was that I hadn't heard from Jane Green. With any normal person, I could have put this down to them being distracted by a family issue or something, but this was Jane Green – the woman who'd once called me from the back of a funeral to ask a question about catering on an upcoming shoot. (It's quite hard to make a decision about tuna or ham when you can hear Great-Aunt Edith's body being committed to the flames.)

Whimsical proclamations about the river aside, Theo had seemed a little more guarded that morning. It was almost like he was cross with himself for being too friendly with me yesterday. I remembered that when the cows were getting rowdy he seemed to have automatically moved behind me, looking for protection. It felt comforting to fall back into our old roles, familiar I suppose. But at the same time, I didn't want Theo to feel like he was in my shadow. I'd much prefer him to take the lead – not be bound by what I wanted to do. I felt a bit like a father teaching his son to ride a bike, running behind and pretending he was still holding on.

We were passing by a willow tree, folded over into the water like someone trying to touch their toes, when Theo asked me if my legs were hurting. I had to bite my tongue. The swelling had barely retreated overnight, and walking had been painful from the get-go. But instead I said, 'Bit stiff. You?'

'Put it this way – I feel like the cast of *Stomp* have crawled into my trousers and are using my thighs for practice.'

'Have you seen *Stomp*? I don't think they practice.'

We walked on without speaking for a while. For so long, in fact, that when Theo said 'I have actually,' it took me a moment to remember what we'd been talking about.

'Someone took me in London,' he said. 'But we had a big fight in the interval, and I left.'

'You . . . stomped off?'

'Yeah,' Theo said. He was preoccupied enough by the memory not to cast judgement on my pun.

'So this was an ex?' I asked.

Theo grunted in the affirmative. Then, after a few moments of plodding along in a distinctly Eeyore-ish way, he sighed and said, 'She was, sort of, you know . . . "the one".'

Never had I seen air-quotes being deployed so gloomily.

'We broke up a couple of years ago. It was a mutual . . . No, actually, it wasn't – she dumped me.'

'Sorry to hear that,' I said. 'This was pretty serious then. Were you living together?'

'Yeah. North London. Highbury.'

'Hang on, really?'

'Yeah?'

'Wow.'

Theo frowned. 'Why is that so hard to believe?'

'It's not. I just had no idea we were living in the same place.'

'Oh right. Well, London's quite big isn't it, as cities go.'

I sidestepped the sarcasm.

'I thought you might know her actually,' Theo said. 'She's a casting director.'

'Oh yeah? What's her name?'

'Barbara. Barbara Nicholls. But she goes by Babs.'

'Ha, amazing, like *Acorn Antiques*!'

Theo smiled sadly. 'That's the one.'

I wracked my brains, but other than her comedy namesake, her name didn't ring a bell.

'So why did you . . .' I stopped. 'I mean, you don't have to tell me if it's . . .'

'Why did we what?' Theo asked.

We looked at each other, and Theo gave the flicker of a smile. This, we silently agreed, was weird. Uncharted territory, in fact. Opening up about our feelings was something we had pretty much avoided at all costs when we were teenagers. Or, at least I had. Some of this was down to Dad and his 'you're the man of the house now' lecturing before he left, and then Mike moved in, and he made Dad look thoroughly progressive.

I don't expect my generation of men will be the last to feel incapable of expressing their feelings either – at least to other men. In truth, I've always found women easier to talk to, especially when meeting as strangers. When a group of men meet for the first time at a party, it's always a race to get the first joke in, and then the evening becomes an exhausting exchange of piss-taking and irony. This, in fact, is the architecture of nearly all male friendships, and to deviate from that feels entirely unnatural, like driving on the other side of the road or walking with only one shoe on.

The comfort of never really exposing frailties is how men can be friends for decades without ever really knowing each other. Because even when they crack – almost exclusively after alcohol has been consumed – and try to tell a male friend that they're scared, or lonely, or depressed, it still has to come couched in sarcasm and self-deprecation, because otherwise it's like jumping out of a plane without knowing if your parachute's going to open. This is why I'm never that shocked when a hitherto boring, emotionless man makes an incredible speech at a wedding. You'll get some middle-aged cousin who you've previously only heard talking about England's goalkeeping issues, or roadworks on the A38, and you're expecting more of the same as they tap their champagne glass with their knife, and the next thing you know they're talking with the eloquence of a poet about how much they love their daughter, how proud they are – and it's all because this is the only fifteen minutes of their lives where they're allowed to show that kind of naked emotion without seven other middle-aged blokes telling them to shut up and have another drink while secretly wishing they were brave enough to say 'yeah, me too.'

As Theo and I crossed a bridge over the reluctant trickle of water below, his half-question still entirely unanswered, I felt particularly aware that time was limited for me to rectify how closed off I had always been with him. If we'd come into our twenties still being friends, I think we might have made progress – but instead it was like someone had pressed pause, and we were still essentially teenagers trapped in the bodies of two thirty-year-olds, proper stubble on our cheeks now but not a fraction more capable of opening up. But without the luxury of time, I realised I was going to have to start upping the ante.

'So why did you break up?' I asked, my voice awkwardly caught halfway between a reporter at a press conference and a precocious child.

'Well,' Theo said, after a pause long enough that I thought he might be about to scupper the conversation, 'I suppose I got complacent. Sort of like I was on autopilot. I managed to fuck up a decent job in the pursuit of something that was never going to happen, and then I got so obsessed with that failure that I just sort of . . . gave up on everything, and that meant I took Babs completely for granted. I tried to win her back by . . . well, it all got a bit dramatic, but let's just say I made things worse.'

Knowing Theo, this sounded suspiciously like he'd tried some sort of overblown romantic gesture and had got too carried away.

'Sorry to hear that,' I said. 'How've you been . . . you know . . . dealing with it?'

That had come out completely wrong – like I was asking him about an embarrassing medical procedure or something. *For fuck's sake, why was this so hard?*

'Well, you know . . .' Theo said, gesturing with his hands in a jolting circular motion, a robot juggler in need of its joints oiling. 'I mean we'd been together since uni so . . .'

'Jesus, really?' I said. 'That's – wow, I thought I'd been in a long-term rel—'

I stopped abruptly, but without looking at me, Theo said, 'It's all right. I know you've been with Amber. It's fine. I don't care.'

Hearing Theo say Amber's name took me by surprise – it made me feel like I'd just plunged into a freezing pool of water.

'How is it being together after all these years?' Theo asked.

We'd just turned a corner past a hedge and found ourselves in a field carpeted with yellow rapeseed. I was having some difficulty speaking. A lump had risen to my throat and I knew if I tried to speak, my voice would be shaky. I was hit by the shock of how badly I wanted to tell Theo everything.

But Theo seemed to take my temporary muteness as reluctance to answer the question, because he said, 'Maybe we should talk about something else,' before striding off into the field, parting the brilliant yellow like a knife through butter.

The route took us away from the river for a mile or so, and we got back to it to find it flowing in earnest, sparkling magnificently in the sunshine.

'I feel a bit cheated,' Theo said. 'It's like a magic trick or something – like someone's turned the tap on.'

I was about to ask him whether he wanted to throw caution to the wind and see if we could go back off-route and find the spot where the water began to flow properly, but the fatigue which had been tailing me all day seemed to pounce, and I asked as levelly as I could if we might stop for a break.

I was grateful that Theo took the opportunity to find somewhere secluded to wee, as it gave me the opportunity to slump to the ground and massage my swollen legs.

I downed several gulps of water, then took out my phone to see if there was any news from Jane. I sat up, heart thumping, as my screen showed that she was actually typing a message right now.

Sorry for radio s. Nephew buggered my phone with marmite. Had to throw it out and get a new one. (The phone, not the nephew, though we'll see on that score too.) Re Regulars – some nibbles, dear boy, but no clear bite yet. Will keep you p'd. P.S. Update on the cyberman's helmet (as it were). Silly gold bastard left it on the 11:49 to Ebbsfleet JGx

It wasn't exactly the news I was hoping for, but at least it wasn't a straight no.

I hauled myself back to my feet as Theo returned, and feigned enthusiasm once again as we set off.

The next couple of miles took us past the sort of places that would sound a bit on the nose if you were a foreigner trying to mock the English: Hannington Wick, Downington, Little Faringdon. All the while, the Thames widened, and we hit something of a milestone when we came to Inglesham, whose stone roundhouse across the bank marks the spot where boats are able to enter the water.

To my relief, it was Theo this time who suggested we had a pitstop. We were bickering good-naturedly about whether it was possible to play a single game of Poohsticks from the start of the river all the way to the end, when, out of nowhere, I was overcome by nausea and had to scramble over to a tree, which I threw up behind. There was no way I could pull the wool over Theo's eyes this time, so I decided to pre-empt it when I came back.

'God, I reckon I must have got food poisoning last night,' I said, sitting down next to Theo. 'Bloody Jack and his terrible hygiene rating.'

I waited for Theo to respond, but he just dragged a stick he had picked up through the grass, then chucked it into the river.

'Maybe I should call and complain,' I added, annoyed that Theo wasn't saying anything. I went to take a swig of water, but my bottle was empty.

Wordlessly, Theo offered me his.

'We can rest a bit longer if you want,' he said.

'I'm fine,' I replied.

'Give it another five? I don't mind.'

'I'm fine, OK?' I snapped, immediately regretting it.

Theo held his hands up in apology.

The moment passed, but I couldn't afford to make another mistake like that again. Even now, the atmosphere – which had been as good as I thought it would ever be between us – felt like it had soured.

But just then, something happened which lifted my mood more than I thought possible. It was another text from Jane:

Hold the phone. Just ran into that funny little bald sod who's now heading up the new commissioning team (quite literally – nearly knocked him flying, like a tiny baby bird). Pitched your idea straight to him. Seemed v v v keen! Think we're on to a winner. More soon, dear boy JGx

I got to my feet, nausea now completely gone. Maybe this was actually going to work. Theo and I would have a TV show together, and he'd never be any the wiser! A swan floated by imperiously. I felt like saluting it.

I looked down at Theo. He was eating a sandwich he'd bought from a riverside café earlier, sitting cross-legged, his hair rippling in the breeze. I felt a surge of affection for him. I had the urge to pinch his cheeks like an Italian grandmother. In the end, I just about managed to restrain myself. But I was eager to finish the last leg of today's walk – to ride this wave of positivity and get some more ideas down together.

I cleared my throat and reached out a hand down to Theo.

'Shall we get going?'

After a moment's hesitation, he took my hand, and I pulled him to his feet.

Chapter Seventeen

Theo

I couldn't quite square the man who'd just thrown up behind a tree with the one who was marching along beside me, a spring in his step. Perhaps that was what the bumpy ride of withdrawal was like.

Lechlade's halfpenny bridge had just come in to view when Joel cocked his ear and said, 'Can you hear that?'

We stopped to listen properly. Music and the odd voice were drifting over from somewhere. Crossing the path, Joel peered through a gap in a hedge and beckoned me over.

'Look,' he said, stepping aside so I could see. And what I could see was . . . the past. About fifteen men, dressed in chainmail and tunics, were milling around, chatting. A chicken was burning on a spit. Someone was gently playing a lute.

'What is . . . what is happening?' I asked Joel, but he seemed equally as nonplussed.

As two of the men roared at each other and drew their swords, Joel and I ducked down so our laughter didn't give us away.

'Well, there's only one way to find out – come on,' Joel said, striding towards the stile that led into the field.

'Really?' I groaned.

'Come on, Theo,' Joel said. 'Where's your sense of adventure?'

The men stopped talking as we approached. I swear I saw one put his hand on the hilt of his sword.

'Hi,' Joel said, flashing them a smile. 'We just wondered what you lads were up to. We're journalists, so I'm afraid curiosity got the better of us. I'm Mack and this is my photographer, Rupert.'

The soldiers sniggered.

Rupert. Of all the names he could have chosen.

'We're rehearsing a battle enactment,' said the biggest of the men.

'You rehearse?' I asked.

The men laughed.

'What, just think we turn up on the day and march around a bit?' the big man said.

I managed to bite my tongue.

'Do you mind if we sit and observe?' Joel asked. 'Could be a story in it.'

The soldiers exchanged looks. The big man nodded. 'Have a seat over there.'

'Come on, Rupert,' Joel said brightly, leading me over to a tree stump where we could sit and survey the scene.

A murky patch of cloud had snuck up on us, and without warning it began to rain hard. With nowhere to shelter, we were quickly soaked. The battle re-enactors mainly seemed unperturbed, although one of them, I noticed, kept looking towards the road, where all their cars were parked.

'I don't suppose your average Anglo-Saxon had access to a Kia Sportage,' I said.

'I'd say not,' Joel replied. 'Skoda Fabia, tops.'

We watched on as the rain continued to fall.

'This really is surreal,' I murmured. 'How old do you think they all are?'

'Hmm,' Joel said. 'Late fifties, sixties? Retired, I'd say, most of them.'

As I watched the men practising their swordsmanship, I felt guilty for having laughed at them before. It was all innocent fun. And at least they had a hobby – one that clearly made them happy. To get to the point where they could retire and indulge themselves in the middle of a rainy afternoon with chainmail and chicken legs, that was surely only because they'd led successful lives beforehand. They'd turned up, knuckled down, done their time and then got out. What had I done? I'd basically given up at the first hurdle and then complained about it ever since, blaming everyone except myself for the failure.

And then there was the camaraderie they all clearly shared. Where was my bunch of mates going to come from by the time I reached that age? As much as I didn't want to admit it, Alice was probably right. I'd been stuck in the shed for so long I'd forgotten what it meant to be out with friends, meeting new people – taking advantage of what the real world had to offer. And if the real world involved necking mead out of a tankard and singing songs of yore at half past four on a Monday then I was all for it. The revelation felt strangely exciting. I wasn't going to pretend that I wasn't missing home, even after only a couple of days – but I could see how much my life had come to a juddering halt, and at the same time, I realised I was capable of getting the wheels moving again – starting with *The Regulars*.

'It's sort of great, this, isn't it?' I said, turning to Joel.

'What, pretending to be a soldier from the past?'

'Yeah, but, more how happy they all are. It feels like they've got all the hard bits of life out of the way, you know? They've slogged through the commutes and the meetings and the pre-meeting meetings. This is pure freedom, isn't it? Aren't you sort of excited about getting to that point in your life?'

After a moment of waiting for Joel to answer, I glanced over and saw that he was looking at the scene with a strange sort of pining, his newfound energy seemingly evaporated already.

'Yeah,' he said at last, his voice gruff. 'Would be nice.'

Just then, one of the soldiers shouted across to us. 'You gonna take photos now for the story or what?'

After a second, Joel got to his feet. He seemed to be pleased to have a distraction. 'You don't mind if I take this one, do you, Rupert?'

I shook my head.

Amazingly, Joel did actually have a camera in his bag. The man hadn't brought a waterproof coat, but he did have room for an SLR that looked like it cost more than a small island. As he bounced off, all Tigger-meets-David-Bailey, I noticed a bit of paper on the grass that must have come out of his bag as he'd removed his camera. I reached down for it, but a gust of wind took it away from me, and I was forced to chase it along the grass towards the others, squirming with embarrassment at my lack of co-ordination. At last, just as I got to Joel, I managed to clamp my foot down on it.

Joel was in full flow, talking to the men and asking them to get into position. He hadn't heard me approach, but, as he saw me at his side, he smiled. It was only a small moment, but it was a smile of such warmth and affection that it left me strangely moved. I suppose just as Joel's mood had been up and down, so had the way I'd felt towards him since he'd turned up on my doorstep. I'd hated him fiercely that day – the brass fucking neck of him appearing unannounced like that. Even after all this time, the pain he'd caused was still raw, and yet here, in this moment, I couldn't deny how good it felt to be with him again, getting into another scrape.

I know that 'in another life . . .' speculation is a dangerous habit, but I couldn't help indulging it now. Because what if there had been another life where things had worked out with Babs, and Joel and I were still as close as we were on course to be when we were kids? For one thing, the day would have come where I'd have asked him to be my best man. I imagined him on a bench somewhere, writing his speech, and then playing his part as the most reassuring presence in the church – adjusting my buttonhole, telling me to take a breath, to remember to actually enjoy myself. A little later down the line, there he'd be – bending down and scooping up his godson or goddaughter, twirling them around in the air, ignoring my half-hearted attempts to stop exciting them this much before bed. All these moments that stretched out into a parallel future that felt agonisingly close . . . was it too much to think we could still sidestep into it, or a life like it, even if Babs wasn't there? In that moment, basking in the warmth of Joel's smile and feeling a great rush of fondness for him, it felt like we probably could.

But then I saw the expression on Joel's face gradually change. It was as if someone had held a painting of him over an open flame until the canvas began to split and tear, revealing another image of him underneath – except this time his face was full of shock, his cheeks colourless. And that's when

I looked down and saw what was written at the top of the page I was standing on.

My Kicking The Bucket List.

Chapter Eighteen
Joel

'Give me that, please,' I said. My voice was calm, but I worried my trembling hand betrayed what I was really feeling.

Theo stood there, unmoved. The rain was beginning to fall harder now, and the wind was getting up.

'What is this?' Theo asked.

'It's nothing,' I said, 'just another project I'm working on.' The page was folded over so that all that was visible were those five words. That was bad enough, but I knew that if Theo looked at anything else on that piece of paper then this was all over. I willed the rain to fall harder, to smudge the words away.

'What sort of a project?' Theo said.

'It's . . . just give me that and I'll tell you, all right?'

After what seemed an age, Theo handed me the piece of paper and I shoved it into my back pocket.

'OK look,' I said. 'It's another TV show I'm working on. Can't go into details. Sorry. It's quite celeb heavy.'

Theo raised his eyebrows.

'Yeah, believe me, I know how much of a dick that makes me sound, but these people and their non-disclosure agreements and everything . . .'

'Oh, right,' Theo said. He sounded disappointed – but in a

way where I couldn't work out if it was because he thought I wasn't committed to *The Regulars*, or if he was just humouring me when I was obviously lying. I felt compelled to double down.

'And besides, I didn't want you to think I had another thing on the go.'

'Huh? Why not?'

'Well, let's face it, when we used to write, you always got annoyed when I got distracted by some new idea when we hadn't finished what we were working on. Remember?'

'I . . . I guess so, well actually, I think that maybe happened once, but—'

'Once? You're joking right? It happened all the time!'

'Jesus, I didn't realise that was such a sore spot.'

If I could just keep him distracted . . .

'Look, I think about those days a lot, OK? And that was always one of your biggest bugbears. I didn't want to piss you off, thinking that I wasn't committed to *The Regulars*.'

Theo folded his arms. 'I understand that, I just . . . Look, I get the feeling maybe something's going on that you're not—'

'Woah, woah, woah,' I said. 'What happened to that speech you gave me when we started the walk, about how we weren't going to talk about anything serious? You've changed your tune! Anyway, there's nothing "going on". I was just trying not to hurt your feelings, OK? And think carefully before you go down that route by the way.'

'Oh yeah? And what route's that?'

'The route where I ask you a few questions about what's "going on" with *you*. Like . . . oh, I don't know – where you're living, for example.'

A sad smile appeared on Theo's face. 'Well, you've got me

there,' he said. 'I've been living in the shed at the bottom of Mum and Dad's garden.'

I was thrown by this. I'd hoped turning the tables on Theo would have made him clam up so we could move on.

'In fact, I've barely left the village, let alone the county, for quite a long time, and if I stop and think about how far away I am from home, I actually feel a bit sick. Oh, and did I mention my job – which I may well get fired from – is writing tweets for a budget burger company?'

'Mate, come on,' I started, 'You don't have to—'

'I know how this goes when I ask you what's going on in your life, but I'm doing it anyway. If you don't want to tell me, then that's on you. So, before we go any further, if you want to tell me something, anything at all – then now's your chance.'

The wind whipped across the field, rippling my clothes. I looked at Theo and tried to find the words, but they just wouldn't come. I wasn't sure what he thought he knew, but this tone of his had me horribly worried. I'd long ago come to accept that he hated me, but to hear pity in his voice, that was a different thing altogether. I didn't want this trip to be some pathetic swansong where Theo indulged me – gave a dying man his last wish while pretending he didn't still despise me.

I made myself look him square in the eye.

'I'm fine, OK? Scout's honour. I was just stressed about this other project. But now you know, so can we get out of here sharpish before we drown in this fucking field?'

I felt movement behind me, and I turned to see a Saxon battalion, weapons drawn, looking confused. Then the big man cleared his throat.

'Are we having our picture taken for the paper then or what?'

*

As we trudged on – the sky brightening, as if the wind and rain had just stopped by to watch our little drama play out – Theo began to pull away in front. I wasn't complaining – I needed to gather myself, to work out how we were going to move past this. I watched as Theo scuffed his way along the path, seemingly incapable of picking his feet up. And then, out of nowhere, he slipped on some mud, arms windmilling frantically until he caught his balance. I couldn't help smiling. Theo had always been able to make me laugh on cue – unintentionally or not – even when things seemed dire. I'd never been able to explain to him just how much I'd needed that back then – how the moments we'd spent helpless with laughter had been like a soothing balm in the days my world got turned upside down.

∞

By the time we were fourteen, we'd developed that cockiness specific to teenage boys, where we knew absolutely everything and most other people were idiots. Teachers began to hate us for how much we larked about. A highlight was the day Mr Barnes, the biology teacher, bellowed, 'Well, you two are *quite the little double act*, aren't you?', and got so angry that he actually cut the lesson short, briefly making Theo and I class heroes.

I was still in the grips of that high that same evening when, out of nowhere, part of the ceiling collapsed as Mum and I ate dinner, sending a torrent of water and plaster down on us. If only that ceiling had held firm for a few more days, when Mum could have had the pick of the local builders – but it just so happened there was only one free. Mike turned up the following morning in his rusty van, and basically never left. There were other things that needed fixing, he claimed. But he seemed to spend most of the time in the kitchen drinking cups of tea which Mum made for him.

One day I got back from school and thought I could hear Mum crying hysterically, but when I rushed into the kitchen, it turned out she was laughing at something Mike had said. Before long, Mum informed me that they were 'dating'.

'Dating?' Theo asked me, sounding disgusted.

We were down at the Thames Head monument enjoying our favourite pastime of throwing stones at a tree. We'd pilfered some cider from Theo's dad, and I was trying to drink it fast enough that I got dizzy and didn't have to think about Mum and Mike.

'Dating,' I confirmed, hurling my stone as hard as I could. 'And then, last night. I . . . heard them.'

'Heard them what?'

'Playing scrabble.'

'Really?'

'No, Theo.'

'So what . . . Oh.' He screwed his face up.

'Yeah.'

'Urgh. That's mental.'

'Tell me about it. But it's worse. She told me he's moving in.'

'Shit. Really?'

'Yeah.'

'Oh.'

'Yeah.'

I threw another stone at the tree. Then another. I didn't really know what it was about all this that made me so angry.

I suppose deep down I knew at some point Mum might start seeing someone else. It wasn't like Dad had died and she was never going to move on. I think she might have even been on the odd date or two, though we didn't talk about it.

Mike quite literally brought a stability to the house – someone to fix things, to drive to the dump and to IKEA. He didn't have kids himself, but there was something generically dad-like about him in those early days – a safe pair of hands. I think Mum worried that I was missing that sort of figure in my life. At fourteen, I was lazy and didn't have any sort of drive to speak of. Maybe Mum thought having Mike around would help with that. But I took against him straight away. I hated how he winked at me. I hated the ripple of fat on the back of his neck, and how he kept clapping me on the shoulder, trying to be matey. But, more than anything, I just felt an overwhelming sense that he was taking advantage of Mum somehow. And *that* was what left me with a burning anger, which just then, as I threw the biggest stone I could find, had me unexpectedly crying, tears running silently down my cheeks.

'Oh . . . um,' Theo started. And I knew that if he asked me if I was OK, I would properly lose it, which I was *not* going to do. Our friendship was about laughing and mucking around and getting away from all the other bullshit. I didn't want to infect it – let Mike change this, like he was changing things at home.

'Let's do something else,' I said, before Theo could ask me anything.

For the rest of the evening, we sat back to back on the ground and wrote sketches. Two years of Theo's indoctrinating had begun to pay off, and it was always a real triumph if I managed to write something that made him laugh. There were two versions of his laugh: there was the Mutley-esque snigger, but then there was the lesser-spotted belly laugh, which made his hair shake like a tree in the wind.

That evening, as the sun went down, we wrote a sketch featuring reality TV shows of the future, as announced sincerely by continuity people:

'Coming up next on Channel 4, it's *Britain's Most Arrogant Babies*.'

'Don't go anywhere, it's time for *Celebrity Abattoir*.'

Even when it got dark and we were shivering in our T-shirts, I wished more than anything that we could stay out, the two of us against the world. But Theo told me he had to get back or his parents would worry.

'Yeah, course,' I said, and I watched him walk across the field until he was just a dot enveloped in the gloom while I trudged home in the opposite direction. I decided not to take the train. I'd rather be freezing and exhausted than get back to what was happening there.

In the event, it turned out they were still out at the pub, and so I lay in my room waiting for them to come home, miserable with anticipation. Sure enough, when they got in, drunk and giggly, they went up to Mum's room and I was forced to clamp my hands over my ears to block out the noise, but it was no good. And before I knew it, I was dragging my knuckles fast across the rough patch on my wall, scraping and tearing the skin until the pain overwhelmed everything else – a great shriek of white noise until at last I couldn't concentrate on anything but the throbbing in my fingers.

It wasn't long before Mike was thoroughly bedded in, like some disgusting tick. His smell seemed to permeate the house.

He'd pulled an armchair around in front of the TV and Mum had started referring to it as 'Mike's chair'. He'd been on his best behaviour for as long as he thought he needed to, because now he thought nothing of bollocking me for getting in late, or complaining to Mum if dinner wasn't on the table – like it was the fucking fifties.

One evening, I heard raised voices and came into the kitchen just as they stopped – but though Mike had clearly had time to take his hand from Mum's arm, I could see the imprint from where he'd grabbed her.

'Mum, what's going on?'

'Nothing, darling,' Mum replied, humming tunelessly and moving to wipe down the kitchen counter, before shooing me out.

A few weeks later, the same thing happened again – except this time I caught Mike with his hand around Mum's wrist.

'Get the fuck off her,' I said, taking a step forward, trying to stand up tall.

Mum quickly saw what was about to happen and stood in front of me.

'Let's all calm down, shall we,' she said.

'No,' Mike snapped. 'He can't swear at me like that. He needs to learn.'

But Mum stood her ground. I could see Mike's fists were clenched hard.

'Why don't you go outside for a moment, get some air, and I'll talk to Joel.' Mum sounded nervous. I hated hearing that in her voice.

Reluctantly, Mike left through the back door.

'Joel . . .' Mum said, but I shrugged her off and sprinted upstairs. I knew she was going to try to justify Mike's behaviour somehow, but I just didn't understand why. I stood by my bed, breathing heavily, and then anger took hold and I swung at the wall, punching it over and over again until my hand went numb.

Of course Mike bought Mum some flowers and me a Play-Station. He said he'd been under lots of stress at work – that he wouldn't lose his temper again. I left the PlayStation in its box. I knew it was only a matter of time before it happened again.

Sure enough, by the time winter arrived that year, they were back to having shouting matches. I appalled myself at how much of a coward I was for hiding upstairs. Dad's words about me being the man of the house taunted me. From that point on, home seemed to simmer with tension. The new rule was I had to be back for dinner every night, but I didn't get why when meals were eaten in silence. Mike sat in his chair in the living room late into the evenings, watching old war films and smoking. I hated the smell of that stale smoke.

One night at dinner, he threw a glass against the wall be-cause he'd had a text telling him a month's worth of work was cancelled. When Mum cleaned it up, she cut her finger on the glass and he called her clumsy. I stood up, as did Mike, but Mum looked at me, desperation in her eyes, and I sat back down, pushing food around my plate and trying not to cry.

All the guilt, all the shame – all the effort of trying to hide how upset I was, how part of me blamed Mum for letting Mike into our lives . . . I just wanted to escape it. The solution came from a kid in our class – Tom – who, it turned out, ran a pretty successful weed operation. I managed to sell the idea to Theo that getting high would be a creative spark for our writing.

'It worked for Lenny Bruce,' Theo mused.

We went to our usual spot by the Thames Head stone, shivering as the lightest of snow fell. We listened to Lenny's *Berkeley Concert* album, sharing headphones. By the time the tape ended, Theo's eyes were half-closed, and he had such a ridiculous smile on his face that I started to giggle.

'What?' he said. 'What's so funny?'

I tried my best to explain, but the more quizzically he looked at me, the harder I laughed, and soon we were both helpless. Sitting in that field with my best friend, laughing so hard it hurt – it was exactly what I'd needed, and in that moment Mike and the horror show at home may as well have been on a different planet. So when Theo jumped up onto the head stone and started talking about us walking the Thames Path one day, I might have been ribbing him with all his talk of 'wenches' and bringing his accordion, but in reality I found myself thinking that as long as I had Theo in my life, the person I knew who could help me escape when things were going wrong, then everything would probably be OK. I grabbed him around the shoulder and we walked off down the lane, swaying woozily, only untangling our arms when we got to his house.

There we ordered pizza and I did my best not to seem too stoned in front of his parents. I'd never spent much time in the same room as his sister, Alice, but despite only being eleven, she was so sardonic and cutting to Theo that even if I hadn't been high, I'd have been laughing like an idiot. She was drawing at the kitchen table, a brilliant caricature of Theo, captioned simply, and brilliantly: 'Theodore D. Poosevelt'. I nearly lost my mind when she slipped it to me under the table. Theo saw what was happening and tried to grab it, but I passed it back to Alice and she sprinted away from

Theo and began doing laps around the living room with her brother in hot pursuit. Theo's Mum, Angie, tried her best to contain them, but she was laughing still – even more so when Geoff, Theo's Dad, began playing the Benny Hill song on an imaginary trumpet.

When everything had finally calmed down, Angie tried to insist that I stayed for ice cream, but I knew that with every second that passed without me forcing myself out into the dark and back home, the punishment waiting for me would only be getting worse. And so I thanked Theo's parents for having me and told Alice to keep up the good work insulting her brother.

Just as I was about to leave, Theo told me he needed to give me something. It was a parcel, wrapped up in seemingly never-ending layers of wrapping paper and parcel tape.

'Early Christmas present,' he explained. 'See you tomorrow.'

My happiness at this unexpected gift was short-lived. I knew I was in trouble the moment I came through the front door at home.

'We were supposed to be having dinner as a family,' Mum said, while Mike simmered behind her at the kitchen table, arms folded.

'But we're not a family,' I said. I pushed past her and made for the stairs, but Mike leapt up and grabbed me by the arm.

'Your mum wants you to sit down.'

I looked at Mum.

'Mike,' she said. 'It's OK.'

'No, it isn't fucking OK,' Mike said quietly, still gripping my arm. There was a stand-off.

I could feel the blood throbbing in my ears as I realised Mike needed to vent his anger, and it was either me or mum.

'Mike,' Mum was pleading now, 'there's no need for this, just let him go now – I'm not cross, really. We can have dinner another night.'

At last, I made up my mind. Mike wasn't going to touch Mum tonight. But just as I tensed – to do what, I wasn't sure – Mike let me go.

'Think I'd waste my energy on you?' He grabbed his keys from the sideboard.

'Oh, are you going out, love?' Mum asked.

'Pub,' Mike grunted, slamming the door behind him.

Mum put on her 'everything's fine' voice and tried to ask me about school, but I shook my head and stomped up the stairs to my room. I lay on my bed and turned up my music, trying to drown out the sounds of carols coming from below. A brief, unlikely rap battle ensued, NWA vs the King's College Choir:

'Straight outta Compton . . .'

'. . . All is calm, all is bright.'

As the urge to scrape my knuckles on the wall became irresistible, I realised I was still clutching the present Theo had given me. He'd wrapped it so tightly, I had to rip the corner with my teeth and prise the paper open. What I pulled out was a binder, the size of a paperback. It was everything we'd ever written together – scripts, sketches, half-thought-out ideas. He'd collated it all.

I flipped the book to its cover. Underneath a drawing of Theo and me, Alice's handiwork, were the words *Joel and Theo: Quite the Little Double Act.*

Chapter Nineteen

Theo

By the time we arrived in Lechlade, the rain had completely cleared, and the final approach was towards the backdrop of a fiery pink sunset. Geese arrowed overhead in perfect formation, reflected in the clear, lazy river beside us. It didn't feel right. It felt like it should still be raining.

We'd barely exchanged a word since we left the battle re-enactors. For a large stretch, the path narrowed so that we had to walk in single file, and Joel lagged behind. All the while, I struggled to reckon with our exchange back there. I wanted to believe Joel – that this 'bucket list' really was just another project, but he had looked so horrified at my discovery, I couldn't accept that was all it was. The internal battle continued until we reached Lechlade's high street, where Joel decided to revert to the cheery bonhomie of Mack the journalist.

'Fancy some fish and chips?' he asked, rubbing his hands together.

'Sure.'

'Lovely stuff,' he replied, whistling loudly. It all felt false, like an actor trying to carry on a high-energy farce despite just having broken his leg in his latest pratfall.

As I stood at the back of the chip shop and watched Joel attempt cheery conversation with the reluctant man behind the counter, I thought back to when we'd parted at Kemble station, where I felt there was something he wasn't quite telling me. And then there were those rumours about his drinking. I remembered a documentary I'd seen about alcoholics where one of their recovery steps was to make things up to people they'd wronged. Was that what the bucket list was all about?

Joel laughed loudly at his own joke and turned around to me, pointing at the battered sausages and raising his eyebrows suggestively. I smiled back weakly, but I had to go outside. The heat and smell of the deep-fat fryer was making me queasy, but not as much as Joel's performance.

When Joel came out, he thrust a bag of chips into my arms and started talking at a hundred miles an hour about an idea he'd had for the next episode of the show. He didn't pause for breath until we'd checked into our crummy B & B, where we were shown to our room by a woman who's opening gambit to us was 'Are you from the hygiene board?'

'We are not, my good lady, so no need to worry,' Joel purred.

The woman eyed him suspiciously, as if Joel were a gentleman thief who coveted her jewels. She led us to our room, while Joel waffled on.

'Let's have a writing session now,' he said, shovelling chips into his mouth, once the woman was gone. He was trying to force energy into his voice, but he looked so tired – particularly now he'd lain down on the bed.

'Maybe a bit later,' I said. 'Or first thing?' I couldn't bring myself to make him stay up any longer. Writing suddenly didn't seem important.

'Sure,' Joel said, tossing a chip into the air and catching it in his mouth. 'Whatever you fancy.'

He put the TV on and flicked to a mindless action film, one with more explosions than dialogue.

I ate a few chips, but I wasn't very hungry. I went to wash my hands in the bathroom. I looked at my reflection. If this was the face Joel was seeing – flooded with concern and awkwardness – no wonder he was trying so hard with his 'everything's fine' act.

By the time I stepped out again, Joel was asleep and snoring. I took the bag of chips off his chest and turned the volume down on the film, watching him for a moment until he stirred. I slipped out of the room. There was a chair at the end of the corridor, next to a window that looked out on the river, just visible in the gloom. I wondered whether Alice was still up. I decided to chance it.

'Well, if it isn't Paul Theroux,' she said as she picked up.

'Well, you know, if Paul Theroux had looked like an unmade bed crossed with a mop.'

I instantly felt better.

'How's things?' I asked.

'Yeah, all right. Bit of drama on the basketball court. Got whacked in the head by some oaf.'

'Shit, really – you OK?' I felt a stab of guilt at not being there to look after her.

'I'll live. I was worried for a little bit that I might end up like James Cracknell, that rower. He got hit in exactly the same place on one of those mad charity voyages he did and he got that thing where you lose your sense of taste and smell.'

'Ambrosia.'

Alice sighed. 'No, Theo, that's custard. *Anosmia*, is the condition.'

'Oh.'

'Anyway, more importantly, how the hell are you? How goes the grand trip?'

I didn't exactly know where to start. 'Well, it was all going quite well. But then something weird happened today.'

'Go on . . .'

'I think . . . I think there's a chance that Joel might be an alcoholic.'

'God, really?'

'Yeah. I mean, I'd read a few rumours in that vein flying around, but it was more just about him partying all the time, you know? But then, today, I found this bit of paper he'd dropped, and it had something about a "bucket list" written on it.'

'Jesus, really?'

'Yeah. He told me it was just some TV project he was working on. Didn't want me to think he hadn't got his eye on the ball.'

'And you don't believe him?'

I pictured Joel, the defiant look on his face in the field.

'I honestly don't know,' I said. 'The thing is – this is what he does.'

'What do you mean?'

I checked back over my shoulder, just to make sure the door to the bedroom was still closed.

'Back when we were kids, there was definitely something going on with him that he never told me about. I asked him about it once, but . . .' I trailed off. The problem was, I knew this was just a story I'd told myself over the years to make myself feel better. It was the 'once' part that I was ashamed of.

∞

I can't remember the exact moment I felt Joel pulling away from me, but once I noticed it, I was convinced it was my fault. Now we were fifteen, my lack of social cachet had become problematic, and he was obviously looking for a way out. The way I clung to him like a limpet was only holding him back.

I started looking for signs he was bored or annoyed when we were together. As soon as I detected the slightest restlessness, I rattled off suggestions for what else we could do, though the options were limited.

'Wanna go to the golf course for a smoke?'

'Nah.'

'Could try and get served at the rugby club?'

'Can't be arsed.'

'Blockbuster?'

'See above.'

'Ha, yeah. Well, just say if you're bored or whatever.'

'How could I possibly be bored, Theo? I mean we could be in Rio, or New York, but we're here. In Kemble. The city that gets eight hours' sleep a night.'

I laughed along, but I couldn't help but take it personally. The problem was, I knew the more paranoid I got, the less fun I was to be around, but it was impossible for me not to panic at the prospect of losing him. This was *Joel*, the person who'd saved me from a life on the margins – the one person who'd taken a chance on me. I thought about him passing me the dry paper towels so I could wipe soap from my eyes, and the moment I'd been able to hold Darren's gaze in the classroom, defiant, all because of Joel's kindness. There was obviously something going on that he wasn't telling me, and I had to find a way of fixing whatever was wrong. I decided that the next time I saw him seeming quiet for no reason, I was going to say something, no matter how unnatural it felt. As it turned out, I didn't have to wait long.

One lunch break, I went to find Joel at our usual meeting spot, but he wasn't there. Eventually I found him by the lockers, staring off into space, oblivious to the two girls who'd just sniggered at him as he stood there with a vacant expression on his face.

'Hellooo,' I said, waving my hand in front of his face.

He blinked a few times, as if I'd just materialised out of thin air.

'Thought we were writing,' I said.

'Oh, right, yeah,' Joel replied. 'Sorry. Forgot.'

'You just been . . . here?' I said, looking around the empty corridor.

'Here and there, yeah.'

Joel scratched at his chin and I started.

His knuckles were bruised purple and the skin was scabbed over.

'Fuck, what's wrong with your hand?'

'Nothing,' Joel said quickly, rolling his sleeve down. 'Come on, let's go.'

We walked down the corridor without speaking. I kept trying to catch a glimpse of his hand, but his sleeve was firmly tugged down, and he was staring doggedly ahead, seemingly concentrating on the door at the far end of the corridor. We were just about to go into the empty classroom where we usually wrote, with Joel just ahead of me, when I blurted out: 'Joel, are you OK?'

He paused by the door but didn't look back. It was like the words I'd spoken had frozen him to the spot. He turned, slowly, to face me. His eyes were wet, his lips strangely twisted as he tried to stop them quivering.

'Please don't ever ask me that fucking question ever again,' he said at last, in a voice that was harsher, lower, than his usual one. Then he turned back and walked into the classroom.

I stood outside for a few seconds, feeling shaken. I'd never seen Joel like that. It was frightening, how angry he was. But at the same time, behind all that front, he had a look in his eye that pleaded with me to ignore what he was saying, to keep going . . .

When I found the courage to open the door, Joel had wiped his eyes, though the faint track marks of tears still stained his cheeks.

'Right then,' he said, suddenly businesslike. 'Let's get this fucker finished, shall we?'

'I . . .' But I felt my shoulders drop. I knew I couldn't do this. 'Yeah,' I said, 'let's get it finished.' Then I turned and shut the door behind me.

∞

I'd not thought of that moment for a very long time. It took me a second to realise Alice was calling my name.

'Helloo-ohhhh. Theo, are you still there?'

'Yeah, I'm here, sorry,' I said, but I still had one foot in the past. I should have been stronger. I should have pressed him further, no matter how impossible it felt. Then, even if he'd decided that our friendship was over, at least I would have done the right thing. Maybe I was being harsh on the fifteen-year-old me, but still, wasn't it true that if only I'd been a little braver, I could have prevented all the shit that came afterwards?

'Well, anyway,' Alice said, 'you sound a bit preoccupied, so I think I'll leave you to it, dear brother. I hope you two manage to sort things out, though.'

'Yeah,' I said. 'Me too.'

I was about to say goodbye when Alice said, 'I'm curious, though. What's it actually been like up till now? Does it feel weird?'

'Kind of,' I said. 'But familiar at the same time. And it's funny, I've started to remember loads of stuff I'd not thought about for years, without us even talking about it.'

'Oh yeah? Like what?'

I couldn't bring myself to tell her about the memory I'd just been lost to. But I told her about the day Joel came in wearing his solidarity eyepatch.

'Wow, I'd forgotten about that too,' Alice laughed. 'And that was, what, two weeks after you'd met?'

'Barely that.'

Alice yawned, which made me yawn too.

'God, it's so weird how things work out, isn't it?' Alice said.

'How do you mean?'

'Well, just think, in an alternate universe, there's another you, who never had a friend at school, who carried on being a lonely weirdo dressed like a P.G. Wodehouse character. And there's another me there too, and I can still walk.'

Chapter Twenty

Joel

I woke with a start, disorientated. My eyes eventually focused on the TV opposite, where someone was running away from the car that had just exploded. I looked around, but there was no sign of Theo. I didn't remember moving my bag of chips over to the dresser. Had that been him?

I reached for my phone and read a text from Mum: *How are you getting on? And have you had any more thoughts about 'Plan B?'*. Before I could collect my thoughts, there was another ridiculous explosion on the TV and I scrambled for the remote, flicking through the channels to find something less hectic. I wished I hadn't, because the next thing I knew I was looking at Amber. It was a repeat of an ITV drama, one of her earliest roles, playing a college student blackmailing a tutor. Seeing her on screen now, pacing up a corridor, pulled me back to the first time I ever saw her.

∞

It was the annual non-uniform day for charity, not long after I'd turned sixteen. For 50p, we were allowed to ditch our school uniforms for the day and wear whatever we liked – within reason, as Theo found out to his cost when he was forced to change his Bill Hicks T-shirt with the slogan, 'If you're in marketing or advertising . . . kill yourself.'

'Where did you even buy that?' I asked.

'Saw it on a website,' Theo said.

'So you saw it . . . *advertised*?'

'Yeah? What's your point?'

'Well isn't . . . Never mind.'

Unlike the rest of the school, I hadn't bothered to think of anything edgy or interesting to wear, I was just in my usual dark jeans and hoodie. Theo, endearingly, seemed so excited by the occasion that he was bouncing along beside me like a self-propelled slinky. My thoughts drifted as he yammered on about a new sitcom he'd discovered.

We'd just turned into the long corridor that stretched the length of the school building, when I was distracted by a flash of yellow at the other end. A girl was walking in our direction, wearing a yellow plaid skirt and matching blazer. At the time, I had no idea that this was an homage to *Clueless*. I would imagine there is still significant damage to the floor at the spot where my jaw hit it.

The girl and I made eye contact, and from that point on as we walked, our eyes were locked together, a missile seeking its target. The journey down that corridor would be the longest twenty seconds of my life. As she smiled at me – a smile that seemed to suggest mischief, nonchalance and shyness all at once – walking became impossible. What was it again, left foot, *then* right? I tried to work out if I'd seen her before. Surely I'd have remembered her.

'Hey,' she said, as we passed.

'Helley,' I said back – half-way between hello and hey. I screwed my eyes shut. How was it possible I'd managed to fuck up 'hello'? I'd caught a faint hint of her perfume. It was citrus-y, orange . . . blossom, or something? Was that a thing? I had no idea. But then again, I also had no idea that for the rest of my life there would be moments I'd catch that scent in the air – in a rush-hour tube carriage, or in a restaurant – and it would catapult me back to this moment.

I made myself count three full seconds after she passed, then I turned. The swish of the girl's hair told me I'd been a second too late to see her looking back. I wanted more than anything to rewind and try that again, but Theo nudged me in the ribs, asking if I was listening to him or what? And the moment slipped away.

A few days later, I was supposed to be meeting Theo at lunchtime as usual, but I'd barely slept the night before, a result of Mike falling asleep drunk, mid-cigarette, in his chair and nearly setting it alight, and all I wanted to do was find somewhere to hide and close my eyes for a few minutes. I told Theo I was feeling ill and heading home, and then I made for the place I'd scouted out earlier – a trampoline in the corner of the gym hall, a secluded spot where I thought I wouldn't get disturbed. I put on some comedy CD that Theo had given me, then leant back and closed my eyes, idly picking at the scabs on my cracked knuckles. But moments later I heard footsteps approaching.

'Hey, that's my spot.'

I jumped, smacking my elbow on the wall behind me. It was *her*.

'Sorry,' I said. 'I can move if you want.'

The girl looked at me for a moment.

'No, don't worry. But mind if I join you?'

'Sure,' I said, doing my level-best to hide how ecstatic I was to get a chance to make up for the 'helley' incident.

She crawled under the trampoline and sat opposite me, arranging her legs so that they were stretched out straight in a mirror image of mine.

'I'm Amber, by the way,' she said, taking a book from her bag. 'I'm new here.'

'I'm Joel,' I said. 'I'm not new. Well, I sort of am.'

'Delighted to meet you, Joel.'

There was something alluringly grown-up about the way she said this.

'What are you listening to?' she asked.

'Erm . . . a band . . . they're called Slipknot,' I said, hoping Amber couldn't see the CD case by my foot which had *Fawlty Towers* written on it.

She wrinkled her nose and opened her book.

'What are you reading?' I asked.

She showed me the cover. The book was called *An Actor Prepares*.

'Cool,' I said.

'Do you know Stanislavski?'

'I . . . Yeah, course. Wasn't he on Graham Norton recently?'

'I don't *think* so,' Amber said, 'given that he's been dead for eighty years.'

'Right, yeah. Must've been thinking of someone else.'

Amber narrowed her eyes, apparently trying to work out if I was joking or not.

'So you want to be an actor then?' I said, possibly overdoing it on the sincerity front to make up for how I'd just come across.

'I'm *going* to be an actor,' Amber replied, smiling. There was nothing haughty or arrogant about the way she said this, just understated confidence.

We started talking about our favourite TV shows. I did my best to think of the most obscure, edgy ones I could, no matter if I'd actually watched them, and Amber scribbled a few down in the back of *An Actor Prepares* which, I saw, was full of other doodles and notes. So she wrote in books. A defacer of literature, no less. I noticed her school tie was arranged with the thin part hanging down in front of the thick part. I decided I should probably start doing that too in future.

'Shit, that looks sore,' Amber said. It took me a moment to realise she meant my knuckles.

'Oh yeah, they're fine really,' I said. But I didn't hide them. It felt too obvious a move to do that now, and I didn't want to invite questions.

'Are you sure? Wait, hang on, I've actually got some stuff that might help.' She reached into her bag and brought out a little tube of something. 'Here,' she said, 'give me your hand.'

'W-what?'

'Give me your hand, come on.' Amber raised her eyebrows expectantly at me.

As Amber reached out towards me, I was more worried about my palm being sweaty than how my knuckles looked. She took my arm gently in one hand, and with the other she squeezed a little of the cream onto my knuckles. She began to rub it in with delicate little circles. It was instantly cool and soothing. After a moment, I looked up. Amber was watching me intently. She looked away, cheeks flushing slightly, and pushed her hair behind her ear.

'All done,' she said, putting the cream back in her bag.

'Thanks,' I said. 'That, um, feels better already.'

'Good.' She assumed the voice of a concerned but friendly

doctor. 'Now, is there anything else I can help you with today?'

I shook my head.

'Are you on MSN by the way?' Amber asked.

Jesus, who *was* this girl? Was MSN the same as ecstasy?

'Huh? No,' I said. 'But I smoke weed quite a bit.'

Amber laughed at this, and I laughed back, even though I had no idea what the joke was. She started scribbling something down in her book, then she tore a scrap of the page out and handed it to me.

'Here's my username. Add me tonight?'

'Definitely,' I said. It seemed crucial I agree. I could find out what she was talking about later.

'See ya then.' Amber crawled out from under the trampoline.

As the lunch bell went, I looked at the scrap of paper on which Amber had written: Xx_LittlePixie_xX. I put the precious cargo in my pocket, and wandered in a daze back to the form room, finding Theo in our usual spot.

'All right?' I said.

'All right. Hang on, I thought you were going home sick?'

'Yeah, I was,' I said, adjusting my voice to a croak. 'But, you know, couldn't be arsed going all the way back.'

'Fair enough. So where've you been?'

I put my hand in my pocket, feeling for the scrap of paper, flexing my soothed knuckles. 'I was . . . nowhere.'

A month passed. Ever since adding Xx_LittlePixie_xX on (what turned out to be) MSN messenger, it had felt like I was living a double life, one that Theo knew nothing about. I would wait for Mum and Mike to go upstairs and then get on the computer in the living room. Amber and I would message for hours at a time, to the point where I'd crawl into bed bleary-eyed only a few hours before I had to get up for school.

With the distance that talking online allowed, I found it easier to open up – it meant I could organise the thoughts rattling around my head into something cogent. But still, when her question appeared one night – 'What actually happened to your hands?' – I couldn't think of how to respond. I must have typed a dozen different answers: brushing it off as an accident, or that I'd got into a fight, or, most ludicrous of all, pretending that I'd come down with a rare tropical skin disease. In the end, after rejecting all of these, the only option I had left was to tell her the truth.

'It's something I do to make me feel better,' I wrote.

I watched the screen, blinking the soreness away, waiting for Amber's response.

'I thought it was something like that,' she wrote. 'It's cool if you don't want to tell me anything about it, but you can if you want . . .'

And so I did, tentatively at first, but before I knew it, my fingers were travelling across the keyboard so rapidly it was like they had a mind of their own, and the more I shared, the more I unburdened myself of all the guilt and shame, the more it felt like I was swimming up through a foetid lake, pushing myself to the surface, where I could finally breathe again.

It helped that Amber had her own pain to share. When you're messed up, I realised, it's easier to talk to people if they're messed up too. She'd been in counselling since she was twelve, ever since she'd found out she was adopted and had run straight to the station, getting on a train to London before quickly running out of money and having to call home.

She'd only been introduced to her biological mum just a few weeks ago.

'It was so strange,' she told me. 'We look so alike, and she even sits in the same way I do. It felt like I was talking to a version of me who'd come to visit from the future. It was nice I guess, but I don't even know if I want a relationship with her – it's so confusing.'

I tried my best to make her feel better, but I wasn't equipped with the right things to say. I just wished there was something I could offer her that was the equivalent of her soothing my cracked hands. The best I could do was think of ways to distract her, which meant sending her a series of (in hindsight godawful) music playlists, and researching books on acting that she could add to her collection. I ordered one online by someone called Uta Hagen, which took weeks to arrive second-hand from America.

I took it from my bag as casually as I could, as if it were a second thought, handing it over and saying I'd just happened to come across it in a charity shop. We were on the fourth of what became our regular rendezvous under the trampoline. I'd been having to make up excuses to put Theo off the scent. I'd pushed past how guilty this made me by telling myself that, fundamentally, nothing was changing about our friendship. OK, so I might not have been writing with him as much, but he seemed just as happy cracking on by himself, as long as I read everything he showed me afterwards. I knew if I just came out and told him I was spending this time with Amber he'd be weird about it, so this felt like the best for everyone.

That morning before I saw Amber for our fourth meeting I'd barely been able to concentrate on anything. Was it natural to be this nervous? I wondered. And the same went for just how much time I spent thinking about her. Whenever I did, it produced an almost painful weight in my stomach that I carried around with me. I didn't understand that at the time. There were moments she smiled at me and my brain felt like it was collapsing in on itself like a dying star. Why was something this exciting so painful and confusing at the same time?

Later that night we talked on MSN.

'Thanks again for the book,' Amber wrote. 'Loving it already.'

I punched the air. My gamble had paid off.

Another message appeared.

'You going to Chrissy Price's party on Saturday?'

'Yeah, probably,' I wrote back. (I had no idea who Chrissy Price was, or that she was having a party, but if Amber was going, then I was too.)

Then, somewhat out of the blue, Amber asked me about Theo.

'I see you two together all the time. He's like your best friend then, right?'

'Yeah,' I wrote. Part of me worried why Amber was asking me this, whether she meant anything by the question. Theo sometimes seemed a bit odd, obviously, but only I was allowed to think that. And I couldn't see a way I could go out with someone who thought badly of him.

'I like him,' she wrote. 'He's really funny in English.'

'Yeah, he's the best,' I replied, flooded with relief.

'Have you told him about Mike and everything?'

'No.'

'What? But why not? You just said he's your best friend . . .'

'It doesn't really work like that.'

147

'How come?'

'Well . . . Theo's, like, completely innocent. He has this lovely little life with his kind, normal family. He wouldn't know what to say. And I don't want him to think I'm this big screw-up.'

'Well, that's cute,' Amber wrote. 'But I still think you should tell him. You can't keep pretending everything's fine forever, can you?'

Just then, I sensed a movement behind me. Mike had been spying on my conversation. He slammed down the glass of water he must have just fetched from the kitchen, ripped the headphones from my ears and picked me up by the scruff of my neck, slamming me against the wall.

'Don't you fucking dare tell people about what goes on this house.'

'Get off me,' I said, glaring back at him. I don't think I've ever hated anyone more than in that moment.

A door slammed and then Mum appeared, face ghostly white in shock when she saw what was happening.

'Mike, stop,' Mum said, darting forward with a determined look and grabbing Mike's arm. But Mike barely seemed to notice. I could see then how angry he was. I tried to signal with my eyes to Mum to leave, that it was OK, but then she dug her nails into Mike's arm and tried to wrench it away. Instinctively, Mike threw his arm back and his elbow caught Mum in the face. She crumpled to the ground, covering her nose with her hands. Sitting there, in her nightie, covering her face, she looked almost childlike. Mike let go and I dropped to my knees, throwing my arms around Mum. After a moment, I heard Mike wrench the power cable from the computer.

'That was an accident,' he said to us. Then he left, taking the cable with him.

As I held Mum, I was already imagining the soothing rasp of the rough wall against my battered hand. But then I thought of Amber and the urge to hurt myself dwindled. There was a party at the weekend. I would see her then. If I could be strong, and just hold on until then, maybe everything would be fine.

Chapter Twenty-One
Theo

Lechlade to Newbridge, 16.4 miles (161 miles to Thames Barrier, London)

'You . . . all right?' I asked Joel, as we prepared to set off to Newbridge. He looked dreadful this morning. Waxy-skinned. Dark bags under his eyes. He looked like he should still be in bed.

When I'd got back to the room last night, I thought I could hear him on the phone to someone, but when I opened the door, the room was in darkness, and I realised he was talking to himself in his sleep. 'Should've told you, should've told you,' he was saying, over and over again, getting increasingly agitated. When it was clear he wasn't going to stop, I turned the light on, and when that didn't work, I prodded him awake with my finger. He looked around and finally saw me, blinking against the light. He seemed startled and afraid.

'You were having a nightmare,' I said, pretending to busy myself with my already unpacked bag.

'Mmm, sorry,' Joel grunted. Then he turned away onto his side. By the time I'd turned the light off and got into bed, he seemed to be sleeping soundly, but I spent the night wide awake, listening to the distant sounds of the Thames lapping on the riverbank, wondering what exactly his frightened words had meant.

'Oh yeah, I'm fine,' Joel said now, casually, stretching his arms out in front and cracking his knuckles. 'Just still feeling the effects of that food poisoning, I guess. I probably look worse than I feel.'

He slung his bag onto his back and marched off ahead.

We made our way down a dusty track to the river, which glittered in the early-morning sun. A boat chugged along, a springer spaniel on its bow, staring ahead like a noble captain. Joel continued his guidebook schtick as we walked, keen, it seemed, not to present me with a silence I could fill.

'We'll see a few things of note today then, Theo. The statue of Old Father Thames at St John's Lock, for instance, and the twelfth-century-built Old Radcot Bridge, which happens to be the oldest on the Thames.'

We were walking on something more recognisable as an actual path now, which meant we kept having to step aside for cyclists. After about an hour, Joel pointed out a Second World War pill box, but that seemed to be the last thing of any interest on the stretch we were walking, which grew increasingly remote and wild.

'Shall we have a breather,' I said, wishing that I didn't sound quite so much like a supportive supply teacher.

We found a patch of beaten down grass and watched the river go by. Joel kept absent-mindedly scratching his legs and his arms as if he had mosquito bites, and he popped two more of his 'hay fever' tablets. I was trying to summon the courage to ask him what was really going on when the trill of a bike bell announced that we weren't alone.

The man looked like he was in his late fifties, completely

bald, with eyebrows that began thin but thickened out at the sides of his eyes, as if they were trying to make a run for it.

'How do, boys?' he said. 'Bob. Nice to meet you.'

'All right?' said Joel and I in unison.

'Fancy an ice cream?' the man asked.

'Ice cream?' Joel replied uncertainly.

It wasn't clear where the man was going to produce said ice creams from. It was then that he turned his bike sideways and patted the pannier at the back. 'B & B's ice creams' was emblazoned across it in bright pink lettering. Not only was this the first ice-cream bike I'd ever seen, it was also a tandem.

'Well then? Fancy it? I've got the lot. Raspberry ripple, vanilla cone, you name it.'

'Not for me thanks,' I said. I glanced at Joel.

'Yeah, me too. Sorry.'

'Right,' the man muttered, looking crestfallen all of a sudden. Just as we were about to turn back to the river, he said, 'It's just, the wife's left me. We were travelling around together, selling this stuff. I'd jacked the job in and everything. IT consultant, you know? We were supposed to be seeing the country. Doing a bit of the Thames Path. It was my brother-in-law's idea. He's into that sort of thing. Well, we'd got as far as Lechlade before she'd had enough. So I'm left here with this ice cream to flog.'

'Cold,' Joel said. Then, when the man looked at him sharply. 'Your wife, I mean.'

'Betty,' he said, giving us a look that suggested we should know who she was just from that single name, like she was a Brazilian footballer. The poor bloke.

There followed a paralysing silence where neither Joel nor I knew what to say. I broke first, excusing myself to 'water

152

the plants' behind the cover of a tree. But when I came back, wondering if I should maybe have invented some excuse so I could rescue Joel from the conversation he'd no doubt be trapped in, I found the two men laughing together as if they were old friends. I couldn't help but feel a little vexed. It seemed my absence had been the key to this becoming a happy scene. I should have known Joel would easily charm the man. And I also should have known that this would make me disproportionately annoyed and jealous. But, most of all, as I watched the ice-cream man gleefully clutching a wedge of twenty-pound notes and wandering off down the path, I should have known that the moment Joel Thompson saw a novelty tandem ice-cream bike, and learnt that it was for sale, he would spend whatever was in his wallet in order to buy it.

Chapter Twenty-Two

Joel

'No,' Theo said. 'Absolutely not.'

'Oh, mate, come on – look at it!' I showed the bike off to him like an assistant on a game show, running my hand along its light blue trunk.

'What are we supposed to do about this though?' Theo tapped the ice-cream box mounted on the back of the bike.

'It's fine, I've paid him for the ice cream as well as the bike. We can eat it. We don't have to sell it or anything.'

'Oh no that would be mad. We're just going to ride a divorced ice-cream man's tandem bike half the length of the country, that's much more sensible.'

This was so much better. Grumpy Theo was my favourite Theo.

'Listen,' I said. 'How about we try it out? If you don't like it, we can sell it on.'

'Yeah, good luck getting full price,' Theo huffed. '*You* can ride it if you want. I'll walk behind.'

'OK, OK, fine.' I held my hands up, admitting defeat. Then I waited for Theo to turn his back. 'Race you then,' I said, grabbing the bike and wheeling it forward, just about managing to mount the front seat and keep the bike upright. I swerved off violently into the muddy lane, feet slipping off the pedals. Eventually I got going properly, momentum doing the work for me, giving my aching legs the respite I'd been craving.

I heard Theo struggling to keep up behind me.

'Oh, for fuck's sake,' he panted. 'Fine. Let me on.'

'I thought you didn't want to,' I called over my shoulder.

'Joel, stop being a dick and slow down.'

'Right you are . . .'

I stopped to let him climb onto the seat behind me, and off we went, unsteady at first, but getting into a steady rhythm.

'This is ridiculous,' Theo said. After a moment, though, I heard him trying to pull the ice-cream box open. 'There better be a fucking Feast in here.'

After a bit more grumbling, I managed to persuade him to ride up front for a bit. This worked even better. Without him being able to see me, it meant I could keep my feet on the pedals but let him do most of the work, giving me valuable time to get my breath back. Twenty minutes later we were practically powering along – Theo's hair blowing gloriously in the breeze.

'Fine, I admit it,' Theo said through a mouthful of ice cream. 'This is pretty fucking great.'

And so we cycled on, hugging the curves of the river, with nothing but the odd duck for company, until some narrow-boats began to pop up. I drank in the smell of the diesel and woodsmoke, waving cheerily to the boaters we passed. We approached a silver-haired couple reading newspapers up on deck, a bottle of champagne cooling in a bucket.

'Ahoy there,' the man called in perhaps the poshest voice I'd ever heard. 'Might I purchase an ice cream from you fellows?'

We slowed a little and I pulled open the box.

'Have one on us,' I said, tossing them up a couple of Magnums.

The man caught them and saluted, and I returned the gesture.

'I feel like we're in *Wind in the Willows*,' Theo laughed.

'Poop poop! The open road, the dusty highway!' I called, and we picked up the pace again.

Now *this* was the life. The sun was on my back, geese were skidding comically onto the water next to us. It was like the whole riverbank was cheering us on. I wanted more than anything to stay in this moment with my friend for as long as possible. Here, my every waking thought wasn't about how sick I was, or how long I had left.

Here was freedom.

Chapter Twenty-Three
Theo

At Newbridge, we managed to luck our way into a room at the Rose Revived pub, a beautiful little place perched just off the river. According to Joel's guidebook, Oliver Cromwell had supposedly supped an ale or two there, so I decided I'd do the same while the sun was still up. Joel told me he'd come out and join me shortly, but after an hour had passed without any sign of him, I went up to the room. I felt oddly trepidatious about what I might find when I opened the door, but Joel was just conked out on the bed, fast asleep.

I considered waking him, but he obviously needed the rest. Instead, I took pen and paper from my bag and headed back downstairs, where I bought a musty pint of ale from the bar and sat in an armchair by the unlit fire. I'd planned to get on with some writing, but I couldn't concentrate tonight. I tried calling Alice, but there was no reply. After a couple more drinks, I found loneliness stealing over me. I knew the sensible thing was to go to bed, but my mind was still too clogged with unhelpful thoughts. By this point, the barman had begun delivering a fresh pint every time I was down to the dregs of the previous one. It was easier just to give in.

On a table by the fireplace, I spotted some complimentary

postcards among the leaflets and maps. I plucked one from the basket and began to write.

My dear sister,

I write to you in uncertain spirits, despite making good progress on our voyage today. You would so love it here. Nature surrounds us in all her majesty. Why, only this morning I saw a moorhen defecating on a can of Red Bull. Such beauty!

I had been meaning to tell you something. I remembered recently about the picture you drew for me to cheer me up after the cricket pavilion bat drama. You really were, and are, very talented. And you've done a better job of looking out for me than I have for you. I'm sorry about that.

Anyway, I think that might be my yearly quota of sincere words used up, so it only remains for me to say this: do you reckon the postman is reading this, right now? I bet he is. I wonder if he knows about the last postman we had who read all our postcards. Such a shame that he 'fell' like that. Terrible business.

Your loving, and admittedly quite drunk brother,
Theodore D. Poosevelt

The barman rang for last orders, and I decided to treat myself to one final pint and a Scotch to keep it company. The harsh tang of the latter on my tongue made me think of Edinburgh – pre-show drinks in the Dagda Bar; Dutch courage. Inevitably, my thoughts then turned to Babs. I wondered what she was doing right now. Whether she was still up . . .

I slid my phone out of my pocket – slowly, as if trying to hide from myself what I was doing, and started composing a text.

Hey. I'm sorry for that call the other day. Things have been a bit weird. I'm on a road trip of sorts. With Joel Thompson. I don't know if you know him?

I deleted the last sentence. And then, imagining quite how terrifying Alice would be when I told her what I'd done, I deleted all of it. But it wasn't enough to stop my mind wandering to those final few months – the terrible decisions I'd made. How I'd not seen the end coming, I'll never know. By that point I was like a blind man stumbling towards a ravine.

∞

After the debacle where I'd quit my proper job on the false promise of writing in the Sky TV comedy department, I had to come clean and tell Babs I was soon to be unemployed.

'Can't you get your old job back?' she asked. I had neglected to mention that I had resigned from that position with the 'corporate pigs' in such a godawful way that I had firmly burned my bridges. I mumbled something about a restructure making that impossible instead.

'Well listen, I'm sure you'll find something else soon,' Babs reassured me. I was lying with my head on her lap while she tangled and untangled my hair. We were doing our Sunday evening tradition, where we lit candles, drank wine and listened to an album from start to finish on Babs's record player – a beautiful vintage contraption passed down by her dad. Our tiny rented flat was full of gorgeous items like that – all of them belonging to Babs, most of which she acquired on expeditions to Spitalfields market. It made me feel very grown-up to be the sort of person who – instead of a coffee table – put their mugs on a crate that looked like it had last been used to drop supplies into Vietnam.

'About finding another job . . .' I said, dipping my toe in the water.

'You're thinking of not getting another one? Are you going to till the land or something? Think we'd have to ask the landlord about that, and he doesn't let us put up posters.'

'Even though we do.'

'True, true.'

'No, the thing is, I think I want to try and write. See where I can get with it.'

'What, so just speculatively?'

'Yeah.'

Babs continued to play with my hair, but she didn't say anything.

'Do you think that's a terrible idea?'

'I'm not saying that.'

'But you're not *not* saying that?'

This time, Babs took her hands from my head.

'Look, I'm not going to tell you what to do. If you want to write, then fine. Great. I'm not going to give you permission, though. You've got to decide for yourself, you being twenty-seven and everything . . .'

'Ouch,' I said. 'Twenty-seven. That sounds like such a real age. I should have achieved something by now.'

'You took the bins out earlier.'

'I did. I was very gallant, given what was in them. I was thinking something more creative, though. How else am I going to die of an overdose and still make the papers – another twenty-seven-club tragedy.'

'Another what?'

'The twenty-seven club, you know – all those people who died at that age.'

'Oh yeah. Who was it again? Janice Joplin.'

'Hendrix . . .'

'Ken Cobain.'

'I'm sorry . . . *Ken Cobain?*'

'Yeah. The Nirvana singer.'

I turned to look at Babs.

'Oh,' she said, closing her eyes. 'I've done that thing where I've got someone's name wrong, haven't I?' And for the next twenty minutes I teased her about Ken Cobain sounding like an avuncular carpenter and Babs retaliated by taking my feet prisoner and tickling them until I submitted.

If only I'd been able to freeze-frame that moment and go back to it. *This is it!* I'd say, shaking myself by the shoulders. *It doesn't get better than this!* Maybe then I'd have just got another proper job and tried a bit of writing on the side – without it obsessing me so much.

But then I read on a comedy website that Joel had been given his own prime-time sitcom that just happened to star his 'long-term girlfriend' Amber Crossley. And my fragile little ego couldn't take it. *It should be me*, I'd think, in my darker moments. Well, I was going to show him.

At first, I made sure that I hid this obsession from Babs. I made a point of being selfless and romantic – cooking dinner every night so there'd be something when she got home from a long day at the office, leaving silly notes in her bag most days, something to make her laugh, getting up early on the weekends and buying coffee and the Saturday supplements. But as the months passed and the script knockbacks came, a slow drip-feed of rejection, my mood soured. I spent more time in the day lying on the sofa, hate-watching Joel's show, than trying to come up with my own. I'd scramble madly to get in an upright position when Babs got home from work. She'd open the curtains and I'd pretend to claw at the sunlight like a vampire. She laughed the first time I did it. She didn't by the fifth.

She caught me asleep with a beer in my hand when she came home from work one lunchtime to pick up something she'd forgotten, and we had the first of many fights about what I was actually doing with my days. Babs told me I needed to start finding a way to help her with the rent. I told her, ludicrously, that she was stifling my creativity by making me think about money. She told me to stop putting notes in her bag – they were getting annoying.

There should have been a piercingly loud alarm going off in my head. But I was too deep into my obsession with Joel and his preposterous good luck. The final straw came when his show won a prestigious industry award. I was supposed to go to some media do Babs's company was putting on that night. By the time I met her in the soulless, aggressively lit bar, I was struggling not to slur my words, having put away a few pints in the shitty pub across the road beforehand, just to take the edge off. The rest of the night was a blur. I remember stumbling and spilling a drink – some furtive sideways glances as I told what I thought was a winning anecdote, but which inexplicably wasn't getting the right reaction. When I woke up the next morning feeling like my tongue had been pebbledashed in the night, Babs was sitting on the end of the bed. That was never a good sign.

'Morning,' I croaked.

Babs looked at me, waiting.

'Sorry?' I tried.

'Yeah, genuine sorrys don't tend to come with a question mark at the end. Thank you so much for ruining a really important night for me.'

'Shit, did I?' I said, sitting up, the room spinning horribly. 'I really am sorry. I'm an idiot.'

I reached for Babs's hand, but she stood up and folded her arms.

'I am so fucking fed up of that excuse, Theo. I honestly don't know if I can . . . I'm going out. I'll see you later.'

As the front door slammed, it was finally the jolt to the brain I needed. Jesus Christ, what the hell was I doing? The words Babs had left unsaid were quite clearly 'do this any more' or 'be with you' or any other terrible combination that meant she was thinking of leaving me. Well, that wasn't an option. I wasn't going to let the only good thing in my life go. What I needed was a plan. Something that made it clear how committed I was to her. *A big gesture.*

A week later, I was standing outside her office just off Great Portland Street, holding a box of chalk. As I began to draw on the road, a few passers-by – tourists, mainly – stopped to see what I was doing. Perhaps they thought I was one of those people on the Millennium Bridge who painted over chewing gum to turn it into art; maybe that I was some sort of Banksy type creating a searing satirical artwork – Thatcher but with the face of a duck or something. *Nope*, I wanted to tell them, *I'm just a big idiot in love.*

As the letters I'd drawn became more visible each time I went over them, a small crowd began to gather. I saw two Japanese tourists gasp and put their hands up to their faces. I smiled and shrugged. 'She might say no,' I said.

Once I'd finished my handiwork, I stood back, looked up at the fourth-floor window, and called Babs's work phone.

'Hello?'

'Hey, it's Theo.'

'Oh hiya, you all right? I'm glad you called actually. I was going to ask you to get toilet paper from the Co-op if you're planning on . . . leaving the house.'

'Sure,' I said, the slight barely registering. 'But I've got a question for you first.'

I could hear Babs typing. 'Yeah what's that?' she said, sounding distracted.

'Actually, why don't you come to the window. You can see it from there.'

'Window? What are you . . . Hang on.'

I squinted up at the fourth floor. Sunlight was bouncing off the window, so I couldn't quite see if anyone was up there. I looked back at the road. Would Babs be able to see the words? They were pretty big. BABS, WILL YOU MARRY ME? P.S. IT'S THEO. I was so proud of myself, especially with the jaunty postscript. What a brilliant proposal story this was going to be. And if a few people took photos and they found their way on to Twitter or BuzzFeed or the local news, then that would just be a nice bonus, wouldn't it?

I was still on the phone. I could hear excited voices in the background. Some whooping. Some laughter. I heard Babs pick the receiver back up, and I held my breath.

'Wash it off, Theo,' she said. Then she put the phone down.

There can't be many more humiliating tasks than clearing your proposal off a busy side-road while trying to keep up the pretence to those around you that she said yes. When I'd finally got rid of it, I found the nearest pub I could and set about getting staggeringly, award-winningly drunk.

Somehow, I made it back to our Highbury flat, only to find a force field had mysteriously developed which made it impossible to get my key into the lock. When I looked at how delicate the panel of glass above the handle was, it seemed obvious that I should put my elbow through it. I didn't even wrap my jacket around my arm. The crunch of the glass seemed so quiet – I'd been expecting the sort of crash of the sound effects you got on the radio – so it was with surprise that I registered the blood blossoming so quickly that it had coated my arm in seconds, and the whole thing seemed so preposterous that I found myself laughing, and stumbling backwards onto the ground.

That was how Babs found me: flat on my back, making a one-winged blood-angel on the concrete.

I needed twenty-eight stitches.

Babs waited for six weeks before she kicked me out.

I didn't deserve two minutes.

∞

The barman shook me gently awake. As I made my way uncertainly upstairs, I realised, with a clarity that had eluded me since the break-up, just how laughable it was to think I ever had a shot of winning Babs back after the way I'd treated her. I'd got my priorities so appallingly wrong, and now I was having to live with the consequences. I thought about what Joel had said when he summarised his life in the showbiz spotlight: 'It's . . . fine'. Was that what I'd thrown everything away for? How had it had taken me so long to see that? I suppose I'd much preferred to live in ignorant bliss. All the regrets and terrible choices I'd made were angling to be noticed like attention-starved children. *Look at* me*! No, look at* me*!*

I paused outside the room, thinking about Joel and what he'd been hiding from me. The ice-cream escapade had been a distraction – I realised that now. I'd fallen for it far too easily. I wasn't buying his bucket list excuse any more. There had to be more to it. What if this really was another example of him shutting me down when I tried to find out if he was OK . . . and I'd just let him? There was a real possibility that I would look back at this moment in years gone by, lying awake at night because I'd failed to do the right thing.

I looked up at the light above me in the corridor, the bulb fizzing as the light wavered. *No*, I thought. *Not this time*. From this moment on, things were going to change. And tomorrow that was going to start with me getting the truth out of Joel.

Chapter Twenty-Four

Joel

I woke shortly after dawn. Theo was snoring softly, each out-breath briefly levitating a clump of hair from his face. Unable to get back to sleep, I decided to slip outside. I threw the stolen coat around my shoulders and pinched Theo's slippers before padding outside.

The bridge had little enclaves for people to stand to avoid traffic, and I stood in the one closest to the centre, leaning out over the river and surveying my domain. The sun was yet to break through the clouds, and a faint layer of fog hung above the river, which seemed to be motionless, as if waiting for the day to begin before it flowed again. There was a narrowboat moored up on the north bank, sleek and royal blue. Two years ago, when *Tooth*'s popularity began to grow and the paparazzi had started following Amber around, we'd seriously considered the idea of getting a boat like this, keeping on the move.

'Even if they find us,' I remember her saying, spearing a strawberry on a fork (then pretending to feed it to me before eating it herself), 'they can pursue us like Diana and Dodi, but the worst that'll happen is that we'll steer into a swan or something.'

I smiled at the memory. As if on cue, my phone vibrated with a message from her.

Hey. So I'm on my way back.

Shit.

The message continued:

Charlotte's buggered off somewhere with some terrible creep who's got a yacht, and I don't really want to be here on my own. I'm in a cab to the airport. You back in London yet? If not, I'll come to Kemble. Been ages since I've seen your ma. I know she's never exactly warmed to me, but it would be good to see her. X

Shit. Shit. Shit.

Without thinking through what I was going to say, I called her.

'Hey, love, you get my message?'

'Hey, yeah – I was just going to say, are you sure you don't want to stay out until the end of the week? Why don't you just try and relax there for a few more days?'

I could hear the desperation in my voice already. I should have waited before I called her – planned it properly.

'I'm not staying out here on my own, Joel. It actually gets quite creepy at night – it's so quiet. Last night I could have sworn I heard voices outside the cottage.'

'The thing is, though,' I said, casting around wildly for something to say, 'it . . . *is* all paid for.'

'Oh, sorry,' Amber said, 'I didn't realise that was your concern. Don't worry, I'll pay you back your half.'

'No, no, sorry, that's not what I . . . Of course you should leave if you're not safe there, if you're not happy.'

In the background, there was a volley of car horns and Italian insults – so elegant and lyrical, even if they were clearly just telling someone to get fucked.

'So where shall I come to then – I've not actually booked my flights yet. Bristol or London?'

'London,' I said quickly. 'I'll try to be back in a few days. Depends on Mum.'

'Oh, the poor thing. And poor you, having to deal with all that. Are you sure I can't come to you, try to take some of the weight off your shoulders? Maybe it'll give me a chance to impress your mum for once.'

'No, honestly, it's fine, you don't need to do that.'

'But—'

'Amber, it's OK! Just head home to Hampstead and I'll see you there when I can.'

I gripped the wall tightly with my free hand. I felt a horrible urge to hurl my phone down into the water. Using Mum as an excuse was about the worst possible thing I could have done. I just wish I'd thought of something better at the time.

'Joel,' Amber said, her voice steady, though I could tell she was worried. 'I'm going to ask you this one more time, OK. So please don't get cross. You made a promise to me that you'd tell me if you started drinking again. That was the deal we made. So please just . . . Are you telling me the truth?'

I looked out over the river just as a heron swooped overhead, its wings disturbing the fog. One of my legs had started to itch. It was more like a deep throbbing this morning, the same way my knuckles used to feel the morning after. How long was I going to be able to keep up this pretence? How many more days could I really last? But then I imagined the alternative, feeling Amber's hot tears mingling with mine as I held her and told her the life we'd built together was crumbling.

'I promise I'm not drinking. I haven't wavered even for a moment.' My voice was a monotone, like a recorded message, but I could hear Amber letting out the breath she'd been holding, and I latched on to it – like a diver who'd run out of air taking oxygen from another.

'I'm sorry I had to ask again,' Amber said. 'I'm so proud of you for staying strong. And I love, you, OK?'

'I love you too,' I said.

The heron had circled around and now swooped down to the riverbank, where it found a patch of grass and stood up tall and statuesque, as if it were posing for a portrait, the final addition to the scene. For a moment, everything was perfectly still. But then a disturbance in the bushes nearby had the heron lifting off, wings beating furiously as it flew over my head, letting out a single strangled cry as it passed.

Chapter Twenty-Five

Theo

Newbridge to Oxford, 13.5 miles (144.6 miles to Thames Barrier, London)

'What a fucking mess,' Joel said, as we looked into the box that was now an ice-cream graveyard.

'I suppose we should have predicted that it was going to melt,' I said. 'Because of how temperature works and everything.'

We ended up having to chuck the whole lot away, but the resulting clean-up operation took a good chunk of time out of the morning.

'We could just stay here today,' I said. 'Find a café somewhere and have a solid writing day. Stay overnight at the pub again.' I hoped Joel would believe my keenness to stay here was because I wanted to get on with the writing. In fact, I reckoned that if we spent a day sitting across from each other – rather than being constantly on the move – it would be easier for me to unlock the door and get him to tell me what was really going on. But Joel wasn't interested. Worse still, any trace of the bonhomie from yesterday seemed to have gone.

When we cycled off, it felt like he was just going through the motions – unable to actually put any effort into pedalling, and when I tried to make conversation just to get things going, his responses were monosyllabic. We went for a stretch of more than an hour without speaking, and the silence was only broken when Joel asked, in a pained voice, 'How far to Oxford?'

'Just a mile or so, I think,' I replied. It was double that at least, but I thought it best to bend the truth a little.

We stopped for a breather at Bablock Hythe, an ancient crossing point of the river the Romans had once used, according to Joel's guidebook. As I watched Joel flicking through the pages, I tried to reach for the best way in to the conversation. But it felt impossible. It was all very well making a plan when you were six pints and a Scotch down, but not in the cold light of day.

'I need to ask you something,' I said.

Joel didn't look up from the guidebook.

'Yeah? What's that?' He put his thumb to his mouth and bit his nail.

I could feel my pulse start to quicken. I was looking down at the water now, letting gravity do the work, the diving board bending under my weight . . .

But just as I went to speak again, a bike bell trilled and a voice said, 'Good morrow! Fine set of wheels you've got there.'

A man with a thin, angular face, sporting a shaving rash so severe it might as well have been a beard, had hopped off his bike and was wheeling it towards us. As he got closer, I saw he was wearing eye-wateringly tight Lycra.

'Lovely day for it, gents,' he said, hands on hips, crotch thrust skywards like a houseplant leaning towards the sun. 'Fellow Thames-Pathers, by any chance?'

'Yeah,' we mumbled in unison.

'Top banana! Mind if I join you gents on this leg? Turn this duo into a trio?'

Joel and I looked at each other. The pause stretched out uncomfortably long.

'Well . . .' I said, but didn't go any further.

'If you want,' Joel added. It was a deliberately rude reply, but the man – who introduced himself as Colin – seemed entirely oblivious.

And so off we went, Colin cycling just behind us. If I thought he was going to be a silent accomplice, I was sorely mistaken. He launched into an exhaustive account of the history of the local area, followed by a lecture on the visible flora and fauna.

'If this guy doesn't shut up soon, I'm going to drown myself in the river,' Joel muttered.

'You'd have to make it past that willow herb and mimulus first,' I replied.

Colin's chatter was relentless, battering us into submission. For the rest of the day, he followed us, unshakeable, like a barnacle stuck to the bottom of a boat. All the while I grew increasingly concerned about Joel. When we stopped for a rest, he slumped down on the grass like a puppet that had just had its strings cut. The next minute, he was scratching so vigorously at his arms and legs, it was like a dog with fleas. I decided enough was enough. I had to find out what was going on, and that meant ditching Colin.

'Oi,' I whispered to Joel, as he clambered onto the front seat. 'You up to trying to lose this guy?'

'Yes, obviously. I've been wanting to all day, but I just wasn't sure if you were up to it yourself.'

Fine, I thought. *Have it your way.*

We began to increase our speed, slowly at first, but before long we were properly motoring.

'Oi, gents!' Colin shouted after us, the anger palpable in his voice. 'Slow down for goodness sake. Ah, bugger.'

I looked behind and saw he'd fallen sideways off his bike into some tall grass, but I couldn't find it in my heart to give a single shit. By now we were flying along at a pace bordering on reckless given the uneven path and tree roots sticking out.

'We can probably slow down now,' I gasped. But Joel seemed determined to keep going, his legs pumping wildly. I leaned to the side at the same time as Joel glanced across to the river, and I saw his face was stuck in a grimace, snot trickling from his nose, his eyes streaming.

'Joel, come on, let's just—'

'No!'

'Mate you're clearly in pain.'

'I'm fine!'

'Don't be ridiculous.'

Joel was in control of the brakes, so the only option I had left was to brace my feet on the ground. My left foot buckled, painfully, and I yelled out in pain, but Joel didn't stop. Eventually I was left with no option but to lean to the side, my weight tipping the bike sideways, and we veered right into the long grass, coming to a juddering halt.

Joel climbed off the bike, gasping for air, and collapsed onto his knees. He braced his hands on the ground and retched. I limped around and tried to help him up, but he shook me off, wiping vomit from his mouth with the back of his hand.

'Come on,' he said after a moment, staggering to his feet. 'On to Oxford.' He had a wild look in his eye, daring me to challenge him.

I just stood there, watching him. I could feel tears forming in my eyes.

'Joel,' I said. 'Please . . . please can you just tell me what's wrong?'

Joel kept his head down.

'Mate,' I said quietly. 'I know I said at the start that we couldn't talk about serious stuff, but . . . this is so fucking stupid. Please. Please just talk to me. I know you're not OK.'

Defeated, Joel looked up at me. He looked fearful now, as if he couldn't quite believe what was happening. As I looked into his eyes, I felt the present giving way to the past, because I realised I'd seen Joel looking this scared just once before, on the night that changed everything.

∞

Chrissy Price's party was invite-only, but Joel seemed suspiciously clued up and confident that we'd get in.

'Who invited you?' I asked him.

'Oh, no one in particular,' he replied.

'But that's not how invites work, is it?' I said. 'What if we don't get in? Have you got an official invite printed out?'

I could almost hear Joel counting to ten.

'Theo. Listen to me. Just be cool, OK?'

'Cool? I'm me! Have you met me?'

Joel sighed. 'Listen, it's a house party in a cul-de-sac around the corner from the village hall. It's not the BAFTAs. We'll get in, OK?'

As he took his jacket off and folded it under his arm, I noticed there were scratches on either side of his neck, as if someone had grabbed him there.

'Let's finish that script at lunch, shall we?' Joel said. 'What did we decide to call it in the end?'

'*The Regulars*,' I replied, distracted. Joel must have seen me looking at the scratch marks because he put his jacket back on.

'That was it,' he said, breezily. 'Oh, just realised I can't do lunchtime. Got the dentist. Some other day soon though.'

I watched Joel wandering off. I stood there for a long time in the middle of the corridor, people passing around me like fish avoiding a weed poking up from the riverbank, and I felt my friend was slipping away. Things just hadn't been right between us since that day he'd forbidden me ever to ask him again if he was OK. I'd hoped that as the weeks went by we would end up back where we used to be – 'the little double act'. But if anything it felt like the distance had grown between us, and I was sure episodes like this, where I'd panicked about something that was supposed to be a bit of fun, were all part of the problem. The party seemed to take on a new significance now – maybe the answer was to show Joel that I could be fun and not so uptight. Perhaps that was the way to get things back on track again.

It was that hope that left me full of nerves on the day itself. That and the little bit of subterfuge I'd had to use with Mum and Dad. They were going to the theatre that evening and asked me to 'babysit' Alice, much to her indignation. She must have said 'But I'm *thirteen!*' at least fourteen times. In the end I took her aside and told her we'd pretend I was going to stay home and look after her. I waited until Dad's car had turned the corner at the end of the drive before legging it upstairs to get ready for the party. Then I grabbed some cans of cider from the fridge and slung them in a plastic bag, and went to find Alice, who was hunched over her drawing pad as usual.

'Right then,' I said. 'Remind me, if Mum and Dad come back early and I'm not here, what are you going to tell them?'

Without looking up, Alice said, 'That you're doing drugs with the Gallaghers at Little Somerford Owl Sanctuary.'

'*Alice.*'

She sighed and looked up. 'Oh my god. Theo! What have you done to your hair?'

'Never mind about that,' I said. Then, 'Why? Is it really bad?'

Alice was laughing like I'd never seen her laugh before.

'You look like the lion from the *Wizard of Oz*!' she wheezed.

I darted over to the hall mirror. The rushed dye job I'd just done on my hair had looked OK upstairs – but now, with its burnt orange tips set against the sickly yellow of the rest of it, I could see how disastrous it was.

'Shut your gob,' I said. 'Remember, if Mum and Dad are home before I am, then tell them I've just had to run over to Joel's to give him that textbook I borrowed.'

'Very believable,' Alice said, wiping her eyes.

I harrumphed and headed for the front door. And with one final dash of Davidoff 'Cool Water', I was out into the balmy summer evening, butterflies flickering in my stomach.

When I arrived at Chrissy's house, the only sign of life was next door, where a pensioner was watching *Countdown*. It didn't exactly scream 'party'.

I knocked, but no one answered, so I let myself in and made my way down the hall, feeling self-conscious when I passed someone I didn't recognise, not sure whether I should say hello. I passed a doorway and someone grabbed me by the arm and yanked me into room.

'Fucking hell, Theo, what have you done to your hair?' It was Joel.

He already seemed quite drunk – certainly drunker than the nine other people in the room. Everyone was standing in a square, backs hugging the walls, as if there should have been a focal point in the middle.

It took a while – precisely the time it took for me to drink two weak ciders – for things to warm up, but the gradual shift towards an evening that constituted a party reached terminal velocity when Tom Pritchard, our weed/gravy dealer, downed a small bottle of vodka in one go before promptly expelling it in several spectacular heaves out of the living-room window. His older brother Mark arrived shortly afterwards in an appropriately vomit-yellow car, but rather than taking Tom home, he just made him splash water on his face and sent him to buy more vodka.

More people began to stream in, the music was cranked up, and someone lit a joint in the bathroom. Joel had seemed morose when I first got there, but his mood had begun to brighten. The ciders flowed, and before long I had forgotten about my terrible lion hair and my stupid, gangly awkwardness altogether, as Joel and I danced around to some terrible local band's EP which was now blasting from the speakers. As we jumped up and down, arms around each other's shoulders, everything felt all right again – back to normal. Me and Joel versus the world. I was gripped with an overwhelming desire for him to know how much he meant to me. But the more I tried to articulate this – shouting over the music – the less sense I made.

'What?' Joel kept shouting. After about the tenth time, I could tell he was starting to lose patience. He seemed distracted, too, looking around for someone to appear. He was basically downing drinks now. When he stumbled away out of the living room, I tried to follow him, calling after him to wait.

'Mate, I'm going for a piss OK?'

'But this is important!' I slurred.

'What then? What do you need to tell me that can't wait for three minutes?'

I felt embarrassed at him chiding me like that. It made it even harder to say what I wanted to.

'I just . . . I just . . .'

'*What?*'

I lowered my gaze to the floor. 'I just wanted to say that, erm . . . I never had a friend, really, until you came along. I was just such a fucking loser, really, and I know I still am – I know all the comedy stuff is nerdy and embarrassing, but having you as a mate just means I'm not such a freak any more. When we write stuff together, even just mucking around with it, it's just the best, and I never really thought I'd have that, and . . .' The words were all tumbling out in the wrong order.

I looked up at Joel, nervously, hoping that he'd have a smile on his face, or even better, that he might say something meaningful back. But he wasn't looking at me. He was looking at someone over my shoulder. I turned around to see Amber Crossley standing at the top of the stairs. I knew Amber from my English class – she was sent out every lesson without exception for being on her phone, but she was always the best person in the class at reading scenes from whatever book or play we were studying.

Amber began to walk down the stairs. When she got to the bottom, she looked self-consciously between us and said, 'Well, here we all are.'

'Hey,' Joel said, smoothing his hair back in a way I'd never seen him do before. 'You know Theo, yeah. Theo, this is Amber.'

'Hello, Amber,' I said, though I hiccupped halfway through her name: 'Am-ic-ber.'

'No, no, it's *Amber*,' she said, as if I'd heard it wrong. It might have felt like she was making fun of me if she hadn't smiled at me afterwards. And it was quite the smile.

'Come on, you two,' she said, 'shall we go for a smoke outside?'

I had never concentrated so hard in my life at simply standing upright. Joel was rolling the last of the weed Amber had brought, and when the joint came to me, I took the smallest pull I could. We were standing in the garden, ignoring a bunch of the others bouncing up and down on a trampoline in the corner. I was slurring my words even worse now and Amber was nodding politely at me, like she was talking to an elderly relative in a nursing home. The next thing I knew, she was prodding me awake. Apparently I had fallen asleep against the shed door with my hands in my pockets. Amber's face was up close to mine.

'You OK there?' she said. It took me a second to answer. I don't think I'd ever stood this close to a girl before. Certainly not one as pretty as Amber.

'Yeah I'm fine,' I managed to say, adding a yawn for good measure, as if the only reason I'd gone to sleep was my growing weariness at this gathering of the Kemble bourgeoisie.

'Right you are,' she said.

'Where's Joel gone?' I asked.

'He's . . . I'm not sure, but listen, do you fancy going on a weed mission? We're all out. Joel said you might have some back at yours?'

'Oh, right, yeah,' I said.

When I didn't move, Amber raised her eyebrows.

'So . . . I'll go get it now then?' I said.

Amber beamed and squeezed my hand.

'Excellent work, soldier,' she replied, and I saluted.

I stumbled back through the house into the road and picked my bike up from the front lawn. I felt pleased to be on this mission. It felt very important that I got it right, that I impressed Amber and Joel as much as I could. It was only when I swung my legs onto the bike that I remembered I'd already packed my stash of weed in my sock, just in case Alice decided to go routing around through my stuff while I was out. I grinned to myself at how happy Joel and Amber were going to be with me. I had visions of them lifting me into the air and carrying me around on their shoulders.

As I turned back to the house, a girl rushed past me to throw up into a hedge, just as an Alsatian started barking relentlessly from the neighbour's garden. I chucked my bike down next to Mark Pritchard's car and steered my way past the heaving bodies crammed into the hallway, which stank of sweat and spilt beer. A group of boys were wrestling on the utility-room floor. I had to jump over them to get to the back door, until finally I was back in the garden. That was when I saw Joel. He was prone on the trampoline, and he wasn't alone. Because in his arms was Amber.

And then everything came into focus. So that's why they'd sent me away. That's why Joel had been busy all those lunch-times, why he'd been so secretive about everything. How had it taken me this long to realise it was all just because of a girl?

I was suddenly desperate to be as far away from Joel as I could. I was vaguely aware of some commotion behind me. I thought I heard Joel calling my name, but I barged my way through the house, determined not to look back. I hauled my bike off the front lawn and set off up the road. My legs were pumping so hard the lactic acid burnt, but I kept on going. My front light was picking up moths and other bugs flitting across the road. The white painted markers on the road were flashing by, the same image over and over again, like I was cycling through a frame of film on an endless loop. I swerved and nearly lost control, regaining it just as I heard a car coming up behind me, beeping its horn. But I wasn't going to pull over to let them past. They could just fucking wait.

As I came around the final corner before my house, a muntjac deer skipped across the road just in front of me, eyes bulging with fright. Instinctively, I jerked the handlebars left and my front light caught the face of Alice, ghostly white, cycling towards me in the other direction. I just had time to see a faint look of surprise cross her face before I heard the car behind me slam on its brakes, and then there was an awful, grinding crunch.

I stumbled off my bike, legs shaking, blood pounding in my ears. I fell to my knees next to Alice, who was lying on her back, eyes closed, looking as peaceful as if she were sleeping. Her helmet had come off her head. It had a huge crack in it. I heard the car doors open. Looking around, I shielded my eyes from the blinding headlights. I caught a glimpse of a yellow door, and realised it was Tom's brother's car. Standing in front of it, silhouetted against the bonnet, were Amber and Joel.

PART THREE

Chapter Twenty-Six
Theo

The time I spent in the waiting room in Gloucester A & E still haunts me. I dream about it regularly, and it's always the same things that I see: a man having a nosebleed into an upturned cap; a child in pyjamas wriggling on the floor as his dad tried to restrain him; a woman wearing a paper party hat smeared with blood. In the dream, they are like animatronic figures, repeating the same actions over and over again, until at last they all wrench their heads around to look at me, and that's when I jolt awake.

Alice was rushed straight through. Dad went with her. Mum and I stayed in the waiting room, but Mum couldn't sit still. She kept getting up and pacing, arms folded around herself, sobbing. When she finally settled down next to me, I rested my head on her shoulder, and whatever it was about me doing that meant she stopped crying for a moment, so I stayed like that, trying not to move a muscle.

At first it looked like Alice was going to lose all feeling below her neck. But after a few days she could feel her arms again.

'It's because of her drawing,' Mum said, with a tearful laugh. 'She wasn't going to let anything stop her doing that.'

I spent as much time as they'd let me in Alice's hospital

room that summer, as her rehabilitation began. I only saw her cry twice. I always knew that she was far braver than me. But I knew then that she was a superhero. Partly because of her determination to get stronger, but mainly because it was only after six weeks had passed that she brought up Joel.

'Where was he driving to anyway?' she asked one morning, almost casually.

I'd decided I wasn't going to tell her the truth – at least the truth as I understood it, that he was chasing after me to explain, or apologise – because that only seemed to make it worse.

'I don't know,' I said. 'Just decided to get in Tom's brother's car, I suppose. Someone must have egged him on. Not that I'm defending him or anything.'

Alice grimaced as she pushed herself up in her bed.

'Have you seen him since?' she asked.

'No,' I replied. 'And I won't. I promise.'

Alice closed her eyes and rested her head back.

'I don't mind if you do. It wasn't deliberate.'

'Well yeah, but that's not the point is it?' I said. 'You can't walk because of that fucking idiot.'

'Thanks for reminding me, bro.'

'I'm sorry.' I reached out and took her hand in mine. A gust of wind got up and the strip blinds clattered against the open window.

'Has he tried to talk to you?' Alice asked.

I hesitated before showing her my phone. There were 128 missed calls. Four were from this morning.

'Yeesh,' she said. 'Has he been to the house?'

'I don't think so.'

'Probably for the best. Mum would probably try and batter him with a saucepan or something.'

I smiled, but not for long, because as Alice shifted position again she winced with pain.

'Aren't you . . .' I faltered.

'What?'

'Aren't you angry with him?'

'I was,' Alice said, after a moment. 'But I've chosen not to be now. There's no point.'

After a moment I stood up and went over to the window. There was something about my thirteen-year-old sister being as calm and stoic as this that I couldn't stand. Where was the screaming and the tantrums about how unfair it all was? Didn't she want me to go and kick the shit out of Joel? To get revenge for what he'd done to her?

'You know it's OK to be angry,' I said, turning back to face her. 'In fact, I want you to be.'

Alice frowned. 'But why?'

'Because look! Look at what he's done to you!'

Alice took a band from her wrist and started to tie up her hair.

'Thanks for the second reminder. Look, if you're going to get all upset, then I'd like you to leave, please.'

'But—'

'Otherwise, I need a wee.'

'Oh.'

'Give me a hand getting into the chariot?'

The chariot was what Alice has christened her wheelchair. It had taken a good deal of practice, but we had a well-choreographed routine now to get her from her bed into the chair.

'All good?' I said, reaching down to pull a stray bit of material away from one of the wheels of her chair once we'd completed the manoeuvre.

Alice nodded. I was about to get back to my feet when she said: 'Of course I'm angry with him, Theo.'

When I looked at her, I saw her eyes were glistening with tears. I'd never noticed what a brilliant blue they were. I took her hand.

'I wish it hadn't happened,' she said. 'I'm spending every moment I'm awake trying not to think about how shit my life is going to be from now on, and my friends are being so weird when they come to visit me because they don't know how to act, and I can't stand that. But you've got to help me by not getting angry. Because it just reminds me that things aren't OK. And the more I can keep pretending that everything's fine, the more everything will be fine in the end. All right?'

I swallowed, hard.

'All right,' I said.

'Good.' She wiped at her eyes with her sleeves and clapped her hands together, as if sweeping the moment away, signalling that this would be the last time we'd speak of it.

'Now that's settled. Onwards, driver. Onwards.'

∞

The atmosphere of the Turf Tavern, Oxford, was raucous. Students in their college-branded hoodies were sinking pints and shots. A kid wearing corduroy trousers at the bar had ordered a yard of ale and was pouring most of it down his front. As people strained to make their voices heard, the volume seemed to be rising exponentially, on target to blow the roof off the place. In a little nook, surveying the scene in silence, were me and Joel.

An hour ago, I'd watched on helplessly as his mouth opened and closed with no words forthcoming, while beside him the front wheel of the tandem – collapsed on its side – turned slowly around, its spokes catching the sunlight.

'Let's just get to Oxford,' he'd said eventually, his voice thick with defeat. 'We can talk there.'

And now here we were, side by side, two glasses of Coke untouched in front of us, sitting in silence. It was almost a competition as to who could be the most still. It felt like as long as we sat like this, the chaos unfolding around us drowning everything out, we wouldn't have to do anything. Suddenly everything was too much – more so when I saw Joel's bag was on the table next to me and the 'bucket list', muddied by my boot, was poking out of it. I closed my eyes. In that moment, all I wanted was to be in the shed, earphones on, keeping the real world at bay.

'I'm going to get some crisps,' Joel said, finally breaking the deadlock. He got to his feet, grimacing with the effort. The way he walked to the bar – head down, hands in his pockets – it was like he was sixteen again.

∞

It was another month after the conversation with Alice before I saw Joel for the first time. I'd started going to the Thames Head stone after school. It was a place I could find some quiet before going back home, or to the hospital. It was a cold September afternoon, a chill wind whipping through the grass. I hadn't heard Joel approach, so it was too late for me to get away. I just sat with my legs pulled in to my chest, my chin on my knees, and tried to pretend he wasn't there.

'Can I sit down?' he asked. A scraggly bit of stubble hung from his chin. There were dark bags under his eyes. His hands looked more cracked and sore than ever.

I didn't reply, but he sat down anyway – alongside me, but with an unnaturally wide gap between us. I thought he might launch into a monologue about the party, try to apologise and make excuses, say how sorry he was, but he didn't. Maybe he had that speech prepared and couldn't bring himself to say it, but in the end we just sat there not talking. After a while he lit a joint. He extended his arm, but I refused the offer, and then once again, but on the third time, I took it. Sometime later, I don't know how long, he said goodbye and left.

The following day, the same thing happened. And the day after that, and then every day for a week, and we never exchanged a word. I was still so confused and angry. If it wasn't for what Alice had said, I do think I might have thrown a punch at him, just to break the tension, to find some way of releasing the pressure valve. The weed probably went some way to stopping me lashing out. It softened all the jagged edges.

The first time I finally spoke wasn't a conscious decision, I just responded automatically after Joel's traditional greeting:

'All right?'

'All right.'

He looked so shocked that I'd replied it almost made me smile. I watched as he composed himself. Acknowledging him was the green light he needed, and he started trying to apologise, until I put my hand up and stopped him.

'Please don't,' I said. 'One day, maybe. But not now.'

'OK,' Joel said. 'If that's what you want.'

I could tell he still wanted to say something, but he seemed to decide that having me acknowledge him was enough of a victory, and so he let it go. I can't remember who asked the question first, but one of us brought up a new show that had started on the BBC that week. At first, as we spoke, it was like we were strangers. Conversation was stop-start. We talked over each other. Everything seemed unfamiliar. It reminded me of coming back to school after the holidays and forgetting how to write. Then I made some stupid joke that made him laugh and it seemed to uncork the bottle. But the look he gave me after he stopped laughing nearly broke my heart. I could see on his face the aching relief that maybe all was not lost. The next thing I knew we were both crying, our heads down – shuffling towards each other and meeting in the middle, putting our arms around each other's shoulders, bound by our sadness. After a moment, self-consciousness set in, and we untangled our arms.

Joel sniffed and cleared his throat. He picked up a stone and flicked it at the Thames monument.

'Do you remember that plan we made?' he said. 'To walk the Thames Path?'

'Yeah,' I said. 'I remember.'

Joel threw another stone. Sniffed again.

'Do you still want to do that?' he asked.

I flexed my toes in my trainers, feeling the material strain.

'Yeah,' I replied. 'One day.'

I said that because I realised then that when we'd been crying just now, it was because we knew our friendship was damaged in a way which meant a gap had opened up beneath our feet, separating us, and that this promise we'd made of a future event, of something so far away that it was the tiniest speck on the horizon, was our way of saying that maybe, someday, when enough time had passed, the fault line beneath us would heal, and we'd make it back to each other.

∞

As I watched Joel standing at the bar, crisps clutched in one hand, phone in the other, I wondered whether *this* could be that moment, no matter how awkward or painful it was going to be. Joel had moved to the corner of the bar, listening intently to whoever was on the other end of the line. I clenched my hands together in my lap, clinging to that thought that maybe this was the point where everything started to get better. But then Joel looked at me, his face pale and afraid, and I watched as the phone slipped from his hand.

Chapter Twenty-Seven

Joel

I could still hear Jane Green barking my name, even after I'd dropped my phone on the floor. She'd been typically phlegmatic as she'd told me that *The Regulars* wasn't going to happen after all. 'I'm going to kill that little bald fucker of a commissioner the next time I see him.'

When I looked over at Theo, he was staring back at me like an innocent puppy that's unable to comprehend why his hitherto kind owner has just shouted at him – it was as if he already knew. I made what felt like an epic journey back to where he sat, wondering how I was going to break the news to him. I stumbled slightly – feeling woozy and hot.

'You OK?' Theo asked, getting to his feet.

I braced myself on the table.

'Let's get out of here,' I said.

Oxford's city centre was quiet, save for sporadic groups of uni-age kids monopolising the pavements, drinking from cans, boisterous and excited. Jane's news had sent me spiralling, and the sight of those kids – in the sweet spot where they were on the cusp of adulthood but without any of the responsibility, their whole lives ahead of them – hit me hard. We passed an off-licence and I came to an abrupt halt, like I'd been caught in a searchlight while absconding from prison.

Theo was so preoccupied that he carried on walking.

I turned to the window. The spirits were shining like beacons. *If you're going to press the self-destruct button, then at least do it properly*, they seemed to say. I took a step towards the door. But then an image came to me of Amber, standing alone amongst the couples and families at baggage claim, waiting patiently for her suitcase, and I stopped, the bottles immediately losing their sheen, their siren calls muffled.

I heard a squeak of tyres and looked across the road to where Theo was being accosted by a cyclist. To my dismay, I recognised Colin, wearing perhaps even more Lycra than before. It was quite possibly the last person we needed right now. I stood in the doorway and watched him try to engage Theo in conversation, only for Theo to tell him – quite calmly, like he was giving directions – to fuck off. Colin went on his way, shaking his head like a disappointed teacher.

I crossed the road and joined Theo. We walked on in silence until we came to a stop on the bridge, looking down at the murky river below us. Across the water stood a pub bearing the name 'The Head of the Thames'.

'Not really the head, is it?' Theo said. 'That's Kemble's only claim to fame.'

'Does seem a bit unfair,' I replied.

Theo looked at me and then back to the off-licence where I'd stopped.

'The answer's yes,' I said. 'I am. An alcoholic, that is. But I've been dry for five years.'

'Oh,' Theo said, confused. 'But then . . .'

'But the damage was sort of already done.'

'What do you mean?' Theo asked, and this time his voice

shook slightly, and I realised he was scared. I just wished there was another way than this – for him to understand without me having to say the words.

'I'm not well, Theo,' I said at last.

A few seconds went by. Theo was looking straight ahead. I wondered if I'd spoken so quietly he might not have heard me. But then he said, 'What is it then? What's . . . actually wrong?'

I looked down again at the swirling, indifferent water below us. I wondered how cold it was. How deep.

'I've got liver disease,' I said. 'Advanced stages.'

Still Theo looked ahead. 'The bucket list?' he asked.

Just then, two boys passed by behind us. One of them kicked a bottle which clunked along into the gutter. His friend cheered. The simple call and response known only to the teenage boy made me smile.

'Yeah,' I said at last. ''Fraid so.'

Theo's breath seemed to catch in his chest. It was as if he'd nearly cried out.

'Fuck, Joel. Liver disease . . .'

'Yeah, I know. They're real fuckers, livers.'

Theo scuffed at the ground. 'And it's all from, you know, the drinking, and stuff?'

'Well, it's complicated,' I said. 'Mostly the drinking. But I fell down the stairs way back when, ruptured the liver quite badly. It basically never properly recovered from that.'

Theo finally turned to face me. 'I didn't know that,' he said. 'You falling down the stairs, I mean.'

'Yeah that's probably because it was after we'd . . . you know, gone our separate ways.'

A breeze had got up. My coat collar was flapping around

my ear. Theo kept looking at it, as if he might reach out and flatten it down.

'But the bucket list,' he said. 'Does that mean . . .' He waved an arm in the air like a reluctant conductor, unable to finish the thought.

'It's not looking good, put it that way,' I replied.

'But what about a transplant?' he said, earnest all of a sudden. 'I mean, sorry, you and the doctors have probably thought of that already, I expect.'

'I'm on a waiting list,' I said.

'Well, that's good, right?'

'It would be, if I wasn't so far down it.'

'Oh.'

'Yeah. It's a bit like trying to get Glastonbury tickets, there's just a little bit more riding on it, and, um, yeah . . . I'm afraid I'm not sure I've got enough time.'

I gripped the railing of the bridge tightly, wishing I had something more hopeful to say. I realised it was times like this, when you're standing in the gaping chasm of your inability to find the words to reassure someone, that you feel at your most useless as a human being.

'And there's really nothing else they can do?' Theo asked, looking back once again to the river.

After a moment where I willed him to look at me, but which went unrequited, I said, 'No. Nothing else,' and did my best to ignore Mum's voice in my head. *What about Plan B?*

We were quiet for what felt like an age. It was Theo who broke the silence this time.

'I'm sorry,' he said.

'Yeah. Well, me too.'

'You don't have to be sorry about this, Joel. Jesus.'

'No,' I said. 'Not that. There's something else I've got to tell you. It's *The Regulars*.'

'What about it?' Theo said. 'Can't that wait? I know we're behind on the scripts but—'

'No, it's not that.' I took a long, deep breath. 'Back in Kemble, when I first came to see you, when you said you weren't going to do the walk, I sort of panicked. The whole reason I'd wanted you to do it was so we could do one last thing together before I . . . And the BBC *were* looking for a new show from me, I promise, but we hadn't discussed anything yet. I called my producer Jane straight away though once you and I had talked, and it looked like it was all set to happen anyway. But Jane called me just now and . . . well, turns out Channel 4 apparently commissioned something similar a while back. I'm really sorry, Theo. If I'd had my time again, I'd have done things differently . . . That goes for a lot of things.'

Theo seemed to be experiencing about ninety different emotions at once.

'It's fine,' was all he said, his voice stiff and emotionless.

We watched the water in silence again. Something that had floated under the bridge caught my eye. It was a yellow washing-up glove, bobbing from side to side in a slow, sorrowful wave.

It was probably too early to say anything, but I wondered now that everything was out in the open whether we could still do the path together. I wouldn't have to keep pretending I wasn't tired. Theo might be up for doing the legwork on the tandem. The image came to me of us coming to a stop at the end of the path – the feeling of satisfaction at completing the journey and honouring our promise, maybe even exchanging an awkward hug. *We've made it. Our last hurrah.*

'I just can't believe it,' Theo said. He folded his arms on the wall and rested his chin on them, looking off into the middle distance.

Tentatively, I reached out and patted him on the back. I'd give him all the time he needed.

'It's OK,' I said. 'Livers, eh? Fuck 'em.'

If I'd looked away then, I might not have noticed it. But I saw it sure enough – the slightest glimmer of confusion in Theo's eyes at what I'd just said.

'Oh, sorry,' I said. 'You were talking about the TV show. Not me.'

'No,' Theo replied. 'No, I . . . That's not . . .'

I waited. But he didn't even bother to finish the lie.

'Wow,' I said, with a mirthless laugh. 'Even for you Theo, that is . . . Fucking hell. Well, it's good to see you've got your priorities right anyway.'

'No, Joel, I—'

'I'll see you around. I'm so sorry to have upset you.'

And with that I left him, wanting to get as far away as I could. After a moment, I heard him lumbering after me. He grabbed my shoulders, but I shook him off.

'That's not what I meant, I swear,' he said, pawing at me, his voice trembling. But I didn't care what he said now. He could protest all he liked, but I knew what I'd seen.

I turned to face him. 'You've made your feelings crystal fucking clear. Now leave me the fuck alone, OK?'

I pitied him. How was he possibly going to get anywhere with his fucking life when his self-centeredness ran so deep. To think there'd been a second on that bridge where I'd nearly asked him for help. Well, I was glad I hadn't put myself through that.

'Please,' he said, 'Just let me ex—'

'No. Just don't bother, OK? It was a mistake, me doing this – I realise that now. I just wish I had sooner, saved us both some fucking grief.'

I paused, waiting for Theo's response, bracing for him to grab me and tell me not to go. But I took a step back and Theo didn't move or say another word. Apparently he'd decided it was easier just to let me walk away.

Chapter Twenty-Eight

Theo

I walked around in the same loop for so long I lost track of time. When I finally made it back to where we were staying, the streets were empty. *The streets were empty, and my friend was dying.* Worst of all, he thought I cared more about a stupid TV show not being made than what was happening to him – and the truth was I couldn't honestly say the news about *The Regulars* hadn't temporarily come to the forefront of my mind, even if it was just for a second. Joel had seen it. He seemed to despise me so much in that moment that I felt I had no choice but to let him walk away. But now I felt a horrible certainty that I'd never have the chance to make things right with him, because when I got back to the B & B and trudged up the stairs, I knew even as I pushed open the door and called his name that he would be gone.

Chapter Twenty-Nine

Joel

I hauled myself off the train at Marylebone and decided to treat myself to an Uber to Peckham. That was the good thing about dying, I suppose: you stopped caring about things like a price surge.

When I got into the flat, it felt cold and damp. This had been where I'd lived during a strange, productive yet lonely time in London. I'd kept it as an office after Amber and I moved in together in Hampstead, but part of me knew I was using that as a bit of an excuse. I always felt there might be another time I'd need to seek refuge here. And that's all I wanted now. To shut myself away here. To not think about Theo, or the fact that Amber was flying home but that I still wasn't brave enough to see her.

I showered, trying to warm myself up, sinking to the floor so I could wash my swollen legs and blistered toes. As I dried off, I caught a glimpse of myself in the mirror. I'd been avoiding my reflection as much as I could lately, and I was shocked by how gaunt and exhausted I looked. What a stupid mistake the walk had been. How many precious days had I just chalked off, and all for nothing? I should never have sought Theo out. Not now, and not after Alice's accident either.

I should have just stayed away.

∞

I was given a suspended sentence of fifteen months at a young offenders' institute after the accident. I'd not been in trouble with the police before, hence the judge's leniency. I still had to do 190 hours of community service, but it felt like a meaningless punishment. The final part of my sentence was paying 'the victim' £2,750. As if that made up for anything. It was an embarrassingly small amount in the context of what had happened, but even then I couldn't afford it myself, and nor could Mum. But Mike could. Mum had been making noises about asking him to move out after the confrontation where he'd pushed me and elbowed her – accident or not. But after this, the grip he had on us tightened even more.

For the second time in my life, a school decided to wash its hands of me. Atherton quietly decided that despite my on par GCSE results it would be best if I looked for another school to attend sixth form. I got a place at a college on the other side of the county because Mum was friends with someone on the board there. While the other kids my age spent their summer holidays lazing in the park or mucking about down by the river, I was doing my community service, which involved a high-vis jacket and picking up rubbish on the side of the road. Every time I squeezed the litter picker, the latest scabs on my knuckles opened up. I almost relished the pain. As morale-destroying as it all was, I still preferred it to the counsellor I'd been sent to. Alan, an oddly thin, grey-faced man – like a haunted pipe cleaner – would ask me how I was doing, and I would say I was fine, and he would say he didn't think I was, actually . . . and then we'd sit in silence while he waited for me to talk about how I was really feeling, which I didn't do, so it all felt completely pointless.

Even though I'd barely talked to anyone since the accident, I was aware of the rumours that were going around. The story of the party had mutated so much by now that the accepted theory involved me deliberately running my friend's sister over after an argument about a girl. I didn't care what people thought about me, I deserved everything I got. But it broke my heart to know that Alice would never walk again and that Theo and his family would be hurting so much. I called Theo every day for six weeks. He never picked up. One day, I got drunk by myself and went to his house, but I wasn't brave enough to knock on the door.

I hadn't seen Amber, either. We texted every day since the accident, and then she told me she wanted to meet up. At first I felt it was too much of a betrayal to Theo. But then the more days that passed, the more I felt myself losing control. I was co consumed with self-loathing that it scared me to think what I might do, and I knew that seeing Amber was the only thing that would stop me feeling like that.

We agreed to meet at her house when her parents were out for the day. When she opened the door, I almost didn't recognise her. She'd dyed her hair a messy white-blonde and her nails were painted black. But that wasn't the only thing that had changed. We didn't feel like the same two people who'd shared those stolen moments underneath the trampoline. It was like we'd both shed our skin.

Amber led me into the living room and came back with some white wine, which she unscrewed and poured into two thin-stemmed, expensive-looking glasses. I felt absurd holding the wine glass, sitting on the pristine white sofa, like we were pretending to be grown-ups. We drank the wine like it was water. I felt a little calmer then. It was easier to talk.

'I'm not really sleeping at the moment,' I confessed.

'Me neither,' Amber said. 'I keep seeing Alice's face, just as we . . .' She trailed off and pulled her knees into her chest. 'And all I keep thinking is that if only Tom's stupid brother hadn't brought his car, then none of it would have happened. Jesus, I mean, I nearly didn't go to the party in the first place because Mum got wind and tried to stop me. If I'd just done as she'd asked, then none of this would have happened.' She started to cry then, restrained at first – using her fingers to blot the tears, but then a sob seemed to ripple up through her, and she fell against me.

At first I sat there, stiff and unresponsive. I think it was because the last time we'd held each other had been in Chrissy's garden. It felt wrong somehow. But then I put my arms around her, pulled her close, breathed in the smell of her hair, which was like woodsmoke.

'I still can't believe it,' she said, her voice muffled by my neck. 'I still can't believe what you . . .'

I tried to speak, but Amber put her hands on the sides of my face, and the words died in my mouth. Our foreheads were touching, our breathing synced. We stayed like that for a while, just being still in each other's orbits. I don't really know who kissed who first. All I knew was that for as long as we stayed in this moment, I didn't have to think about the party, or Mike, or anything else. We stumbled upstairs to Amber's bedroom, our breathing ragged, stopping every few moments to kiss.

Afterwards, we lay on her bed, facing each other, listening to the rain falling gently against the window.

'Are you OK?' I asked.

'Yes,' Amber said. 'That was, you know, unexpected.'

'Yeah,' I murmured. Then, after a moment: 'You know I didn't come here with that in mind, right?'

'I know,' Amber said. 'That's not what I meant. I thought that we maybe would, one day. But I just pictured it differently. There'd probably have been some stupid song playing, candles, or whatever. But I'm glad it wasn't like that.'

'Yeah, me too,' I said.

I shifted onto my back and Amber wriggled down and rested her head on my chest.

As I ran my hand through her hair, I realised how calm I felt – how right *this* felt, the weight of Amber's head on my chest, the warmth of her. It was like up until that moment I'd been trying to walk with a piece of jagged glass in the bottom of my foot, and now it was finally gone.

'I can't wait until I can move away from here,' Amber said. I didn't reply at first. We'd talked before about not wanting to be in Kemble all our lives, but it felt serious now – not just a throwaway comment where we tried to outdo each other with our rebelliousness.

'Right, yeah. Is that the plan, then? You know, for definite?'

'Yeah. I'm set on drama school. A London one, if I can get in.'

'You will,' I said. 'You definitely will.'

We were quiet for a moment. The unanswered question hanging in the air. *London.* It could be a new start for both of us. Maybe the only option I had left was to leave everything behind.

After a while, Amber fell asleep. I looked up at the ceiling. There was a cluster of white stars stuck to the wallpaper. As the light outside faded, they began to glow. And for the first time in a long time, I felt a faint stirring of hope.

Chapter Thirty
Theo

I woke feeling groggy and disorientated. I swung my legs out of bed, and as my foot reached the floor, I felt something underneath it. I reached down and picked up a piece of paper, swearing when I realised it was a note from Joel. I must have dislodged it from the bed when I'd come in.

> *Theo,*
> *I'm sorry about all this. You were a great friend to me, and I will never forget that. I shouldn't have got angry. It's not your fault.*
> *Joel*
>
> *PS I've sent the full script on to Jane Green at the BBC, just in case things change.*
> *PPS I've left the bike round the back. Not sure I could get it on the train to London.*
> *PPPS I'm sorry about the damage on the wall. Bill me for it. Flat 4, 121 Prospect House, Peckham Rye.*

It took me a moment to spot what he was talking about – then I saw the fist-sized dent in the cheap plasterboard wall that separated the bedroom from the bathroom. I crossed the room to inspect it closer, imagining Joel so consumed with anger that he'd lashed out like that. I stood there for a long time, listening to the city hum, wishing I could rewind everything. Instead of Joel writing that letter with a bruised and bleeding hand, he could have been explaining to me what the weeks ahead held in store while I did my best to reassure him.

What the fuck had I done?

I explained about the damage to the indifferent receptionist as I checked out. I fetched the bike and wheeled it down to the river, calling Alice as I went. I wasn't sure what I was going to tell her yet – I just wanted to hear her voice. She didn't pick up, but she messaged me soon after:

Soz, Patrick Leigh Wanker, can't talk. Out for brunch with someone.

I looked at the tandem, which I'd leant down on the grass. It was such an absurd thing even when there were two of you to ride it, but now it was just me, it looked tragic. It was like the thing was cursed – Bob the ice-cream man was now finally free, and I'd have to find the next innocent fool to pass it onto.

Alice messaged me again:

OK fine you've wangled the truth out of me with your ceaseless interrogating. Yes it is Dan Bisley. I am annoyingly nervous.

I typed a reply, feeling numb, like I was on autopilot.

Don't be nervous – you'll be great.

Yes I'm well aware of that, Theo. Something odd about this, though. Think it's because he seems very 'nice'. Bit disconcerting. Might throw a sausage at his head, just to check he's not a robot.

Maybe don't do that, I replied.

Too late. He's on his way back from the toilet. I'm cobbing a Cumberland at him in 3 . . . 2 . . . 1 . . .

Well, good for her, I thought, reflecting on the fact that maybe, just maybe, Alice not having my constant presence to deal with meant she'd actually found the time and headspace to do something for herself.

I watched as a rower cut through the water, so serenely that he barely disturbed it. I edged closer to the bank – the water looked black and filthy with oil, too murky to see the riverbed below.

With some difficulty, I climbed onto the front seat of the tandem, horribly aware of the empty seat behind me. I noticed a sign a short way along that signalled London ahead of me, Kemble behind. I had no idea which way to go. I reached into my pocket and took out Joel's note. Behind me, I heard a shout – a strangled sort of yell, growing louder as the source of it neared me. For one ridiculous moment, I thought it was Joel – that this had all been an elaborate prank that I'd be furious about for a very long time before I started to see the funny side. But then something hard connected with my side, the note flew from my hand onto the bank, and before I knew it, I was toppling towards the putrid, oily water, bringing the bike and my bag with me. I had just enough time to see my assailant fleeing before I plunged into the water.

It was Colin.

Chapter Thirty-One

Joel

I woke in Peckham at dawn, pulling the curtains open to reveal a cloudless sky, brilliant sunshine gilding the leaves of the trees that lined the edge of the park. I wondered what Theo was doing. He'd be headed home to the cosy embrace of his family, I expected – coming up with a story about why we'd decided to end the walk early. In a way, I was grateful to him for how he'd behaved. It made me realise that trying to salve the blisters of the past was a fool's errand – I should have been concentrating on filling my dwindling future with something more worthwhile. As I stood at the window, I watched a passenger plane arc overhead, its undercarriage glinting in the sun. And then I remembered my bucket list.

I spent the rest of the morning on my laptop bouncing from website to website, giddy due to my self-imposed rule that money was no object – that this was all about packing in as much fun and luxury as I could. Then I called Mum.

'Joel! I've been so worried. Are you OK?'

'I am, but we've had to cut the walk short.'

'That's . . . a shame,' Mum said, not entirely convincingly.

'But I've got something much more exciting planned,' I said.

'Exciting? Oh, now come on, really, that's the last thing you should—'

That was when I started playing fado music from my laptop and held my phone up to the speaker. After a while, I brought the phone back to my ear.

'Well, that's rather stopped me in my tracks,' Mum said.

As I'd expected, she cycled through all the reasons she couldn't go to Lisbon – she didn't want me spending money on her, she had book group, the plants needed watering. But I knew I'd hooked her with the music. I could feel her resolve weakening as I mentioned the sea, the music, the food . . . It may have been a decade later than promised, but I was finally taking her away.

∞

Two years had passed since Alice's accident. Despite our reconciliation of sorts at the Thames Head, Theo and I had drifted apart. We did meet up a couple of times afterwards, but the damage felt irreversible, and it seemed to be a question of which of us would pull the plug first. One evening, when I knew Mike would be out, I invited Theo over to watch a new sitcom that was starting that night. But the first scene featured a car crash that was played for laughs. We sat there in excruciating silence as the studio audience howled. The episode ended, I turned the TV off, and Theo said he should probably be getting home. There were no big speeches, no eulogies for our friendship. We both said 'see you soon', but we knew neither of us meant it.

A few weeks later, I saw him pushing Alice in her wheelchair in town and I crossed the road to avoid them, feeling guilty and ashamed. I watched them making their way along the high street. The idea of being in their lives as if nothing had happened was fanciful. I didn't see Theo – even in passing – for a long time after that.

Given that our friendship had fallen by the wayside, that also meant the end for our writing. Coming up with stuff on my own was uncharted territory, but I'd found myself wanting to, even if just to distract myself. I'd been spending every free minute I had with Amber. We'd sit at opposite ends of the sofa and she would devour every word written about acting and theatre while I wrote scripts, even sending a few sketches on spec to shows on the air. It was freeing, to have complete creative control – although I concede that sounds preposterously lofty given that I was mainly coming up with jokes about badgers and jam.

Looking for further tips to improve, I went on the BBC Writers' Room website and discovered a new talent competition that they were running, which came with the chance of winning a place in the writers' room for *Get in the Van!*, a sketch show they were trialling on a new digital channel. With Amber's encouragement, I threw myself into it – working whenever I had free time from college coursework, honing a script I'd started about a rural battle of the bands competition, and sent it off.

I'd thought nothing more about it until the morning of my eighteenth birthday in July, when I got an email from someone called Jane Green at the BBC, congratulating me rather brusquely for winning the competition, telling me that I should report to her in London at the start of October for my month-long stint in the writers' room. By then, Amber had been auditioning for drama school, and that day she was down in London for her fourth try-out at Mountview. I decided not to message her in case she'd not had good news herself.

Instead I went to the Thames Head for a solo, celebratory pint, trying to ignore how strange it felt to be taking that rite of passage without Theo.

A few more legal pints later, now pleasingly woozy, I got a call from Amber – she'd got in to Mountview. I celebrated so loudly in the pub that all the locals swivelled on their bar stools and fixed me with murderous looks for spoiling the morose atmosphere. But I was too proud of Amber to care.

That evening, we went to the golf course that overlooked the village. Amber brought a tent and blankets and we drank cheap cider under the stars to toast our success.

'Have you told your mum about London?' Amber asked.

'Yeah,' I said.

'How did she take it?'

'Oh, you know, about how you'd expect.' The truth was I'd told Mum about the month I'd be spending in London in the writers' room, but she didn't know that Amber and I were setting up there permanently, which, of course, meant leaving her on her own . . .

Ever since Mike had stumped up the compensation money for Alice, the hold that he had over us seemed to placate him in some way. It was all about power, I think. In the last few weeks, he'd started making me go on a few jobs with him – hauling equipment around, going out to get him lunch – all unpaid, obviously, but then I owed him, so I couldn't refuse. But now I had the chance to get away from him for good.

When I finally screwed up the courage to tell Mum that I was moving permanently, she immediately burst into tears. But as I tried to apologise, saying I wouldn't go after all – that I'd come back as soon as my placement was done, she stopped me.

'No – that's not why I'm . . . I'm just so proud of you.' She cupped my face in her hands.

Just then Mike's van crunched into the driveway. Mum and I exchanged a look. How was he going to react? I saw a flicker of fear in Mum's eye.

'Mum,' I said, taking her hands in mine. 'Why don't you come to London? You don't have to stay here. We could get away from him – both of us.'

But before Mum had time to answer, Mike appeared, slamming the front door with such force that the house seemed to shake.

'That Bulgarian wanker has stitched me up on two jobs today with his quotes,' was how he announced himself as he stomped into the kitchen.

Mum and I stood there just looking at him – seeming, I knew, guilty. We may as well have had escape plans stretched out on the kitchen table.

'What's going on?' Mike said, tossing his keys onto the counter, where they fell like smashed glass.

'Nothing,' I mumbled.

Mike looked at me, then Mum, eyes darting back and forth between us.

'Come on,' he said, 'Out with it.'

I looked at Mum. 'Didn't you say you needed a lie-down. Why don't you go upstairs for a bit?'

'I . . . well, I . . .'

'Come on, it's OK,' I said, forcing a smile. I ushered Mum into the hall and hurried her up the stairs, following on behind her.

I heard the bottom step creak under Mike's weight.

'Don't make me ask you again,' he said, voice quiet now. 'What's going on?'

I stood at the top of the stairs and made myself face him.

'Mum and I are moving to London,' I said. 'I'll pay you back the money in instalments.'

Mike considered me without saying anything, scratching at his chin, the sound of nail on stubble like a match igniting. As he began to climb the stairs, I clenched my fists, willing myself to stand tall, but tears born of fear and hatred pooled in my eyes.

'Of course he's crying,' Mike sneered 'No fucking bottle.'

I heard Mum opening the bedroom door, and it was like a starter pistol had been fired, because I wasn't going to let her get hurt again, not today, not ever. I launched myself at Mike, who was nearly at the top of the stairs, throwing my skinny arms at him wildly as I tried to land a punch. But Mike simply sidestepped, and I barely connected a glancing shot as my momentum saw me flying down the stairs, my right side taking all of the impact as I slammed into the edges of the steps on the way down, my head taking the final blow.

When I came to, I tried to struggle up, but I felt Mum's hands on my shoulders, and her soothing voice telling me it was OK, and then she laid me gently back down.

'Where am I?' I croaked.

'In the hospital, darling,' Mum said, 'but you're OK, everything's OK.'

'Where's Mike?' I asked, agitated, but Mum shushed me softly and said, 'He's gone, love. Don't worry. He's left,' and my eyelids fluttered and closed.

After the doctors had finished checking me over and told me to rest, Mum sat by my side and explained what had happened. It would seem that Mike had been planning his exit for a long time. He was going in with his brother on a bar in Malaga. His tickets were already bought and he was just counting down the days. He hadn't stuck around after I'd fallen, presumably because questions would be asked about how I'd come to hurt myself. I don't think either Mum or I mentioned the police – we just wanted the whole thing over. It would only be later that the CT scans and X-rays determined that the fall had left me with abdominal bruising, a broken rib and a laceration on my liver. I may have thought the whole thing was done, but Mike's last act – stepping aside to avoid my punches – was unwittingly his most violent.

I stayed in hospital to rest for a few days. Amber came to visit me, but I was so dosed up on painkillers, it all passed in a bit of a blur. I just remember her kissing me softly, and me worrying – absurdly – at how unattractively cracked my lips were.

The following evening, when I was feeling a little more lucid, I came around from a nap to find Mum at my bedside, her arms wrapped around herself as she tried not to wake me with her crying.

'Hey, it's OK, Mum,' I mumbled. 'No need for that.' I reached my hand out towards her and she took it, warming it in her own, pressing it against her cheeks. She was trying to speak, but sobs escaped every time she opened her mouth.

'I'm so sorry for the life I've given you,' she said. 'I should have protected you.'

I tried to sit up. 'Mum, please.'

She was trembling now, like she'd just been rescued from freezing water. I tried to find more words to reassure her, to make her realise I didn't blame her, that I loved her, but every time I tried to speak, it just seemed to make her more upset. Eventually, I shifted over enough so there was room next to me and pulled her gently towards me. She lay at my side and I stroked her arm, trying to calm her. We stayed like that until it got dark outside, and the room was bathed in a rich orange from the street lamp outside the window. I was still at a loss to know what to say to Mum about everything. I just wanted to draw a line under it all – to think about a future where we could be a family again, just the two of us.

'Mum,' I said.

'Yes, love.'

'If you could go on holiday – absolutely anywhere. Where would you go?'

Mum stirred and pushed herself up. Her face was smudged with tears.

'What?' she said, when she saw me smiling. 'Have I got great big panda eyes?'

'Afraid so. But they're very fetching great big panda eyes.'

Mum laughed, then sniffed and wiped her eyes.

'So . . .?'

'Well, I've always wanted to go to Portugal. Your grandad always talked so fondly about it. He was your age, you know, when he spent that summer in Lisbon.'

'Let's do it then,' I said. 'You and me. We could go to all his old haunts if you know them.'

Mum looked over at the window, eyes closed against the orange light. It was like she was reaching her face to the sun. It was like we were already there.

They let me out of hospital the following day, and I spent two weeks recuperating at home with Mum. In Mike's absence, the whole place seemed lighter somehow, as if the sunlight was finally allowed in. The first thing I did when I was strong enough was persuade Mum to drive us to the tip. There, we held hands, and together we pushed 'Mike's chair' over the side and watched it crash to the ground.

I wish I could have stayed longer at home with Mum, to bask in our new-found freedom, but soon Amber and I were packing up to head to London. As I gathered up my last few things, wincing every now and then with the pain in my ribs, Amber stood on the threshold. She seemed unsure whether to come in and help. Mainly, I suspect, because of the noticeably cold smile Mum had given her when she arrived. The accident with Alice loomed large over everything, and I knew too that Mum felt it was Amber who was pushing me to move away. I tried to explain to her how that wasn't the case, and how Amber had been there for me when Mike was at his worst, but it didn't seem to help much.

'You should get to know her properly,' I said, after Amber had given us a moment so say goodbye. 'You can still come to London – the offer's there.'

Mum hugged me as tight as she dared without hurting my bruised ribs. She flicked a bit of fluff off my shoulder and looked me in the eye. 'I'm sure you and Amber like each other a great deal,' she said. 'And London will be wonderfully exciting for you both. But don't let yourself get too carried away. First love can be such a powerful thing, but try to remember how young you are.'

I held my tongue. I wasn't going to part on an argument, and I knew that she was just trying to protect me. Instead I said, 'Order some holiday brochures and get the Lisbon research going, OK? We can start saving up now, try and book it for next summer. How does that sound?'

'That would be lovely,' Mum said, hugging me again. She couldn't help but squeeze me a little tighter this time, but I didn't show her that it hurt.

I loaded up my last bag and joined Amber in the back of her cousin's car. As we drove off, I looked back at Mum and called, 'One last thing.'

'Yes, love?'

'Just so you know, your glasses are on top of your head!' We moved off, and I waved back at Mum until we were around a corner and out of sight. I tried not to think about the moment she closed the door behind her, alone now with unhappy memories of what had gone on in that house. But I'd be back to see her soon, I told myself. Just because she was out of sight, it didn't mean she'd be out of mind.

Amber and I ended up taking a sofa bed in a house near Morden at the arse end of the Northern line. Our flatmates – who we saw less often than the resident mice – were a bunch of other struggling arty types. We may have been broke, but I loved exploring the city with Amber – even if we were limited to wandering the streets until our tired feet brought us to a pub where we'd nurse a drink all evening. We settled into a routine where we'd meet up on the South Bank after our respective days writing and acting. There, we'd minesweep as many drinks as we could in the BFI bar and try to sneak in to whatever was showing in the cinema screening rooms downstairs. Then, afterwards, we'd stroll along by the river, acting out our favourite scene from whatever gloriously pretentious art-house thing we'd just watched, seeking out a Waterloo sunset before we caught the last tube home.

I was doing my best to forget about Mike, but I began to have nightmares about him. At least once a week, I'd dream he was chasing Mum down a hallway which would get smaller and smaller – until it was like one of those false perspective paintings – and then at the point where there was nowhere for them to go, Mike would reach out to grab her and I'd wake, sometimes crying out. Amber would soothe me by curling her body in to mine, staying awake with me until I finally drifted off to sleep. Each time I woke like that and felt her arms around me, I dreaded the thought of her absence. The idea of coping with everything by myself seemed unthinkable.

Time had moved glacially in Kemble, but in London the days flashed by. Before I knew it, we had been there for two years. I'd impressed Jane Green enough during my competition placement for her to throw me into other writing rooms, and I was making just enough money from those gigs to get by. Being a decade younger than most of the other writers, I'd naturally been treated with a fair amount of suspicion, bordering on hostility at times. It made me even more determined to prove myself – more often in the pub than at the writing table itself, which was fine by me, because I'd survive the hangovers better than them and get a head start in the mornings. When I had a few nights off booze, I realised that the nightmares came more often. Luckily those days became rarer – there was always some party or other – either with our flatmates or one of Amber's drama-school friends. Even on Sundays there'd be Bloody Marys in our local, cheap red wine and anarchic, rule-bending Scrabble to finish off the weekend. It was a constant cycle between drunk and hungover, but as long as Amber was there, it didn't matter. She was like a hangover cure and the best cocktail I'd ever had all rolled into one.

'Charming,' she laughed, when I told her this one morning.

'You sound like some dreadful Bukowski character. You'll be calling me "one hell of a dame", next.'

The conversation moved on, but later, as we lay on the sofa, she turned to me and said, 'What you said earlier. The cocktail thing. That's not all you think of me as, right?'

'No, course not. I just meant you make me happy all the time, whatever we're doing – that's all. I don't know what I'd do without you.'

Amber seemed to stiffen. At the time, I couldn't see why that might have given her pause. Wasn't that what relationships were all about? Weren't you supposed to be lost without the person you were with? As I unscrewed the top of another bottle of corner-shop Chianti, I had no idea that the exchange was the first hairline crack on an icy pond.

By the time Amber had graduated from drama school, she was already getting cast in modest parts in plays, and the odd advert on TV – which I recorded and played back on an endless loop, especially when she was out for the evening and I found myself at home alone. I'd sink a bottle of wine and marvel at how that was my girlfriend on the TV, looking bemused at an anthropomorphised indigestion tablet. On the first night I saw her on stage, at the Young Vic, playing Portia's attendant in *The Merchant of Venice*, I was so stupidly proud of her as she spoke her lines that I very nearly lamped the man next to me who'd chosen that moment to unwrap a sweet so loudly, at least to me, that it was like he'd let off a firework. I came back for the next few nights – plus the Saturday matinee – but there were only so many times Amber could sneak me in.

I missed her horribly when she was working, so I filled the void in the pub. I had regular drinking pals from the comedy world – particularly now I'd shown my writing chops and a working knowledge of 1950s radio sitcoms. There'd always be someone I could persuade to get stuck in with me in one of the pubs around the corner from whichever office we were in. I'd time it so I'd return home when Amber arrived back from the theatre. It turned out she'd absolutely got my number with her Bukowski dig, because secretly I quite liked the romance of it all – the boozy writer coming home to his West End star. I loved this adventure we were on – except the times when Amber had to go away.

It was the August of our third year in the city when she agreed to head off on a summer jaunt with Charlotte, a friend from Mountview. I grumbled to her about how I'd miss her, diving onto the floor and wrapping my arms around her ankles.

'You'll survive for five whole days without me, my love,' she laughed.

I clung on without showing any sign of releasing her, to the point where I wasn't sure how much I was still joking.

'Why don't you go back and see your mum?' she said as I walked her to the Tube.

'Yeah, I'll think about it,' I replied. I'd barely been back to Kemble since we'd come to London. I hated being back in the house. The brightness that had arrived in the wake of Mike's absence seemed to have faded. Mum looked so much older with every visit. The guiltier I felt about not going back to see her, the harder it was to get on the train.

The moment Amber disappeared into the tube station, I sent out a generic text to my address book asking who was around for a drink. Someone called Danny, who I had a vague memory of being introduced to on a night out a few weeks before, replied saying he was off up to the Edinburgh comedy festival for a few days – hoping to crash as many corporate events and neck as much free booze as he could – and his mate had dropped out if I wanted to come.

'I'm in,' I said, without thinking about it.

I met him that afternoon at King's Cross, and we started drinking on the train up. The rest of that day was a blur, as we bounced from pub to pub. I had a vague memory of laughing in the wrong place at a serious bit in a show we went to see, then getting into an argument with one of the performer's friends as I left. Next thing I knew, I was being shaken awake by Danny, who was trying to tell me I'd been shouting in my sleep. I was so confused and scared at first that I nearly threw a punch at him.

The next morning, dazed, cold – in the strange twilight between drunk and hungover – I wandered out into the murky Edinburgh streets, sunglasses on because even the sun straining against the slate grey clouds was too much. There were so many tourists and people handing out flyers, the streets felt cramped, and great waves of claustrophobia stole over me. Was it too early for a drink? I knew that would calm me down. But nowhere was open yet.

Every street I turned on to was rammed with tourists. I pushed my way past an Australian trying to explain haggis to his bored teenage sons, nearly tripping on the uneven cobbles as I did so. I ignored four bright-eyed students flyering for shows that night. One was so insistent that I listen to his jaunty patter that I shoved him away and told him to fuck off, then tried to apologise while his friends pushed me away. I felt the air being sucked from my lungs. Spots appeared in my vision. I just about made it around a corner to a quiet side street, taking in great gulps of air. I had my hands on my knees, concentrating on the flyer on the pavement beneath me to keep me present. I looked at the faces of three people dressed as mimes giving whacky looks to the camera, and that was when I realised that one of those mimes was, unmistakably, Theo.

I reached down and peeled the flyer off the ground. The text above the photo read *The nineteenth national student comedy grand final! Sheffield Revue vs Cambridge Footlights*. I pulled my phone from my pocket, wincing at the newly acquired crack on the screen. Behind the smashed plastic, I could just make out the date. The final was tonight.

Chapter Thirty-Two

Theo

The B & B receptionist actually gasped when I opened the door. They were used to the little trill of the bell announcing a fresh-faced tourist, not the swamp monster that had just crossed the threshold.

I was dripping with oily river water, and my hair was coated in mud and gunk. When I tried to explain that there was no reason for alarm, my chattering teeth betrayed me, and I'm not sure adding a Hannibal Lecter impersonation into the mix helped my cause much. After I regained the power of speech, I tried, with some difficulty, to convince the receptionist I was the man who'd just checked out.

'Yes, well, I'm very sorry, but I can't help you,' the receptionist said. 'Company policy,' she added, a thin smile on her face.

'You've got a company policy for *this*?'

The receptionist's smile flickered and died. She glanced at the phone next to her, as if she were about to call some sort of emergency security.

'Please,' I said. 'I just want a quick shower and somewhere to dry my clothes for a bit. I'll pay . . .' I reached for my wallet, but it wasn't there. 'Oh God . . .' I scrabbled desperately in my trouser and coat pockets, my fingers tingling with cold. I pulled out a wodge of soggy notes and held it out to her, like a toddler on a beach scooping up wet sand and presenting it to their mother as a gift.

'I'm afraid I can't help you,' she repeated, wrinkling her nose. 'Now, if you wouldn't mind . . .'

I left with as much dignity as I could, which was hard given that I squelched with every step I took. I walked aimlessly down past the cathedral, just trying to warm myself up. Eventually I arrived at the bridge where Joel and I had ended up. I braced my hands on the wall and wished more than anything that I could rewind twelve hours and play out the scene again – do everything differently this time.

As I watched a houseboat chugging past, I realised that this had been the second time Joel and I had found ourselves at each other's throats on a bridge as darkness descended. I was the one to walk away that time.

∞

'We are now approaching Edinburgh Waverley. All change, please. All change.'

I couldn't quite believe it. I was actually here, at the Edinburgh Fringe, the daddy of all comedy competitions – not as a punter, but as a performer, in the final of the student comedy awards no less. We had got to the quarter-finals in my first year at Sheffield, and then the semis in second year – and now, at last, third time lucky in my final year, we'd made it to the very end. If we beat Cambridge in the final, then we'd have a chance to develop a TV pilot with one of the biggest production companies in London. This. Was. It.

But as excited as I was at that prospect, it was nothing

compared to how thrilled I was that, shortly north of York, Babs had let me hold her hand in broad daylight, in public. We may have been together three years, but her no-public-displays-of-affection rule had remained enforced up until now.

I had fallen impossibly hard for her from the moment we'd met and, as was my custom, I had resolved to be bold and confident and ask her out on a proper date immediately. Sure enough, just five and a half weeks and four aborted attempts later, I did. The first part of the sentence had gone quite well, but I was soon in freefall, making very little sense. Babs was looking at me the way someone might when faced with a piece of modern art: is this thing incredibly complex and brilliant and I'm just missing something, or is it just a dildo strapped to a wok . . .?

'Are you OK, Theo? It's just you do seem to be speaking in tongues.'

'Ha! No, I'm fine! What I was *trying* to ask, was whether you, you know, maybe, wanted to, sort of, go for dinner or something.'

A smile spread out slowly on Babs's face.

'With me,' I added.

'Thanks for clarifying,' Babs said. 'You know I'd been wondering if you were going to ask me out. I know boys can occasionally be a bit thick when it comes to seeing the signals, but I did kiss you the other night. That's quite a straightforward one where I come from.'

I looked back at her dumbly. She rolled her eyes and placed her arm in mine, like she was helping a doddery old man cross the street.

'Where are you taking me out to then?' she asked.

Hmm. I hadn't got that far.

It turned out I was taking her to hell itself. I hadn't had a clue what sort of place I should book, and so chanced my arm on somewhere which vaguely promised 'fusion' – nuclear, judging by the taste. The waiters were horrible, the music too loud. There *was* mood lighting, but unfortunately the mood was 'seven-year-old's birthday party in a provincial bowling alley'. But for some reason it didn't seem to matter. With every new snipe from the sarcastic waiter or dreadful song on the speakers, Babs seemed to find it more and more funny. As we left, drunk on a pitcher of warm margaritas, I kept trying to apologise, but she stopped me and said, 'Listen, it's one of my favourite things in life when something's so hilariously awful it somehow becomes good – so stop worrying. There's nothing like making the best of something bad.'

We turned a corner and came by a bar that was blasting out indie music.

'Come on,' Babs said, taking me by the arm, and soon we had joined the few bedraggled-looking indie kids shuffling on the dance floor. We drank beer from plastic pint glasses and danced in that way which runs the full spectrum of ironic and earnest, and then the DJ put on 'Love Will Tear Us Apart'.

'Well, if we're going to be cliches about this . . .' Babs yelled in my ear, and before I could ask her what she meant she was kissing me, and I was lost in lager and ambiguous food and cigarette smoke, and it was singularly the best kiss I'd ever had, and it is yet to be surpassed.

Two weeks later, halfway through watching a film – I can't recall what now, and I doubt I knew at the time given how nervous I was – we had sex for the first time. Afterwards, as I raised myself up on my single bed and saw how the dusting of freckles on Babs's shoulder were lit as if in spotlight by

227

the shaft of dawn sunlight creeping through the curtains, I wondered if she was thinking what I was: that this was all that mattered now, that conceding our bodies to each other in this way removed meaning from everything else, and that I'd never felt so attuned to the beauty of the world. Just then, Babs patted me smartly on the bottom.

'That'll do, pig,' she said, then instantly fell asleep.

Oh.

As I lay there, realising that perhaps Babs wasn't quite the romantic that I was, but feeling delighted nonetheless, I thought about what she'd said on our first date – that there was nothing like making the best of something bad. I listened to the soft sound of her breathing and thought about how different I felt already to the kid who'd arrived at university racked with insecurities and doubts. Maybe, I hoped, Babs was going to make the best of me too.

In the following three years, I don't think we spent a night apart. Even once we'd moved out of halls and were schlepping across the city to the other's shared flat. We'd successfully cemented our places in the Sheffield Revue, which I put down to fate – that our blossoming romance had made our success inevitable – and which Babs had put down to the fact that only seven people auditioned.

The third part of our trio was a tall blond boy called Luke, who was paper thin with mesmerising cheekbones, like Bowie's Thin White Duke. We were 'mentored' – and I use the term lightly – by a guy called Steve, a balding, pot-bellied former comedy writer who now lectured in English part-time. Babs, Luke and I came up with sketch ideas and performed them to Steve, who, at best, told us they weren't shit, and, at worst, started clawing at the air as we performed, like he was trying to expunge our words from ever existing. Eventually we cobbled together forty-five minutes of material to perform.

The student competition involved early rounds where rival universities performed on the same bill, and then the audience would vote on who they preferred, like a battle of the bands competition. Before our first show against Hull, I remember pacing around backstage, trying to psych myself up. I couldn't hear the audience on the other side of the curtain, but I knew it was going to be a bear pit – the braying drunks of the London comedy store combined with the ferocious atmosphere of a Detroit rap battle. When we finally got out there, the vibe was more local library – which set the tone for most times we'd perform.

We probably deserved to go out in the quarters that year, but I thought we were robbed in our second year to go out in the semis. But finally, in our third year, we made it through to the grand final – and this time we were ready for it. Term finished in June, so we had a couple of months to wait before heading up to Edinburgh. Babs's parents had a place in Northumberland, and they were travelling in Canada that year, so Babs and I got to spend the summer together in their little cottage by the sea. In the day, we'd walk along the beach and take day trips out to the Farne Islands to watch the puffins. In the evenings, we'd cook on the Aga and read by the log burner. When I was younger, I'd scorned the idea of that sort of domesticity. But those warm nights in the kitchen with Babs, getting distracted every few minutes because I wanted to kiss the nape of her neck – I think they were the happiest of my life. So much so that when the Edinburgh festival rolled around, I secretly wished we could have a bit more time in the cottage. But the moment our train pulled into Waverley

Station, I started to get nervous and horribly excited all over again. Just one more knockout performance and we'd have every talent manager and TV commissioner in town trying to snap us up. It was all or nothing now.

To get to where we were staying, we had to run the gauntlet of the Royal Mile, weaving as fast as we could through the hordes of people handing out flyers and the street performers with their head-mics and smug patter.

'Just juggle the knife and fuck off on your unicycle,' Babs muttered.

'Marry me,' I said, thankfully in my head.

It was almost too perfect.

The final was held at a grimy pub called The Tron. I'd been expecting something slightly grander, in all honesty. I was still feeling a bit underwhelmed, but with a few minutes to go until showtime, the audience started to file in – boisterous and loud – and before long the place was packed, a proper sense of tension in the air. In that moment, it really did feel like it could be the start of something – the sort of intimate venue which a camera crew would return to when making a documentary about a performer's life: the place where it all started. As that particular fantasy washed over me, I had to run to the backstage toilet and throw up.

After a less than cordial coin-toss, the Cambridge Foot-lights team (Tristan and Hugo – naturally) chose to perform first. We watched them by peering through a curtain at the side of the stage. It was clear we were up against some stiff competition.

If we were hoping for a rousing, British-underdog-film-style speech from Steve, then we were sadly disappointed. He'd got stuck in to the free booze backstage and was fast asleep under his coat. We sat in silence like stoic civilians in an Anderson shelter, the laughs from next door the falling bombs. Then the Cambridge boys took their final bow to enthusiastic applause. Babs, Luke and I exchanged determined looks. It was showtime.

It was so hot on the tiny stage that I thought I might pass out. Our timing was off from the start, and Babs fluffed a line that she'd never stumbled on before. The laughs were polite at best. I was sweating. My hands were slick with it.

A quick one-man bit from Luke where he played a depressed vet got some more solid laughs, and then, praise be, the wine snobs sketch got easily the biggest reaction of the night. We dived backstage for a quick costume change. Babs gave me a thumbs up and a big grin, and I felt relaxed for the first time since we'd stepped on stage. This was all going to be OK.

From then on, we were on a roll. Even the surly grasshoppers sketch, which had played to silence in the semi-final, got proper laughs, and they just kept coming, in wave after glorious wave. Babs, in particular, was having an absolute stormer. In her solo sketch, where she played a vicar with anger management issues, her blistering riposte to a carefully chosen front-row member was so perfect that I nearly missed my cue. What a moment to realise just how much I was in love with someone, watching them dressed as a clergywoman viciously berating a cowering stranger.

Before I knew it, we were at our closing sketch – Napoleon public speaking. This required the three of us to change costumes again, so we'd pre-recorded a parody of a budget airline advert which played out to the audience as we swapped outfits. As I stood in the wings, adjusting my military jacket,

I could feel it in my bones that this was going to the best we'd ever performed. We were going to take the roof off.

I was first out on stage, and I waltzed on with an extra bit of swagger. I looked out into the crowd, making eye contact with everyone in turn, nodding to myself as if I knew some secret that they didn't. Wonderful pockets of laughter were erupting just at this. It was like fireworks going off. And it was contagious. So much so that I took a gamble and carried on simply prowling the stage, making eye contact with every audience member once again as the laughter grew and grew. I went for one last sweep of each row, and that's when I saw him. Joel.

He was in the back row, a beer in his hand, looking straight back at me, a smile on his face. Suddenly, I wasn't on stage any more. I was sitting back to back with Joel on dewy grass. I was lobbing stones at the Thames monument. I was kneeling by Alice on the cracked tarmac.

My staring schtick had gone on for just too long now. The laughter was dying away. The audience was growing impatient, and I heard someone clear their throat, someone else whispering to their friend. My eyes refocused on Joel, and I felt my stomach plunge. He was covering his mouth with his hand. His smile was gone, and now it looked for all the world like he was trying to obscure an unpleasant sneer.

'Theo!' Babs hissed from behind the curtain. There were a few relieved laughs at this. Perhaps they thought my stalling was deliberate.

I probably could have salvaged things if I'd said something then. I did try to get my first line out, but my tongue felt flabby and thick. My mouth was getting drier by the second, and my body was growing numb, like a hunter had shot a dart into my neck. Standing – even breathing properly – was becoming ever difficult, and all the while, the silence grew. I finally managed to muster a few words, but by that point Luke and Babs had appeared at my side, taking me by each arm.

'I'm sorry, sir, you appear to have wandered into the wrong sketch,' Luke said, anger – out of character – palpable as he spoke. There were some sniggers, but unkind ones.

'We'll be back in a minute, ladies and gents,' Babs said in a strange, forced 'comedy voice' I'd never heard her use before.

They'd nearly led me off the stage. Looking back, if I'd let them get me off, then maybe they'd have recovered and got the audience back on side. But just at the last minute, I managed to wrench my arm away from Luke, determined to keep going.

'Theo . . .' Luke said, all pretence gone now.

I turned to Babs, but she had her eyes closed. And then I knew it was over.

I felt my shoulders slump. 'Please,' I said, in one last feeble attempt to keep going. 'I can still . . .'

Someone in the audience knocked a glass over, and I heard it roll along the wooden floor for an interminably long time before it came to a stop. I looked up and saw Joel on his feet, making his way towards the exit. I felt a shock of anger, and I barged past Luke and through the curtain, into the dressing room, where Steve was sitting, his hand in a monster bag of Doritos.

'You done then?' he said, through a mouthful of crisps. 'Sounded like it was going pretty well.'

But I didn't stop. I charged through the dressing room and down the stairs, wrenching open the stage door and storming out into the street, where I stopped to take in big, hungry lungfuls of air, just in time to hear our closing theme tune play over a sarcastic round of applause, and to see Joel, hurrying away around a corner, jacket collar pulled up high, like someone hastily leaving a crime scene.

Chapter Thirty-Three

Joel

They say that in any given day in Edinburgh you can have weather from each season. The dial had stopped around mid-winter in February by the time Theo caught up with me on the North Bridge, with icy torrential rain fuelled by a swirling wind.

'Oi,' Theo shouted.

I kept walking, head down. I'd been drinking pretty solidly all day and I was unsteady on my feet, unable to get away as fast as I'd like.

'Joel, I know you can fucking hear me.'

The game was up. I slowed to a halt and turned around.

'All right?' I said. 'Listen . . . mate, I—'

'Don't call me "mate",' Theo spat. 'What the fuck were you doing in there?'

'Well, I . . . I saw your flyer, I wanted to see the show.' I scrabbled in my coat pocket to find the flyer, although I don't know what I was trying to prove.

'Right,' Theo said, jaw clenched. 'Thought you'd just come and sit at the back and take the piss.'

'What? No, god no – of course not, I was there . . . you know, just to see it – to support you.' This was all coming out wrong. I was trying so hard not to slur my words and I could tell from Theo's darkening expression that I sounded insincere.

'Right, and that's why you waited till I was looking at you and started laughing all sarcastically, is it? That stupid little smile on your face – like you couldn't believe your luck how shit I was. Is it not enough for you to be living *my* fucking dream in London – yeah, I read you won that BBC thing, I know what a big shot you are now.'

'Theo . . .'

'What?'

A blast of wind slapped freezing rainwater into our faces.

How could I tell him that I hadn't been laughing at him – that I'd actually been overcome with such pride, with such a fierce feeling of love for my old friend, that I'd been desperately trying to stop myself crying. Theo! With his big silly face and his big mad hair. He'd been so fucking good up there. I had no idea he could act, but he was a natural.

'I just wanted to see your show, that's it,' I managed to say, glad that the wind and rain were lashing down even harder so he couldn't hear my voice wobbling.

'You came deliberately to put me off,' Theo snarled, shoving me in the chest. Such was my state that I was nearly knocked off balance.

'No, I – honestly, that's not it.'

The rain came at us again. We had to step aside to let a family hurry past. I tried to use the distraction to get away. I couldn't bear seeing Theo like this, but he grabbed my arm and yanked me back.

'Why is it you're so determined to ruin my life?'

'I'm not, Theo. I just . . .'

'What?'

'I saw your face on the flyer, and it reminded me how much I missed you, OK?'

This seemed to throw him. I saw his anger die down for just a moment. When he spoke again, he sounded plaintive.

'OK, fine but . . . couldn't you have just called me or something? Sent a text? *Anything* but just turn up like that. You do realise, don't you that . . .' He pointed back in the direction of The Tron. 'We were going to win, I *know* we were.'

'I know, you were so good, honestly!'

Theo didn't acknowledge the compliment.

'You know I worshipped you,' he said. 'That day in the music block – stopping me from getting hurt. I still think about that day all the time.'

I took a step towards him. 'Yeah, well, I know you'd have done the same for—'

'All I think about,' Theo interrupted, his voice growing louder, 'is how I'd give anything for you not to have been there. Yeah, I'd have taken a beating, and more afterwards. I'd still have been the weirdo in the stupid clothes who everyone hated, but at least I'd not have had those years trying to hang onto the coat-tails of someone who obviously didn't want me there, at least my sister would . . . would . . .' He was crying now, the tears mingling with the rain. An ambulance came flying past, siren wailing.

Maybe it was the booze, maybe it was because Theo's words and the anger behind them had left me reeling, but in that moment, hearing him mention Alice, all I wanted was for Theo to know the truth.

'You know I'll never forgive myself for that night,' I said, 'but there's something you need to know about what happened to Alice.'

Theo was wiping his tears away roughly with his sleeve. At the moment he heard me mention his sister, he stopped, stock-still, just staring at me. The city seemed to melt away. It was just us and the rain and the swirling wind.

'What do you mean?' Theo said.

'I'm . . . It was . . .'

I tried not to picture Alice smashing onto the bonnet. The awful noise it made.

Theo clenched his fists.

'*What*, Joel?'

But I couldn't do it. I'd promised myself I wouldn't.

'I'm just so sorry,' I said.

Theo waited for a moment, presuming there was something else I had to say. When it was clear that there wasn't, he shook his head slowly from side to side. Then he looked me up and down, as if trying to quantify just how much he hated me.

'Well, thanks for that,' he said, his voice hollow, all the fight gone out of it. 'But it doesn't change anything, I'm afraid. So please can you just promise me one thing?'

I knew what he was going to say, but it didn't make it any easier to hear.

'Never come near me or my family ever again.'

With that, Theo was gone, cutting a path through the jostling tourists.

Fireworks were exploding above the castle, purple and green sparks splintering the gloom. But I barely registered them. I was imagining what might have happened if I'd gone through with it – if I'd told Theo the truth. That it hadn't been me behind the wheel that night. It had been Amber.

Chapter Thirty-Four

Theo

I squelched back to the spot of my unexpected bath. The bike and my belongings had been completely consumed by the river, and I didn't much fancy diving in to retrieve them. The only thing I still had was my phone, which had been in my pocket when I fell, and which appeared broken beyond repair. I realised that the bit of paper flapping in the breeze on the grass was Joel's note. I stooped to pick it up.

I supposed the sensible thing to do would be to use my remaining cash to buy a train ticket home. But then what? Just carry on with my life as if the whole trip had been a dream – forget about Joel and what he'd told me? It was unthinkable that I could just go back to how things had been before. But then again what other choice did I have?

I was beginning to shiver again, so I started off on the path as if I were still following the route. As long as I kept walking, I wouldn't have to make any sort of decision about anything. I was putting one foot in front of the other, and that was all that I would concentrate on. Before I knew it, I'd got to Abingdon, where the river opened up wide, like arms stretching out, inviting me in. Even though a pair of painful blisters had formed on my heels, and I was in desperate need of a hot meal, I kept on going. The moment I stopped I'd have to face everything again, and I wanted to put that off for as long as I could.

By the time I got to the village of Clifton Hampden, it was so dark I could barely see my hand in front of my face. My feet were killing me. Each step was agony. I'd managed to draw out some emergency cash by phoning the bank from a payphone in Culham, but I just couldn't bring myself to trawl the B & Bs looking for a room, trying to explain my appearance. Instead, I found a rowing boat moored on the side of the river and managed to climb underneath the layer of tarpaulin which covered it, where I lay shivering, occasionally drifting off into fitful sleep.

It was in Henley-on-Thames where I finally broke. It had taken me two days of nearly continuous walking to get there from Clifton Hampden. I was exhausted, but every time I stopped, even just for a moment or two, my thoughts would turn to Oxford, and Joel angrily marching away from me, so I kept on moving. But after another night half freezing to death hidden on a boat, hammered by torrential, filmset-style rain, my legs had completely seized up and so I admitted defeat and decided to go to the pub instead.

I found a place that looked grotty enough that they wouldn't care about the state I was in, and bedded down in a corner to nurse a Guinness. A TV was on in the corner showing snooker. What a tedious game this is, I thought. Who actually watches this rubbish?

Two hours later, I couldn't believe that Higgins had missed such a regulation black off its spot at such a nail-biting moment in this pivotal frame. The coverage came to an end. A welcome distraction gone.

'Another?' the barman asked.

'Yeah, thanks,' I said.

He brought a fresh pint over and I deposited a lot of dirty coins onto the table, which he swept contemptuously into his hand. A memory came to me of Rex – the boy from halls – paying with a similar pile of shrapnel for a pint of snakebite on my first night at uni. What was he doing now? I wondered. He was probably a banker or something. My derision burned hotly for a second – a brief, satisfied sneer at what a sell-out he'd be. But then another thought hit me. Yeah, he's probably got a young family too. A nice house just out of town. Friends. And what the fuck had I got?

Just then I looked up at the TV to see the familiar opening credits of *The Tooth Hurts*. It was a repeat of last year's Christmas special, a particularly farcical episode where Karen and her boss Nigel go abroad to present at a dentistry conference in Italy but get picked up at the airport by the wrong driver and find themselves having to cook Christmas dinner for the Mafia. I'd read the synopsis in the paper, but for some reason it was the first episode I hadn't been able to bring myself to watch.

There was no sound on the TV, but the subtitles were on. '[Audience laughs]' kept coming up, which seemed almost sarcastic, even though I had to admit that this was one of the better episodes, mainly because of how self-aware it was about its ludicrous premise. In fact, I became so invested in it that when two old lads at the bar started arguing good-naturedly with each other, I looked around and glared at them until they were quiet. The episode seemed quite different in tone the longer it went on. A lot of scenes were played straight – following the tradition with sitcom Christmas specials where they go quite dramatic. I remember boring on about this to Joel. He didn't seem to be listening at the time, but maybe he was after all.

We'd reached what seemed to be a climactic scene. Amber's character Karen had phoned her sister Meryl for her advice, because – as the audience has known all along, but she's only just realised – she's in love with Nigel, despite being married to useless, boring Brian. I tried to picture Joel writing all this. Had he got an office somewhere? Had he just done it in his flat? Perhaps he was watching the rerun now.

On the screen, Karen was crying.

'What am I going to do, Meryl?' she sobbed.

'Listen, Kaz,' Meryl said. 'This world's a funny old place. You, me, everyone – we're told when we're kids how our lives are supposed to go. Get a good job. Buy a house. Get married. Have kids. Settle down. But there isn't really a plan for after that, is there? You don't plan for falling out of love with the person you marry. Or your kids hating you. Or your job going to shit. I mean, Christ, look at me, I'm like a walking advert for how not to live your life. But you know what? The only regrets I have are for the people in my life I've cared for who slipped through my fingers. Because those people you have a proper bond with – the ones who turn everything from black and white into technicolour, they're the ones you should never give up on. I remember this friend I had from school – Chloe, her name was. We were inseparable. Never went anywhere without each other. But then we got a bit older and fell out, and we stopped speaking. And, you know, it's been twenty years, but I still think about her. I wish I'd fought harder for that friendship. I wish I'd told her I loved her. So when it comes to Nigel—'

But the rest of Meryl's speech would have to wait. I was up, making my way to the exit, my drink untouched, and then out into the night, the chill of the evening rippling through me. I'd barely moved a muscle since Meryl had mentioned the people who 'slip through your fingers', but now I was walking on purposefully, the pain in my feet dull and distant. I didn't know whether Joel had deliberately written that scene in the hope that I'd see it, but either way, each word that flashed up on screen had felt like an electric shock. Earlier, I'd already felt myself sliding back into my usual warm bath of regret and self-pity, because wasn't that so much easier than refusing to accept that this could be my fault, and – more than that – that I could still actually *do something* about it? Well, I was done with that way of thinking.

I'd just enough cash to buy a train ticket to London. I didn't know how much time Joel had left, but there was no way in hell I was going to let the last conversation we ever had be that argument in Oxford. I was going to make things right between us, whatever it took. I just hoped he'd let me try before it was too late.

Chapter Thirty-Five

Joel

In Laurie Lee's memoir *As I Walked Out One Midsummer Morning*, he leaves his Gloucestershire home in summer 1934 and walks all the way to Spain, via London, with nothing but the clothes on his back, a violin and a stick. Ninety years later, I was waiting for a taxi to take me to the train station where we'd travel to Gatwick before getting a flight to Lisbon, with nothing but a new iPhone, a laptop, chargers, European plug adaptors, two pairs of sensible shoes, multi-weather clothes – because you could never really tell, could you? – a laminated travel and accommodation itinerary, a travel pillow, a back-up travel pillow, noise-cancelling headphones . . . and my mum. Truly, Lee and I were kindred spirits.

Mum had come down to Peckham the previous evening. Her train had been delayed and we ended up going to the pub on the corner for a late dinner – every single detail of which, from the square plates to the water glasses, Mum had categorised as 'posh'.

Our taxi to the station arrived shortly after seven the next morning. It was a cold, grey day, mist drifting over the park opposite my flat. I had to ask the taxi driver to wait as Mum told me she was going to the café on the corner to buy a sandwich and a coffee. At first, I thought they were for us, even though we'd had breakfast, but then I saw her cross the road and put them at the end of a bench where a homeless man was curled up asleep.

As we got into the taxi, Mum reached across and held my hand.

'Now, I know I promised I wouldn't ask again, but are you sure you're up to this?'

Her eyes were wide with concern, searching mine for signs of any reluctance. I smiled and told her I was feeling fine, even though the nausea had been particularly bad that morning. I was dreading the flight.

I rested my head back against the seat and looked at my watch. Amber was probably on her way to rehearsals already. She was back from Italy to record this year's *Tooth* Christmas special. I could sense her patience was close to breaking point when I'd called her the previous day to tell her I was taking Mum away for a few days, to see if that would finally lift her spirits.

'Of course,' she said, though the disappointment was clear. I couldn't exactly blame her. She had come home to work, a granite grey London, and an empty house, while I was suddenly off in the opposite direction, to clear skies and sun-warmed cobbles. I was hoping that a week in the sun, resting and recovering from the walk, would help bring some colour to my cheeks – to slow my decline even a little. But I knew that when I got back at the end of the week, I was going to have to tell Amber the truth. As the taxi pulled away, I closed my eyes, wondering if the conversation would be more or less hard than the one where I thought I'd lost her forever . . .

∞

I might not have realised it, but the four years after that night on the bridge with Theo in Edinburgh had seen me in ever quickening freefall, and I was about to hit terminal velocity. On the surface, that may have seemed unlikely, given how well things were going for my career, and how much I was living the high life as a twenty-five-year-old – out most evenings with a revolving crew of industry people hanging on my every word, my profile having grown and grown. But the truth was, having a drink in my hand was the only time I wasn't miserable. In the mornings, when I was sober, I could feel nothing but dread waiting to assail me as soon as I opened the front door. It was the same feeling as when you realise the tide's coming in quicker than you think, and you know you need to act fast not to get cut off. When I got that first pint in, it was like being back on dry land, the spitting, foamy waves forced into retreat.

Amber had wanted us to move out of the Morden flat and find our own place, now that we were both earning good money, but I didn't really want to. It felt like too much responsibility. I think there was part of me that still liked being in the slightly shitty digs with our now regular flatmates – a Norwegian couple called Emil and Markus, and a stoner called Chris – because they were my age but still wanted to drink and get high all the time, and it gave legitimacy to my behaviour.

Amber was now being regularly cast in proper TV roles – steadily building up her reputation. It meant that she was away a lot filming. Before, when that had been the case, I'd found it hard to be apart from her, but at least then it was mostly because I *missed* her, whereas now it was solely because I *needed* her. It meant I'd feel resentful when she went away, spiteful too, and those were the times I'd really hit the drink hard.

There was a month when Amber was off in Cardiff shooting something where I was on an almost continuous bender, aided by some coke that Markus had picked up. Things came to a head the night Amber came back. Normally I would have made sure to stop drinking the day before she returned, but I must have got my timings wrong. I was woken by Amber letting herself in. I came to with a start. I was sitting at the kitchen table, head on my arms, still in last night's clothes. My mouth tasted vile – cold chips and vomit. There were empty cans and bottles everywhere. My credit card, covered in white powder, was next to my hand on the table. I tried to hide it, but Amber saw. She stood by the counter, arms folded.

'What, no "Hey, honey, I'm home"'? I said, aiming for humour but landing on bitterness.

'Do you want to tell me what's been going on?' Amber said, like a teacher coming across a group of students up to no good.

I scratched at the back of my head, feeling the grease in my hair.

'Oh, you know – just been entertaining a few acquaintances. Anyway, tell me of your adventures. Is Cardiff as wonderful as they say?'

'Please don't try and breeze past this. You're not half as charming as you think you are. I mean, look at the state of you.'

'I'm fine,' I said. I got to my feet, trying to force a smile onto my face. 'Look, OK, I've had a bit of a big one – but I'll clean up and then let's go out for a meal. Somewhere fancy.' I made to go towards her, but Amber took a step back.

'I don't want to do that. I don't really know what I want any more.'

I could feel panic rising inside me. 'Hey, come on, there's no need for that. You're overreacting.'

'Don't tell me what I'm doing,' Amber said. 'You're acting like this is a one-off. But this has been every night for god knows how long now.'

'OK, now that really isn't fair,' I said. 'Look, why don't you go and have a bath and I'll get everything tidied up, and then we can go out.'

'I can't do that, because the bath's filthy. In fact, the whole flat's filthy. It's like I'm living in a teenager's bedroom.'

I threw my hands in the air. 'I said I'd clear up!'

'That's obviously not the point I'm making, is it?'

'I don't know! I don't know what's got into you.'

Amber looked around the kitchen again, daring me to follow her gaze, to see the state of it. 'Is this always what happens when I go away?'

I sighed and slumped back into the chair. I nearly reached for an open bottle of vodka but just about managed to stop myself.

'Joel, tell me the truth.'

I felt anger overriding the panic. I didn't like being interrogated like this. When it was clear I wasn't going to answer, Amber grabbed her keys and made for the door, stopping at the last second and turning to face me.

'I can't stand seeing you like this,' she said.

She was closing the door behind her when I muttered, loud enough so she could hear, 'Yeah that's right – go off and leave me again.'

She threw the door back open. 'Oh I get it now. I understand.

This is all *my* fault. That would be so much easier for you to believe, wouldn't it? Well, you know what, I am so tired of being your carer, Joel. This hasn't been an equal relationship for a very long time. I think . . . I think I need some time away from you. Don't try and contact me, OK?'

I felt a great weight clamping down on my chest, a tightening vice.

'Wait, no,' I said, getting back to my feet, 'don't say that – please just give me a chance. I'll get my shit together, stop all this – I promise.'

I tried to take her hand, but she smacked it away.

'Don't,' she said. 'Please don't.'

I backed away, half-tripping over a bottle. My hand still stung where Amber had slapped it, and that pain, and the voice of self-destruction now willing me on, meant I found myself reaching for the most spiteful thing I could think of to say.

'So that's it, is it? Even after what I did for you that night.'

After the door slammed, all I could hear was Amber's sobs as she hurried away. I sat very still for a moment – and then I burst up out of my chair and ran out into the street, looking wildly around and shouting Amber's name, but she was gone. I trudged back to the flat. Sitting in the wreckage of the kitchen, there was only one person I could think of to call for help.

I arrived back home in Kemble the next day. The moment Mum opened the door and took me in her arms, I started crying. The sobs were so violent that I was terrified they wouldn't ever stop. When they finally did, I was so exhausted that I had to lie down on the sofa. Mum covered me with a blanket and sat down with me, gently pushing her hand through my hair. For the next three weeks she mopped my brow and rubbed my back as the shakes took hold of me. She made me soups and stews, and when I felt up to it, she'd walk me to the end of the road and back. I felt so ashamed that she was having to do this for me. But I don't know what I'd have done without her. Or maybe I do. It would have been so easy to carry on down the path of self-annihilation . . .

After a month, I was strong enough to go out by myself. I went for long walks, breathing in the country air as deeply as I could, hoping it would purify me. Only once did I nearly slip up – standing for forty-five minutes outside the Thames Head pub in the rain, shivering and stuck to the spot. But I managed to push past it. As I warmed myself in the bath at home later, I allowed myself a small moment of pride, but then I thought about how Amber was still refusing my calls, and it all felt like too little too late.

I cancelled my upcoming work, thankful that I'd stopped partying before I'd squandered the last of the money I'd made since I got to London. As time went on, I got into a routine where I'd get up just after dawn and walk all morning, slowly increasing the distances. I enjoyed being up before everyone else, save for the odd dog walker. It was so peaceful. The boredom I'd abhorred, I now relished. I bought a pedometer and counted my steps – the ones I'd taken overall, and the ones I'd taken before I thought about having a drink. I tried to do the same with thoughts of Amber, but that was impossible. I missed her terribly still. I had been so poisonous to her, and all she'd ever done was love me. In my lower moments, I nearly messaged her to tell her about the milestones I'd achieved. *Three months without a drink, now.* But I knew that didn't count for anything. It wouldn't make up for how I'd treated her. The drinking may have made things worse, but it wasn't the cause of my behaviour – it was just the end product of a man who'd never tried to deal with what was underneath it all.

After six months, I decided to move back to London. I had to get back in the saddle with my job, my residual cash now pretty much gone.

'Are you really sure, darling?' Mum said. 'You're welcome to stay for as long as you want.'

It made my heart ache to hear her say that. She made it sound like everything had been normal. Like I'd just come home for Christmas and she was inviting me to stay for New Year's too. I had taken some comfort in seeing how Mum seemed to have found her sense of self again. She'd started a book group and was volunteering at a charity shop twice a week. She'd made new friends through both. The garden had become her pride and joy. But even though both of us were better, we still hadn't sat down and talked properly – not about why I had arrived home in such a state, and certainly not about Mike, or the accident. I don't know whether Mum thought if she tried to rake over the old coals I'd have clammed up or bolted straight to the pub. Perhaps I would have done. But in the end I left without us having anything close to a heart-to-heart.

Thankfully, I still had enough of a reputation intact that I got some writing work straight away when I got home. That meant I could afford to rent a flat in Peckham, the place I'd eventually buy. I had a desk by the window that looked out over the park. There, I wrote and wrote like it was the only thing keeping me alive. I was so prolific that days would pass at a time without me seeing anyone.

After a trip to the dentist, which ended in farce as the

dentist and his assistant had a big falling out about something in full view of everyone in the waiting room – I got home and wrote feverishly about what I'd just seen. It had been so dramatic – but there was real pain there too, when the dentist reappeared and had to put on an act, as if everything was normal. I wanted to write a show that captured the pathos of pretending. When I pitched the idea to Jane, she thought it was too dark, too sad. Would I be open to collaboration to get the tone right? The old me would have run a mile, downing pints in the pub and haughtily dismissing the suggestion as my sneering contemporaries applauded me for having such integrity. But I realised that was all bollocks. This was real life – you had to make compromises.

As I waited to meet my would-be collaborators, I got a text from Markus, my old flatmate. He had proposed to Emil and they were having an engagement party at the end of the month. Did I want to come? It took me a while to reply. I'd been in a couple of situations where drink had been around and I had just about coped, but that wasn't the reason I hesitated. It was because I knew Amber would be there.

I walked around the block three times before I went into the bar. I spent the evening chucking sparkling water down my neck and having near heart attacks every time the door opened. I was talking to Markus's sister, Astrid – a tall, striking woman who'd told me how bored she was approximately eight times in the ten minutes we were together, asking me if I knew where she could get some coke – when I felt a tap on my shoulder.

'Hi,' Amber said, with a shy smile.

'Hey – hello!' I replied, too enthusiastic, too manic with forced this-is-normal-isn't-it? happiness.

We hugged slightly awkwardly, our cheeks jarring as we air-kissed, like strangers meeting for the first time. Before we could say another word, Emil had whisked Amber away to meet someone, and that was that. She was like a shooting star rushing across the night sky.

I managed to escape Astrid and headed to the roof terrace, which had emptied as rain began to fall. I smoked a cigarette in the cold. This was a trick I'd stumbled on which allowed me to escape when I felt the urge to drink. I'd just lit a second when I heard the glass door slide open and turned to see Amber.

'You got a spare one of those?'

'Sure,' I said, offering her the pack.

After several attempts to spark my lighter, Amber said 'Wait, might be easier if I just . . .' and pulled me gently by the shoulder so that she could use the cigarette in my mouth to light hers. She turned and looked back indoors. 'Emil and Markus then, eh?'

'Yup,' I said. 'All very grown-up.'

'Was that Markus's sister you were talking to when I arrived?'

'Yeah. Astrid.'

'She seemed nice. Very pretty. I bet she does yoga.'

'Probably,' I said. 'We didn't really get that far.'

Down below us, a motorcyclist and a cabbie were having a shouting match.

'Ah, London,' Amber said. 'How I've missed you. With your rain and your anger.'

As I'd gathered from the papers, Amber had been in Berlin filming a police drama for the last few months.

'How's Germany then?' I asked.

'Oh, you know,' Amber said, swirling her cigarette in the air.

'German?'

'German.'

'I thought it might be.'

Amber shivered against the cold. I started to take my jacket off, but she shook her head.

'You look well, by the way,' Amber said. I saw her glancing at my glass. I was having to fight the urge to tell her exactly how long I'd been on the wagon.

'I was going to say you look like a movie star,' I replied. 'But then you always did.'

Neither of us said anything for a moment, but then I saw Amber's mouth twitching into a smile and I broke.

'OK that sounded far less cheesy in my head . . .'

Amber laughed. 'Oh it's not that. I was just thinking how ridiculous it is to think of me in the same context as the words "movie star". This show I've been putting my blood, sweat and tears into is clearly going to be a disaster, and the director – Francois – is a nightmare.'

'How so?'

Amber stubbed out her cigarette.

'He gives direction like this.' She took my shoulders in her arms and put on a pained expression. 'Amber, zis is not *truth*. Where is your *truth*, darling?'

'Yikes,' I said. 'And where is your *truth*?'

Amber shrugged and turned back to face the city. 'Oh god knows. Wherever it is – I know it's telling someone that it was a mistake me taking the part and that I should never have left London.'

I went to take a sip of my water, but my glass was empty.

'Well, for what it's worth,' I said, 'I'm sorry if I played any part in that decision.'

'You didn't,' Amber replied. There was nothing reproachful in the way she said this, it was just a fact.

Just then, the glass doors opened again. It was Markus.

'Heyyyyy, you two,' he slurred, swaying a little as he came over. He threw his arms around us both. I could smell tequila on his breath. 'And why are you not inside dancing, please?'

'Ah,' Amber said. 'Sorry but I've suddenly remembered I've broken both my ankles.'

Markus looked at me. 'Jooooel?'

'Me too I'm afraid – what are the chances?'

Markus threw his head back theatrically. 'Urghhh, you two. It's just like the old days. Always on the edge of the party. Always *together*.' He bopped both of us on the nose in turn and giggled to himself. Then he heard a song he recognised and began dancing his way back inside, where Emil arrived at the same time to jump into his arms. Amber and I watched them dancing as the other guests stood around in a circle, cheering them on.

'They look so happy,' Amber said, sincere, but unmistakably sad. She shivered again. I knew we'd have to go inside before long.

Ever since Amber had come out to the terrace, I'd been trying to find a way to steer the conversation to a place where I could apologise for everything I'd done, but the words I'd planned to say just seemed so facile.

'So,' I said, 'I don't really know where to start when it comes to an apology. I don't even know if you want to hear it.'

Amber's expression didn't change. She'd obviously been expecting this.

'Would it help,' she said, 'if I were to pre-empt what I imagine you're about to say?'

I laughed a little nervously. 'Maybe, I don't know.'

Amber took a breath, then started to speak, deliberating over each word, becoming more sure of herself as she went.

'I think you want to tell me that you're sorry for taking out your pain on me. That you loved me but partly for the wrong reasons – because a big part of what drew you to me was because I helped you escape when things got hard.'

Amber looked at me as if to say 'right so far?' and I nodded.

'You want to say that the drinking got out of hand and the worse it got, the more you needed it, and by the end you barely recognised yourself, especially when you said what you did about Alice's accident to me that night. You wanted to self-destruct in the biggest way possible, and that meant saying the worst thing you could think of to the person you loved the most.'

I had the strangest urge to drop my glass and see if it shattered, because it felt like I was dreaming. 'But that's exactly . . . basically word for word. How did—'

'Because I know you, Joel. Because I love you.'

My heart skipped a beat at her use of the present tense.

'Oh,' was all I could muster in response.

'I knew I had to leave you that night,' Amber said. 'I could have stayed and tried to stop you drinking – paid for rehab or therapy and made sure you kept the appointments and stayed on track, but—'

It was my turn to jump in. 'But that would have meant I'd have been doing it for you, rather than myself. There'd always be a part of me that wanted to burn it all down again. The resentful part that didn't like that you'd made me get better.'

Amber nodded. 'I think that sounds about right,' she said.

There was a blast of noise from inside. We looked back to see people forming a line, grasping each other's waists.

'Wow,' Amber said. 'I have to say, I hadn't predicted a conga.'

'Me neither. It's almost charming, isn't it?'

Just then, Astrid and an equally haughty friend stepped outside – obviously not conga people – and Astrid produced a telltale plastic baggy.

I turned to Amber. 'You know, I've always wanted to say this phrase, but I've never found the right moment until now.'

'What phrase is that then?' Amber asked.

I made my elbow into a crook, and Amber slipped her arm inside.

'Shall we get out of here?' I said.

We had to wait for the conga to pass, like we were at a level crossing as a cumbersome goods train trundled through. It felt even colder when we finally got outside again, and this time Amber accepted the offer of my jacket. This, more than anything, gave me hope.

We walked south towards the river, talking about everything and anything, switching topics every ten seconds, going off on tangents, going from serious to trivial, heartfelt and ironic, silly and mature. It was the way that only two people who know each other completely talk when they've been apart – where there never feels like there's enough time to say everything because there's always a new spark that sends you off in another direction.

By the time we'd run out of steam, we had walked up and down the South Bank and were standing on one of the little jetties that juts out into the river by the Oxo Tower. It was the early hours of the morning now. Looking around, we were practically the only people I could see. The last revellers had made their way home. The morning joggers were yet to appear.

As I stood with my arms braced on the jetty wall, I felt Amber rest her head on my shoulder. It was so good to feel her touch again. I tried my best not to spoil the moment by asking whether she could see a future for us, but I heard the words spilling out of my mouth before I could stop them. 'When you're back from Berlin, do you think we—'

But Amber squeezed my arm tight, signalling me to stop. We stayed quiet and still, listening to the gentle lapping of the river on the bank. Eventually, Amber lifted her head from my shoulder.

'I still need some time,' she said.

'Of course.'

She hadn't said no. That was all that mattered.

Then she leant up and kissed me on the cheek. 'I'm so glad you got better.'

I didn't see Amber again, or even hear her voice, for another six months. But I emailed her and asked for her address in Berlin, and we began writing letters to each other. I wrote until my hand seized up. It felt easier to talk like this – for me to try and explain why I'd ended up in the state I had.

I barely socialised with work people those days. I'd got tired of people telling me I should 'just have a drink, for fuck's sake'. I never really felt like leaving my flat, but I was lonely without any company too. After a week without a letter from Amber, I walked past a pub and felt a dangerous longing. I managed to push past the temptation, but it still scared me. The next day, I booked my first therapy session.

The following week, I was sitting in the waiting room when

an email popped up on my phone from Jane Green.

Hope you're sitting down, m'boy. Can confirm that *The Tooth Hurts* has an official green fucking light!

I stood up and sat down three times in a row. Another patient in the waiting room eyed me nervously.

I began to think of that waiting room as my happy place, because even though the sessions were painful and left me completely drained, it was where I'd received the good news from Jane, and then, before my sixth session, I had another message that had me doing my jack-in-the-box routine again. This time it was from Amber.

Hey. So here's a funny thing. I've just been offered the part for the lead in a sitcom on the BBC. I gather you might be involved. I'm flying back tomorrow for a meeting. Dinner? X

∞

The taxi jolted to a stop and I opened my eyes. The driver mumbled an apology. A fox – the reason we'd stopped – trotted past.

'Little chap looks like he's on his way to work,' Mum said. She had her handbag on her lap, tapping away at it as she watched London go by. She was wearing a wide-brimmed sun hat, newly bought for the holiday. As she looked out of the window, a sliver of sun that had forced its way through the clouds caught her face. In that moment, I could imagine her when she was young – younger than I was now. I realised with a pang of sadness how little I knew about her at that time in her life; how I couldn't remember seeing any photos of her before she'd had me. I was determined to find out all I could on this holiday, to build that bridge to the past.

'That hat really suits you,' I said.

Mum beamed, and her cheeks flushed a little. 'Why, thank you.'

When she looked back to the window, she was still smiling. It was a smile that made my heart swell and ache at the same time.

Chapter Thirty-Six
Theo

I came to on a park bench in Peckham.

As I struggled to get up into a sitting position, so stiff with cold that it felt like my bones had fused together, I saw that someone had left a sandwich and coffee – presumably for me – at the end of the bench. I was all set to tuck in to the sandwich, ignoring the implications of what this meant for me and my life, when I saw someone sleeping on a bench a little further on who obviously needed the food more than me, and I left it with him instead.

The train journey the previous evening had been surreal. I'd managed to get a table seat all to myself – one benefit of looking and smelling like some sort of river creature, I suppose – and I kept falling asleep, only to be jolted awake as the train swayed. I remember waking and looking out of the window. I could just about see through the gloom, and it looked somehow like we were travelling through water – but after a moment I realised it was just the way the grass in the fields was moving in the breeze that made it look like wind rippling the surface of a lake. Then, what felt like moments later, I was being prodded awake by a cleaner with a litter picker, who told me we were in London. As I left the train, I caught sight of a poster advertising tickets for the studio recording for this year's *The Tooth Hurts* Christmas special. The fact that just the studio records were being given their own poster showed what a juggernaut the show was – I'd never seen that before.

Going through the barrier, I'd felt a rush of something approaching nostalgia. There's always something undeniably romantic about getting off the train in London, especially under Paddington's arches. That was the moment a pigeon flew so close to my face that its wing touched my mouth. And then I remembered that I hated this stupid city and all that it stood for. I wiped my mouth with my sleeve – replacing pigeon with river – and took out Joel's note, the one he'd written to me in Oxford. *I'm sorry about the damage on the wall. Bill me for it. Flat 4, 121 Prospect House, Peckham Rye.* My phone was dead thanks to the river incident, so I had to ask a reluctant stranger to let me borrow his phone to look for where Joel's road was. Once I had it memorised, I set off to get on the tube, reading the rest of Joel's note again as we went down the escalator. *You were a great friend to me, and I will never forget that.* 'Were' a great friend. That was the part that stung. Joel had obviously decided our briefly rekindled friendship was over, and after the way I'd behaved how could I blame him? I didn't know what I was going to do when I got to his house. What if he refused to let me in? I thought about him arriving on my doorstep in Kemble what now felt like months ago – jamming his foot in the French doors so I couldn't close them. He hadn't given up then, so neither would I . . .

But after the eighth time I'd pressed his buzzer with no reply that evening, I wasn't sure what else I could do. Either Joel wasn't there – in which case I had no idea where else to look, or, perhaps worse, he *was* there, knew it was me outside, and didn't want to let me in. A third, even worse option revealed itself. What if his condition had deteriorated after he'd left? What if the walk had been too much for his body to take? I began jamming my fists on all the other buzzers. The few people who answered told me they couldn't help. Defeated and exhausted, I'd sloped across the road and slumped onto a bench. Someone had left an old oversized fleece there. Not stopping to think why, I'd lain down on the bench and pulled the fleece over me like a blanket, willing some answers to come to me as I slept.

Now, stretching my arms out over my head, trying to get the blood flowing again, I prayed the morning would bring more luck. I crossed back over the road to give Joel's buzzer one last try. But there was no answer. I spent the rest of the morning doing slow laps of the park, willing the sun to break through the stubborn bank of clouds above. I leaned against a bus shelter and pondered my next move. I desperately didn't want to give up this early, but I wasn't sure what else I could do. More galling still was that if I did have to admit defeat and head home, I was very much out of money, which meant finding a phone box and calling Alice, or Mum and Dad, and asking them for help getting back. The idea filled me with shame.

At that moment, I heard a woman at the bus shelter next to me say, 'Now, you sure you've got the tickets?'

'For the hundredth time yes,' her friend said. 'You do realise we're going to be about four hours early?'

'Sorry, I'm just too excited. I've never been to one of these recording thingies before. And anyway, all I can think about is whether Karen and Nigel are going to get together.'

I swung around and stared at them. They exchanged looks

and turned away, closing ranks – a textbook London manoeuvre so as to avoid an interaction with an unwelcome stranger. But I knew what they were talking about already. It was the *Tooth* Christmas special recording. The only person in the world who might be able to help me find Joel would be there. I wasn't done yet.

Three hours later, the familiar beacon of Television Centre appeared up ahead. I'd tried to slip onto the bus without paying, using the two women as a shield, but the driver was wise to it and chucked me off. Without money to get a cab, I'd had no choice but to get to the BBC on foot. The last stretch of the journey had been agony. One of my walking boots – not built for being dunked in the Thames – was done for, the front flapping open with every step like an animatronic mouth. Blisters begat blisters begat blisters on my toes and heels. I was sweating copiously, and the smell of that mixed with the still-wet gunk on my clothes left a lingering stench. *Riverbed, pour homme.*

There were some paparazzi knocking around outside, laughing and smoking together. I joined the back of the ticketholder queue just as the doors opened. By the time I got into the building and to the front of the line, I realised I hadn't exactly planned for what I was going to do next. I looked straight ahead and attempted to ghost past the man in the BBC lanyard who was checking people's tickets.

'Excuse me, sir, have you got your ticket?'

At the last second, I affected an offhand manner. 'What's that?'

'Your ticket, please.' A smile, but a firm voice, eyes wandering over my filthy clothes.

'Oh, no, I don't need one.'

The security guard clasped his hands together in front of him, fingers interlocked. 'I'm afraid you do.'

I let out a weird, high-pitched chuckle. 'No, no – I'm not making myself clear. I don't need a ticket because I'm an old friend of Joel Thompson's. And Amber,' I added. 'Amber Crossley?'

'Yes, I am aware of who that is.' The smile was gone now. 'Have you got a guest pass?'

I patted my pockets, theatrically – left and right trouser, inside jacket, in case it was with my silver cigarette case and silk handkerchief. One of my hands came away with a muddy smudge.

'Afraid not,' I said, my voice now taking on a posh drawl. But I wasn't Simon Russell Beale on my way for Martinis with Alan Yentob, I was a disgusting swamp monster, and there was a subtle but noticeable shift in atmosphere as another man with a lanyard appeared and steered me to one side.

This wasn't looking good.

'Please,' I said, 'just give Amber a call. My name's Theo Hern. She'll remember me.'

'I'm afraid I can't do that, sir,' the man said. 'The cast are uncontactable this close to the recording.'

Desperate times called for desperate measures. I lowered my voice. 'Look, I promise you I'm not insane. I do know Amber. And I need to speak to her, urgently, about a mutual friend of ours who is seriously ill and vulnerable. She is the only one who can help me find him. So please – I'm begging you.'

The man gave me a sympathetic smile. I felt a glimmer of hope. But the smile was clearly one he reserved for all the weirdos and fantasists who claimed they knew Amber Crossley. How many men had he had to eject from the premises as they told him that *you don't understand, me and Amber are deeply in love – she'll realise that one day soon, don't you see?!*

'Please, sir,' the man said, gesturing towards the exit. It made it worse that he was being so kind, keeping his voice low, trying not to humiliate me.

My shoulders slackened. All pretence gone now. Head down, so as to avoid the stares and sniggers of the stragglers lining up with their tickets, I shuffled out of the building through the revolving doors. As I pushed my way outside, I was hit by a blast of cold air and the blinding flashes of cameras. I shielded my eyes but was too late to stop myself from bumping into someone coming at speed from the opposite direction.

'Sorry,' I grunted, stooping to retrieve the phone I'd just knocked from their hand, before looking up to see that it belonged to someone I'd not seen in a very long time.

'It's OK, he's with me,' said Amber Crossley.

Such was my relief at seeing her, I had temporarily forgotten about my appearance. So when I reached out to hug her, babbling away in an excited stream of consciousness, it had been something of a code red for the security guys, who forcibly yanked me away and bundled me into a side room.

'Reggie, it's fine. This is Theo, he's an old schoolfriend. He doesn't . . . normally . . . look like this.'

I smiled weakly.

Apparently satisfied that I didn't pose a threat to Amber, the security guard let go of me and, after fixing me with a final look of disgust, left the room. For the first time, I properly took in Amber. She was dressed in jeans and an oversized grey hoodie – the picture of an actor in dress-down mode. She was taller than I remembered, and there was something slightly different about her nose, but when she smiled, I was suddenly fifteen again, shy and awkward, finding it difficult to know how to hold myself.

'You know, it might have been best to call ahead,' Amber said.

'I would have done, but . . .' I pulled my phone from my pocket. The screen was caked in gunk.

Amber took it from me, holding it between two fingers, and knocked on the door. Someone opened it and Amber said a single word – 'Lucas'. Seconds later, a man in a Breton striped T-shirt with bleached blond hair appeared and held my phone up to the light. 'Water damage?' he asked.

Amber nodded.

Lucas – I presumed – disappeared without another word, taking my phone with him.

'He's a lifesaver when it comes to technology,' Amber said, applying some sort of lip balm. 'The amount of phones I've dropped in baths and sinks and hot tubs.' It might have been my imagination, but I was pretty sure she blushed slightly after the casual use of 'hot tubs'. 'Anyway . . .' she said, looking me up and down again. I realised she was waiting for me to explain.

'It's quite a long story,' I said. 'It ends up with me falling in a river.'

'Christ, are you OK? Do you need a blanket or something? I can ask Lucas—'

'No no, it's fine.'

'As long as you're sure.' Amber held my gaze for a moment.

'God, it's been years, hasn't it?' She sounded a little stiff, suddenly, and an awkwardness descended. It was then that I realised this was the first time we'd spoken since Alice's accident. I wondered if she'd ever thought of getting in touch.

There was a burst of activity outside – I caught a snatch of conversation about 'lighting checks'.

'They'll want me in make-up soon, I expect,' Amber said, 'So was there anything in particular you came to see me about, or . . .?'

'Well . . .' I began. Was this fair on Amber, to bring up Joel and his illness just before she went out in front of the cameras and a few hundred superfans to perform in a light-hearted comedy show? It was a small concern in the grand scheme of things. But the decision was made for me when Lucas appeared once more to take Amber in to make-up.

'Why don't you come to my dressing room, have a glass of wine there?' Amber said. 'You can watch the recording on a monitor.'

The next thing I knew, I was being led into the bowels of the studios, through brightly lit corridors, past extras and camera operators and runners and clipboard-wielding floor managers and studio managers, down into Amber's dressing room. There were bulbs bordering the mirror, herbal teas and ointments in wrinkled tubes, all the accoutrements of a star. The monitor in the top-left corner of the room showed the audience filing in. The set on the stage was the familiar setting of the dentist's office, with the reclining chair and various charts and posters on the fake wall.

A glass of white wine appeared out of nowhere. I swivelled in my chair and noticed the script for that evening's episode on the edge of Amber's dressing table.

The Tooth Hurts
(Xmas Special II)
'Filling Time'
Written by Joel Thompson

The title was one of those puns that fell into the 'so bad it's good' category. I imagined Joel typing it out, then deleting it, then doubling down and retyping it. And then I imagined a world where I'd been there with him, sitting across a desk in our office with corkboards filled with Post-its, half-empty coffee mugs everywhere. He'd have looked at me with a sly grin on his face. 'How's this for a title, then?' And we'd have debated it for far too long, forgetting to eat, forgetting we had homes to go to . . .

I knew that life wasn't possible now, but the need to find Joel – to tell him how I wished we could have had that, if things had worked out differently – that felt stronger than ever.

I was up on my feet, applauding, as Amber came into her dressing room. With retakes and scene changes, the recording had taken nearly three hours – but I'd been rapt throughout.

'You were fantastic,' I gushed.

'Thanks, Theo.' She seemed surprised to hear me compliment her like that.

I poured her a glass of wine and began rhapsodising about her performance. 'The way you delivered that line about the tractor – oh, and your *face* during the root canal scene.'

'Yes, well, I just say the lines, don't I? It's the script that's so good.'

Though there was a little forced false modestly in her tone, Amber did have a point. So it wasn't the most sophisticated thing in the world, but it just *worked*. Everything about it was so full of heart and warmth, and that the audience were still laughing and ahhhing after all the retakes was just a remarkable achievement. Joel's achievement.

'Anyway,' Amber said. 'What was it you wanted to—'

But before she had a chance to finish her sentence some enormous hooped earrings attached to a person swept into the room in a cloud of perfume.

'Darling, you were absolutely terrific. Your best yet. Such a fucking pro with the great unwashed too – you had them absolutely eating out of the palm of your hand.'

Amber nodded her head in a mini bow.

The woman looked at me and recoiled. 'Christ alive, who is this?'

With difficulty, Amber finally removed some fake eyelashes.

'Theo, this is Jane Green – the show's producer. Theo's an old friend, Jane.'

'Is he now?' Jane said, looking me up and down without even trying to conceal her disgust. 'And what's he doing here?'

I gave Amber a look: *Why is she talking about me like I'm not actually here? She can see me, right?*

It was then that I clocked her name. Jane Green. The person Joel told me he'd sent our script to.

'Well, sorry, matey boy, but I need the star,' Jane said. 'Amber, darling, we've got that call with Hank in LA.'

'Now?'

'Yes. Five mins. I expect he's finishing off his smoothie or waxing his balls or something.'

I snorted with laughter. Jane turned and gave me daggers.

'Sorry, champ, time to go.' Keeping a safe distance, she

started to usher me out, flapping her arms at me like I was a wasp threatening a picnic.

'Hang on, wait,' Amber said. Her eyes were suddenly full of concern. 'Theo, this isn't about Joel is it, the reason you're here?'

Jane whipped her head around. 'Joel? What about him?'

But Amber still had her eyes fixed on mine. 'He told me he's been with his Mum for the last week,' she said.

'Really?' I said. 'But that's . . . not . . .' I faltered. So Joel hadn't told Amber about the Thames Path. But why? I suppose that the idea of him coming to see me to try to make amends, walking two hundred miles in the process, was something she'd have tried to talk him out of.

Amber was smiling ruefully. 'I knew it,' she said. 'I knew he wasn't telling me the truth. And he told me this morning he was taking her away, Jesus Christ.'

Jane looked at Amber and tapped her watch. Amber raised her eyes to the ceiling and let out a long, steadying sigh. Then she began to collect her stuff, suddenly businesslike.

'I'm sorry, Jane. Please can you cancel the call?'

Jane started to say something, but Amber cut her off.

'I've got something much more important than Hank to worry about. Where are you staying tonight, Theo?'

I shuffled my aching feet. I wasn't sure I was ready to admit that a park bench in Peckham was pretty much the only option open to me.

'Well,' I said. 'I hadn't really got that far to be honest . . .'

In the underfloor-heated bathroom of Amber Crossley's Hampstead home, I peeled off my disgusting clothes and lowered myself into the bath that was just the bearable side of boiling. I was past caring about my appearance by this point, but when we got to her house, Amber told me she needed some space to think, and sent me upstairs.

As I scrubbed myself clean, the water gradually turned to the shade of the Thames. I must have looked like a news-footage seagull being cleaned up by the RSPB after getting caught in an oil spill. I was still exhausted, but I felt better for having washed off all the grime. As I dried myself after-wards, I looked in the mirror and decided there and then that when all this crap was over I'd finally get a proper haircut, something an adult would have. Maybe I'd stop eating cereal for dinner and get an ISA. All I'd need to do then was make some money to put in it. At least I had a working phone again. As Amber had promised, Lucas had worked his magic and managed to revive it, handing it to me just I got into the taxi with Amber. I'd prayed for a message from Joel, but no luck.

I wrapped a towel around my waist and transferred my stinking clothes to a bin bag. Amber had put a clean T-shirt, jumper and jeans on the floor outside. They were a size too big, but I'd never been more grateful for fresh clothes. It was only as I made my way downstairs that I realised they must belong to Joel.

When I came into the living room, I found Amber pacing around it, phone in her hand.

'I've called him twenty times but it keeps going to voice-mail,' she told me. 'I've tried all of his old haunts too – all those Soho bars, and all his old writer pals, but no one's seen him. He must have known I'd do that. He'll have found somewhere new to go. I just don't know if he'll be on his own or what.'

'Shit,' I said. It hadn't occurred to me that this was what Joel was doing, but Amber was clearly convinced. 'I mean, if he's off drinking then . . . how's his body going to handle that?'

Amber kept pacing. 'I don't know,' she said, her voice strained. 'Christ, he'd been doing so well, too. It's going to set him back god knows how far. I'm just praying we hear the keys in the door any minute. All I want is for him to know I'm not disappointed in him, you know? Because that's exactly what he'll be worried about. Every time he thinks of it, he'll have another pint.' She stopped dead. 'Hang on, wait – his office, the Peckham flat, we should—'

'First place I went,' I said. 'Sorry. No joy.'

'Oh,' Amber said. She sat down on the very edge of the sofa, looking disproportionately small against it. I stood there rather awkwardly, not knowing what to do. Then Amber looked up at me. 'I've just realised I haven't actually asked you why you've been looking for him.'

I cleared my throat and sat down at the other end of the sofa. 'We've been walking the Thames Path together.'

'The Thames Path. What, that's where he's been? With you?'

I nodded.

'But why on earth wouldn't he have just told me that? Oh, wait, hang on. Is this . . .' Amber looked to the ground, chastened suddenly. 'There was that thing you promised each other. Your trip. I remember him telling me about it years ago. I suppose . . . I never thought you'd actually do it.'

'Me neither,' I said. 'He turned up on my doorstep out of the blue. I wasn't going to go at first, but . . .' I trailed off. I realised that I was about to mention *The Regulars*. My brain jump cut to Joel on the bridge in Oxford, disgust on his face.

'That was why he lied,' Amber said, more to herself than

to me. When she spoke next, she avoided my eye. 'So, did he . . . I'm assuming that he told you everything then.'

'Yeah,' I replied, fiddling nervously with my hands now. 'I honestly don't know if he'd planned to. But we'd got as far as Oxford and that's when it came out. We . . . we had a bit of a falling out about it. No, that's actually bullshit – I was a complete fucking idiot about it, and that's when he left. I've been trying to find him to . . . to say sorry, to try and make amends.'

Amber was trying very hard not to cry now. I knew I should go over to comfort her, but I was way out of my depth – I didn't want to make things worse. Even still, I shook my awkwardness off and moved closer to her.

'You mustn't be angry at him,' she said. 'He told me he wasn't going to tell you, no matter how many times I asked him to. Said he didn't want to get in touch with you after what happened in Edinburgh. He thought you'd be too angry to even hear him out.' She was crying in earnest now. 'I'm so sorry, Theo.'

I didn't quite know how to handle this. Why had Joel told Amber he wasn't going to tell me he was sick? What difference did it make?

As I patted Amber awkwardly on the back, I was blinded by a sudden flash that came from the window, and I recoiled.

'What is it?' Amber asked, whipping around. 'Oh, the fucking paps.' She jumped up and ran over to the window, throwing the curtains closed. When she came back to the sofa and sat next to me, we grew silent, lost in our own thoughts. We stayed like that for a long time. I suddenly felt overwhelmed by tiredness. I hadn't realised just how drained I was. It had been the adrenaline keeping me going these last few hours. But now I was fighting a losing battle to stay awake, especially as every time I shifted, the sofa seemed to give a little, like I was falling into quicksand. I thought I'd just rest my eyes for a moment, give my brain a quick refresh.

But the next thing I knew, cold daylight was flooding the room.

'Bollocks,' I mumbled. I went to get to my feet, but then I realised that Amber had fallen asleep against me, her head resting on my shoulder. I suddenly felt a bit sick. This was horribly strange: wearing Joel's clothes, in Joel's house, with Joel's girlfriend sleeping next to me. I stood up, taking a few steps away from the sofa. My movement woke Amber, and after a moment where she got her bearings, she reached behind for her phone.

'Anything?' I asked.

Amber shook her head. Even so, this felt like the most likely place he'd come back to, and if he did – in the grips of a drinking binge – I didn't want this to be how he found me.

'I think I should probably go,' I said.

Amber got to her feet. 'You sure you don't want to stay a bit longer – have breakfast, maybe?' But I knew she was just being polite.

'No, but thank you.'

Amber smiled at me, but her eyes betrayed how worried she was. I felt an urge to reassure her, to make her feel better, even if I didn't really believe what I was about to say myself.

'Look, I'm sure he'll be back any minute,' I said.

'Yes, I'm sure you're right.' And although Amber's voice wavered a little as she said this, her smile as she crossed the room to hug me was now a genuine one.

'Will you phone me as soon as he does?' I asked.

'Of course,' Amber said.

Just after we'd exchanged numbers, there was a noise outside the window. Excitement mixed with trepidation flashed across Amber's face as she crossed the room and opened the curtains just a chink.

'Still just the paps,' she muttered. 'It's almost like they can sense something's wrong, the fucking ghouls.' She looked over at me and said, 'Oh . . .' before stopping herself. It took me a moment to realise her concern – me leaving through her front door wearing Joel's clothes . . . that wasn't exactly ideal.

'Don't worry,' I said quickly. 'I'll go out the back way. If there is one?'

'Well, there sort of is, but . . . well, follow me.' Amber took me through the hallway into the ground-floor bathroom. 'It'll mean climbing over that wall and sneaking through those gardens. I don't know if you can actually get out that side.'

'I'll take my chances,' I said, opening the window – an act which took more strength than I was anticipating.

Just as I was wondering if I'd always be cursed to immediately follow up even the most vaguely filmic lines with an act of physical ineptitude, Amber put her hand on my arm.

'I'm sorry again,' she said, 'about Alice.'

I nodded.

It was only when I was at the other side of the garden that it struck me as odd that she'd said, 'sorry *again*', despite the fact we hadn't mentioned Alice at all since I'd shown up. I looked back, but Amber had gone, and so there was nothing for it but to carry on, pushing my way through wisteria, wet leaves showering me with autumn rain.

Chapter Thirty-Seven
Joel

I was looking out to sea, counting down the seconds as I tried to predict when the sun would finally disappear behind the horizon. London felt a million miles away.

The flight out had been an unusual experience. I'd only flown first class once before when I was taken out to LA for meetings, and I didn't remember a huge amount about it, because – predictably – I'd used the opportunity to get black-out drunk. But this certainly made a pleasant difference to the usual experience of hurtling through the air in a coffin full of farts, being press-ganged into buying duty-free vodka. The best thing about it was how excited Mum had been. She's never been the most sociable person in the world, but she was so giddy she began chatting to everyone within reach – quickly winning over even the taciturn businessman who'd initially tried to ignore her.

When we landed, Mum said goodbyes to everyone as if parting from long-lost friends. We took a taxi through the blistering heat into the winding cobbled streets. I'd booked the nicest Airbnb place I could find – a beautiful old apartment with a private terrace overlooking the old town. Our host, Ruben, was dressed in that effortlessly stylish way continental European men do, like an investigative journalist who played saxophone in a jazz band in his spare time. He showed us around the apartment and ran through the usual spiel of how everything worked. Every time I thought he was done, I started to thank him, but then he would remember he hadn't explained the shower, or the air con, or the rubbish, or the TV, or the kettle. Mum watched him explain all this with such a look of bafflement on her face – *why*, her look said, *does this man think we need the toaster explained?* – that I found it very hard to keep a straight face.

'What do you want to do first?' I asked Mum when Ruben finally left.

She wandered over to the window, where sunshine streamed through the shutter.

'How are you feeling?' she asked, opening the window. Fado music drifted in on a warm breeze.

'Fine – honestly,' I said. 'I just need to make sure I drink lots of water.' I picked up a brochure from the table. 'We could do the castle – or the ceramics museum's supposed to be good. Whatever you want – let's do it.'

Mum turned around, a twinkle in her eye. 'In that case – what I *really* want . . . is to go and sit in the sun with a glass of something and read my book.'

'Now that,' I said, 'sounds like a plan.'

We found a bar with a sprawling patio that looked out over the port – cocktails (or mocktail in my case) in hand. They were hilariously over-the-top affairs with half the contents of a fruit bowl upended in them. Mum was asleep within approximately eight seconds, book resting on her chest. I got up and adjusted the umbrella so that she was in the shade.

Having forgotten, as I always did, to buy a book at the airport, I'd picked something donated from former guests at

Ruben's place. There were only three books: a John Grisham, collected poems of T.S. Eliot, and a book cheerily titled *Serial Killers of the World*. Naturally, I went with Eliot. (I'd read the Grisham. And the serial killer book was in German.) I leant back in my chair and stretched out my legs. They had swollen up quite a bit on the plane but were better now the air could get to them. I opened Eliot and took a gulp of sugary something-or-other. I'd never much been one for poetry, but I was pleasantly surprised by how much Eliot spoke to me. I was so lost in it in fact that the next time I looked up the evening was waning and the sun was melting into the sea.

I looked over to where Mum had been sitting, to see whether she was ready to find somewhere to eat, but she wasn't on her lounger any more. I sat up and scanned the terrace. It took me a long while to spot her as she'd wandered quite far away. My heart had started to beat that little bit faster. It was a strange moment – a role reversal of sorts, for a son to be scanning a crowded area, concern rising at the thought his parent had wandered off. It was only as I arrived at Mum's side that I saw she was crying.

'Hey, what's wrong?' I asked.

But she stood impassive, looking out at the sea as tears dripped off her chin. Eventually she turned to me. 'I've been a terrible mother,' she said.

This hit me like a knee in the midriff.

'That's nonsense,' I said. 'What's brought all this on?'

Mum waved a hand at the view in front of us. 'Look how you're spoiling me. When all I ever did was bring misery to your childhood.'

I put a hand on her arm. 'I think maybe this is the cocktails talking. For one thing I've been promising to take you here for years. Some son I've been.'

But she shrugged me off. 'This isn't a competition. I'm your mum. It's my instinct to protect you, to give you the best life you could have. And then I go and do a thing like bring . . . that man . . . that violence, into the house.'

This was the first time Mum had even mentioned Mike since the day he'd gone. I wondered how often she'd torn herself to pieces with all these thoughts. If only I'd been around more to save her from them.

'Mum,' I said softly. 'None of that was your fault. He was a vicious, controlling bully who took advantage of your good nature. You see the best in everyone, and that's not something you should ever change.'

Mum was shaking slightly, now, the emotion threatening to overwhelm her. I put my arm around her shoulder, steadying her.

'Y-you know all I wanted was for us to be a family again, after your dad left. I didn't want you to grow up without someone to do the things I couldn't. I never thought . . . I will never forgive myself for not being able to keep you safe.'

I could feel the lump growing in my throat. It made it almost impossible to speak without crying myself.

'Please, Mum,' I said, my voice thick, almost a croak. 'You have to promise me that you'll stop thinking like that. That's not who you are. That's not who you've been to me. You are the kindest, bravest, most selfless person I know. These last few years have been the happiest of my life, and there's no way in hell I'd have been around to experience them if you hadn't put your life on hold to help me get better. I was nothing but dismissive and distant to you for years, yet you never wavered in your love for me, not for a single second. I love you, OK? And who knows how much time I've got left, but after what we've been through, I reckon we deserve to squeeze as many drops of happiness out of it as we can, don't you?'

At this, Mum turned to me, and we embraced. I was crying more than her now. The way she held me. The way she rubbed my back. It felt like I could have been a kid again – after a fall, just needing a hug to make everything OK.

We made our way back into the old town, Mum's arm looped around mine.

'Are you hungry?' I asked.

'Not especially,' she said. 'You? How are your energy levels?'

'Pretty good actually.'

In truth, I was reaching my limit, but with every step we took, it was like we were growing closer, and I didn't want that to stop. Even when Mum asked, for the hundredth time, if I'd been able to find anyone else to help me with 'Plan B', I couldn't get cross, I just told her I was working on it, even though I wasn't.

The streets were quiet. It was a Sunday in the tail-end of the tourist season, but it still felt a little eerie, like we were actors wandering through an empty set. Fado music was drifting over from somewhere. As we walked, Mum began to hum along.

'My favourite, this one,' she said, but almost instantly the music stopped – as if the musician were shy and had been interrupted mid-practice.

'Ah shame,' Mum murmured.

We began to wind our way up the cobbled street to the top of the hill where we were staying. I needed every ounce of strength to keep my legs working, but I was determined not to let Mum catch on. We rounded a corner. A busker was counting the change in her straw hat, her acoustic guitar lying in its case.

Mum and I had walked on a little further when the idea occurred to me. I stopped and Mum looked at me, concern etched on her face.

'You OK, love?'

'Yeah fine. Listen, what's the name of that song you were humming just then?' I asked.

'It's called *Gaivota*,' Mum said.

'*Gaivota*,' I repeated. 'Give me one sec.'

'Joel, where are you . . .'

When I caught up with the busker, it took me a while with the language barrier for me to explain what I wanted her to do. But after a fair bit of pointing towards Mum, saying '*Gaivota*' a lot, holding out twenty euros and doing a gesture a European footballer might do when he's imploring a referee not to send him off, the busker finally understood what I was saying.

I beckoned Mum over. By the time she'd reached us, the busker was all set up, and even with the first chord, Mum clapped her hands to her mouth as she recognised what she was hearing, tears – happy ones this time – glistening in her eyes. The busker felt her way tentatively into the song, which was slow, somewhere between sad and hopeful. After a moment, I turned to Mum and reached out my hand. She tilted her head to the side at first – *really?* – but then she took my hand and rested her head gently against my shoulder. There, on the cobbles, under the stars, we moved slowly in time with the music. It was hard to tell who was leading who.

Chapter Thirty-Eight

Theo

I was the only person to depart the train at Kemble. I was still in Joel's clothes, though these too were now dirty from where I'd had to scramble over a fence at the end of the row of gardens outside Amber's house.

I couldn't face going home just yet, so I sat on a bench and watched two pigeons fighting over a crust of bread. I tried to picture Joel – where he might be now. Amber would know him better than me when it came to a drinking relapse, but for some reason I couldn't imagine him at the bottom of a bottle somewhere.

The minutes ticked by as I sat on the bench. I ached to be back home with Mum, Dad and Alice, but that strength of feeling bothered me now. Of course I missed them and wanted to see them again, but part of that longing was rooted in the fact that the life I'd left had been such a safety blanket. To go back there now, give in to it – settling back in the shed, fighting off Dad's attempts to evict me every few months – it would be a way of forgetting about Joel. Time is a great healer, as the cliche goes. And just as the scar on my arm has faded, so would the blisters on my feet, and so would my memories of Joel. But that felt like the biggest cop-out. I didn't want to go back to how things were before.

When I eventually got back to the house, I realised I must have lost my keys in the river. I rested my head on the door and pressed the doorbell. But there was no answer. I looked through the frosted glass of the door for signs of life. The hall light was on, but I presumed only because under British laws all dads leave hall lights on no matter how small the chance of burglary.

I went next door to Alice's. As I approached, I heard the sound of basketball on flagstone. Through a gap between the fence and wall, I watched as Alice aimed a shot at the hoop the other side of the patio. It hit the backboard but bounced over the top of the hoop. Alice collected it, wheeled herself back to her original position, and tried again. She shot a further five times without success, but scored with her sixth. Her expression was unchanged throughout: quietly determined.

I was on the verge of calling over to her when I heard another voice.

'You're nearly as good as me.' A man with biceps the size of Scarborough wheeled into view.

Alice raised an eyebrow. 'You do realise that's the only reason I'm dating you, don't you, petal? I'm just here to steal your skills and then it's over.' She threw the ball harder than strictly necessary into the man's midriff.

'So we *are* dating then,' the man said, throwing the ball back.

Alice spun around, aiming at the hoop.

'I'm thinking about it, Daniel,' she said, scoring with her shot.

'Oh, it's "Daniel" is it now?'

Holy shit. Daniel. *Dan.*

I went to back away so as not to disturb them, but I managed to trip on the grass verge and fall into the drainpipe.

'OK, interesting development, I think there's some guy watching us from over there,' Dan said.

Shit.

'Jesus, Theo?' Alice called.

'Oh, hi there,' I said, tapping the drainpipe with my knuckle as if I might have been sent from the council to do some sort of survey.

'What the hell are you doing back here? And why are you dressed like that?'

'It's . . . sort of a long story.'

'Riiiiight. Oh, this is Dan by the way. Dan, this is my brother, Theo.'

Dan and I nodded at each other. Then there was a pause.

'So are you going to come round or are you just going to stand there like a weirdly well-dressed Worzel Gummidge?' Alice said.

I smiled. I'd missed her a lot.

When I went around into the garden, Alice had gone inside to get something, so I was forced to make conversation with Dan. I got the impression Alice had done this deliberately to save herself from the awkwardness, which was a very astute decision given the patter I came out with.

'So . . . Magic Johnson. Was he basketball?'

'He was,' Dan said. 'I mean . . . about thirty years ago.'

My only other bit of basketball knowledge was the film *Space Jam*. Thankfully Alice reappeared to save my blushes. Or so I thought.

'So are you so successful already that you've bought yourself a whole new wardrobe?' she said.

'Yeah, well, about all that . . .' I toed at bit of loose stone on the ground. I didn't really know where to start.

Dan, who'd sensed the brewing awkwardness, cleared his throat. 'I should be getting going, really. Big day tomorrow and all that.'

'Oh yeah?' I said. 'Let me guess, a vital game in the A-league? The Gloucester Jets versus the Cheltenham . . . Ladybirds.'

Dan looked at me evenly. 'Not quite. We're having our Labrador put down. Choccy.'

Behind him, I saw Alice put her head in her hands.

'Ah. Sorry,' I said.

'Oh don't worry,' Dan replied. 'I mean, I guess to some extent he was the best friend I've ever had, but that's by the by.'

'Right. Yeah. Sorry.'

'No, no, don't be,' Dan said. Then he sniffed and added, 'Loyal, too. A real hero.'

'All right that's enough,' Alice said.

Dan grinned. 'Sorry, Theo, only messing. He was about a hundred years old and he was my stepdad's anyway, I'm just there for moral support.'

He reached up and slapped me cheerily on the back. I tried not to act like my chest cavity had just exploded. The way Dan and Alice were looking at each other, I reckoned I'd have to brace myself for more punishing blows like that in the years to come.

'Well then,' I said, after Dan's taxi had disappeared around the corner.

But Alice put a hand up. 'Nope, you first,' she said. 'Wait, what alcohol does this tale require?'

I considered this. 'Got any whisky?'

'Yeesh,' Alice said. 'I'll have a look.'

She returned a while later with a dusty-looking bottle without a label on it.

'Can't get the stopper out,' she said, handing me the bottle without a huge amount of confidence in her eyes that I'd be any more use. Eventually I managed to pull the stopper out with my teeth and spit it onto the floor.

'That made me feel like a sea captain,' I said.

'Yes well, enough prevaricating, Moby Dickhead. Are you going to tell me what's happened or what?'

And so – over more whisky than was sensible – I did.

By the time I'd finished talking, the empty bottle was dripping with dew.

Alice had listened with a consistently even expression, apart from her eyes widening when I revealed the truth about Joel's bucket list. When I got to the part in Oxford, I forced myself not to alter the story.

'I keep telling myself that he'd got it wrong – I hadn't really been thinking more about the TV thing than him, but if he saw that in my face, then it has to be true, doesn't it?'

Alice peered at me through the gloom for a long time without speaking. Then she said, 'I'm not going to try and make you feel less guilty, I'm afraid.'

'No, of course not, I don't want you to,' I said, though I knew that probably wasn't true.

'Look, whatever happened, *happened*,' Alice said. 'You can't go back and fix that. But you tried to find him afterwards, didn't you? You wanted to make up for it. The fact he's hiding from you and Amber shows there's deeper stuff going on with him – stuff he needs to figure out for himself.'

I was about to say that I thought it was more likely he was

off getting trashed – all because I'd been such a terrible person to him. But I managed to stop myself. For once in my life I wasn't going to make this all about me. Joel's entire life was crumbling around him; there were things far more concerning to him than my selfishness. I would sit by the phone waiting for Amber's call, and as soon as that happened, I'd be ready to do whatever I could to help.

Just then a car slowed in the road. I thought it might have been Dad's, but then it set off again.

'Where are Mum and Dad then?' I asked.

'Mini-break in Shropshire. They're back tomorrow. You can sleep on my sofa if you want.'

'Nah, that's OK. Have you got your key? I'll just sleep in the shed tonight, I think.'

'Ah,' Alice said. 'About that . . .'

I slept on Alice's sofa that night after all. She hadn't been able to bring herself to explain there and then, but after I'd made us a cup of tea the following morning she took me over.

'What *happened*?' I asked, surveying the square of sun-deprived grass where the shed had once sat.

'Mice,' Alice said. 'Apparently they were nesting there, all hanging out like a Disney film.'

I realised I was holding my mug at an angle which meant tea was slowly dripping on to the grass.

'So where's all my stuff then?' I said.

'Dad boxed it up and moved it into the dining room.'

'Oh. Right.'

Alice took a sip of tea, then she said, 'Sorry, do you want me to give you a moment or something?'

It was hard to tell if she was being serious or not. As I

looked at the spot where the shed had stood, I realised it was relief I was feeling. I was glad it was gone.

'Come on,' I said, 'let's go back inside.'

Inspired by the cause of the shed's demise, we put *Basil The Great Mouse Detective* on my laptop and Alice agreed to help me sort through all my boxes. I had my phone next to me and I kept glancing at it, willing there to be a message from Amber saying she'd found Joel, but to no avail.

I was sorting my old notebooks into keep, chuck and 'not sure' piles. It depressed me how little the quality varied from year to year. Something I'd written when I was twelve was indistinguishable from ideas penned when I was twenty-four. Even the handwriting had barely changed. The 'keep' area was thin on the ground. Most of it had come from Alice, who I suspect had only done it to keep my fragile ego intact. We sifted in silence for a while, watching Basil fighting Rattigan on Big Ben.

I lifted a tattered copy of the *Blackadder* script book out of a box. Underneath it there was a smaller book.

'This film is hell of a lot darker than I remember,' Alice said. Then, after I didn't respond, 'What's up?'

Slowly, I raised the book so she could see it.

'Joel and Theo: Quite the Little Double Act,' Alice read. 'That's my drawing of you both, isn't it? Holy shit, I'd forgotten about that. We did two, right? I remember you copying out all the jokes and the scripts into the one you gave Joel. Took you hours.'

I opened the pages and started to read, and suddenly I was fourteen again, in physical pain from laughing at a character Joel was doing, marching around his bedroom as a General with amnesia. It was as if someone had yanked me down through the pages. When I finally stopped reading I felt like I had come to after a long dream. The film had finished. Alice had obviously decided to leave me to my reminiscing.

My emotions had gone through a violent tug of war as I read through the book. There was stuff in there that still made me laugh – certainly more than my own solo ramblings. But with each punchline there came the sting of unfulfilled potential. If only we'd managed to stick at it without everything else getting in the way. I held the book in my hands, running my finger over the title lettering, anger building as I thought about what a waste it had been. And then I realised that actually, no, I wasn't going to just sit by my phone and wait for Amber's call, hoping for the best. I was going to find Joel and bring him back home, and what's more, I knew exactly how I was going to do it.

I grabbed my phone and dialled Amber's number.

'Amber, it's Theo. You've not had any word, have you?'

'No, still nothing,' Amber said. She sounded bereft.

'Don't worry,' I said. 'We're going to need a bit of help – but I'm pretty sure I've thought of a way we can get to him.'

When Amber and I had finally finished talking through the plan, the afternoon was slipping away, but as it did so, it seemed to take all my doubts with it. Because this time I was sure of it – I was going to get my friend back.

Chapter Thirty-Nine

Joel

I suppose I could have told myself that I had my phone off in Lisbon for noble reasons – that I wanted an authentic experience where I wasn't glued to a screen, to really engage with Mum. But the truth was I knew having it on would mean having to speak to Amber, having to lie to her again. At the same time, I didn't want her to be worried about me, so I knew I'd have to check in with her eventually. When I went to, two days after my impromptu dance with Mum, I was shocked to see quite how many missed calls I'd had from her. I jumped as my phone rang in my hand – but this time it wasn't Amber.

'Joel, m'boy!'

There was, remarkably, a pause.

'Hi, Jane. Everything OK?'

'Yes, yes, sorry – listen, I've got some rather fucking interesting news for you.'

That was a bit more like it.

'Go on . . .'

'It's about your show. The one you and that other chap wrote.'

I nearly dropped the phone. Surely not . . .

'The thing is,' Jane said. 'It turns out there may be hope after all. Rumours are that the rival Channel 4 thing might be a dead duck. Anyway, the powers-that-be want to meet. Soon as possible. Just with you,' she added. 'All a bit cagey. You know how they can get.'

'Right,' I said. 'But—'

'I've got a good feeling about this. I can read that little weasel I spoke to like a book. But time is very much of the essence. They want to make a decision by the end of the week. That means meeting A-sap. Three o'clock tomorrow. I'll text you the restaurant details, OK?'

'But, Jane, I'm in—'

'Sorry, bad signal, can't quite hear you. Anyway, see you tomorrow, dear boy.'

With that, she hung up.

I sat on my bed for a long time. I hadn't harboured even the tiniest speck of hope that *The Regulars* could be revived. But why did they just want to meet with me? Were they trying to cut Theo out of the picture?

My phone buzzed again. The restaurant info from Jane. I drew my knees up to my chest. To be at the meeting would mean leaving Mum behind on her own. I listened to her humming to herself on the balcony. She'd told me earlier she thought she might go off to do a bit of solo exploring, adding that she just fancied a little alone time. I knew that it was more likely she was trying to save my embarrassment at slowing her down, as the heat and steep streets had taken it out of me the previous day. A small voice inside me said I could easily get a flight home tomorrow morning, see what the meeting was about and come back. Another told me that violated what this holiday was about. As the voices fought, Mum came back inside. She read my face in an instant.

'What is it? What's happened?'

She came and sat down on the bed next to me, and I told her everything about *The Regulars*, and the call from Jane Green.

'Well,' Mum said, when I'd finished. 'I think it's rather obvious what you should do.'

PART FOUR

PART FOUR

Chapter Forty

Joel

Perhaps for the first time in my life, I was early for a meeting.

Jane had chosen a private members' club for the lunch – all plush drapes and full of twenty-somethings talking about their start-ups. It made me feel old. The table was in a booth hidden away in a barely lit corner. When Jane arrived, I'd already got through a bottle of sparkling water and was on to another. I don't know why I felt so nervous. I suppose I was just out of practice. I used to wing my way through these meetings, but it had been a while. And I'd usually have a few glasses of something to take the edge off.

Jane's behaviour wasn't exactly helping today. She ordered a Martini and drank half of it in one go, and was unusually sketchy on the details of which executives were coming, what they were going to ask me, and what the deal was with Theo being omitted from the conversation. The idea of getting in touch with him appealed about as much as walking over rusty nails, but it still didn't feel right he wasn't included – especially as I might not even be around to see the thing air. Maybe I'd just insist that Theo be in charge of it all – let him have his show; see how happy it made him in practice.

Jane downed the rest of her drink and ordered another one straight away, barking at the waiter like a drill sergeant. This really wasn't like her at all. She kept looking to the door and tapping away manically on her phone. She sent one final message and put her phone into her handbag, which she'd placed on the table.

'So, I'm afraid, there's something I need to tell you,' she said.

'Let me guess, they've cancelled?' Jesus, what a pain that would be. What a wasted trip.

Jane sighed. Then, quite unexpectedly, she reached over the table and took my hand. In the process, one of her chunky rings nicked my finger, and a little cut opened on my knuckle. I felt a faint sting – a ghostly impression of the pain that had gone before.

'I want you to know I wasn't happy about this, and that I only agreed to help them because they promised they had a bloody good reason,' Jane said. 'I don't like lying, but apparently this was something of an emergency.'

'Jane,' I laughed, 'have you had a bump on the head or something? Why all the weird secrecy – can't you just tell me what's going on?'

But she ignored me, snatching her newly arrived drink straight from the waiter's hand and taking a huge gulp. She glanced at the door again. I followed Jane's gaze, and then felt my stomach give a painful lurch. There, walking towards me, hair bouncing with each nervous step, was Theo. And then, as if perfectly choreographed, he moved to one side to reveal Amber just behind him.

'Sorry again, dear boy,' Jane said softly, getting to her feet. She gave Amber and Theo a curt nod as she passed, which they returned, before approaching the table.

'Can we sit down?' Amber asked.

I folded my arms, looking at them both in turn. I felt a flash of anger at how perfectly matched their solemn expressions were – as if they'd rehearsed all of this.

'You two make quite the team,' I said. 'You do realise that I've flown back from Lisbon for this? My mum is out there on her own.'

Amber and Theo exchanged looks. I clenched my fists under the table. I hated this – the subterfuge, the little unspoken language they seemed to have developed.

'Please,' Amber said, 'can we sit?'

I shrugged. 'Be my guests.'

They slid on to the booth on either side of me, a pincer movement which infuriated me even more.

'It was hundreds to get a return flight that short notice, by the way. Cash or cheque's fine, whatever's easiest for you both.'

'You don't have to pretend, mate,' Theo said calmly.

'What? I'm not fucking pretending.' I yanked down my collar. 'This isn't fake tan, *mate*. And . . .'

It was only as I looked at Theo again that it began to dawn on me what he'd meant, and I felt a great rush of panic hit me head-on, like I was standing on a hilltop, bracing myself against a powerful wind.

I didn't have to pretend . . . because Theo had told Amber that I was dying.

I braced my hands on the table. Amber and Theo both moved towards me – concerned I might collapse, or maybe that I was going to push past one of them and make a run for it. I couldn't bear to look at Amber. This wasn't supposed to be how it happened. One of my legs was shaking uncontrollably. Every sound in the restaurant – the braying laughter, the cutlery scraping off plates – was amplifying in my head, a furious cacophony. Then Amber took my hand, and everything was quiet again. I turned to face her, and our eyes met.

'I'm so, so sorry,' I said.

'It's OK,' Amber said. 'I'm just so glad I've found you again.'

I heard Theo clear his throat.

'Joel, I—'

'Shut the fuck up, Theo.'

I sensed him shrink back into his side of the booth.

'Hey,' Amber said, gently. 'Don't be angry at him, please. He was just trying to help.'

But I barely heard her. My mind was racing, now. I was imagining Theo picking up the phone, dialling Amber's number – or finding out where the house was in Hampstead and turning up out of the blue. I turned to glare at him, but he was looking down at his feet.

'Look at me,' I said. When he didn't, I slammed my fist on the table and said it again, louder. The conversations on neighbouring tables stopped abruptly, heads turning in our direction, but I didn't care.

Theo looked up reluctantly.

'What made you think you had the right to do that?' I asked.

'Joel,' Amber pleaded, but I could feel the anger taking hold of me, and I welcomed it, because the longer I could take it out on Theo, the longer I could avoid facing Amber. Blood from the tiny cut on my knuckle was blossoming now, a dark red bead trailing down the side of my hand.

'I bet you loved the drama of it, didn't you?' I said. 'I bet you told yourself you were doing the right thing – that you were being honourable or something.'

'I'm sorry,' Theo said in a small voice. 'I thought she had a right to know. I didn't want to lie.'

I let out a mirthless laugh. I couldn't actually believe it – the fucking audacity of the man. 'Wow, what a weird moment to choose to find some balls for the first time in your fucking life.'

'Joel, that's—'

'Oh what, sorry, you don't agree?' I said, clenching my fist tight now. 'Let me remind you of the facts, shall I? Let's see – I tell you I've got liver disease, and yet you're more concerned about a TV show not getting made.'

'But—'

'Not content that you've hurt me enough, you decide to wait until I'm on holiday with my mum before telling the woman I love that I'm dying. I mean – Jesus fucking Christ, Theo, I can't wait to see what you've got planned for an encore.'

Theo had gone very pale, his eyes wide. He looked scared, like I might hit him, but there was something else lurking there too – something I couldn't read.

'You're looking slightly confused. Sorry, did you think this was going to be more of a laugh? That maybe I'd just say, "Don't worry about it, pal – plenty of good fodder for the eulogy – anyway shall we be really naughty and have a starter *and* pudding?"'

I thumped the table again and a knife clattered onto the ground.

'*Say something*, for fuck's sake.'

But Theo was looking at Amber, who was sliding along the booth away from us.

'Amber,' Theo said, 'you knew . . . didn't you? Please say that you knew. That's what we were talking about at yours that night, right . . . *Right*?'

Amber was starting to hyperventilate. I went to move

towards her, but she put her hand up to stop me, breathing faster all the time.

'What . . . are you both . . . talking about?' she said in between breaths. 'Tell me. Tell me now what is happening.'

I turned to Theo. He looked like he might be sick.

'You told me you knew,' he said. 'That night at yours. You said you knew.'

'That – that's not what I . . . I was talking about Alice.'

'Alice? What do you mean? What are you talking about?' Theo moaned.

Amber tried to stand, but stumbled. I leapt up and tried to take her hand, but she wrenched it away. The maître d' began marching smartly towards us from the other end of the restaurant, sensing trouble from afar. Theo was on his feet now too.

'Look can we just slow down for a second,' he said.

'Oh fuck off,' I said, enraged at Theo thinking he could ever be the sensible one among us. It was his fault that Amber had found out the truth about me like this, in the worst way possible – he didn't get to have a say in anything any more.

'No, *you* fuck off,' he snapped back. 'For fuck's sake, Joel, I didn't say anything I thought Amber didn't know. All I told her was that you were with me for the week – that you hadn't been with your mum. I didn't say anything about your . . . about what's happening with you, OK?' He turned to Amber, hands clasped together in front of his chest as if in prayer. 'Amber, please can you tell me what you meant about Alice?'

Amber looked at me. As I finally realised what was going on, I shook my head, eyes wide – trying to signal that she didn't have to tell him. But it was too late.

'When I said I assumed Joel told you everything, I thought

302

we were talking about Alice,' Amber said, clutching the booth for support. 'Theo, it was me behind the wheel. I was the one who hit her. Joel kept telling me to stop, but I wouldn't listen. And then I let him take the blame for me, because he thought he had to, because I had all these grand plans to be an actor. Theo please believe me – there's not a day that goes by when I don't feel guilt about what I did. And I know that doesn't make anything better – not for Alice, not for you . . .'

Theo shook his head, uncomprehending. 'No,' he said, 'but that can't be right . . . that would change . . .'

The maître d' arrived at our table. 'Is everything OK?' he asked.

Theo looked at him like he'd seen a ghost. 'No,' he said at last. 'No, not really.' Then he turned and walked away, reaching up to grab his hair with both hands, dropping them only to throw the door open, and then he was gone.

Chapter Forty-One

Theo

I heard car horns blaring. It took me a moment to realise the cause of the noise was me. But I couldn't cross the road any faster; it felt like I was wading through mud.

A montage in sickening sepia was playing over and over in my mind – Joel and Amber stepping out of the car, their feet crunching on broken glass . . . me and Joel in tears at the Thames Head stone . . . shouting at each other on the North Bridge through the wind and the rain. And then there was the night at Amber's, where it was clear now she thought we'd been talking about Joel taking the blame for her for Alice's accident. *'He told me he wasn't going to tell you, no matter how many times I asked him to . . . I'm so sorry, Theo.'*

All this time I had been burning with anger for something he hadn't done. And now he was dying, and there was nothing I could do to make up for it. As I stepped up on to Waterloo Bridge, walking with my head down, tears stinging my eyes, all I could think was, *It should be me.*

I slammed into someone coming the other way.

'Watch where you're fucking going.' The man I'd walked into rounded on me. He was bald, with a thick gold earring in his ear and a mottled purple birthmark scalded across his cheek.

I stood there, looking at him.

'Got something to say?' he snarled.

I could see the thrill of excitement in his eyes that the weedy, pathetic-looking man who'd shouldered him wasn't backing down. And I wasn't. Because I wanted pain, and I wanted punishment. So I took a step forward and shoved him as hard as I could. I swear I saw a glint of glee in his eye as he drew his fist back. The punch connected hard just below my right eye. I collapsed sideways onto the ground, then I felt a boot slam into my ribs. I might have been eleven again, Darren kicking the crap out of me on a cold stairwell. I covered my head with my hands, vaguely aware of voices, of car horns blaring once more – and then the pain stopped abruptly, and there were hands – gentle this time, on my shoulder, and someone was saying 'Jesus, Theo – is that you?'

I took my hands away from my head, pushing the hair off my face, locking eyes with my rescuer. Her hair was cropped much shorter than when I'd last seen her, and she was wearing glasses when she'd always worn contacts. But there was no mistaking her. It was Babs.

Chapter Forty-Two

Joel

For one ridiculous moment, I thought I could try to pretend this was all a big mistake, that Amber had misheard what I'd said, but the way she was looking at me meant I knew that was impossible.

After Theo had left, we'd sat down next to each other in the booth, our foreheads gently resting together like the first time we'd seen each other after Alice's accident all those years ago. I held Amber's hand until her breathing finally levelled out and she was able to speak again.

'How long have you known?' she asked.

'About a month,' I said at last.

'What about . . . Oh god, Joel, I can't even say it . . .'

'They're not sure,' I said.

'And there's nothing . . . I mean surely there's *something* . . .'

I swallowed hard. 'I need a transplant, but there are hundreds of people ahead of me on the waiting list. I . . . It doesn't look like there'll be enough time.' Now, finally, I was saying the words I'd dreaded for so long – and it was worse than I could have imagined.

'And you've known about this for a month,' Amber said, only now fully taking this in.

'Yeah,' I whispered.

'So, hang on, all this time,' Amber continued, carefully separating her hand from mine, 'you've kept it from me.'

'The thing is I—'

'I can't believe it . . . you've been lying to me this whole time.'

She shifted away from me on the bench.

'It's not like that,' I said.

'What is it *like* then?' Amber shot back, her voice trembling.

'I just couldn't bear to,' I said. 'After all I've put you through in the past – I didn't want to tell you until I absolutely had to.'

'And you thought that's what I'd want – like I'd be grateful, or something? Like I'd look back and go, well, at least I got an extra month in the dark.'

'But—'

'Joel, we could have spent this time together trying to come to terms with this, trying to be strong for each other – that's what a relationship is. This is real life and we face all that it throws at us *together*.'

She stood up.

'You know what, I should never have let you take the blame for what happened to Alice. That poor girl. God I was such an idiot, and so selfish.'

'Amber, please just—'

'But do you know what's worse, Joel? I let you think that it was noble to do something so self-destructive. And now look what's happened. I'm sorry, but – I don't know if I can bear . . . I think I need some time on my own, OK?'

As I watched her go, I felt the strangest sensation come over me. It was the feeling of stumbling across someone else's tragedy – walking past a ring of people crowded around a body while someone half-seen through a forest of legs tries to resuscitate them, yet I knew if I were to push my way through the crowd and look down, it would be me on the ground, glassy-eyed. Lifeless.

Chapter Forty-Three
Theo

I'd pictured various scenarios post-break-up where I ran into Babs in the street. They normally involved me doing something gallant. Often on a horse. Her rescuing me from a fight I'd started with a man who looked like an extra from *Hook* wasn't one of them, funnily enough.

At first – once I'd established I hadn't been knocked unconscious and this wasn't a dream – I tried to brush the whole incident off, asking Babs polite questions: 'So what brings you to London then? Work, I expect.' But all the while I felt the bruise under my eye swelling, and it's hard to sound interested yet aloof – *lovely to see you but I really must be getting back to my girlfriend; did I mention she's a yoga-teaching nuclear physicist who speaks nineteen languages?* – when you're slowly losing vision in one eye.

'I think we need to get you to a doctor,' Babs said.

'Oh no, no need for that,' I said brightly. 'So did you get the train down or . . .?'

Babs took a clean tissue from her bag and carefully dabbed at my cheek while I winced. She was standing very close to me. When I stopped babbling, she became aware of our proximity and took a small step back, glancing at her watch.

'How about we get you to a barman instead then? I've got

an hour or so to kill before I need to be at King's Cross. You're not feeling concussed, right?'

'Nah, definitely not. He barely touched me.' (I'd deal with the irreparable long-term brain damage another day – this was a drink with Babs we were talking about!)

We found a pub around the corner and Babs ordered a pint of Guinness for me and white wine for her, along with some ice. She dropped a couple of cubes in her glass – the rest she wrapped in a scarf and gave to me to press on my cheek.

'Jesus that is going to be one hell of a black eye tomorrow. You've not got any modelling jobs lined up, have you?'

'Just Dolce & Gabbana. But they're only shooting pecs and abs, so should be fine.'

'That's a relief,' Babs said. 'Cheers then.'

We clinked glasses, and drank.

'So,' Babs said, 'I'd ask "how are things?" but I'm guessing they're perhaps not completely brilliant?'

I took another sip to buy me some time. 'I suppose they've been better. But it's all relative, isn't it?'

Just then a man and woman in their early twenties greeted each other awkwardly at the bar in the way only people on a first date can. There was a handshake, a hug, and a kiss on one cheek. The boy went for two, but the girl left him hanging. I wondered what their fate was. Would this be their only date – she having to send a text refusing his offer to meet up again, citing a lack of chemistry? Or was this the start of a long and happy relationship – the awkward ballet of how they'd greeted each other at the bar on their first date making it into the groom's well-received speech?

'Do you know those people?' Babs asked.

'No. I was just . . .' I picked at some candle wax on the table. 'Well, I was just thinking that was us, once.'

Babs turned to look back at the bar. 'I'd never have worn those shoes. And he's much taller than you.'

'That's not quite what I meant.'

Babs sighed. 'I know. I'm just trying to stop you getting all sentimental and nostalgic. At least wait until I'm drunk.'

'What's wrong with me getting all sentimental and nostalgic?'

'Because I know you too well. It'll start with you being quite sweet and talking about us and what it was like when we first met, and it'll end with you getting very, very upset about pubs from your youth that have closed down and confectionary that no longer exists.'

'Fair enough,' I said. (I'd stopped listening at 'quite sweet'.)

'Come on then,' Babs said. 'You can't keep putting it off.' She gestured to me to press the ice to my face, and I complied. 'What got you so upset that you picked a fight with a man twenty times your size?'

I dabbed tentatively at my eye with the improvised ice pack, then lowered it to the table. Part of me still didn't want to soothe the pain.

Babs was looking at me expectantly, so I gathered myself and began to tell her about the last week. By the time I'd finished the whole story about Joel, and our walk, and his diagnosis – and what Amber had just told me in the restaurant – the ice had melted into a large pool of water.

'Gosh, Theo, that's awful. Poor Joel. Liver disease is such a fucker. Do you remember my cousin Max? His best mate went through this last year. In the end – well, it doesn't matter, I imagine Joel's explored that, but . . . and, Jesus, I can't believe that he took the blame for Amber too. Have you told Alice yet?'

I shook my head. 'I was thinking about how – or if – I was going to do that when I walked into that guy.'

'When you say "if" . . . do you think you might not tell her at all?'

'I don't know. She's got a right to know, obviously. I just don't know what good it will do her. It might make her revisit the night it happened – that won't be good for her at all.' I don't know whether I was still too shocked to properly process how I felt about Amber, now that I knew the truth. It changed everything, of course, but at the same time it changed nothing. It had been an accident. I'd always known that. Did it really matter who had been behind the wheel? One thing I did know was that I hadn't got the energy left for more years of pointless anger.

'Well, you know Alice better than anyone,' Babs said. 'I'm sure you'll make the right decision.'

'Well, I suppose it's just . . .' I stopped. I looked down at where the puddle of water on the table was spreading. I thought again of the tarmac, of crunching glass. And the pool of blood. 'Actually,' I continued, 'I don't think that's really why I don't want to tell her. I'm not saying it's not part of it, but I think the main reason is . . . because I feel guilty.'

'Guilty?' Babs said. 'How do you mean?'

I chewed my lip.

'Well, the thing is, I have spent the last decade of my life hating Joel. I told myself that it was because he ruined Alice's life, but what happened in Edinburgh isn't that far behind. Alice managed to forgive him before she'd even got out of hospital. Thirteen years old, her whole life turned upside down, she was working out how to move past it all, even though she was still angry at him. But I was the one who'd make her sit through his TV shows and curse him and never let her forget the past, all because I needed him to be this villain, the reason for all my failures. I wasn't prepared to admit that it was down to my own lack of talent that I didn't succeed. So I think when I was walking along the bridge back there, I was trying to convince myself that I shouldn't tell Alice the truth because it would be painful for her, but deep down I knew it was really because I'd feel so ashamed of what I've done all these years. I've built a fucking bonfire with all my hatred and self-pity, and made Alice sit around it with me, because it's so much easier blaming someone else for everything that's gone wrong. And now I know that the thing I used to fan those flames . . . it wasn't even his fault.'

I took a long gulp of my drink, reflecting that me working out in real time what a selfish arsehole I've been my whole life, and telling Babs all about it in great detail, was another scenario that hadn't made it in to my top ten for when we bumped into each other. The thought made me let out a strange little laugh.

'What's so funny?' Babs asked.

I didn't even bother lying.

'I don't think you're an arsehole, Theo.'

I raised my eyebrows.

'OK, I may have thought that at times, but I know you've got a good heart underneath it all. And, look, it's just taken a punch in the face and half a Guinness with your ex and you're already getting better.'

'Cheaper than therapy, I suppose,' I replied, and Babs smiled, and that made my heart hurt. I knew what I was about to say was a mistake, but I was past caring. 'I miss this,' I said quietly. 'I miss *you*.'

Babs sat back in her chair.

'Hey, come on,' she said, throwing her hands up. 'I was having a nice time. Weird, obviously, but still nice.'

'Sorry. I just . . . losing you is my biggest regret, you do know that, don't you?'

Someone behind me laughed very loudly. It was the boy on the date. *Yeah, laugh it up now, you fucker,* I thought.

'Do you really want to do this?' Babs asked.

'What?'

'Oh, you know – the big post-break-up chat. Because you know me very well, Theo. I'm not going to sit here and tell you it was a huge mistake that I ended things. And even if I did, would that actually make you feel any better?'

'No,' I admitted. 'Probably not. But given that I've just been punched very hard in the face and come to the conclusion I've been an arsehole for most of my life, I'm not sure I could feel much worse.'

Babs put her elbows on the table and cradled her chin in her hands while she spoke. 'I don't know if you could tell, Theo, but it really, really, *really* hurt hearing your voice again when you called me the other night. But do you know why? It was because when you first started speaking, I pictured you when we'd just got together. The kind, selfless, silly you. The person who made me tea every morning in halls. Who made me feel better when I'd fucked up an essay by doing that stupid little dance you did, shaking your willy around.'

I blushed. The willy dance. How could I have forgotten *that*?

'*That* is the person I fell for,' Babs continued. 'But then, you

314

started droning on about the TV show, and it was like we'd fast-forwarded a few years and we were in London, where all that bitterness and selfishness had taken hold of you. And I just remembered thinking what a shame it was that you chose to give in to all that – that even when you proposed to me, it was because you were scared of losing me rather than because you loved me. When I put the phone down, I felt relieved, because I've always worried that ending things was a mistake, but after speaking to you, I realised I'd done exactly the right thing.'

She sat back in her chair, clutching her wine glass, waiting to see how this had landed.

'OK, you were right,' I said, after digesting what I'd heard. 'I didn't really want to hear that.' I tried to smile to show I was joking. But it was hard when I was hurting so much, and not just from the punch.

'Theo,' Babs said, leaning forward and taking my hand. 'That version of you I fell in love with is still there. I know it is. It sounds like you're starting to figure out a way you can be that person again – you just need to dig deep and keep going.' She squeezed my hand, and I squeezed back. Then, in two swift motions, she looked at her watch and reached up to tilt my chin to one side, so she could inspect my bruise. 'I'm supposed to get my train now,' she said, still examining my eye. 'But maybe . . . Look, I could always get the sleeper train later or get a hotel or something. I don't really like the idea of leaving you like this.'

'Oh, well . . .' I started. 'I suppose . . .' I trailed off.

'It's no biggie,' she said.

'Well . . . I don't . . .'

'Look, I need the loo. If you decide you want me to stay,

then mine's another wine. And get some more ice for your bruise.'

I watched her walk away. The idea of spending a whole evening with her . . . what a bonus that would be. I'd barely asked a question about her own life. We could get to that over dinner. We could reminisce about old times and I'd do my best not to get sentimental. Now that she'd said it, I wanted so badly to show her that I could still be the person she fell for. But as my mind went into overdrive, Babs's phone lit up with a message.

Can't wait to see you tonight. I've missed you x

The background photo underneath the message was of Babs and a man with red hair and a fulsome beard. The photo was taken at arm's-length, at what I recognised as Arthur's Seat in Edinburgh. In the brief moment before the screen went dark again, I recognised just how happy Babs looked in the photo. It was the smile of someone in the fierce grip of new love. It was then that I realised that the best way I could show her the old me, the one who still thought of others before himself, was to let her be happy – starting with making sure she got home tonight to the person lucky enough to be waiting for her.

'Are you sure?' Babs said, when she came back from the loo.

'Yeah. But thank you again for, you know, rescuing me and everything.'

'Any time,' Babs said. It looked like she was making to leave, but then she stopped.

'Fancy walking me to the Tube?'

Finally, a question I had an easy answer for.

'Absolutely.'

We walked along the Embankment. As I looked down at

the river, I couldn't quite imagine how it would have felt to have got this far on the walk with Joel. It would have been weeks still until we'd got here onto the home straight. I suspected in that time I would probably have found a way to mess things up, whatever Joel might have told me about what he was going through. That wasn't a self-pitying thought. It was just the truth.

I wondered whether I'd ever see him again. Did it make a difference now that everything was out in the open? I just wished there was a way I could make up for what I'd done in Oxford, but time was against me.

As a police speedboat shot up the river, I realised there was something I'd been meaning to ask Babs, something which she'd glossed over but which had lodged in my mind to return to later.

'Earlier, you mentioned your cousin.'

'Yeah, Max.'

'Max, that was it. You said something about his friend having liver disease, and then you said "I imagine Joel's explored that". What did you mean?'

By the time Babs had finished explaining, I'd slowed down and come to a halt.

I apologised to her for the change of plan, but I had to go, and go now. We hugged goodbye and I ran to the road and flagged down a taxi. As we shot south over Waterloo Bridge, I felt more alive than I'd done in years, trying not to get my hopes up too much – a task made impossible now that I could imagine a distant future where Joel and I would start the Thames Path again, and that this time we'd make it to the end.

Chapter Forty-Four

Joel

I'd forgotten what this felt like. The anticipation of that first sip. It would be like rain after a drought. I tipped the whisky bottle back and forth. The golden liquid seemed to glow despite the gloom. I was lying in the dark on the bedroom floor in my Peckham flat. Above me, I could just make out a spider in the corner of the room up by the ceiling. It was reeling in a fly that moved its wings hopelessly against the spider's silk.

'Sorry old chap,' I said, raising the bottle to the fly.

I'd tried calling Amber after I'd left the restaurant, but she didn't reply. She sent me a message saying she'd get in touch again when she felt ready – her tone officious, like we were office colleagues who'd fallen out over a spreadsheet.

I had my clammy fingers on the bottle top. I could feel it giving way. At the sound of my buzzer going, I dropped it.

Shit. Amber had changed her mind.

I rolled the bottle under the bed. The buzzer went again. The button that opened the front door from my flat had long since broken, so I couldn't let her up from here.

'I'm coming!' I shouted, though I doubt she could hear me. I yanked open my flat door and got to the stairs just as exhaustion hit me head on. I hadn't quite realised until now just how much the upheaval of the last few days had taken out of me. Hugging the banister tightly, I made it to the bottom, fighting past the spots that threatened to obscure my vision. I stood there for a second, trying to get my breath back, fearful at how angry or upset Amber would be when I saw her face. But when I opened the door, I was met by the sight of Theo – one hand pawing nervously at his shaggy curls. His right eye was swollen half shut, a dark red bruise underneath it. But I didn't really care what had happened. I didn't want to know why he was here. He wasn't Amber, and so I didn't fucking care.

'Sorry, Theo, not now, OK?'

I went to shut the door, but Theo jammed his foot in the way. We both looked at his squashed foot.

'Please,' Theo said. 'It's important. Just give me ten minutes, that's all I'm asking for.'

Theo sat at my kitchen table while I made tea. As the kettle boiled, I went into my bedroom and retrieved the whisky from under my bed. I took it to the bathroom and poured the whole lot down the toilet.

When I got back to the kitchen, Theo was prodding gingerly at his eye.

'Got any ice?' he said.

I looked in the freezer but all that was in there was some own-brand chicken nuggets. A grim reminder of my time here during the break-up. I held the bag up and raised my eyebrows at Theo, who shrugged and nodded. I chucked the bag over and he pressed it to his face.

'I'm sorry for tricking you into coming to see us,' he said, as I handed him his tea. 'I'd got my wires crossed with Amber. She was convinced you were off on a bender.'

'So I gathered. Actually I was reading poetry on holiday with an old-age pensioner.'

Theo winced. Then winced again at the pain this caused his eye.

'You going to tell me what happened?' I asked.

'Well,' Theo said, 'I walked out of the restaurant having found out that, you know, my best mate *hadn't* in fact been the one who'd paralysed my sister, and I wasn't really looking where I was going and ended up shoving a man the size of a grizzly bear, who then punched me very hard in the face.'

It was my turn to wince.

'It gets worse,' Theo said, adjusting his medicinal nuggets. 'Someone came to my rescue.'

'How is that worse?'

'It was my ex. The one I was telling you about.'

'What, Babs from Acorn Antiques!?'

'The very same,' Theo said. 'Whereupon we retired to a pub and had "The Big Post-Break-Up Conversation", which largely involved me realising what a prick I've been, all the while looking like this.' He briefly removed the nuggets and gave me a sarcastic double thumbs up. 'How about you?' he asked. 'What happened after I left?'

'Hmm. Not a huge amount better. Amber pointed out that lying to her was probably just about the worst thing I could have done, then left, saying she needed some time to think. So I decided to walk home, which made me feel dreadful. And then I bought a bottle of whisky . . .' I stopped.

Theo looked worried. 'Did you . . .?'

'No,' I said. 'Poured it away just now. Stupid, really.'

'Have you not got a sponsor, or whatever they are?'

'No. I've thought about it. But doesn't seem much point now . . .'

Theo lowered the nuggets and slid them away.

'That's what I've come to talk to you about actually,' he said.

'It's all right,' I said. 'You don't have to apologise about Oxford. I should have just been clear about everything from the start. I shouldn't have lied about the show. It was stupid.'

Theo sat forward. 'It doesn't matter – I still reacted how I did. It doesn't excuse that.'

'But—'

'Please, just let me finish.' Theo clasped his hands together tightly on the table. I nodded at him to continue. 'When I was with Babs earlier, and I told her what you were going through, she mentioned something about her cousin whose friend had the same thing. But her cousin was able to help.'

I went very still as Theo talked. If this was going where I thought it was . . .

'They had all these tests,' Theo continued, 'and they were the right sort of match, and the cousin became something called a living donor. They cut a chunk of his liver out, and used it to replace his friend's, and it worked, and he's better now.'

It made me want to smile, hearing Theo explain this in the most Theo way possible. He made it sound like a story a six-year-old had written rather than a relatively recent result of incredible advances in surgery – and the thing that my mum had been on at me about ever since the doctor mentioned it: Plan B.

'So,' Theo said, 'what I've come here to say is . . . well . . . that's what we can do, isn't it? I mean, I can do that. For you. Become your donor.'

I looked at my old friend, with his half-closed eye, his mad mop of hair, his earnest, hopeful face.

'When the doctors told me about that option,' I said, 'I made a promise that I'd never ask anyone.'

'Why on earth would you do that? That's insane.'

'You wouldn't understand.'

'Try me.'

I put my hand over the top of my tea. Kept it there until steam dripped from it.

'I'm not prepared to ask someone to go through all that when it's my fault for being so reckless with the drinking.'

Theo frowned. 'I thought you said it started with that time when you fell down the stairs.'

'Yeah, well . . . it probably wouldn't have escalated if I'd not drunk so much.'

'But even so, the drinking – that's an illness in itself, isn't it?' When I didn't reply Theo continued, haltingly. 'Addiction. That's not your fault either.'

'It doesn't matter,' I said. 'I have to face the consequences. I'm not going to ask someone to go through something so life-changing. It's months of recovery. Horrible trauma on the body. And,' I raised my voice over Theo's, 'it might not even work.'

'But that's the point, you're *not* asking anyone,' Theo said. 'I am here' – he jabbed his finger into his chest – 'and I am offering. So let me help you.'

I felt a tiny flame of hope, long since extinguished, flicker back into life.

'You do realise that it's not guaranteed that we'd be a match,' I said. 'If we're different blood groups, say, then it's over already.'

'I know,' Theo said. 'I was googling it all on the way over. But we don't need to worry about the blood type, do we?'

I looked at him blankly.

'Don't you remember that biology lesson with Mr Barnes?'

I rubbed my eyes. 'Funnily enough, no.'

'You do – the one where he cut the lesson short and called us "quite the little double act".'

An image came to me of Mr Barnes and his reddening cheeks.

'Oh yeah, I do – but what's that got to do with it?' I asked.

'We'd been learning about blood the previous lesson, right? He'd asked us to find out our blood types if we could. We started doing that stupid routine when we told him ours, where we pretended to be blood particles.'

'You've lost me, Theo.'

Theo sighed and turned to his right, addressing someone who wasn't there.

'All right?'

He turned to his left, responding to his own question, and continued this back and forth as he spoke.

'All right.'

'How you feeling?'

'Oh, negative.'

'You?'

'Oh, negative.'

It gradually dawned on me what he was saying.

'Oh,' I breathed.

'O *negative*,' Theo said.

Chapter Forty-Five

Theo

Joel and I talked long into the night. By the time he went to bed and I lay down on his lumpy sofa, I felt like I was tipping the balance in favour of him letting me help him. I was wary, though, of a U-turn overnight. I could just imagine him saying he'd thought it over and changed his mind.

I woke early, neck stiff from the draught coming through the window. I took in the flat properly for the first time. The place seemed sparse, lacking personality. The furniture was all the cheap IKEA stuff. When Joel first got successful, I used to picture him at home – writing in some swanky study; framed posters of his shows on the wall; a constant stream of famous friends and agents – Joel holding court, swirling red wine around his glass as everyone hung on his every word. And all the while, it looked like I'd been wrong. This, here, felt like a lonely life. It was nothing like the warmth and homeliness of the place he shared with Amber. I thought about her there now – curled up on the sofa, trying to process the impossible. If Joel refused my help, there would be days in the future when she'd feel his absence more keenly than others. Christmas. Warm summer evenings, golden sunlight never enough to melt the cold grip of grief. Well, that wasn't going to happen. I simply refused to consider it.

When Joel came through in his dressing gown and we exchanged morning grunts of greeting, I watched him nervously as he made tea. His legs looked horribly sore from where he'd been scratching them.

'I'm sorry,' he called over the rising sound of the kettle, his back to me. I jumped to my feet and marched over towards him, ready to refute all his arguments and tell him I didn't care what he said, that I would take him, by force if necessary, to the hospital, and we were going to do this. When he turned around, I was much closer than he was expecting, and he jumped.

'What?' he said. 'What is it?'

'What were you going to say?' I asked, fists clenched at my sides.

'I was going to say I'd make you toast but I'm out of bread.'

'Oh right.'

'Sorry.'

'No, doesn't matter. I'm not very hungry.'

'Me neither.' He drummed his fingers on the countertop. 'So I called the hospital.'

'That's great!' I said. 'And?'

'They've managed to arrange an emergency consultation for this afternoon.'

'Brilliant!' I said, clapping my hands together.

Joel sipped his tea and looked at me over the top of the mug.

'You make it sound like we're going to Alton Towers.'

'Hey, come on . . .'

'No, I know,' Joel said. 'Let's just not get our hopes up, shall we?'

*

My hopes were very firmly up precisely until we arrived at the entrance of King's College Hospital. Joel walked on ahead of me, but I froze, thinking of the waiting room at Gloucester A & E. The vomit. The blood. Mum sobbing.

Joel turned around, realising I wasn't at his side. He walked back towards me.

'You OK?' he asked.

'Yeah – yeah fine. I just, er . . .' Did I imagine it, or did I see a trace of scepticism in Joel's eyes, as if he might have been expecting me to back out? Real or not, it was the thing that pushed me on, and I was the one who strode forwards first and went through the door.

Thankfully we didn't have to wait too long before we were taken in to the office of Dr Ashraf Abbasi. She was short, with close-cropped black hair and beady brown eyes. Several flourishing pot plants were dotted around the room. Determined to take any positives I could, I decided this was a good sign.

Dr Abbasi recapped Joel's situation and then we arrived at the possibility of us being a match.

'The fact you have the same blood type is a very good start,' she said. 'We will need to do extensive testing, nevertheless, and I must give you the warning now: given the severity of Mr Thompson's liver damage, this operation would involve taking roughly sixty per cent of Mr Hern's liver, almost all of the right lobe, in order to replace Mr Thompson's liver entirely. And that's a lot of liver, OK?'

'OK,' Joel and I said in unison.

I couldn't help but picture the operating theatre – or at least the sort I'd seen on TV. The tubes down my throat. A nurse wiping blood away as the doctor made that first incision. I felt a pressure start to grow on my chest. I sat forward and then back, trying to shift it.

'Are you OK, Mr Hern?' Dr Abbasi asked.

'Yes, fine,' I said quickly, keen to show I was in peak health. 'Carry on.'

'If the operation is a success, and your body accepts the transplant, Mr Thompson, then your new healthy liver will grow to around ninety per cent of the size of your original one – this will take four months, give or take. And, Mr Hern, yours will grow back to its original size, maybe a little quicker.'

'That's incredible,' I said.

'Yes, but what are the risks?' Joel asked. 'I mean, of the operation itself.'

Dr Abbasi tilted her heard from side to side. 'Well,' she said. 'All the risks that come with putting the body through so much. Blood clot, pneumonia, bile leakage, wound infection . . .'

'Ha,' I said, half to myself.

I saw Joel and the doctor looking at me.

'Sorry, it just sounded a bit like you were commentating on a very depressing horse race: It's Blood Clot followed by Pneumonia – but Bile Leakage is fast approaching with two furlongs to go . . .'

Silence.

'Perhaps you could remove Theo's brain while you're at it,' Joel said, though he smiled all the same, which made me feel the best I had all day.

Joel and I were separated for testing for the rest of the afternoon and the following day. MRI and CT scans, endless blood and urine tests, a heartbeat-assessing echocardiogram, several X-rays – and all topped off with a four-hour psychological assessment from the hospital, followed by a separate session with an independent assessor from the Human Tissue Authority (my least favourite rappers – though I didn't have the energy left to make that joke out loud, which was probably for the best).

I understood the need for all the physical stuff, but the psychological part of it just felt like we were wasting time. I knew they were only doing their job, but the HTA test in particular frustrated me. The point of it seemed to be to make sure that I didn't feel like I was being pressured into doing this – that I had a choice. Well, in some ways they were right to be concerned, because I *didn't* have a choice, but only because I knew that this was something I had to do if I ever wanted to look myself in the eye again, and the fact I was terrified of the surgery and how painful it was all going to be, let alone the recovery, was entirely irrelevant.

Finally, after a second exhausting day of tests and assessments, I was allowed to leave the hospital. Dr Abbasi told me that given the severity of Joel's condition, the process to see if we were a match would be fast-tracked, but even then we'd have to wait at least four more days before we found out.

I found Joel outside, sitting on a bench. He was holding something between his fingers, turning it back and forth. When I sat down next to him, I realised it was a ring.

'What's that?' I asked.

'It's a ukulele,' Joel said, still staring at it.

'No, I know what . . . I just meant . . . I mean, is it yours or . . . ?'

'It's an engagement ring, Theo.'

'Fuck, really? For Amber?'

'No, for him.' Joel nodded at a traffic warden across the road who was picking his nose. 'We're starting a new life together in Paraguay.'

'Yeah and what happened to sarcasm being the—'

'OK, OK, sorry,' Joel said, putting the ring back in his pocket.

The traffic warden's eyes lit up as someone pulled into a parking space that was clearly off limits, and he waddled off towards them.

'How long have you been planning to propose?' I asked.

Joel puffed out his cheeks. 'Few months, I guess. We were supposed to be going away together. Then I got the diagnosis, so . . . not ideal, timing-wise.'

'No,' I said. Then, after a moment: 'You don't have to explain if you don't want to, but . . .'

'Why didn't I tell her?'

'Well, yeah.'

Joel reached out to itch his leg, but then stopped himself, clenching his fist.

'I've been thinking about that a lot too,' he said. 'The story I've been telling myself is that I wanted to keep her happy for as long as I could, even if that meant staying away from her, keeping her at a distance. But, if I'm honest, I'm not sure that's why.'

'What do you mean?'

'There's a simpler answer: I was terrified of the actual moment I had to tell her. I didn't think I could handle it.'

'Have you told Amber that?' I asked.

'No. I haven't had the chance. She's still too angry. Or at least she was. She wants to see me later.'

'Well, that's a good sign,' I said. 'You know, I only spent a little bit of time with her, but it's obvious that she loves you an insane amount. I mean, I don't see the attraction myself . . .' Joel smiled. 'But, if you tell her what you just told me, I'm sure she'll understand.'

'Well we'll see,' Joel said. 'I really hope so, Theo.'

A thought struck me. 'And you'll tell her about this, right? About what we're hoping to do.'

But this time Joel didn't say anything. After a moment, he passed me the key to his flat. I hadn't noticed it when we'd been on the walk, but I saw now there were scars on his knuckles, like faint chalk marks. Joel glanced at me and I looked away, but then he held his hands out, closing and unclosing his fist, as if testing he still had mobility.

'Do you remember the day at school when we had that argument – where I told you not to ask me if I was OK ever again?'

I nodded.

'The truth is that Mike, the guy Mum was . . .' He stopped and gathered himself. 'Mike was hurting us. Me and Mum. And if he wasn't being violent, he was being intimidating and controlling. Sometimes it just got too much, and I didn't know how to cope, and I'd end up taking it out on a wall. Hence . . .' He balled and unballed his fists again, showing me the scars properly this time. 'I got it into my head that you wouldn't want to know about it – that it would be too hard for you to hear and it would make things weird between us, and all that time we spent mucking around together was like my happy place, you know? For some reason I could talk to Amber about it, though. It was just . . . it felt easier. And then a few days before the party, things escalated with Mike, which is why I was so desperate to talk to her that night. When Amber realised how upset I was when you'd seen us together and left, she ran to the car to try and come after you – she was desperate to make everything OK between us, because she knew how much you meant to me. I know it's too late to say this now, but if I had my time again, you know I wouldn't have shut you out like that, right?'

It was jarring, to feel everything fall into place with such a heavy thud. So much made sense now.

'I'm so sorry you and your mum had to go through all that,' I said. 'I knew you hated Mike, but I didn't have any idea that he was . . . about what he was doing.'

'Yeah, well, they're clever, people like Mike. They make it feel like it's somehow your fault and that you shouldn't talk about it.'

I shook my head. I was burning with anger at what that man had done – the way he'd silenced Joel. Then something else occurred to me.

'You told me one of the reasons your liver got damaged so easily was because you'd fallen down the stairs. Was that . . .?'

Joel nodded.

'That piece of shit,' I muttered. 'Do you ever think about what he's doing now?'

Joel shrugged. 'Not really. In my drinking days, at the worst of it, I'd try and find him on Facebook. But I sort of scared myself, thinking about what I'd do if I did find him. All the bravado from the booze. But it doesn't matter what he's doing to be honest, because fuck him. We won in the end. Me and Mum.'

We sat with our own thoughts in silence for a while after this.

'Do you want to get a coffee or something?' I asked eventually.

'I think I just need a bit more time on my own,' Joel said.

'Of course. I understand.' I got to my feet. 'That stuff about Mike,' I said. 'I'm really glad you were able to tell me.'

Joel was looking ahead, but he nodded to show me he'd heard.

I was about to leave him to it, but then I realised there was something else I needed to say.

'I haven't told you this, but it was Alice who convinced me to do the walk with you,' I said. 'She forgave you a long time ago, for that night. Or at least what she thought happened that night. I just thought you should know.'

This time, Joel looked at me. He tried to say something, but then he stopped. I got the impression he was too choked up. But then he smiled at me, and that said far more than any words could.

Chapter Forty-Six

Joel

I rang the doorbell rather than going in with my keys, just in case Amber didn't want me in the house yet – or at all, in fact. But when she opened the door, she pulled me gently towards her, holding me for a moment, and pressed her lips against mine. But just as I was losing myself in the moment, she pulled back and gestured for me to go down into the living room. I took the conflicting gestures to mean that she loved me but wanted answers. A fair bargain.

'Do you want to go first?' I asked, after we'd sat down.

Amber nodded.

It was the practical questions she wanted answering first. How long had I been ill before I went to the doctor? When had they first diagnosed me? When had they told me how serious it was? I answered the questions faithfully and slowly, like I was giving a statement to the police. Amber showed no particular emotion as I spoke, but I could sense a sort of crackling energy trembling below the surface. Then we got to the hardest part.

'Why didn't you just tell me?'

It felt like the vice was back on my heart, squeezing it to the point it might burst. The pain travelled down into my stomach, spreading greedily now. When I finally spoke, the words seemed to come from somewhere else – they were the words of the boy bracing himself against his bedroom door, waiting for angry footsteps on the stairs, listening to his mother whimpering in the next room.

'I was too scared.'

The tears I'd been holding back breached my defences, and it felt like my lungs had been punctured as I struggled to breathe. Amber threw her arms around me, holding me so tightly it hurt, and I breathed in her scent, felt the warmth of her, and the fierceness of how she loved me. With my head against her chest, I could hear her heart hammering so furiously it was as if it were trying to beat for the two of us.

'It's OK,' she kept saying. 'I love you. It's OK.'

We were clinging to each other like we were lost in a violent swell, facing the waves, refusing to give in. We stayed like that for what could have been hours before we slowly pulled apart.

'There's something else I need to tell you,' I said.

Amber kissed me softly on the forehead. 'What's that, my love?'

As calmly as I could, I began to explain about the living liver donation, watching Amber closely as what I said sank in. When I got to the part where I told her I might have found a match, she grabbed my hand.

'Who?' she said urgently.

'Well. It's Theo.'

'Theo?' Amber breathed, incredulous. 'What, *your* Theo?'

'Yeah,' I said, grinning. 'My Theo.'

Amber cupped her hands over her mouth. 'Oh my god, Joel, this is incredible, I can't, I mean—'

'We don't know if we are for sure yet,' I said, hope flaring in me despite my best attempts to suppress it. 'We're definitely a blood match, but there are other test results we're waiting on.'

'And when do you find out?'

'Within the next couple of days. And if that's the case, they can fast-track me for the operation given how . . . well, how advanced everything is.'

It was almost comic, the range of emotions playing across Amber's face in those few seconds. It was like watching a time-lapse camera trained on someone watching a thriller. It sent a great wave of longing through me. Longing for a future with her at the centre of everything. And that's when something came to me.

'There's another thing I wanted to say – but brace yourself, because I'm afraid it involves poetry.'

Amber laughed properly now, and grabbed my hand even tighter.

'When I was away with Mum, I came across something that T.S. Eliot wrote and I haven't been able to get it out of my head. He's banging on about flowers and talking birds – I might be paraphrasing slightly there – but then he mentions "the still point of the turning world". I couldn't stop thinking about that phrase. I was going round and round in circles, trying to work out why that stuck with me, and then I realised something. It's you. And it has been ever since we first met. Because ever since then, no matter how much life has tried to knock me off balance, I know as soon as I'm with you that the chaos will clear. You're my still point. You always have been. And I've taken that for granted. So, if we get through this, then I promise to do whatever it takes to be yours. And I'll never shut you out again.'

At this, Amber launched herself at me, her mouth seeking mine, and I made a mental note to invite Eliot to the pub with Stanislavski the next time he was free. I owed him a pint.

Later, we lay together on our bed, Amber's head on my chest, listening to the gentle buzz of activity outside: Families out on walks. The low rumble of planes descending into Heathrow. As I stroked Amber's hair, I thought of the moment in her old home all those years ago, lying in her bed, limbs tangled, feeling hopeful for the first time about what lay ahead. I realised something then. If I could go back and speak to that kid, I'd tell him that it didn't matter about the future, about the twists and turns ahead. What mattered was right there in front of him. And that I should spend the rest of my days searching only for the kind of happiness that exists in moments like that – where you hold the one you love, as the world goes about its business, quiet and gentle, as if trying not to wake you. Because, in the end, that's all that really matters.

Chapter Forty-Seven

Theo

I'd been staring at my phone all morning, waiting for it to ring. I was still in Joel's Peckham place, and I felt cheered that things had obviously gone well enough with Amber for him not to have come back. But it had been four days since we'd left the hospital and I was starting to properly worry now. I'd spoken briefly to Alice, just to let her know that things had gone well in my attempts to make up with Joel, but I hadn't said anything about the donor situation yet. I didn't want to tempt fate.

Inevitably, I was in the shower when Joel rang. I'd propped my phone up by the door so that I could see when someone called, and I nearly slipped on the wet floor as I went to grab my phone with soapy hands.

Joel cut to the chase. 'They want us to come in,' he said.

'Bloody hell, OK. I mean, is that good? Did they say anything about the tests or what?'

'Dr Abbasi just said we should come in and see her. Amber's on set and I can't get hold of her, but I'm leaving in an Uber now. Pick you up en route?'

'Yep.'

'OK, see you soon.'

It all felt so ordinary, like we were arranging a working lunch. But as soon as I slid into the car and saw how ill Joel looked, everything felt horribly real.

'Bit of a bad night,' he explained.

'You OK?'

'I'll live,' Joel said, but I wasn't quite ready for gallows humour yet.

'Do you think it's a positive sign that we're both being asked to go in?' I asked as our driver looked for the best place to drop us off. 'Surely if they were going to tell us we aren't a match there'd be no need?'

Joel drummed his fingers on his knees. The sound seemed strangely amplified in the quiet of the car. I wound the window down, trying to get some air.

'Honestly? I don't know,' he said.

The car pulled up by the hospital and I jumped out, a ball of nervous energy. I walked around to Joel's side and waited for him to do the same, but he seemed to be having some difficulty.

'You all right?' I asked, opening the door.

'Sort of. Feel like all the strength's gone out of me all of a sudden.'

'Right. Well, not to worry, shall I . . .' I reached my arms out awkwardly. I wasn't sure what Joel needed at first.

After a few failed attempts, he said, 'Just, give me . . . *That's* it.' He held my arm and I took his weight, pulling him to his feet. I thought of the moment we'd met after Alice's accident, when we put our arms around each other's shoulders, trying to fight back tears. As we inched our way to the hospital entrance, me supporting Joel as best I could, I couldn't help but feel pride at how we'd finally found our way back to each other. It might have taken a while, but sometimes that's how things have to work out – one foot in front of the other, one step at a time.

Chapter Forty-Eight

Joel

When Theo and I tried to hug Dr Abbasi for the third time, she laughed and threatened us with the water pistol she used for her pot plants. It was official: Theo and I were a match. They would book us in for the operation as soon as they feasibly could. Dr Abbasi attempted to give us the serious news – that there was still a chance my body would reject the portion of Theo's liver, that the operation would last six hours and that testing indicated I might be at risk of having an allergic reaction to the anaesthetic – but, like the idiots we were, we were too excited to listen. I'd been trying so hard not to get my hopes up, but now it was like a valve had been undone, releasing all the pressure. When I tried to call Amber, my hands were shaking too much.

'Mate,' Theo said, 'Shall I . . .'

He took the phone from me and brought up Amber's contact, pressing call and passing me back the phone. When I finally got through and told her the news, she didn't say anything at first. I think, like us, she'd been trying to prepare for the worst, so it took her a long time to find her voice, but when she did, she was talking at a thousand miles an hour, attempting to shut down an entire day's filming to come and see me. I might usually have protested, but getting to hold her in my arms while we shared the good news was too good to turn down.

Theo and I walked out of the hospital in a daze.

'I'm going to go home today, see my family,' Theo said. 'But I'll be ready to jump on a train as soon as we get the green light.'

'Of course,' I said. We walked on for a bit while I worked up to what I needed to say. 'Listen, I haven't even begun to . . . to actually say to you how much . . .' Just then my phone rang, and I took it out of my pocket.

Theo, thinking it was Amber again, clapped a hand on my shoulder and said, 'I'll see you soon, OK?' and walked off to flag a taxi. He had such a skip in his step I thought he might be about to break out into the Morecambe and Wise dance.

The call was from an unknown number. I prepared for the PPI scammer; the car insurance chancer. But a familiar voice greeted me, albeit without its usual bombast.

'Joel, it's Jane Green.'

'Oh hello. You changed your number?'

'No. I was just rather worried you might not pick up, after the whole lunch affair.'

'I see,' I said. 'Well, I think I'll let you off. After what I'm about to tell you, I think you'll probably see why.'

I found a bench to sit on and explained everything to Jane, who listened without interruption, if you didn't count the monosyllabic swear words which she launched like mortars at every twist and turn of my story.

'Well, dear boy, I suspect that this will make what I am about to tell you even more significant. Hold on to your fucking hat, because I've got some more news about *The Regulars* . . .'

By the time we'd finished talking, I had sat down and stood

up from the bench seven times, the phone clamped to my ear still. I must have looked like a hostage negotiator being given some particularly demeaning instructions.

When I lowered myself gingerly into the taxi taking me to Hampstead, all I wanted was to close my eyes and wake up when I got there. But there was one final phone call I had to make.

'Joel!'

'*Olá*, Mum. Quick question: are you sitting down?'

Chapter Forty-Nine
Theo

It was a peculiarly welcome sight: the top of Dad's head above a hedge, the occasional flash of those lethal garden shears of his. When I went through the garden gate, I found Mum and Alice sitting on the patio with mugs of tea. Mum jumped up and came over to hug me, while Dad clambered down the ladder, waving at me like Edward Scissorhands, and came over to ruffle my hair (thankfully having lost the shears by the time he got to me).

'I've run out of explorer-cum-travel-writer puns to insult you with,' Alice said with a grin. 'Can you just imagine I've thought of a really good one?'

'Yeah, why not,' I said.

'Tea?' Mum asked. 'Can't wait to hear about your big trip. Are there photos? Do we need to find the thingy lead, the scart thing, for the big telly?'

'Um, maybe later,' I said. 'I actually need to tell you something first.'

'Oh, OK,' Mum said. 'Nothing's wrong is it, darling?'

'No, I'm fine. Let's just . . .' I gestured to the French doors and led them inside.

Dad slid a chair aside so Alice could come to the kitchen table. Then he and Mum sat down opposite me. It was strange, this. We were never the sort of family that had 'family meetings' or big talks. They were looking at me expectantly, but I didn't quite know where to start.

'Is this about Joel?' Alice prompted.

'It is,' I said. 'I found out this week that . . . well . . . there's no easy way of saying this, but it turns out he wasn't the one driving the car that hit you. It was Amber Crossley.'

Nobody said anything at first. Then Alice blinked rapidly a few times, like she'd just been exposed to a very bright light, and said, 'Well, I wasn't expecting that.'

'I'm afraid I'm a little confused,' Dad said. 'He wasn't in the car?'

'No, he was,' I said. 'But he was trying to get Amber to stop. In the end, he decided to take the blame for her.'

'But . . . why?' Mum asked.

'Because he was – and still is – very much in love with her. But also because he is a generous, decent, selfless person. And that brings me on to the second thing I need to tell you, because let's face it, those aren't exactly qualities that I've shown any time recently.'

'Now that's not true,' Mum protested.

'I'm afraid it is,' I said. 'I've parked myself here, relying on you all to look after me, stopping you from living your lives. I've been miserable, and I've been angry at the world, and you've all had to put up with it. I forced you to evict me.' I turned to Alice. 'You've always been far more mature than me when it came to Joel. You wanted to move on, but I was the one who never let you forget what happened. It's time that I actually did something to help someone else for a change. Luckily, I've been given a pretty big opportunity to do just that.'

I saw Mum take Dad's hand as I started to tell them about Joel's liver disease, and that it was so advanced that he had run out of all options apart from one.

'What's that?' Dad asked.

I looked down at my hands as I answered. 'There's a way where someone with a healthy liver, who's a match for Joel, can donate a portion of theirs which can replace his. A living donor. And it turns out I'm a match. We've done all the tests. We're just waiting for a date for the operation.' I kept my eyes down. I felt strangely embarrassed, like I'd just revealed a big secret I'd been keeping from them for years.

'Oh, Theo,' Mum said. 'That's really quite something. Are you sure about this? Have you thought it all through? Is there not somebody else who might be a match?'

'Not that he knows of. But it doesn't matter, he needs it now,' I said. 'I've not stopped thinking about it since it became a possibility, and the only thing that's worrying me is whether it'll work. I'm not backing out. I owe it to him.'

Alice, to my astonishment, was crying.

'Fucking hell, Theo, please get over here now so I can hug you, you big idiot.'

Ah, that was more like it.

I moved around the table and she yanked me by the sleeve down towards her, hugging me with her fiercest ever grip. After a moment, I felt Mum's arm around me, and then Dad's. In the middle of it all, I squeezed my eyes shut, and focused on just how happy I was that I was about to do them proud.

The call from Joel came the next morning.

'We're on,' he said. 'A week today.'

'Yes!' I yelled, like we'd just won the World Cup or

something. I thought I heard a familiar voice in the background. 'Do I take it things are OK again?'

'Yeah, everything's good,' Joel said.

'Well, that's excellent news.'

'Yeah. Listen, hang on a sec.' It sounded like Joel had gone into another room. I heard a door shutting. 'Again, obviously it goes without saying that—'

'Whoa, whoa, whoa – I'll stop you there. I am doing this, OK? You're not talking me out of it. Not to put too fine a point on it, but at this stage, even if you miraculously got better on your own, I'd still march in there and tell them to chop me open – see if some passing stranger needs an upgrade.'

Joel laughed – a proper hearty laugh – and it made me feel like I'd come in out of the cold.

I woke on the day of the operation to find a crisp autumn morning waiting for me, a thin layer of mist hanging in the air. Dad had suggested we all drive down to London together rather than getting the train. As we wound our way through Kemble's country lanes, I gazed out of the window, watching the trees and fields slide past, thinking of all the adventures Joel and I had been on around here. On those endless summer days of school holidays, we would do anything to assuage our boredom, to try to make time go faster. If only I could go back and tell myself that it might feel like time was dragging, but it was actually pelting along at an intergalactic speed, that I should dig my heels into the ground and savour every last second of it.

We were going along a narrow road – the trees reaching their branches out across it towards each other, blocking out the light – when I felt the first throbbing pulse of nerves. It started in my stomach and spread outwards. I gripped the seat belt until it dug painfully into the webbing between my fingers.

I noticed Alice looking over at me.

'Mum?' she said.

'On it,' Mum replied from the front.

I was about to ask what this little exchange was all about when I saw Mum reach into the glove compartment and bring out a CD, which she slipped into the car stereo.

'We present the all-weather Goon Show.'

There was a short blast of jazz, and then:

'And tonight we bring you the story of . . . The Stolen Postman.'

It was my favourite episode of *The Goon Show*. I didn't have it on CD, so Alice must have bought it specifically for this journey. As the gentle lunacy of the episode began, I felt my shoulders beginning to relax. I released my grip on the seat belt.

Without looking at me, Alice reached across and squeezed my hand. And then it was like the four of us were off on a summer holiday, in Dad's old Saab, waiting to be the first person to say 'I can see the sea!', feeling all our troubles ebbing away.

Chapter Fifty

Joel

When we got to the hospital, I asked if we could walk around the block before we went in. This was only partly down to nerves. Mainly I wanted to keep on walking because I had Amber on one side of me and Mum on the other, and I liked it far too much to let go.

Amber and I had collected Mum from Gatwick a few days before. Never in my life did I think I'd be one of those people involved in a tearful reunion at arrivals, but there we were, a tangle of arms, Mum saying, 'I can't believe it – I just can't believe it' over and over again. The best part was that it seemed to thaw the last stubborn bit of ice that separated Mum and Amber. I sat in the front of the taxi and listened to them discussing Lisbon, genuine affection in their voices.

Mum happened to casually mention the name Martin a few times – a chap she'd met while breakfasting in what became her favourite café. 'And then Martin said this very funny thing about the waiter . . .' 'Martin was ever so kind helping me with my bags and the taxi . . .'

Amber and I had exchanged glances in the rear-view mirror.

'Sue, does Martin live in England?'

'I believe he does,' Mum said.

'And did Martin perhaps give you his contact details?'

Mum gasped with faux shock.

'I will not even deign to answer that question.' But after a moment, she took a bit of paper from her bag and started gently fanning herself.

'Sue!' Amber said. 'Is that . . .'

'I don't know what you're talking about, dear,' Mum said, trying not to smile. From the mirror, I could just make out the word Martin, followed by an email address, written on her makeshift fan.

Mum stayed with us in Hampstead up until the operation. I was determined to squeeze every drop of happiness that I could out of those few days. I probably tired myself out more than was sensible, but taking Mum to Columbia Road Flower Market and going on walks around Hampstead Heath went some way to making up for leaving Lisbon halfway through the holiday, although Mum's continuing case of mentionitus when it came to Martin had helped somewhat with my guilt. That wasn't to say the idea of another man in Mum's life didn't worry me, but he'd clearly been kind and generous to her so far. If he did arrive on the scene properly I'd be watching him like a hawk to make sure that was how things continued. I had visions of taking him aside outside the house, reminding him of his promise to have her back by ten while Mum covered her face, mortified.

When she, Amber and I finally walked into the hospital, it was just in time to see Theo and his family arrive. I knew they were coming with him, but I hadn't really thought about what seeing them all again would feel like. Inevitably, there was something of an awkward stand-off – a solid metre of daylight between the two groups. I felt Amber increase the pressure a little as she squeezed my hand. I gave her a reassuring squeeze back. She was worried, I knew, about seeing Alice.

'All right?' I said to Theo.

'All right,' he replied.

There was a pause, which was ended by Mum walking over and pulling Theo into a hug. 'I can't tell you how grateful I am,' she said. 'You are a wonder, Theo.'

Theo's cheeks went pink. "S'nothing,' he mumbled.

Mum turned to Geoff and Angie. 'You should be ever so proud of him,' she said.

I sensed Geoff shutting down his automatic response – to make a knowing joke about Theo: 'he's not so bad when you get to know him' or something, in the way only a dad can. Instead, he smiled and said, 'We are.'

'Hey there,' Alice said, looking at Amber and me in turn. We said hello back, then Amber cleared her throat and said, 'Alice, would you have a moment to talk later? We could get tea or something.'

Alice paused for a moment, then looked at me and Theo. 'Well I gather these two are going to keep us knocking about here for god knows how long, so yeah, let's.'

It was only a brief exchange, but it seemed to make everyone relax.

Theo and I hung back as everyone shuffled into the waiting room. Theo looked a little green around the gills.

'You OK?' I asked.

'I'll be fine when we get in there,' he said. He pointed at our families ahead of us now beginning to chat politely, like they were at a coffee morning or a church fete. 'Well, this is surreal.'

'Agreed. But amazing all the same.'

'Yeah,' Theo said, his voice wobbling a little. 'It really is.'

We had to wait a little while before someone came to collect us, which didn't help with the nerves. As we were taken through the endless warren of corridors, I kept the image in my head of the first moment Theo and I had ridden off on our tandem, the sun on our backs, the years rolling away, doing my best to channel that hope.

Chapter Fifty-One
Theo

Dressed in a paper gown, lying on a gurney, I felt my nerves begin to fail me, despite what I'd told Joel. The room felt airless. I started to worry that if I had a panic attack that would somehow mean they couldn't do the operation and then I'd have let Joel down again. Thankfully, the feeling passed by the time a porter came to get me.

I felt a lot better when I saw the others again. They had obviously been well-drilled – by Dr Abbasi, I suppose – to smile reassuringly at me when I came in, and some of them were better at smiling on demand than others, which made it look a little bit like they were characters in a farce trying to hide an unconscious nun behind them. After a few minutes of chatting, everyone relaxed a bit, and I felt my heart rate slowing.

Mum hugged me one final time, whispering 'We love you so much' before she stood up. Dad gave my foot a little squeeze. 'You'll be right as rain in no time, OK?' And then Alice leant across and hugged me, passing something into my hand as she left. It was a drawing she'd done. The scene showed the two of us sitting in her garden, drinking whisky under a starry sky. The caption read: 'To Theo, *still* the bravest idiot I know'.

Joel was in a room next to the operating theatre. I felt for him, because he would have the longer wait. My operation was set to take around six hours, but Joel had to be nearby to go straight into theatre as soon as I was done. 'Apparently it's "against protocol" for me to go for a curry and a pint,' he said, when I was wheeled in to see him. 'It's PC gone mad.'

'What next?' I said, with a sad shake of my head. 'No smoking in the operating room?'

The nurse wheeled my gurney around so that Joel and I were facing each other, toe to toe. The nurses said they'd give us a few minutes alone together.

'Shall we just hide?' I whispered, once they'd gone. 'See how long it takes them to find us?'

Joel glanced over at the door. 'Yeah, why not. You go first and I'll just say you ran away, and then when they're off looking for you, I'll make a break for it too.'

'OK – deal.'

There was some movement outside the door and we both looked over – was our time up already? No, we had a little longer.

'So,' Joel said. 'Are you . . . you know, scared?'

'Nah,' I said. 'Are you?'

'Nah,' Joel said, waving his hand dismissively. 'Absolutely not.'

Chapter Fifty-Two
Joel

I had never been more scared in my life.

Chapter Fifty-Three
Theo

I had never been more scared in my life.

Chapter Fifty-Four

Joel

'Actually that's bollocks, I am actually incredibly fucking scared,' I said.

'Me too, obviously,' Theo replied.

I'd been weighing up whether to tell him about Jane Green's call. If you were to tell someone perhaps the best news they'd ever had immediately before an operation, would that mess with their heart so much you'd have to delay it? Because, as it turned out, a change in 'creative direction' at Channel 4 meant they'd decided not to go ahead with their pub-based sitcom, which meant that the BBC did want *The Regulars* after all, and were keen to get Theo on board – especially when they read what I'd sent on, which I'd told them was mostly Theo's work. Looking at him now, I felt like he could actually do with having something positive to focus on.

'So, I had a call from Jane,' I began.

'Oh yeah?' Theo said, distracted still.

'The show's back on,' I continued. '*The Regulars*. BBC back on board.'

Theo looked at me. I looked at Theo.

'You know what I've realised,' he said, putting his hands behind his head and stretching back, brow furrowed.

'Go on . . .'

'Life's just absolutely fucking mental, isn't it?'

'Quite possibly the most profound thing I've ever heard,' I said, smiling to myself as I saw the happiness spreading through Theo like a nurse had come in and attached a drip full of it to him. It made me think of the teenage him: the innocent, optimistic kid who sent scripts to major TV channels at the age of thirteen with genuine hope in his heart that they'd get made. It also reminded me of something else he'd written – something we'd never actually talked about, and which I felt compelled to tease him about now.

'Here's a question,' I said. 'Do you remember that time when I found that thing you'd written called *My Ideal Girlfriend*?'

Theo froze. 'Don't think so,' he said, suddenly trying to look casual, throwing in a yawn for good measure.

'We must have been about fourteen. You told me it was a character monologue, but I never quite believed you.'

'Hmm, not ringing any bells.'

'Let me refresh your memory,' I said. I cleared my throat and began to recite: '*My ideal girlfriend writes poetry, but never tells anyone about it. She knows about French New Wave and takes a Super 8 camera on holiday . . .*'

That was when Theo gave up the pretence.

'Oh god, please stop! Shut up! Blah blah blah blah!' He was raising his voice, trying to drown out mine.

I showed mercy and stopped.

'You know I nearly sent that to a girl in my English class until you made fun of it,' Theo said. 'I owe you one for that.'

'Well, you *are* about to give me a sizeable portion of one of your most vital organs, so I'd say we're about quits.'

Theo nodded.

'You know what the worst part of that thing I wrote is?' he said after a moment.

I shook my head.

'It's still true. All of it.'

That made me laugh the hardest I had in ages.

'Not to wipe that grin off your face,' Theo said, 'but I've been thinking about something a bit more serious. About what we spoke about on the bench the other week, about Mike and everything.'

'Oh OK,' I said. 'I mean, way to ruin the jazzy mood I'm in . . . but go on.'

Theo shifted on the gurney. 'I was just thinking that, touch wood and everything goes fine today, in the future, if we find ourselves going through something hard or worrying, whatever it may be . . . we should tell each other, right?'

'That sounds like a good plan to me, Theo.'

I could hear movement in the corridor outside. It was nearly time.

I cleared my throat. 'Listen, I'm rubbish at this sort of stuff, as I think you've probably realised by now, but . . . I want you to know something. I can't think of a better friend than you. And I feel very lucky to have had you in my life.'

At this, Theo nodded, his bottom lip trembling a little. He couldn't quite manage to reply, but instead he stretched out his leg, and we tapped our feet together, once, twice.

Chapter Fifty-Five

Theo

Dr Abbasi came in and explained that they were ready for me, and the anaesthetist made his way over to my bed. Looking at Joel, I felt compelled to say something that placed us together in the future.

'By the way,' I said, 'you do know we're definitely going to finish that walk, right? Start to finish this time.'

'Abso-fucking-lutely,' Joel said. 'Even if we do the whole thing with Colin next to us.'

We couldn't help acting up then for Dr Abbasi's benefit, but also, I guess, to distract ourselves from our nerves. We asked her stupid questions about whether she'd ever had a patient spontaneously combust, while she steadfastly ignored us, until it got too much for her and she let out a big sigh.

'You two . . .' she said.

Us two, I thought, exchanging a smile with Joel and lying back down. *Quite the little double act.*

The anaesthetist was young, with wispy blond hair, and had a spot of what looked like mustard on his chin. I made a note to tell him when I was conscious again. Now didn't seem the right time. As he told me to hold the mask in position over my nose, I could feel my heart thumping harder and harder in my chest.

Don't fuck this up, don't fuck this up, I repeated to myself, concentrating as hard as I could on trying to stay calm.

The anaesthetist finished attaching the drip to the back of my hand, took hold of my arm and placed it on my lap, and told me to count backwards from a hundred. I was at eighty-five, the room was beginning to fall away, when I heard what I thought was Joel's voice, sounding very distant. It was hard to make out, but I think the words he said were, 'Love you, mate.'

'*Love you too*,' I said. But it was hard to tell if the words had made it out of my mouth, because everything was fading, fading, until it was just darkness.

Chapter Fifty-Six
Joel

One year later

I closed my eyes and listened to the wind rushing through the trees. In the distance, there was the gentle growl of a combine harvester. A cloud that hadn't received the memo moved reluctantly away from the sun, and I felt a warm glow return to my face. The grass beneath my legs was soft and springy. I shifted upwards so that my back was against the stone warmed by the morning sun – the stone which marked the start of the Thames Path. How strange yet familiar it felt to be back here again.

It was set to be another beautiful day, the kind of late summer Saturday which England thrives in, where barbecue smoke is never far from your nose, where garden furniture gets brought out of the garage for one last hurrah, and everyone, for a few hours at least, slows down enough to remember that life can be pretty great.

I closed my eyes again and tried to picture Theo's face the day we'd met here last year. Had he looked nervous and apprehensive as he pushed open the gate, or was there at least the hint of a smile on his face when he saw me? I wondered – as I had done so many times – what would have happened in an alternate universe where we'd done the whole walk without me telling him I was ill. I had a vision of us standing by the murky waters of the Thames, down from Greenwich, saying an awkward goodbye before going our separate ways – then, a few months later, he'd have turned on his phone and read on the BBC news page, or from some equally impersonal messenger, that I'd died. Would he have cried for me? Would he have still been blinded by hatred for what he thought I'd done to Alice – and in Edinburgh?

I realised I was absent-mindedly scratching under my T-shirt. I couldn't be sure if the scar that stretched from my stomach to my chest still really was itchy, or whether it was just psychosomatic, a reminder of the episode that I knew would define the rest of my life.

'Colin would be delighted.'

'Whatever happened to him I wonder?'

'He's probably in hiding deep in the Bolivian jungle, waiting for the day Interpol track him down on charges of assault.'

'Probably.'

I'd been doing a lot of this, lately – imagining whole conversations with Theo, as if he were standing right beside me.

As if he were still here.

∞

The operation had been a complete success, that far. They had removed what they'd needed to of Theo's liver without a hitch and had sewn him up – they couldn't have been more on the home straight. But after the precious cargo had been taken away, beginning the short journey to the room I was just going into, a blood clot began to travel from Theo's leg up to his lung. It all happened very quickly after that apparently.

I often wonder whether he was still with us when I went under – whether we'd have at least been alive at the same time so that perhaps even though he was unconscious, some semblance of understanding registered: they had got what they needed.

The hardest thing was how long it took me after I'd come around to understand what had happened. It just didn't make any sense. I was the one who should have been dead. It was only when Dr Abbasi calmly talked me through it that I finally got it.

I still haven't been able to revisit those dark hours that followed. I don't think I ever will. To be filled with so much rage and fury and sorrow, but to be so weak that I could barely move . . . It was like the stories you hear of people with 'locked in' syndrome, screaming as they try to make themselves heard, but no noise escapes. When they told me that the signs were looking good – that my body had accepted Theo's liver – the only part of me that registered it was the one that wished it wasn't true. I didn't want to get better. I wanted to die. Because what had I done? What the *fuck* had I done?

It was probably harder for Amber than it was for me in those first few weeks. She was devastated about Theo, of course she was – but she also wasn't able to show relief or even joy that I was getting better, because I was so utterly broken at what had happened, about what I'd made my friend do, that thinking of anything beyond that made me convulse with shame and self-loathing. Mum and Amber saw me through those early days together. It will be a long time still before I'll be able to show them the gratitude they deserve.

I don't remember much about the memorial service. The

whole day had an unreal quality to it. It rained so hard the church roof leaked. I got caught in the downpour outside, but I hadn't even noticed I was soaked through. I gave a soggy, faltering speech. None of the sentiment came out properly. I kept getting my words muddled. I'd wanted it to be funny, the way John Cleese was at Graham Chapman's funeral, because I remember Theo making me watch that video a hundred times, and it clearly meant something to him. But I lost my nerve. It wouldn't have been right. I couldn't look any of his family in the eye. The guilt was too much.

I was sitting outside afterwards in my hospital wheelchair when Alice wheeled up beside me. We hadn't spoken since Theo had died. She, out of everyone, was who I was most scared of talking to.

We looked on as Theo's distant relatives helped themselves to the buffet.

'Why do people feel the need to eat at memorials?' Alice asked.

'I'm not sure,' I said. 'It feels like one of those things that we just do and never question why.'

'I wonder who was the first,' Alice said. 'Some big burly Viking got a bit peckish after all that setting fire to the boat and pushing it out to sea business, and thought, you know what I need now – an egg and cress sandwich.'

I smiled.

We were quiet for a while, then Alice said, 'I'm trying to imagine what he'd make of all this, you know. I can sort of picture him looking down, all that hair bunching up over his eyes and just going' – here she morphed into a very accurate impression of her brother – '*Oh what, me? I'm the one that carked it? Well, that's just fucking typical, isn't it.*'

I laughed even through the shock of Alice recreating Theo's grumpiness so well.

'Anyway,' Alice said, 'how's that ol' liver of his holding up in there?'

I brought a hand to the place my scar was, still tender to the touch. 'Pretty good so far,' I said.

'Does it feel weird?'

'Yeah,' I said. 'Really weird.'

There was so much I wanted to say to Alice, but I knew I'd be no more coherent than the speech I'd given earlier. Alice seemed to know what was going on in my head.

'It's OK,' she said. 'It's all so hard. Let's not try and make sense of it now. We'll just tie ourselves up in knots.'

'OK,' I said. 'But when you're ready, do you promise to come and see me, or call, however you want to do it?'

Alice nodded. I thought she was about to go, but she turned and put her hand out, and I took it, and we just stayed like that for a while.

When she gave my hand a little squeeze and went to move away, I said, 'Alice – please . . . can you just . . . I just need you to know how much I loved him. He was so brave. Braver than I'll ever be. He really was my best friend. Even in all the years we were apart, I never stopped thinking about him.'

Alice took a moment to compose herself, then she lifted her head and said, 'Promise me something?'

'Anything,' I said.

Nine months later I was pacing the stalls of the theatre inside BBC Broadcasting House, waiting for everyone to arrive. Amber was the first, and the way she embraced me instantly made me feel a hundred times better, though I still had butterflies about what was about to happen.

Mum came through the door next, waving when she saw me. Martin, with his bristly moustache and twinkling blue eyes, followed behind her, carrying her coat. He had lived up to his reputation so far, and I'd never seen Mum so happy. I guided them to their seats, and confirmed to Mum twice that yes, the little bags of popcorn were indeed free.

A little later, when Geoff and Angie appeared, and then Alice, with her boyfriend Daniel at her side, I felt myself starting to freak out. I'd seen them since Theo's memorial, and we'd talked at length, but even as they did their selfless best to rid me of my guilt, and the interactions became easier, I was still a bag of nerves each time we met. Amber took my hand and whispered in my ear that everything was going to be OK, and it was that which gave me the strength to go over and greet them. Alice and I hugged. Angie and Geoff said hello, and when Geoff patted me on the arm and asked me how the liver was – I was so overwhelmed and grateful that I couldn't stop myself welling up.

'Hey, come on now,' Angie said. 'No tears today. That's not what Theo would have wanted.'

'I bet it would be in fairness,' Alice laughed. 'Ideally, he'd want this to be broadcast on every available channel in the world and for there to be some sort of mass crying outbreak like when a North Korean leader dies.'

'Oh give over,' Angie said, but she smiled all the same. 'Shall we go and find our seats then?' she asked me.

'Yes, you're just over there.'

The lights were dimming as the last cast and crew members trickled in.

Just before the Herns went I said, 'You don't have to or

anything – I won't be offended in the slightest if you don't want to, or if you're keen to get back home, but—'

'We're coming to dinner, yes,' Alice said. 'Amber and I sorted the restaurant already, don't worry – she said you were, quote, *a bit stressed* about finishing the edits or something. Come on, Ma and Pa – let's get you sat down.'

I smiled at them all as they left. I was nervous about the dinner, but the fact they were coming at all, and that it had been a joint effort by Alice and Amber, left me with a good feeling.

I took my seat next to Amber. I couldn't quite believe that this was happening. All the people I loved most in the world were sitting around me. Except one. I felt a lump growing in my throat again.

'Are you OK?' Amber whispered.

I tried to speak, but I couldn't find the words.

'Hey, it's OK, you don't have to explain,' she said, wriggling down and putting her head on my shoulder in the way she always does.

The lights dimmed, and white text appeared on the dark screen.

The Regulars
(Cast & crew screening)
Episode one – Whose round is it?
Starring Amber Crossley
Written by Theo Hern

'Hey,' Amber whispered. 'They missed your name off the credits!'

I kissed the top of her head. 'Don't worry, that was me,' I

said. 'This was always his dream more than mine. It's my one chance to let him have his moment.'

The opening scene began, like all those jokes you don't hear any more, with a man walking into a bar. As he opened his mouth to speak, I raised my eyes to the ceiling and thought, *We did it eh, mate? We actually did it.*

∞

A butterfly had settled on my rucksack.

'If you're thinking of hitchhiking to London, it's a bloody long way my friend,' I said. I checked for the hundredth time that morning that the engagement ring was in my pocket. It felt good to be worried about that again.

Just then, my phone vibrated. It was a message from Alice.

Ready to see it in all its glory?

YES, I replied.

I opened the photo Alice had sent through and gasped. She had gone above and beyond, and absolutely outdone herself. Leaning up against the wall of a pub – in glorious British racing green – was a tandem.

Alice: The pub's agreed we can lock it up around the back until you get here.

Me: Perfect, thank you. How much do I owe you?

Alice: Oh, nothing. You kept your promise. That's all I wanted.

At the funeral, Alice had asked whether – for Theo – I would walk the Thames Path. And get to the end this time. She didn't like the thought of that particular adventure of ours going unfinished.

'As soon as I'm strong enough,' I'd said. 'I promise.'

I had decided to walk the path to Oxford – to where Theo and I had got to, and then do the rest on the bike. I knew I'd get some funny looks, or maybe even the odd wag asking me if I'd forgotten someone. But that was the point, I definitely hadn't. Because when I was cycling I'd imagine Theo was on the back seat, and when the sun was behind me I'd pretend there were two shadows ahead, instead of one.

The butterfly took off, and that felt like my cue to get to my feet. I pulled the rucksack onto my shoulders and tightened the straps, turning to look at the path that cut a faint line across the fields. The river, and all its history, were waiting for me. There was nothing left to do now but start walking.

Author's Note

I walked most of the Thames Path, in three stints, in autumn 2015, summer 2017, and spring 2019. I chose that particular national trail partly because I was taken with the idea of walking from the source of something to its end, experiencing nature in all its majesty, and partly because I have no sense of direction and it's quite hard to get lost when you're following a river (although I did manage it. Twice). I was indebted to Joel Newton's excellent book, *Thames Path*, a no-nonsense guide to the route. If – and I heartily recommend it – you do decide to take on the TP, you should know I have taken one or two liberties with the path when it comes to bicycle accessibility. As much as I love the idea of two people saddling up their tandem and following in Joel and Theo's tyre tracks, the route is a public footpath and so cycling isn't allowed (nor cycleable, in most places). I'm afraid once I'd had the idea it was too hard to resist, so for a more sensible guide to the path, Joel Newton is your man.

Acknowledgements

Thanks to my incredible – and incredibly patient – editors, Harriet Bourton and Tara Singh Carlson, for challenging me to dig deep with this book, and who helped make it so much better. I still have Stockholm syndrome but, you know, in a good way. To my ever-wise agent, Laura Williams, who listens to my nonsense on a weekly basis and never complains. I owe you many pints. To everyone at Putnam and Orion, especially Chrissy Heleine, Nicole Biton, Katie McKee, Ashley McClay, Ashley Di Dio, Virginia Woolstencroft, Katie Moss, Olivia Barber, Jen Hope, Esther Waters, Dominic Smith, Declan Kyle, Nigel Andrews and Linda McGregor. To the gang at Headline for all their support. To all at Greene & Heaton, espcially Kate Rizzo. To Ben, Holly, Lucy, Emily and Fran, for just the right balance of encouragement and piss-taking. To Georgie, for making everything better. Finally, to my family, who I missed an awful lot during the last year. Here's to better days ahead.

Don't miss Richard Roper's hilarious and life-affirming debut . . .

This wasn't a love story . . .
Until she turned up.

MEET ANDREW.

Everybody likes Andrew. But they don't really know him. They know what he's told them – that he's happily married with two kids. Living the kind of life that's either so boring it's true, or so perfect it's a lie . . .

ENTER PEGGY.

Peggy arrives in Andrew's life in a burst of kindness and possibility. For the first time in ages, Andrew feels alive again. So now that he has everything to lose, can he risk it all and tell Peggy the truth?

'Charming, humorous and life-affirming tale about human kindness'
BBC